Pandora's Box

1

Winter Hansen

Contents

Dedication

To my son Colt Wes Hansen:

May your curiosity always outweigh your fear of the unknown.

To my husband, Daniel Ray Hansen:

In my darkest of times, you were always my light.

To my father, Robert Wes Carlyon:

You instilled in me a sense of self power to be unapologetically myself, you have always been my greatest supporter.

To my sisters: Sapphire Ellison Grace Carlyon, Brianna Alaythia Lisette Carlyon, and Whisper Anavah Carlyon:

May you always work hard and never believe anyone who says you cannot achieve *your* definition of success.

A Letter to My Readers

When we're young we read these incredible stories of a hero that cannot be defeated. Stories of magical places, villains with supernatural powers, and universes and worlds that don't exist anywhere else. We're taught that the hero always wins, that magic is always good, and justice is always served, but then we grow up in the real human world where the hero doesn't always win, magic doesn't exist, and justice hardly ever is served. We lose the creative and imaginary child that everyone has within them to the system that tears creativity down by its very bones and builds conformity on top of it.

As I was growing up, being the eldest of six children- four girls and two boys, I had expectations set on my shoulders. I was expected to be the bigger person, expected to be the example, expected to be self-sufficient, and expected to be the adult that I certainly wasn't at the time. The majority of my family is super religious and I was raised by people who expected women to be small, meek, and in the background. I was taught that women married and submitted to their husbands, to build the home, and to have as many children as God blessed them. I was watered down, stripped of my color, and forced into a box that I would never fit in and then chastised because the box that I was expected to conform to was in fact too small.

Because when you come from a family that is high achieving, they will never see you as who you *are*, but only for what you *do*.

They will never see the potential for your version of greatness, only the things that they deem important and worthy of being praised for. When you do not meet their level of perfection you are labeled as not good enough and told to try harder. The thing is, everyone has a different definition of perfection, and if you're always striving to be someone else's definition, you'll only burn yourself out because it is *impossible* to meet everyone's expectations simultaneously.

For the longest time, I looked in the mirror and *hated* the reflection that looked back because I wasn't their definition of perfect or worthy of love. I was broken, and with every attempt I made to be who they wanted me to be, I became less and less shrinking myself to fit in the box. Shrank myself to fit the cookie cutter mold they said was what I was meant to be. Then one day, I picked up a book. I picked up a book about a detective who solved mysteries and Winter disappeared. I lived in the world of Nancy Drew, I *was* her. I could tune out the entire world, travel to somewhere that only existed in my mind, and be anywhere or *anyone*.

When my mom committed suicide when I was 14, I lost a piece of me and for a long time blamed myself for her death. People told me that I should have called, should have visited, should have heard her side of the story, but I had made the decision no *child* should have to. I told my mom that she couldn't hurt me anymore. I had said no, you're not *allowed* in my life anymore and at 14 years old I built a wall around my heart because the person who was supposed to protect it was the one to destroy it. I *refuse* to continue repeating the same story of the generations who came before me. If I must shoulder the weight of their traumas, then so be it— I will *ensure* the cycle ends with me.

I am no stranger to pain, no stranger to fear, no stranger to grief.

When I was 16, I was raped and sexually assaulted multiple times by my boyfriend at the time and when I begged for help from church leaders, I was told I made it up, was told it was all in my head. When I was 22 years old, my husband and I wanted to create a family after the emotional turmoil of whether I even *wanted* to have kids. Then I miscarried- *twice* within a couple of months of each other. It is a great agonizing pain, the feeling that the body that was defiled in the most nefarious way, now refuses to allow you the joy of turning sexual trauma into something beautiful that gives life and I spiraled.

Depression is like bobbing out alone at sea and right when you think you've learned how to *swim* something yanks you under and you fight for just a breath, just a break in the enormous waves causing you to sink.

I don't think my husband knew what he meant when he said it, but I distinctly remember a time when I told him I was sinking and he told me that mermaids don't drown. *So* instead of fighting the water, why not learn to *thrive* in it? It will never go away, but I get to *choose* how it affects me. What was painted as ugly scars of my life, I get to wear as badges of *survival*. So why *not* write a fantasy book where I get to choose how the story is told? *So,* in the deepest of postpartum trenches after the longest awaited arrival of my rainbow baby son, Colt, I started writing Pandora's Box.

I've made a lot of decisions in my life out of fear; fear of retaliation, fear of loss of control, fear of people in my life I was supposed to be able to trust, but decisions made in fear are *reactive* and to truly be living, decisions that you make for your own life you must be *proactive*. Do it for *you*. Everyone gets *one* narrator in their life and only *one* story to tell, so why would you let someone else dictate how your story is written? My favorite places have always been fictional and when I read a really good book I get attached to characters as if they truly existed in the real world, because for *me* they *do.* Writing a story was even more intimate than I had imagined, and these characters are a part of me, like some of my closest friends.

So, if you too love books because you love to disappear into a world where *anything* is possible, I hope that you'll pick up your sword and join me in the world I created. Because when we lose our sense of creativity and imagination, are we truly human anymore?

From the deepest part of my heart,

There is no greater redemption story than wearing the *scars* of wounds that others inflicted to destroy you as *badges* of fucking **honor**.

Winter V Hansen

Chapter 1

I tapped my toe impatiently against the tile, my jade green eyes flicking to the simple rose gold watch for what felt like the eighth time. Twenty minutes had passed since I'd asked for that forensic evidence. This was my first stop of the morning, gathering files for a case I had been assigned to just last week—a homicide. The kind that didn't make the news, but had too many questions stamped onto it to be assigned to a newer detective.

With a sigh, I smoothed my long auburn ponytail over my shoulder and crossed my arms over my beige long-sleeve shirt—it was about as uninspiring as the building I was stuck in. The movement made the hem of my grey slacks brush the tops of my black heels, and a sudden shiver rippled through me. No matter the season, precinct twelve's forensic wing, one of the few dull buildings on this planet, always felt like a frozen tundra. I had hope the day would kick off with something more productive than waiting. There was a lot riding on this case—which was why they had handed it to me. Someone who was analytical. Ambitious. Thorough. And I was stuck here, still waiting on Cathy.

Where was she?

Shifting from one foot to the other, I adjusted the badge on my hip. *Precinct 12 Detective* gleamed up at me. I ran my thumb over the raised black letters, lost in thought. Ever since my promotion, the badge had felt like a burden rather than a mark of honor.

When my father, Harrison Vaughn himself—our brave and fearless commissioner—had promoted me, his expression had been filled with unbounded pride. Even when I was a little girl, he had dreamed of me following in his footsteps, eventually becoming Raos commissioner myself—and those were some large shoes to fill. The shadow of expectation followed me wherever I went.

I glanced around the office again—empty. Everyone who normally would have been bustling around filing paperwork seemed to be busy preparing for the big precinct ball. A groan rose in my chest as I remembered I was an attendee. Extravagant parties had never been my thing, but as a Raos detective, I had quickly learned that public perception was both important and vital. I raised my watch again, my ivory skin contrasting against the links. Six in the morning. It was way too early for this.

With a sigh, I tapped the small bell on the raised stone counter, it's chime echoing brilliantly through the empty halls. Leaning forward, I nearly pressed my nose against the glass that separated the lobby from the back of the building. My eyes scanned through the massive shelves, stacks of files, and beat up books. Still, not a soul in sight. Leaning one elbow on the countertop, I brushed a speck of lint off my slacks impatiently. If it had been up to me, I would have worn combat boots and tactical pants all the time, but formal wear was both expected and enforced here.

"Ah, Detective Vaughn, I apologize!" Came a light and airy voice. Cathy bumped a bookshelf as she rushed to the front, sending papers skittering everywhere like confetti. "Oh dear." She blushed quickly working to stack the papers back where they had been. I bit back a grin. Cathy was new to forensic keeping, but she was always incredibly keen on details and very organized—that is, when she wasn't busy accidentally dumping papers into the floor. Her dark brown hair settled in large curls around her face, a dramatic contrast to my fiery red. Her head barely rose over the tall desktop as she peered at me.

"I had a hard time finding the rest of the evidence files. They were moved to a different wing since we've been renovating." Her breath came out in huffs, like she had been sprinting around flustered. She slid the filed stack neatly underneath the glass panels separating us. "No worries! Thanks for grabbing these, Cathy!" I said with a nod. She smiled back at me, her light skin crinkling around the corners of her blue eyes. "Anytime, Detective." she said and I watched as she rushed away, her small body tucking between the shelves. I would feel incredibly claustrophobic working as a forensic keeper, I thought to myself before turning and heading for the front door. My heels clicked against the floor as I walked through the doors. A rush of cold air blasted my face, blowing loose strands of auburn hair against my cheeks.

Spring had just arrived on Liarta, my home planet, and as April shifted into May, the icy chill had finally begun to thaw. It was beginning to be replaced by something almost pleasant. A more mild tempered weather. The planet itself was massive and reminiscent of the ancient human planet Earth. Just as her ancestor had, patches of lush greenery formed soft, mossy carpets between golden skyscrapers that spiraled skyward. Thought there was plenty of land, the structures were tightly woven into golden arches that rose higher and higher in silent contest.

Only the elite lived here—politicians, celebrities, and the disgustingly wealthy. Every surface gleamed with artificial perfection. The rest of the humans lived on our sister planet, Cappurn—a cold, harsher world with a fraction of the population. Snowy, inhospitable, and wholly forgettable. Today, it seemed, the weather had gotten confused on which planet it resided and the chilled air bit against my nose and ears. I silently wished I had worn my coat for the walk to and from my squad car.

Since the city of Raos had been growing at an exceeding pace, Commissioner Vaughn petitioned for the forensic department to have en expanded building separate from the precinct. A wonderful investment for the forensics team—a minor inconvenience for the rest of us.

I rushed to where I had parked, tucking the files tightly against my chest. It was an older car, made before the sweep of new technology. Black but faded to almost an ash grey from the unrelenting light from our system's star, Aurelios. The freshly placed Precinct 12 stickers gleamed up against the faded paint of the car door. I pressed my thumb against the reader on the window's side triggering a click and the door swung open with a reluctant creak. Sliding into the driver's seat, I set my belongings on the passenger side and put the car in drive, speeding away. The car hummed beneath me, silent and smooth, gliding along the elevated expressway like a whisper through silk.

Aurelios light danced off the skyline ahead, where countless towers stretched towards the clouds like gilded fingers, each golden surface glittering like water. Some of the building twisted impossibly upwards with gravity defying elegance, while others floated above their bases—levitating through some miracle of engineering I had long since stopped questioning.

Below, the city pulsed with life. Hover-trams zipped between platforms suspended in midair, casting soft neon trails in their wake. Pedestrian walkways glowed with soft blue light, winding between levels like threads in a massive web, dotted with people in sleek, minimalistic attire. On either side of the highway, enormous digital billboards projected 3D ads into the sky, their holograms shimmering just past my windshield—entertainment teasers, biotech enhancements, even planetary vacation packages. The golden buildings weren't just status symbols, they were power hubs, data centers, and vertical ecosystems all wrapped in radiant alloy designed to reflect both light and heat. Overhead, droned flitted about like lazy birds between towers. Some delivered packages, others no doubt meticulously scanned traffic. Liarta may have looked like a dream, but the deeper you dove into it, the more you saw the layers—opulence built on tension. Perfection laced with secrets.

And I was headed right into it's heart—Precinct 12.

Chapter 2

Precinct 12 was as glamorous as a Liarta precinct could be. When my father had been sworn in as commissioner, he had designed it to symbolize Liarta's pride—shiny, extravagant, and overly grand. In my opinion, it had all been unnecessary, though my opinion had never really mattered. I was just a detective, after all.

I walked through the giant glass doors, a large indoor fountain bubbling quietly welcomed me in. Its water curled into intricate arcs, winding over itself, similar to the architecture of Raos, our capital city. Decorative vines clung to the stone walls surrounding me, and my heels clicked against the shiny black tile as I made my way to the reception desk. The stack of forensic evidence shifted in my arms, and I adjusted it back into its folder.

The precinct lobby was quiet this particular morning. No one waited for Margaret to call them to the desk as I passed the line of neatly arranged white lobby chairs. Reaching the receptionist desk, I tapped my fingers against it's surface and nodded to Margaret through the giant glass panes. Her ash grey hair shone in the Aurelios light as she gazed at me through her ruby-red framed glasses.

"Morning, Margaret," I said with a nod as I badged through the turn styles. "Morning, Detective Vaughn." She tilted her head slightly as she continued, "Lieutenant Smith said to inform you he's waiting for your interrogation of the suspect they just brought in." She slid some paperwork under the slats in the glass. "Thank you," I responded, taking the stack. Excellent—more paperwork I inwardly groaned to myself.

Turning left at the front desk, I made my way down the hall with just the click of my shoes to keep me company. The last decade had been significant for police technology, including the addition of the new atom scanners. These scanners worked on all kinds of atoms, not just metal. They could detect anything used in making weapons or explosives with pinpoint accuracy. The influx of endorsement money from Liarta citizens had allowed the city to fund them, although some were still wary of the AI integration. I scanned my badge and stepped slowly through the scanner's blue light, the massive stack of papers growing heavier in my arms with each step.

"State your name and credentials," an AI voice said. "Pandora Vaughn. Detective," I replied, holding my badge up to the camera. The light scanned me from top to bottom. "Detective Pandora Vaughn identified. Clear," the AI voice confirmed, and the sliding glass door whooshed open in front of me. I slid through, clutching my papers as they flapped in the draft. "Have a great day!" the voice beamed as the door whooshed shut again behind me.

Casually, I walked through the open area at the back of the police department toward my desk. Gentle chatter filled the air as officers discussed their cases between work stations and the smell of freshly brewed morning coffee wafted towards me. Setting my stack of papers down with a soft thud, I dropped into my chair and leaned back, my gaze drifting to the towering floor-to-ceiling wall of windows beside me.

Despite the crisp breeze, it was a beautiful day—Aurelios' rays warming my skin through the glass. Outside, people strolled leisurely along the walkways, sipping their coffees and moving like ants in a colony, each absorbed in their own routine. They never seemed concerned with the world around them, simply going about their day on autopilot, lost in the tasks at hand.

"Detective Vaughn." A male voice boomed behind me and I sighed gathering my wits. I knew exactly whose voice that was, and I hadn't been mentally prepared to deal with him this morning. "Morning, Lieutenant Smith. It's a beautiful day," I responded, spinning in my chair toward the direction of his voice. He skimmed right over my attempt at small talk as his glacial blue eyes landed on mine, stern and pointed.

"Adam Fritz is in room four." His grey mustache twitched with each word. He pressed the pad of his pointer finger into the surface of my desk, looming his height over me. "Only keep him as long as you need. I don't need the media catching wind that we've got Mr. Fritz here for questioning. Understood?"

"Understood," I murmured, the smile fading from my face. Lieutenant Smith had a reputation for being a hard ass. He ran the precinct efficiently, though few would have called him approachable. Personally, I had always seen him more as a grumpy grandpa. His thick gray eyebrows perfectly matched his mustache which twitched more as he scanned the room. Noticing his presence, the other officers quickly wrapped up their conversations and hurried back to their stations. I rolled my eyes.

"Don't think that just because your father is commissioner, you get special interrogation privileges either," he said gruffly. His gray suit jacket hugged his frame tightly, and I almost imagined he saw it as his own personal cape of justice. "I never do," I responded, crossing my arms over my chest. If anything, my father being commissioner had put a target on my back. That had been something I learned a long time ago. Anything

I achieved in Precinct 12 had been the result of my own hard work—never special privileges.

"If that's all, I need to head to room four. We wouldn't want Mr. Fritz to wait any longer than necessary." I stood, clutching the forensic file Cathy had given me that morning in my hand. Smith narrowed his eyes, skimming them over the file I held. His jaw tightened in silent warning and his eyes flicked back to mine, but he said nothing—just turned on his heel and strode away. Uniformed officers quickly moved out of his path, lowering their gazes, hoping to avoid bearing the brunt of his foul mood. With a sigh, I made my way toward the interrogation room.

Let's get this over with.

I peered through the one-way glass at the suspect seated inside the room. He leaned back in his chair, his dark brown hair perfectly smoothed to the side, not a strand out of place. His navy blue suit—neatly pressed and impeccably tailored—flexed slightly as he moved, the row of brown buttons glinting under the light. He casually turned his wrist, most likely checking the time on his gaudy gold watch, before clasping his hands together. As he leaned forward, his eyes flickered toward the mirrored glass, and for a moment, it felt as if his gaze could pierce straight through my chest. I smoothed down the front of my slacks, grasped the door handle, and entered the room.

"Good afternoon, Adam Fritz," I addressed the suspect, my tone even. Pulling out the metal chair across from him, I cringed at the grating sound as it scraped against the floor. "Will your attorney be joining us?" I asked. He remained unfazed, his expression unreadable. "He seems to be unavailable at this time," he said slowly, narrowing his eyes. "Would you like one appointed to you, Mr. Fritz?" I continued. His eyes narrowed further. "Do I need one?" he asked cautiously. "Do you understand why you've been brought in today?" I asked, lowering myself into the chair.

Crossing one leg over the other, I leaned in slightly. If I was going to be a female detective in a male-dominated field, I might as well leverage my strengths instead of fighting my weaknesses. People didn't often find me physically intimidating, so I opted to make them uncomfortable instead. Considered statuesque at six feet tall, my slender frame lacked the imposing bulk that commanded immediate fear. Instead, I relied on pressing my male suspects' imaginations—often, that alone was enough to get the information I needed. I pressed my lips together, keeping my expression neutral as Mr. Fritz studied me. After a pause, he finally spoke.

"Yes, I understand you are working on a case you believe I can assist with." Another deliberate pause. "However, I must inform you that I have not come across any information I can disclose—to you, your department, or your colleagues." He leaned forward, narrowing his eyes. "I haven't told you the details of why you were brought in yet, Mr. Fritz. How could you possibly know that you have no information that would benefit me?" I asked, tilting my head. "What information could you possibly think I have to bestow upon you, Detective?" His voice was steady, his posture unwavering as he matched my advance.

His confidence was undeniable, but I knew better—whether or not he was directly involved, he potentially knew who was. Politics came with a certain level of privilege, and ever since his election as Raos governor, Adam Fritz had been known for having dirt on everyone. Many suspected that blackmail was the very reason he had climbed the ranks in the first place. Most citizens of Liarta doubted his election had been legitimate at all, whispering that his victory had been orchestrated by his father—the president of the very planet I served under. Of course, any fraud claims had conveniently disappeared just a month after. Just like clockwork. I leaned back in my chair and casually opened the file I had tucked under my arm. My fingers lingered on its edge as my eyes flicked over the label briefly before continuing.

Amy O'Rayne

The name had been unfamiliar when the case landed on my desk a week ago. Amy—5'6", blonde, slightly curvy—she wasn't someone who stood out in any particularly remarkable way. But the circumstance of her death had been anything but ordinary, instantly piquing my detective instincts. She had been found in her car, parked outside the office building where she worked. Initially, there had been no signs of foul play. The vehicle had been locked with the engine running, idling until it was empty of gas. She had been wearing office attire—a blue long-sleeve blouse, black pencil skirt, and black kitten heels—as if she had no indication of what that day would bring to her. It hadn't been until she failed to show up for work for an entire week that anyone had taken notice.

When officers arrived to question her coworkers, they found her car tucked away at the very back of the building's parking lot. Inside, Amy had sat eerily still, her head gently taped to the headrest and her hands folded neatly in her lap as if she were simply taking a quiet break. By the time I arrived on the scene, officers had dusted the car for prints—but found nothing. Not even her own. The interior had been spotless. No crumbs, no fingerprints, no stray belongings. It was as if the car had never been used, let alone driven. Just Amy, sitting upright, staring out the windshield—frozen in time.

The absence of prints hadn't surprised me. Whoever had

done this had a professional touch. What had struck me as odd was the complete lack of personal items. No purse, wallet, phone, or even a lunch bag. Either the scene had been meticulously staged, or the killer had taken everything with them. The autopsy report had only deepened the mystery. The lab had detected traces of vecuronium—a paralytic. A small injection site found at the back of Amy's neck indicated how it had been administered.

But the real questions remained—when, where, and *why?*

"It is my understanding that you filed a missing person's report for your secretary, Amy, earlier this week. Is that correct?" I asked, opening the file and sliding her photo across the table, pinning it down with my fingers in front of him. Mr. Fritz leaned in slightly, studying the image before giving a slow nod. "I did. She failed to show up for work starting Tuesday morning." His response was brief, his tone measured. Then, he leaned back in his chair, crossing his legs and folding his hands over his knee, settling into a posture of practiced ease. "I assumed she was either still missing, or you had found her in unfortunate circumstances," he sighed, his expression soft and unmoving. It was so quiet after he stopped talking I could almost hear his watch ticking away on his wrist. I narrowed my eyes at him. "Why didn't you report her missing on Tuesday, Adam? You waited until Sunday evening and were at home—not at work—when you finally made the call."

Adam remained unfazed and didn't move an inch. "I was unaware that she had been missing. I have secretaries who fail to return to work all the time, Detective. Miss O'Rayne was the third secretary I'd had this year. I didn't think anything of Mrs. O'Rayne's disappearance until she failed to collect her paycheck on Sunday, which she normally did." He pressed his mouth into a firm line. "Quite honestly, Detective, she was my best secretary thus far, and I'm disappointed something happened to her." I scraped my chair back and leaned forward, pressing my palms firmly against the cold metal table. My face hovered just a foot away from his, "Mr. Fritz, if you could drop the theatrics and tell me what you know about her disappearance, I'd appreciate it."

Adam pursed his lips, his eyes narrowing. "Detective, I don't know anything about Amy's disappearance, and I'd caution you against insinuating that I had any involvement." There it was—the politician's wall. Whether he was guilty or not, politicians were trained to put up a defense, deny everything, and minimize any chance of implication. But Adam wasn't as polished as others I had interviewed. He was young, inexperienced, and lacked the careful calculation of seasoned officials. He didn't have to be clever, though. He knew that no matter what, his father would bail him out before anything could stick.

"April fifteenth at eight p.m., Mr. Fritz. Where were you, and who were you with?" Adam let the question hang in the air, thick with accusation. "I was with my wife. We were getting dinner at Pine Meadows, the upscale restaurant across town—you know the one." He studied me, folding his hands and bringing his elbows up to rest on the table, inching his way into my space. I felt the warmth of his skin leeching into mine as he paused, seemingly to ponder something. "But I do believe you knew that, Detective, so why am I here? What do you wish to interrogate me about that warranted me taking time out of my day to answer your questions?" A smirk rose on his face as his minty breath dusted the loose strands of hair away from my face. My breath hitched in the back of my throat, which had suddenly gone very dry.

I had known Adam since our school days. We were never close, but we had always been aware of each other in passing.

The girls had found him incredibly charming—he had a natural ability to captivate people with nothing more than his presence.

"Adam, would you care to explain what Biltmore Pharmaceuticals has to gain by funding your election campaign?" My voice echoed off the walls as I forced myself to maintain composure.

"If you must know, Detective," he began, sitting back in his chair. He picked a speck of lint off the front of his suit jacket as if he didn't have a care in the world. "Biltmore Pharmaceuticals backed my campaign due to their interest in my and my father's proposed legislation regarding prescription medications and narcotics. The current tax on sedatives, narcotics, and paralytics hindered their ability to conduct proper research and develop other essential, lifesaving drugs. The proposed bill would provide a tax break, allowing them to redirect those funds toward advancements in areas such as cancer treatments." He shrugged, then glanced around the room with an air of disinterest.

"Mr. Fritz, are you aware of a drug called vecuronium?" I questioned, tilting my head slightly, trying to get a read on his new demeanor. "No, ma'am. I do not preoccupy myself with specific drugs unless directly influenced by them. That is for the doctors and nurses to occupy themselves with." He returned his gaze to me, adjusting his watch, the gaudy metal glowering at me from across the room. "Mrs. O'Rayne had five times the appropriate dose of vecuronium in her system when our officers found her," I stated, crossing my arms over my chest.

Adam sighed, "So, you have found her." He leaned back slightly. "Detective, I have no idea where she got the drugs. Yes, Biltmore Pharmaceuticals is owned by my family and was funding my campaign, but they have never visited my office or supplied us with any medications. If she went behind my back and communicated with the company, that would directly violate her contract." Bobbing his head, he added, "My lawyers will need to be informed—just in case legal action is necessary." I straightened, tapping the edge of the file against the table. "Mr. Fritz, when was the last time you were in contact with Mrs. O'Rayne?"

The fluorescent lights in the interrogation room casted a stark white glow over Adam, accentuating the sharp angles of his features and the firmness of his jawline. The precinct lighting was never forgiving, aging everyone under its glare, yet he remained undeniably striking despite it. His suit jacket strained slightly across his broad shoulders, the fabric pulling taut with subtle tension. He had always been athletic, even in his younger years—his dedication to his appearance unwavering, sometimes even to a fault.

"Monday afternoon, after I returned to the office to grab some paperwork from her. She said goodbye for the day around 3 p.m., clocked out, and left my office—I assumed to go home," he replied. "And after Mrs. O'Rayne left that afternoon, how did you spend your evening?" I pressed, growing tired of the back-and-forth with this man. One moment, he tried to charm me into distraction; the next, he acted as though I had utterly deflated his confidence and wasn't worth a moment of his time. This wasn't the first time Adam Fritz had sat in my interrogation room—but it was the first time he was the prime suspect in one of my cases.

"Detective, I made several work calls from my office, which you can verify in my call log, and I drove home around five o'clock to pick up my wife for dinner. My Mercedes has a tracking app—you're welcome to check that as well," Adam stated matter-of-factly. Then, glancing at his watch, he added, "Are you arresting me, or am I free to go? I have an appointment with an investor in thirty minutes, and I don't intend to keep him waiting." He pushed back his chair to stand.

"Sit down," I snapped, my tone firm. Half-rising, he hesitated for a moment before slowly lowering himself back into his seat. "Amy was found dead in a car that wasn't hers, parked in your office lot, after being missing for a week. You were the last known person to have contact with her. One of the companies funding both you and your father's campaign is the only manufacturer on this planet producing the paralytic drug found in her system. She had no signs of struggle, meaning she was either killed in her sleep or by someone she *trusted*. Her bank records show a $500,000 deposit from your company's payroll at 2:45 p.m.—just minutes before she left your office. Meanwhile, you claim you stayed alone for another two hours before driving home to meet your wife. Would you care to fill in any gaps for me, Mr. Fritz?"

Silence.

The air vent above me hummed, its stale breeze brushing against my back as my heart pounded in my ears. Adam blinked a few times, processing the information. "I was not aware of any wire transfers to Mrs. O'Rayne in that amount. A discrepancy of that magnitude would have been flagged by my personnel and brought to my attention. The funding for our campaign has never been accessible to my employees—it is always managed solely by my father or me. Mrs. O'Rayne had no clearance to handle those funds, nor would she have had access to the pharmaceuticals locked away in a facility that neither I nor any of my employees have ever visited. As for Amy's passing, I had no idea she was gone. I understand why you'd assume I have answers, Detective, but I don't." He said and I exhaled sharply, pressing my fingers to the bridge of my nose as my professional facade cracked just slightly.

"Adam, do you realize how much evidence directly links you and your family business to this case?" I asked, setting the file down on the table between us. "Even if you didn't personally kill her, a judge is going to look at all of this and see one thing—irrefutable proof that Amy died because of you." My voice grew a little louder as my frustration built. I was getting absolutely nowhere. "Adam, can you at least tell me if you recognize this vehicle?" He obliged, leaning forward to examine the image.

At first glance, it appeared to be a standard base model sedan, but a closer look revealed unusual modifications—only adding more questions to an already convoluted case. The black four-door sedan had slightly tinted windows, but the most peculiar detail was its upgraded anti-theft flush door handles, which could only be unlocked using a thumbprint—prints that had been meticulously wiped clean. A scan of the vehicle had failed to emit any VIN or registration, and its AI module had been destroyed. It was as if Amy's existence had been erased entirely. Adam furrowed his brow. "It looks like a Mercedes, Detective, but I've never seen this model before. It looks brand new—maybe even a prototype?" He leaned in closer, studying the details with more interest.

"I feel like I've seen that car before, though. *Somewhere*," Adam murmured, tilting his head as if reaching for a distant memory buried deep in his mind. I didn't have time for this. "Where would Amy have gotten this vehicle, Adam? A prototype like that would be well beyond what she could afford on a secretary's salary." I slid the photo back neatly into my file. "I'm not sure. Is that why she stole five hundred thousand dollars from my company?" He lifted his gaze to meet mine, flipping the interrogation back on me.

"No. The money was never used. When our officers finally

accessed her bank account to verify its contents, the entire amount remained untouched." He studied me briefly, his eyes flicking over my face before scanning the rest of me as if searching for something—perhaps a tell, a sign of doubt. Then, he exhaled. "I don't know how to help you, Detective. I truly have no answers to give." His voice was calm, but I sensed the truth beneath the surface. Adam didn't know what had happened to Amy, which made him uneasy. Someone close to him had been eliminated, and he had no control over it.

"You're free to go, Mr. Fritz. Officer Jenkins will escort you out of the precinct. Thank you for your time." I turned on my heel, ready to leave the room. "Detective?" Adam called after me, his voice smooth, almost playful, changing from how it had been mere moments ago. I paused but didn't turn around. "Do make our next meeting a little more *pleasurable*," he cooed.

I hurried out of the interrogation room and headed back to my desk, my heart pounding steadily in my chest. Damn him for getting under my skin. Weaving through the maze of desks, I reached mine and slammed the files down with more force than necessary. Exhaling, I ran my shaky fingers through the loose strands of hair framing my face, tucking them back into place.

"Ah, Pandora, how did interrogating Adam Fritz go?" A bright, familiar voice pulled me from my thoughts. My spirits lifted as I turned to see Detective Ivy Zephyr—an exceptional investigator at Precinct 12 and my best friend. She was a petite woman with a personality far larger than her frame could contain. Her blonde, shoulder-length hair was neatly secured in a tight bun, not a strand out of place. Dressed in dark green slacks and a crisp black button-up blouse fastened to her chin, she exuded an air of precision. Organized. Composed. Effortlessly put together. She never faltered, never sweated. It was admirable and almost infuriating.

"He didn't tell me anything I didn't already know, unfortunately," I sighed, sinking into my chair as stray strands of hair slipped around my face again. "Isn't he your only suspect?" Ivy asked, settling gracefully into her roller chair across from me. She crossed one leg over the other, her badge gleaming under the overhead lights—Detective, Precinct 12. An exact match to mine.

"He *was*," I groaned, resting my forehead against the desk. "The man didn't even know she was dead. My detective instincts tell me he's not our guy—though I'd love nothing more than to take Adam Fritz down by the kneecaps, trust me." Lifting my head again, I twirled a pen between my fingers before huffing, "He couldn't even identify the vehicle. Incredibly unhelpful." Ivy smirked, "He's always had a way of getting under your skin,"

"You. Also unhelpful." I shot her a glare before sighing. "You need to head back to their office," she said, pulling a stack of case files from her filing cabinet. "See if anyone else saw her that day."

"Uniforms already questioned everyone. I don't know who else we could ask that would actually give us anything useful." I gestured toward the mountain of paperwork on my desk. "Besides, I need to go back through all of this. I'm ridiculously behind." Before Ivy could respond, the office doors burst open. Two detectives marched in, dragging a thrashing suspect in handcuffs. The man kicked and twisted, his fangs flashing as he snarled at his captors. Ivy and I both snapped our heads toward the commotion just as the two detectives leading the parade came into view—Detective Chance Kamar and Detective Luke Nesnah.

Oh *joy*.

Chapter 3

Almost in perfect sync, Ivy and I turned to face each other. No words were needed—we both knew what the other was thinking. Not the two of them.

I had dared to hope I'd get a day without dealing with those two. Wishful thinking. Detective Chance Kamar and Detective Luke Nesnah were, without exaggeration, the bane of my existence. Combined, their superiority complexes could fill the precinct with enough hot air to suffocate us all. Chance's boyish antics were enough to drive me up a wall—even if he was Ivy's boyfriend. And Luke Nesnah? His mere existence made me want to set myself on fire.

"Here we go," I muttered under my breath, earning a sharp flick to the arm from Ivy. "Cut it out," she scolded, shaking her head before returning her attention to the spectacle unfolding before us.

"Next time we tell you to come in for questioning, it'll be a lot easier on you if you just cooperate," Chance grumbled as he shoved the suspect into a holding cell and slammed the door shut. "Seems like it would've been easier for you, too," the suspect shot back with a smug grin. "Looks like I gave your buddy there a nice parting gift." He jerked his thumb toward Detective Nesnah, whose lip bore the evidence of a recent scuffle—a dried smear of blood from a split bottom lip. Detective Nesnah snarled back at him in response.

I bit back a satisfied smirk. Ivy and I watched in silence, neither of us daring to break the tension. The room was so still you could hear a pin drop. "Yeah, well, look who's sitting behind bars now, tough guy," Chance quipped, clicking the lock into place with finality. Detective Nesnah loomed over the cell looking broody and irritated. His jaw was drawn tight and his eyes stormy.

So, the *usual*.

I watched as Chance lumbered over to our cluster of desks at the back of the room. The usual chatter among officers resumed, filling the air with a familiar hum. "Morning, ladies," he cooed, leaning down to give Ivy a quick peck on the lips. She blushed. His blonde hair was perfectly slicked back and his green eyes shimmered with amusement.

"Detective Kamar," I drawled, rolling my eyes toward Ivy. "Who's that?" She nodded toward the suspect, who was pounding his fists against the cell door and taunting the nearby officers. The two closest to him looked wary but focused on their paperwork. "Just a junkie making a scene in front of the locals—same old, same old," Chance replied with a smirk. "Isn't that Casey Lament?" Ivy asked, leaning around him further for a better look. "Yeah, third time this week. He's probably looking at a longer sentence this time. He can't seem to mind his own business—keeps preaching on street corners about how we're all doomed to the Nephrians or some crap." Without hesitation, he grabbed Ivy's coffee off her desk and took a swig. "Your coffee's cold," he noted, setting down the cup. She just shook her head at him, exasperated but unsurprised.

Out of the corner of my eye, I caught Detective Nesnah at his desk. His thumb swiped over his lip, wiping away the last trace of blood. He leaned back against his chair, muscles shifting beneath his shirt, utterly unfazed by the earlier scuffle. He was tall—even taller than me by about two inches—and built like he spent every spare moment in the gym. His dark brown curls sat in a disheveled heap on top of his head, each strand seemingly at war with the others, refusing to settle in one direction. The deep bronze of his skin contrasted sharply with his dark hair, making him impossible to ignore.

I found myself watching the steady rise and fall of his chest as he kept his eyes closed, lost in thought. I wondered what was running through that self-assured, infuriating mind of his. Surely nothing good. His eyes snapped open as if he had heard my thoughts from across the room locking onto mine with unnerving precision. My breath hitched, heat creeping up the back of my neck. His piercing blue gaze felt like it was peeling away layers, seeing straight through me. I quickly looked away, a shiver running down my spine.

"Pandora!" Ivy snapped her fingers in front of my face, jolting me back to reality. "Sorry," I muttered, rubbing my temples. A headache was starting to form, creeping in like an unwelcome guest. Between this damn case and the two insufferable buffoons in the room, I was convinced this day was going to be the death of me.

A loud buzz from the intercom echoed overhead. "Officer training in one hour," a voice announced. I groaned. The first Friday of every month meant mandatory training for all on-duty officers, and once again, I had completely forgotten. "Forgot again, didn't you?" Ivy teased. I let out a sigh and nodded. Just when I thought today couldn't get any longer. "I'll meet you on the training court in five minutes," she said, rising from her seat. Chance patted her shoulder before striding off toward the men's room. The once-busy precinct grew quieter as officers filed out, heading toward the locker rooms. With a resigned breath, I tucked my papers into my desk and followed the crowd.

***

The locker rooms at the back of the precinct were old and built from cinder blocks, their walls lined with freshly painted blue lockers. Wooden benches sat in the middle of the room, and the air carried a stale scent that somehow still felt familiar. It reminded me of the academy days—grueling, exhausting, but oddly comforting. "Pandora!" One of the newer female officers called through the room as she waved me over. I wandered toward her, pulling the door to my locker open. The metal groaned on it's hinges.

The fresh coat of paint gleamed under the locker room lights as my eyes scanned over my name printed boldly on the front of it. Detective Pandora Vaughn. "I didn't see you here yesterday evening, take a personal day?" she asked, plopping down onto the metal bench. Officer Katie Perdecky was a force to be reckoned with and one of our newer uniformed officers at Precinct 12. She had pulled her jet-black hair into a long braid, which she absentmindedly twirled before letting it rest at her waist. Hazel eyes locked onto mine with an intensity that always made it seem like she was preparing to eat me for lunch. "No, I was working from home," I replied, "And good morning to you, too." I said flashing a grin.

She pulled a granola bar from her pocket and took a huge bite before opening her mouth to speak again, "You look like hell." She lilted and I huffed a laugh. That was Katie—blunt to the point of being jarring, but I appreciated her honesty most days. She was an acquired taste but one I found myself drawn to. "It's been a long morning," I admitted, rubbing the back of my neck as I pulled out black cargo pants and a matching tank top. "I hope you grabbed a coffee," she continued, taking another bite of her granola bar. "I heard training's gonna be intense today. Sparring and range duty."

I rolled my eyes. Just what I needed. I changed into my training clothes and sat on the bench to lace up my combat boots while Katie lounged, casually observing the officers filing in and out. Her muscular frame was hard to miss, her toned legs flexing against her black training pants. "So, what do you think of Detective Nesnah?" She asked. I coughed in an attempt to mask my surprise. "Nothing right now. He's new." I muttered, tightening my laces. Katie leaned forward, resting her elbows on her knees. "Didn't he come from Precinct 10 across the city?"

"He was reassigned for a case here," I answered, keeping my voice even. Her hazel eyes narrowed, "Which case?"

I shot up from the bench, rubbing my hands together, "Let's get going. Wouldn't want to miss training." She chewed her last bite slowly, her gaze sharpening. "Right. Wouldn't want to miss training," she echoed, crumpling her granola wrapper and flicking it into the trash. Shrugging, she stood and jogged toward the door leading to the training field. "See you out there." Her long braid swung behind her as she disappeared through the doorway. It closed with a soft thunk. I pressed my hands to my temples, inhaling deeply. I would not let him get under my skin today. I needed to stay focused. Gathering my bearings, I pushed open the door to the training field.

The cool shadow of the concrete passage leading to the field provided brief relief against the day's warmth. My boots scuffed along the ground, their rhythm matching the steady march of other officers heading toward the field. Stepping into the open, I squinted against Aurelios' glare and shielded my eyes. The massive training field stretched before me, the grass soft beneath my feet as I approached the cluster of officers gathered in the center. I glanced up at the towering walls of the training dome—high but not completely enclosed. The morning light peeked just over the edge, bathing the field in golden light. The padded interior and looming dome might have felt suffocating if the space weren't so vast.

Chance strode across the lawn, his broad shoulders flexing in the Aurelios light. As he reached me, he bumped his shoulder against mine with a smirk. "Itching for some training?" he asked, waggling his eyebrows. "More like itching to get it over with," I huffed. "Leave her alone, she's grumpy today." Ivy jabbed him in the shoulder, making him clutch his chest in mock offense, mouth agape. I rolled my eyes.

"I hate training day," Ivy continued, flicking a speck of dirt from under one of her bright pink nails. "We all just get hot and sweaty rolling around with each other." She muttered. "Sometimes it's fun to be hot and sweaty and roll around on each other." Chance snorted. Ivy's cheeks turned pink as she coughed, trying to hide her embarrassment.

A feral grin spread across his face as he gazed at her face which was growing a deeper and deeper pink with every second that passed. I bit my lip, chuckling to myself. "What are you laughing at?" Chance turned his grin on me. "You're the sweatiest of all of us!" He threw his head back in laughter, his teeth gleaming. Heat crept up my neck. "Well, at least I put in the work instead of cracking jokes the whole time," I shot back. "Hey!" he protested. "Who says I can't crack jokes and crack spines at the same time?" I rolled my eyes even harder. As much as his antics could be exhausting, I'd learned to keep up with Chance's relentless humor. He caught me off guard now and then but throwing in my own little jabs made his constant teasing easier to endure.

Finally, officer Mark Daneer strode onto the field, clipboard in hand, the Aurelios light glinting off his nearly bald head as he scanned the gathered officers. Behind him, his assistant, Officer Yari Truce, trailed closely, her blonde ponytail bouncing against her shoulders.

"Alright, listen up. We're doing combat training today. Pay attention to your assigned pair," Daneer called out, dragging his finger down the clipboard as he read the names. "Jenkins, you're with Young. Smith, you're with Lando. Trace, you're with Fikes. Zephyr, you're with Nesnah." Ivy let out an audible groan but made her way toward their designated training ring. My jaw tensed as I watched Nesnah follow her across the field. "Vaughn, you're with Kamar," Daneer finished, his voice carrying over the field. "Pair up! We're working through exercises twelve through eighteen in the combat manuals."

The moment he finished, the officers dispersed to their designated training spots. "I didn't expect to get paired with you today," I muttered, tightening my ponytail with a firm tug. "Yeah, looks like Daneer is pairing opposite sexes today," Chance remarked, stepping into the marked ring painted onto the grass. He rolled his shoulders and stretched his arms, loosening up for the session. I caught the way his gaze flickered toward Ivy and Nesnah, his jaw shifting as he took a deep breath. "She's fine. She can handle herself," I reassured him. He turned his attention back to me, a grin forming. "Oh, I know. Tiny but mighty. If anything, I feel bad for Nesnah,"

Chance stepped forward, cracking his neck with a sharp snap. "Alright, Pandora. Let's see what you've got."

I dropped into a ready stance and watched as he mirrored me. The muscles in my legs coiled like a loaded spring, eager to launch. We circled each other, carefully adjusting our footing, our movements echoing across the field as we waited for one of us to make the first move. He shot his arm out with a sudden burst of energy but I dodged swiftly, rolling to the side. "You'll have to be faster than that," I taunted, steadying myself. "Who said that was as fast as I go?" he countered, inching toward me. I didn't back down, pressing forward until there was barely a foot between us. "I—" Before I could finish, he grabbed my forearm and yanked, shoving me backwards to the ground with his weight pressing down on me. I'd let my mouth get ahead of me and lost focus.

I gritted my teeth and pulled my leg up between us, driving my knee into his chest to create space. "What's the deal with you and Nesnah?" he asked, shifting his weight to pin me at the hip. "Why is everyone so interested in *Detective Nesnah*?" I snapped, gripping his wrist to keep him from locking my arm. "So, something is going on between you two?" His eyebrows lifted knowingly. I twisted beneath him, freeing my right leg. "Nothing is going on," I hissed, snaking my arms around his and trapping them against me.

Using the momentum, I bucked my hips, flipped him over, and pinned him beneath me, my arm pressed firmly against his throat. Chance, ever unbothered, remained calm and calculating, his expression unreadable. My mind raced—what was he planning next? "If nothing was going on, then why do you seem so worked up about me asking?" he mused, his voice slightly breathy beneath my grip.

He was distracting me and it was working.

I tried to ignore him, but he kept studying my face, his sharp gaze unwavering. He shoved my hand straight up without warning, forcing me to brace against the turf. Our faces were mere inches apart, his breath hot against my skin. "I've known you long enough to tell when something's bothering you. Did he say something to you?" Chance asked, his voice low and probing. I furrowed my brows, confused. And then, in a swift motion, he flipped me and pressed his chest against mine. "Also, never underestimate your opponent when pinned beneath you," he murmured.

He moved so fast that I had barely registered what was happening. With a sudden shift, he hooked his leg under my arm, rolled to the side and arched his hips, locking my arm straight. The moment I felt the pressure of the arm bar, I tapped. Chance grinned wide and jumped to his feet. I huffed, frustrated, but shook it off as I stood. "Again," he ordered. I took a ready stance and immediately threw a jab at his chin. "I heard he was assigned to your mother's case," Chance said.

I froze.

Seizing the moment, he grabbed my wrist and redirected me, causing me to stumble forward. Whipping back around to face him, I glared as he curled his finger in a taunting *come here* motion. "What do you know about my mother's case?" I demanded. Aurelios was beating down on the training arena, the heat radiating off the ground. Sweat slid down my back, and my ponytail clung to my damp neck. Chance wiped a bead of sweat from his brow, creeping toward me again, "Only what Ivy told me—that it's still open and that he's the lead detective."

This time, he dropped his shoulders and charged. I barely had time to brace before his shoulder met my hips, and we both hit the ground with a heavy thud. I scrambled for a hold, feeling his weight shift as he gained the mount. My boots scuffed the turf, my movements frantic, like a beetle flipped on its back. With a sharp thrust, I drove my knee into his chest. He coughed, loosening his grip just enough for me to roll him onto his back. "It is," I hissed. "And he is."

Wasting no time, I moved again rolling onto my shoulder and sliding behind his body. My arm coiled around his neck as I adjusted my grip. I only had seconds—I needed to move fast. I tucked my hand under my opposite arm, locking my legs around his waist. His fingers dug into my thighs as he gripped tightly, trying to break free. He bucked, but it only drove him deeper into my hold. The friction of the turf burned against my back, but I refused to let go. Tightening my arms around his chin, I squeezed until he tapped out—finally. Leaning forward, he wrapped his arms around his knees, silent for a moment as he processed.

"Why is it still open?" he asked, turning his head to look at me. I stood, letting my arms hang slack at my sides. "He says he has to investigate all potential causes of death," I replied, grinding my teeth. Chance exhaled, shaking his head. "I don't prefer him, but he's a good detective, Pandora. The higher-ups wouldn't have reassigned him unless they thought it was necessary." We locked eyes, the irritated tension thick between us. Sweat dripped down my back, my frustration mounting. "The higher-ups are my father and he wants the case closed," I said flatly. "I know," he admitted. "That man has been through enough."

His gaze flickered toward Ivy, who was throwing sharp elbows at Luke's face. "She can't stand him either." He admitted and in one fluid motion, Chance rolled off the ground and stood, shaking his arms before settling into a fighting stance. "Again," he commanded. Rolling my shoulders, I dropped into position, ready for more.

We sparred for another hour, taking turns tapping each other out until the training officer finally called for a break. By now, Aurelios had shifted lower in the sky, casting long shadows across the field and offering us some much-needed shade. Chance extended a hand, hauling me up from the ground. I dusted off my cargo pants, bits of turf falling in clumps. He chuckled, and I shot him a glare.

Ivy bounced over, bumping her shoulder against mine. "How

was it sparring with stick-up-my-ass over there?" I asked, cutting a glance toward Detective Nesnah. He stood at a distance, casually leaning against the wall, watching us. "Oh, ignore him that's what I do," she said, waving a hand dismissively. "It's Friday—we should go to Lady Emerald after training for some drinks." She twirled her ponytail, grinning like a schoolgirl. "Come on, it'll be fun. Just like the academy days."

I remembered those nights—countless Fridays spent in that bar, just the two of us, long before Chance came along. "I don't know," I started, rubbing the back of my neck. "I still have a lot of work on the ca—"

"Pandora," she interrupted, pouting dramatically. "It's one night. You're allowed to have a life." I chewed my lip, glancing at Chance. He shrugged. "One drink," I relented, pointing a warning finger at Ivy. "Only one." She pressed her lips together, but the slow grin spreading across her face told me she had other plans. "Only one," she repeated, feigning innocence.

"Alright, officers, we're moving on to range certification," Officer Daneer called out, his voice cutting through the chatter. "Those of you actively assigned firearms, report to the range." He flipped through the papers on his clipboard, pointing at a few officers as he spoke. His assistant, Yari, nodded furiously, scribbling notes before following him off the field.

"Onward!" Chance declared dramatically, pointing toward the range. Ivy and I sighed in unison, shaking our heads as we trudged after him.

Chapter 4

The shooting range was organized into individual lanes, each marked with an officer's badge number. Sturdy walls divided the sections, provided each officer with their designated space. I made my way to my lane as Ivy slid into the one beside me.

Unholstering my pistol, I set it down in front of me. The sharp clatter of metal against metal echoed throughout the room as officers checked and loaded their firearms. I cleared mine, my fingers fumbling slightly as I loaded the rounds into the magazine.

Officer Daneer entered, scanning the room. "Looks like everyone's here," he muttered, double-checking his clipboard before setting it on the table near the door. "Alright, let's make this quick. I don't want to be here all day. Fire in three-round bursts—torso, torso, head. You must score 90 or above to qualify. Any questions?" He glanced around, but no one spoke. We all shook our heads in response. "Listen for my call." He said as I turned, holstering my weapon and slipping on my earmuffs.

My hand hovered over my hip, ready, as I fixed my gaze downrange. The paper target stood motionless several yards ahead, its silhouette waiting. Taking a deep breath, I steadied myself. "Fire," Daneer commanded.

In a swift motion, I unholstered my weapon, my shoulder snapping my arm into position. I aligned my sights, taking a steady blink before squeezing the trigger.

Bang. The first round tore through the target. The trigger clicked as I eased off, allowing the firing pin to reset.

Bang. The second shot followed precisely, slicing through the paper like a hot knife through butter. I released the trigger one last time, feeling the mechanism reset beneath my finger.

Bang. The final round erupted from the barrel in a flash—but the target displayed only two clean holes. Frustration simmered beneath my skin as I reholstered my weapon and chewed my lip.

"Hold fire," Daneer called. He scanned the room, waiting for each officer to confirm they were ready to continue. I nodded sharply, adjusting my stance, my feet grounding firmly beneath me. My hand hovered at my holster as I forced myself to block out everything else, centering all my focus on the paper ahead. "Fire."

I snapped my weapon up.

Bang. Hit. Bang. Hit. Bang. *Miss*.

I hissed through my teeth, my lips curling in frustration. What the hell was going on? "Reload," Daneer ordered from his position. With a sharp breath, I shoved rounds into my magazine, my movements tense and rigid.

Ivy peeked around the dividing wall, tilting her head in silent question. I exhaled heavily, my gaze lifting toward the ceiling. She didn't press, simply retreated to her row. I swallowed hard, re-holstering my weapon. Daneer scanned the line, waiting for our confirmation. I gave a curt nod. "Fire." My hand twitched as I aimed and pulled the trigger.

Bang. Hit. Bang. Hit. Bang. *Miss*.

A curse slipped from my lips, sharp and unfiltered. Heads turned. Heat crept up my neck, but I refused to meet their eyes. Instead, I gave Daneer a stiff nod and turned away. This was bad. *Really* bad. I had earned the badge of excellence on nearly every range certification. The last time we did this, I was the only officer to hit every mark—zero misses. Yet today, my shots were slipping.

The paper target stood still, yet it taunted me from afar—two more rounds. If I missed the third shot again, I wouldn't qualify. I clenched my jaw, bracing myself. "Fire." I surged forward with renewed focus, sending metal flying down the range.

Bang. Hit. Bang. Hit. Bang. *Miss.*

My fingers felt ice-cold as I slid my weapon back into its holster. A tremor ran through me, and my mouth went dry. The paper target swayed slightly, its chest riddled with bullet holes. The edges of each perforation curled backward like moonflowers blooming under midnight light.

A numbness crept into my toes, and my knees wobbled under my weight. I inhaled deeply, flexing my fingers to steady them.

Last chance.

"Reload." Came his voice and I roughly forced bullets into the magazine before snapping it back into the pistol. I swallowed hard, keeping my eyes on Daneer as he scanned the room. I returned it to the holster, the weight of it hanging pulled against my hip. My hand hovered, poised and ready.

"Fire." Came his last command. Time slowed and the pistol hissed as it slid from my holster, rising into the firing position. My forearm muscles coiled as my hands locked together, snapping the weapon into place. I aimed, my heartbeat slowing to a near stop.

Bang.

The first round buried itself in the head of the shadowed silhouette.

Bang.

The second nestled perfectly beside the first, the paper

shuddering from the impact.

Bang.

I watched as the final round sliced through the air. Time seemed to freeze as it struck just above the first two. A perfect triangle. Dead center in the silhouettes head.

"Weapons down," Daneer instructed, removing his earmuffs. I exhaled, setting my pistol on the metal table with a hollow clang. Pressing my palms against the cool surface, I closed my eyes and prayed I hadn't obliterated my qualification by going against protocol.

Daneer didn't acknowledge me. Clipboard in hand, he moved methodically from one end of the room to the other checking targets.

"Young, pass. Lando, pass. Fikes, pass. Nesnah, pass. Kamar, pass." Daneer moved through the room, his eyes flicking from targets to clipboard as he checked off names. "Zephyr, pass." She peeked around the divider, her eyes widening as she registered what I had done.

Then, he stopped in front of me. I stood rigid under his gaze, my breath steady, though my pulse hammered beneath the surface. He glanced down the range, inspecting my target, then narrowed his eyes as he turned back to me.

Silence.

The kind so thick, a single pin drop would have shattered it. Slowly, he lifted his clipboard, the rough scratch of his pen the only sound in the room. I remained motionless, waiting.

"Vaughn." He exhaled, shaking his head. "Must you always test the rules?" I sucked in a slow breath through my teeth, resisting the urge to smirk. "Three shots to the head on the last round." He tapped his pen against the clipboard. "Risky. Had you missed even one, you would have failed." His lips pressed into a firm line. Then—"Pass."

I released a slow, measured exhale, relief washing through me. Ivy groaned, rubbing her temples. "Risky," Daneer muttered, shaking his head.

Risky, indeed.

Chapter 5

The pavement glistened with just finished rain as my sneakers padded against it. Training had ended hours ago, but I was headed to Lady Emerald to meet Chance and Ivy. I had agreed to *one* drink. Since the academy we hadn't set foot in the older bar on the east side of town, but once, it hosted our group as regulars.

I pulled open the enormous glass door leading into the bar, squeezing myself through boisterous frat boys hollering about a recent game. I peered around the busy bar, searching for my friends. Ivy waved frantically from the pool table they procured near the back. As the bar neared the busiest hour, I weaved through the cluttered tables and laughing crowds.

"You look great!" Ivy grinned, tugging one of my belt loops. Her blonde hair bounced in ringlet curls against her shoulders. "Although, must you always wear black and denim in your free time?" She pouted her lip, "You'd be stunning in a dress."

I rolled my eyes, suddenly self-conscious about the tight black, long sleeve-shirt and denim jeans I paired for the outing. My burgundy hair cascaded over my shoulders settling like a curtain around me.

Ivy looked as breathtaking as ever—her blue A-line dress falling to mid-thigh and her chunky glitter heels practically illuminating the darkness. I couldn't help but think that I'd be unstoppable if I possessed even a fraction of her confidence.

"Finally, you made it—we almost started without you!" Chance called out, tossing a pool cue my way, which I managed to snatch from mid-air. "Well, the case isn't going to crack itself," I retorted, chalking the cue. "Enough chatter—let's play," he declared, placing the cue ball on the table.

"Who's first?" Ivy chimed in, practically bouncing with excitement. "How about you girls kick things off?" Chance suggested. "I haven't even had a drink yet!" I protested, shaking my head. "I'll get you one," he assured me, with a grin. "What can I get for you, milady?" he asked, taking an exaggerated bow and peering up to read my reaction. I bit my lip to hide a smile.

"A bourbon, neat," I replied, bowing slightly at my waist as I played along with the charade. His smile broadened. "Right away," he announced before hurrying off to the bar. Meanwhile, Ivy began arranging the pool table.

"So, what happened at the range today?" she asked, the clacking of pool balls punctuating her words as she gathered them. "Nothing," I shrugged. "Oh, come on—you hit the target's head three times in a row during your last round and nearly botched your certification. I wouldn't call that nothing." She shook her head from across the table. I shrugged again, "I was bound to mess it up anyway. I might as well make it interesting."

A smile spread across her face. "Well, you certainly left an impression. You're lucky, Officer Daneer decided to consider that a pass." I sighed deeply in response. Missing so many shots had stung my pride, and the mounting frustration had led me to be reckless during the final round. I knew better, but I did it anyway—and I was well aware that if I tried any more cowboy antics with Officer Daneer, I'd be in serious trouble.

I watched as Ivy aligned her cue for the first shot. With a sharp crack, the pool balls scattered across the table, and the solid purple ball slid into a pocket with a satisfying whoosh. Setting up for her second shot, she struck the cue ball. It raced down the table, clacking against its peers yet failing to send any into the pockets. "Your turn," she called, playfully waggling her fingers at me.

Chance soon returned with my whisky, which I downed in one gulp before setting the glass on our table. "Alright, one more coming up," he declared dramatically as he exhaled and stood back up. "Hey, I said only one," I pleaded. He simply grinned and replied, "You didn't specify—only one to sip on. A swig as soon as you got here doesn't count." With that, he headed back toward the bar without another word.

I grumbled under my breath, but Ivy sidled up to me. "Relax, you should have fun once in a while," she coaxed with a smile. "Fine. *One* more," I huffed, snatching the cue she'd been balancing on her palm. "Hey!" she protested. I shot her a glare, and she pouted. "Alright, my turn."

Leaning over the pool table, I rested my fingers on the felt as my chest brushed gently against the wood. I steadied my hips and lined up my shot. Tensing my arm, I drew the cue back and then swiftly sent it forward with precision.

Crack—the white ball collided with the others, scattering them across the green felt. The striped orange ball teetered on the edge of a pocket but didn't fall in. A groan escaped me. Today was not my day. Shaking my head, I stepped back to let Ivy choose her next shot as she prowled around the table, slowly assessing where everything had landed.

"So, this case of yours..." Chance's voice floated over the bar's growing chatter as he returned, "Did anything come from questioning Adam Fritz?" he asked, handing me my second whisky while taking a swig of his beer. "No, he was incredibly unhelpful. He gave me the runaround and claimed he knew nothing about her disappearance," I murmured into the rim of my glass. Chance nodded. "Have you questioned anyone else from Fritz Co. or just Adam?" he inquired watching as Ivy lined up her cue. "We spoke with a few employees, but the only person present at the time of her death was Adam. He insisted he was busy making business calls until he left and didn't see her when heading home that evening. Unfortunately, his alibi checks out," I said.

Crack. Ivy took her shot, sinking two of her solid balls—and one of mine. "Damn," she groaned, leaning her head back in disappointment. "You sank one of mine. My turn!" I laughed and strode to the opposite side of the table.

The bar grew louder as more Friday-night regulars filed in, the atmosphere growing wild and charged. I brushed past Ivy and leaned against the table studying the layout with my fingers poised against the fuzzy surface. It was very well known that I was terrible at pool, however I ignored the lingering pessimism in my brain and let the cogs whir as I aligned my next shot.

Another loud crack marked my attempt as I entirely missed my target, the cue ball bouncing off the others loudly announcing my embarrassing shot. "Yikes," Chance chuckled. "You're a great shot with a pistol, but pool just isn't your game."

Heat flushed my neck. "No, I've never been good at pool," I admitted, shaking my head as I leaned against the wall beside our table. "Alright, let's say Adam didn't do it," he shrugged, leaning against the wall beside me. "What if he hired someone to do it?" I nodded and turned my head to him. "I considered that possibility too. There are no withdrawals from his personal accounts—at least none large enough to warrant further investigation. Everything appears business as usual. In fact, he's been spending significantly less lately, and I can't quite figure out why."

My eyes scanned the room. In one corner, a group of scantily clad women chatted and waved daintily at a lone man at the bar. He raised his glass in response but remained seated as they pouted and resumed their conversation. I cocked my head. He looked vaguely familiar.

"You're thinking it has nothing to do with Adam," he stated rather than asked. "I don't feel that he's involved, no," I replied, taking another sip of my whisky—savoring its sweet flavor before letting it burn down my throat. "Do you have any other suspects?" he asked tilting his head. "No, we're back at square one," I sighed.

Ivy then took her shot sinking one of her balls, then walked past us to line up her next attempt. *Crack. Crack.* The sounds marked her second and third shots without pocketing her remaining pieces.

I pushed off the wall, calculating my move. She had already sunk plenty, leaving only a couple of the solid-colored balls on the table—and I was far behind.

Shifting my weight, I leaned more heavily on the table and widened my stance. Ivy glared at me from across the table. "Come on, Vaughn. You can't possibly think you still stand a chance," she taunted with a grin. "Never back down," I murmured as I lined up my shot.

The cue ball raced down the table, and Ivy remained unfazed as it clacked around, pocketing two of my balls in the pockets nearest her. "There you go—making a comeback," Chance called from against the wall, grinning. I shot him finger guns as I prepared for another shot.

The cue danced again, sinking another one of my balls. I pumped my fist in the air and laughed, "She's back!" while playfully sticking my tongue out at Ivy. She rolled her eyes, and Chance snickered. "I'm going to get another drink," Ivy announced sashaying away. Her blonde ponytail brushed her shoulders with attitude. I lined up my next shot, striking one of the striped balls but failing to pocket any. I shrugged, "Guess I'm only halfway back."

Ivy set her drink down nearby and retrieved her cue. "Anyone else notice Detective Nesnah over there? He's here all alone," she observed, gesturing with her nearly full drink toward the bar. Ah, so that's why he looked familiar.

Scanning the crowded room, I found him, indeed, sitting alone at the bar, swirling a half-full glass of whisky while his eyes remained fixed on the news playing overhead. "He's always by himself," I noted with a shrug. We exchanged glances, but no one said another word.

"Alright, let's see if I can swing this," Ivy declared, rolling her head back and forth as she cracked her neck. With a playful push of her hips, she nudged Chance aside, prompting him to raise his hands in surrender. Grinning at him, she leaned forward. Her dress lifted precariously, revealing the back of her bare thighs as she took her shot.

Crack. Ivy sank two more of her balls—only one was left. Surely, she would win. With a flourish, she pointed to the pocket closest to the us. "That's the finishing pocket," she declared, leaning forward one last time.

Crack. She sent the ball hurtling down the table. It collided aggressively with the black eight ball, ricocheting off before thudding against the leather rim and finally slipping into the pocket. "I win!" she cheered, clapping her hands together. I bowed dramatically as she sidled up to me. "Well played," I said, nudging her with my shoulder as she grinned wider.

"Alright, I think I'm calling it a night," I announced, hanging the cue back on its shelf. Ivy pouted. "So early?" she asked, her shoulders sagging slightly. "I've got work waiting for me at home." I rubbed the back of my neck, feeling a mix of awkwardness and regret for dampening the fun. "Don't worry about your drinks—I'll take care of the tab," Chance offered, raising his glass in my direction. "Thanks," I smiled. "See you guys Monday."

I grabbed my bag and shuffled toward the front door. Squeezing through the crowded room, I realized I'd have to walk past the bar to exit. I gritted my teeth, hoping he wouldn't notice me as I sidled through a group of girls on a bachelorette fling and edged past full tables.

I was almost there.

"Detective Vaughn," a deep voice rumbled. I swallowed hard, feeling my shoulders slump. The door was so close—I had almost executed a clean escape. "Detective Nesnah," I responded, turning to face him. He didn't bother responding, his eyes fixed on the news playing above the bar. "I'd say it's good to see you, but it never is," I clipped, setting my elbows on the bar to stare him down.

He pursed his lips, took a swig of his drink, and finally turned his icy-blue eyes toward me. Good god, they were mesmerizing. I blinked as the hair on my scalp stood on end, and my mouth suddenly went dry.

"Mouthy, as always," he quipped. I shook off my daze and narrowed my eyes, my face flushing. "Arrogant, as always," I shot back, anger bubbling within me. "Do you ever have anything kind to say?" I asked my neck tense with irritation. "That depends," he replied, downing the rest of his drink and setting the glass on the bar top with a clink. "Do you have anything kind to say back?"

He shrugged on his black jacket, and I caught a glimpse of a motorcycle brand emblem—something I hadn't expected, considering hardly anyone rode motorcycles anymore with everything being automated.

"You don't deserve anything kind said to you," I huffed, crossing my arms. "Then why say anything at all?" he countered. "Because you spoke to me first," I retorted, glaring at him. "Ah, my mistake," he murmured, scooting closer.

The bar's noise faded into a muffled hum as he leaned toward me. "Have a good night, Detective Pandora Vaughn," he smirked. "And you, Detective Luke Nesnah, have a deplorable one." I hissed in response, my voice barely a whisper.

He grinned as he slid off his bar stool and dipped his chin in my direction in a haughty farewell. Before I could retort anything most likely arrogant and sassy he turned on his heel and strode out the bar's front door.

I exhaled the breath I'd been holding, glancing over at Ivy and Chance who were frozen and staring at me. My lips parted as if I could explain what had just happened from across the bar, but words failed me. Ivy raised an eyebrow and gestured toward the door in a silent *what the fuck?*

I threw my hands up in exasperation and shook my head. Yeah, what the fuck, indeed. Exchanging one last look with Ivy, I waved goodbye to my friends and stepped out into the Liarta night.

Chapter 6

I trudged silently toward the parking lot behind the bar, my boots squeaking on the pavement. What was he playing at? His behavior was infuriating. I kicked a rock with my shoe, sending it skittering down the sidewalk. "*Have a good night.*" I scoffed to myself—what a cocky, arrogant—

"Evening, Detective." A male voice interrupted my thoughts and I froze in my tracks. Leaned against my car was a man with a slow, unsettling smile. I didn't recognize him—at least not at first. His wavy brown hair fell to his shoulders, untamed and a little nappy, and his body language was tense. His brown eyes narrowed as he regarded me.

"Evening," I replied quietly with apprehension. "I saw you in the bar and figured I'd come say hello." He gestured broadly to the empty parking lot around us. A chill of unease ran down my spine. "So, you decided to come talk to me in an empty parking lot just as I'm about to leave in my car?" I asked, remaining perfectly still. "I don't mean to frighten you, Detective," he said, frowning. "I only wish to talk." Fear crept up my spine but I stayed rooted in place as he stepped closer.

"Do you remember the case you had several months ago—a woman named Aiya Malone?" My eyes widened, and the hair on my neck stood on end. With that, I recognized him immediately. His dark eyes, the round, chubby face, even the freckles I had once found endearing—until I had uncovered evidence that he had murdered his wife in cold blood.

"You're her husband," I said, rocking back on my heels as I prepared to bolt. "The one and only," he replied with a shrug and a wide, menacing smile. Even his teeth looked predatory as he prowled toward me in the dark. "But you're supposed to be in prison," I whispered, my voice softer than intended. "You see, I was. *You* put me there." He took another step forward and I instinctively retreated slowly. "But I have since freed myself from the legal system's grip," he continued, his face angling downward. Anger pulsed in his eyes as I took another step back, reaching for my bag.

"Ah, ah, Detective. I wouldn't if I were you."

Before I could react further, hands gripped my arms from behind. I whipped my head around to see a tall, black-haired man baring his teeth, his grip firm and unyielding. He was massive—there was no way I would win that fight.

I whimpered as I turned back to face Mr. Malone. "You see, Detective, I maintain that I was wrongly charged for the murder of my *wonderful* wife, Aiya." He advanced until he was only a foot away. From his back pocket, a knife gleamed as he drew it out and tested its sharpness with his thumb.

"What are you planning on doing, Mr. Malone?" I asked, shifting against the man restraining me. I turned and bared my teeth in defiance. He just grinned. "Me? I'm going to make you pay for your wrongdoings, Detective," he hissed, pressing the blade to my throat. "I want to see the fear in your eyes, just as Aiya had when I slit her cheek to cheek." His hot breath washed over my face.

I raised my chin and spat in his face. "Ah, now that's not so nice, Detective," He retorted and slashed the blade down my arm. I hissed in pain as blood seeped through the tear in my black sleeve.

"Now, Detective," he murmured, returning the blade to the tender spot on my neck, "I was paid a great deal of money to make you disappear, but if you don't cooperate, I can take my precious time with you." I blinked my mouth already forming the most eloquent *fuck you*, but I was cut off before it ever left my lips.

"I'd take those hands off her if I were you,"

I bristled at the voice. It was undeniably *his* voice. I hadn't noticed him leaned against my car, one leg casually crossed over the other, until right now. Malone narrowed his eyes at him.

"And who do you think you are?" he demanded, waving his knife in his direction while remaining planted in front of me. "Detective Luke Nesnah," He replied, his gaze shifting from Malone to the man holding my arms. The badge on his hip flared as it reflected the dingy lighting in the bar's parking lot. "If you let her go, I'll let you live."

The large man restraining me leaned his head all the way back and guffawed. As *loudly* as he possibly could. Malone grinned ear to ear. "Detective, it's two against one. You can't possibly think you can take both of us," he sneered, flicking a speck of dirt from his pant leg.

"First, it's two against two, and second I don't have to take out both of you—you're holding the highest-ranking marksman in our precinct right now," he gestured toward me. I swallowed hard, my heart racing as he continued, "I just have to level the playing field." He smiled smugly.

The cogs worked overtime in my brain as I tried to work out what he was trying to discreetly tell me. What was he implying?

Before I could fully register what was happening, Nesnah snapped his pistol upright and fired two shots. I jumped as the hands holding my arms suddenly vanished. The giant man behind me wobbled, then collapsed onto the pavement with a heavy thunk. Malone whipped his head toward me, but I darted forward elegantly drawing my pistol from my waist.

Bang. Bang. Bang.

Malone crumpled like a mighty oak face-first into the asphalt. Nesnah lowered his weapon, his eyes skimming to mine—blue, oh so blue. With my arms still raised, I watched my pistol tremble in my grip. My breath froze in my lungs, but I forced myself to focus.

It's fine, I'm fine—everything's fine.

The metal clattered as I clumsily reholstered my gun, steadying my breathing. "See? Level playing field," Nesnah murmured, reholstering his weapon. He leaned over, observing the three shots I'd sunk into Malone's skull—just like range certification. Oh, the irony.

I glanced around at the two bodies lying on the ground and released a shaky breath. Nesnah said nothing, merely watched me from a distance. "He..." I began, but the words died in my throat. "Is no longer a problem," he finished. "Oh, for fuck's sake," I hissed, closing the gap between us.

"What is your deal?" I jabbed a finger in his direction. "No deal. I just saw you needed help," he replied with a shrug as the tension rolled out of his shoulders and he leaned against my car again. I bared my fangs at him. "I don't need help from you. I can take care of myself," I growled, throwing my hands on my hips. "Clearly," he said, gesturing toward the two bodies laid to rest behind us. I scoffed, forcing a breath out. "Must you always be so... so..."

"Helpful?" he quipped, tilting his head at me. "You nearly got yourself killed—and for what?" I growled. "Why do you care?" he asked, raising an eyebrow. "I don't," I hissed through my teeth in his direction. Seeing me worked up just seemed to make him more cocky as he couldn't hide the grin that spread across his face. He bit the inside of his cheek in an attempt to mask it, but I had already caught on.

"I'm just saying it would be incredibly inconvenient if you dropped dead before closing my mother's case." I ground out but paused, surveying the scene again. "What a mess," I muttered, rubbing my palm against my forehead.

What an absolute mess.

***

The back of an ambulance bay wasn't a place I usually ended up in my line of work as a detective, yet here I was, getting patched up by a scrawny, blonde EMT. He worked with easy confidence, his brown eyes focused on the wound as he tied off the bandage with a practiced, deliberate pull.

His uniform collar had slipped slightly, revealing a glimpse of a black tattoo curling up his back. Curiosity got the better of me, and I leaned in for a closer look. He glanced up at me clearing his throat. I quickly straightened, warmth rising in my cheeks just as a voice rang out from across the parking lot.

"Pandora!" Ivy called, and a wave of relief washed over me as we both turned toward her. Chance lifted the caution tape, and the two of them ducked under and made their way over.

"What happened? Are you okay?" she asked, grasping my shoulders and scrutinizing me. "I'm fine," I muttered, brushing her arms away. Her eyebrows furrowed with worry as she scanned the area, and she gasped when her eyes fell on the two bodies draped in white sheets. "Are those—"

"Mr. Malone and a henchman," I interrupted, sliding off the back of the truck. Ivy paled. "Didn't you put him behind bars for murdering his wife last year?" she asked, glancing at Chance, who wore a concerned expression as he watched Detective Nesnah deep in conversation with another detective across the lot. "I did. He decided to pay me a visit," I replied, testing the tight, sore bandage on my arm that had thankfully staunched the bleeding. "He said someone paid him to make me disappear," I added quietly, careful not to alert the uniforms swarming the scene. "What do you mean?" she asked, cocking her head.

"Why would someone pay him to make you disappear? That seems strange." Chance interjected, still watching him from a distance. "Why is *he* here?" he gestured toward Detective Nesnah. "He's the reason I'm not the one under those white sheets right now," I groaned quietly.

"What? He was *there?*" Ivy's mouth dropped open. "He took down the mountain of a man over there," I said, swinging my arm toward the massive figure who had pinned me down that now lay on the pavement like a forgotten pancake. Ivy and Chance exchanged a look—I'd have to ask them later what that meant in private.

"Did Malone say who paid him?" she asked, turning back to me. "He didn't. And since we can't exactly interrogate him now, I'm not sure how we're going to get that information," I replied, rubbing my temples as the headache from earlier caught up with me. My eyes scanned the crime scene and froze when they met his.

Leaned against a squad car, the expression he wore seemed amused and his blue eyes bore into mine. "Who would want you dead?" Ivy asked tutting over the bandage on my arm. I swatted her away again and shot eye daggers at her as if to say *leave it alone*. "If I knew, you'd be the first person I'd tell." I said with resignation.

"Looks like you're all set, Detective Vaughn," the EMT said with a smile as he packed away his medical supplies. "Thanks,"

I replied, watching him slam the ambulance bay doors closed. "Stay safe, Detective." He nodded, climbed into the driver's seat, and pulled away. I gingerly rubbed my bandaged arm—that would be sore for a while.

"I'll take care of that one." I gestured toward Detective Nesnah, who still watched our group from a few feet away. "You sure?" Ivy asked, scrunching her nose at him. "I'm sure. Go home." I waved them away. Ivy lingered momentarily before Chance grabbed her arm and pulled her away from the scene. She shot me another look over her shoulder, but her chest dipped in a sigh as she followed Chance out of the parking lot.

I took a deep breath and braced myself. Why did he get under my skin like this? He was just a detective—a detective from an entirely different precinct, at that. I sauntered over to the squad car he was casually leaned against. He watched me approach with curious eyes as I rested my shoulder against the car door.

"Detective Nesnah," I said, exhaling. "Detective Vaughn," he countered, a slight smirk curling at the edge of his mouth as his gaze traveled from my boots up to my face. "Now listen to me," I said, folding my arms over my chest and avoiding his eyes. He remained silent.

Good, at least he's receptive.

"I don't know what kind of power trip you're on, but it needs to cease immediately." I watched as the medical examiners loaded the bodies of my assailants into the waiting ambulances. They struggled with the larger one, even with two of them—if I weren't so irritated, I might have found the scene amusing.

"I can handle myself. I don't need a babysitter or a bodyguard. Your job here at Precinct 12 is to finish the case you were assigned and then be on your way. We liked things just fine before you stepped foot into our precinct." I turned to him. "Or is that too much to ask, Detective?" I challenged, raising my eyebrows.

He leaned his head back against the car and gazed into the night sky. "You know, you can see Feros and Gayle tonight from here," he said, pointing upwards at our two sister planets flickering in the night sky. I followed his finger, glancing up at the looming planets above. "But you can't see Cappurn." He fixed his gaze on me. I narrowed my eyes.

"What?" I sneered. "I understand you think you know everything about your mother and her death. And I get that it's hard for a detective like you to sit back while someone else takes control." He began to explain, but my anger and irritation took over. "You know nothing, Nesnah," I hissed.

He raised his pointer finger, silently indicating he wasn't finished. I bared my teeth, then snapped my mouth shut. "I will do my due diligence on your mother's case, just like in any other case I'm assigned. And I won't apologize for being in the right place at the right time before you met an unfortunate end. I understand you hate me, but I ask that you stop interfering with my investigation." His words cut into my ego bit by bit.

I clenched my jaw, trying to form words that weren't just hysterical screams. After a moment of opening and closing my mouth, I raised my chin and leaned in close, getting in his face. He just blinked at me utterly unfazed.

"*Fuck you*," I whispered.

"When I close her case, I'll be leaving Precinct 12 to return home to Cappurn—and I'll be long gone from your hair." He smiled and strolled off, leaving me fuming like an idiot. "And why can't you close her case now?" I shouted after him, so angry it felt like steam was pouring from my ears.

"Well now, detective, I thought I said no more interfering," he called over his shoulder as he disappeared around the corner. I yelled in frustration, kicking the squad car's tire. What a

condescending, self-righteous man.
   Just ugh.

Chapter 7

I pulled up to my house, the warm lights welcoming me home. "Casa de Vaughn," I murmured to myself as I parked in the driveway.

I opened my car door and looked at my small, modern cabin tucked away in the woods at the outskirts of Raos. The entire front was built of smooth, black stones stacked together, accented by oil-rubbed bronze light fixtures at the corners. Green hedges clung to the stone, interspersed with wild snowdrops emerging from their winter rest finally enjoying the spring weather here on Liarta. Trees hung over the black metal roof like a comforting blanket while soft, warm light spilled from the porch fixtures onto a well-worn, knitted hammock that gently swayed in the frosty breeze.

The scent of cedar wood trailed toward me as I grabbed my belongings from the passenger seat and locked my car behind me. I walked toward the large, dark wood front door and my sneakers crunched on the slate-gray pea gravel. There was no visible handle—only a tiny blue light shimmered along the edge of the frame.

I pressed my thumb against it, and a gentle chime sounded. The door clicked and slid open into a recessed area of the adjacent wall. I stepped into the entryway as the door closed behind me, fastening securely into place. Inside, the lights glimmered on and I slipped off my shoes as I descended into the lower level of my living room.

"Mayra," I called, setting my things down on the pale green couch. "Yes, Detective Vaughn," an AI voice chimed overhead. "Please warm my living room and kitchen," I requested. "Yes, Detective Vaughn," she replied, her tone bright as Christmas bells.

Instantly, a fire roared to life in the large stone hearth at the center of the room. I shrugged off my trench coat and hung it on the metal coat rack in the corner. Warmth seeped from the fireplace as its curling flames cast dancing shadows throughout the space. I crossed the room and passed the back wall made entirely of glass. The light bled into the night outside, caressing the trees with pale yellow tendrils. Peering above the tree line, I gazed at the endless sky.

He was right—both Feros and Gayle loomed in the dark sky tonight.

Feros, the only planet in our solar system so rich in iron it looked as if it were bleeding, radiated with steady beats of light. Brick-red sand and soil—so fine it crunched under your boots like fluffy snow—blanketed its surface, coating massive, layered rock formations. Swirls of various sediments adorned serrated boulders scattered about as if their existence had been forgotten. But not as forgotten as the Feros mines.

Once there to deplete Feros of it's iron rich resources, the mines sat abandoned and cast aside. Just a shadow of lingering thought to the once active work sites. The mining operators—once criminals on Liarta, had been shipped off to work for the government in the mines. This work was given in exchange for their freedom. I, however, had never heard of anyone being allowed to return as a *free* person.

Occasionally, higher-ranking officials were taken to the mines to see what their money was funding—though only when funds ran low, and the people of Liarta needed reassurance that their money wasn't disappearing into a sinkhole. Arguably, it was, which was why the Feros mines had been decommissioned and forgotten almost entirely.

Gayle, on the other hand, gleamed with pride. I had never visited Gayle but remembered being told the tales of its beauty. The planet's surface was almost entirely covered by turquoise water so clear that even the deepest caverns appeared to be mere inches away as you glided over them. The land was scarce, yet every inch was lush and a vibrant green—images of trees taller than skyscrapers, deep mossy water caverns, and shores of amethyst sand brushed through my mind.

Gayle was an ancient planet predating human existence. Its beauty was undeniable, but what had fascinated me even more was the species that called Gayle home. It was believed that the planet's earliest inhabitants were the precursors to the water creatures known as the Gaythe.

With iridescent scales covering their entire bodies, Gaythes were celebrated for their stunning beauty and deadly prowess. Their faces, a pale purple hue formed from scales so fine they resembled human skin, were framed by slatted gills and crowned with hair that looked as if it were made of smoke, trailing wistfully from their scalps.

They were swifter than other aquatic species and stood nearly eight feet tall on average. Their voices purred like a contented cat and could envelop you like a warm blanket—lulling you into a false sense of security or even drawing you toward a watery grave. That is, if provoked.

Gaythe scales, when harvested from a living creature and sealed onto armor, offered unmatched protection. However, if the Gaythe died before scale retrieval, they turned coal black and brittle as ash. The species had known little fear until their numbers began to dwindle from poachers. Very few humans visited Gayle, and for good reason.

I glanced at the shiny plaque on the wall whispering at me. "Detective of the year." It beamed proudly, and I scowled. Hardly—I had hardly earned that title. My father had pressed so adamantly for me to be named detective of the year at the last station meeting that no one objected, despite the dread pooling in my stomach and the protests I raised. He had practically radiated pride when I was handed the plaque at a public press conference, hoping it would convince me to take some time off to process and grieve my mother—his wife. Instead, it only fueled my hatred for Detective Nesnah for keeping her case open.

My head pulsed with pain, and my arm throbbed under the bandages. I walked silently through the hallway to my bedroom, surrounded by dark blue and green walls. Once inside, I slid off my socks and tossed them into the wicker laundry bin by the bathroom door. Then, I opened my deep mahogany armoire, threw my knitted ivory pajama set on the bed, and padded into the bathroom.

I flipped the switch, and the sharp light immediately hurt my head. I rubbed my temples, trying to ease the throbbing. In the mirror, my reflection glared back and purple shadows under my eyes sank them deeper into my hollow face. I turned the shower on, setting it to blistering hot. The droning sound of water hitting white tiles filled the bathroom.

I shoved my service weapon into the locked drawer beside my bed and stripped off my clothes piece by piece, carelessly tossing them on the floor then trudged to the shower.

Recessed in the wall and tiled from floor to ceiling, the shower boasted a grand head jutting out from the tile. The steam billowed in large puffs as I slid under the scorching water, letting it burn against my skin. Pressing my forehead against the icy tile, I groaned. Today had been incredibly draining and I was no closer to cracking my case than yesterday.

My skin blazed as I scrubbed my hair clean careful to keep the bandages wrapped around my arm dry and rinsed away the suds until they disappeared down the drain. Shutting the water off, I limply pushed the glass door aside and grabbed a towel from the wall. I padded the fluffy fabric over my wet skin and wrapped it around my head.

Standing naked before the mirror while brushing my teeth, I noticed my arms looked less full and my ribs pressed against my skin as if begging for relief. I had never been a small woman—my frame had always been full—but the stress of my latest case and grieving my mother had stripped away both muscle and weight.

She had been breathtaking—a woman with jade-green eyes and coppery red hair billowing like chiffon in the breeze. Her eyes crinkled at the corners when she smiled, softening her chiseled features. Though short in stature, her gregarious personality filled every room. She loved nothing more than to surround herself with other passionate, like-minded souls.

She was an ember that, when set against kindling, would blaze with such ferocity as to consume anyone in its path—feisty yet soft and kind. I ached to hold her, to wrap my arms around her waist as she quietly brushed my hair and whispered in my ear. I longed to hear her voice, to feel her presence once more.

I spat my toothpaste into the sink, rinsed it away, and removed the towel from my head brushing solemnly through my wet hair. I returned to the bedroom, snapping the lights off as I went.

Pulling on my pajamas, I answered the beckoning of my bed. I sighed as I slid into the emerald sheets, lying back and staring out the floor-to-ceiling window where cool moonlight poured in. In my view, the planets looked so far away, yet each teemed with life—creatures and people going about their steady lives. It was as if I was frozen in a time when my mother still existed while everything and everyone else continued on.

My eyelids grew heavy, and sleep began to claim me. Outside, a soothing breeze picked up, skittering leaves against the house as I finally drifted off.

Chapter 8

"Mom? I'm home!" I called, dropping my bag onto the marble kitchen counter. The groceries thudded against its surface. "Mom?" I repeated unpacking vegetables and placing them in the sink to be rinsed. Only silence answered. I paused, setting the bag aside to listen—no footsteps, no greeting.

A chill prickled along the nape of my neck. It wasn't like her to ignore my return home. My heart raced as I unholstered my service weapon and raised the sights. I crept slowly toward her bedroom. "Mom?" I whispered, stepping lightly through the dark hallway. My footsteps were barely audible on the hardwood. I held my breath, straining for any sound.

Soft weeping drifted through the slightly ajar door. I nudged it open with my toe, and the color drained from my face. There, on the edge of the bed, sat my father with my mother's cold, grey hands clasped in his. She sat upright, as pale as paper, her glazed eyes fixed in a sorrowful, empty stare—utterly soulless.

I froze.

"Pandora," my dad murmured as he slowly turned toward me, still holding her hands. I felt as if I was made of stone, unable to breathe or move. "I found her like this thirty minutes ago," he whispered, his voice trembling. "There's no one else here. She had her tea on the table and book in her hands when I got home." his eyes pleaded with me.

At last, I met his gaze. He looked disheveled and

tear-streaked, his bloodshot eyes revealing deep sorrow. Still in his commissioner uniform, his shoes shone brightly. My body trembled as he said, "Pandora, please... put down your weapon." I didn't move. "Pandora, that is an order—as your commissioner, stand down." his voice grew firmer.

Quivering, I fumbled to reholster my weapon, its clack echoing in the heavy silence. My mother lay before me, a lifeless shell of the vibrant woman she once was. Her copper hair framed a dull, expressionless face, her eyes stripped of their usual glow.

"Call it in, Pandora," he said, turning back toward her. I stood frozen still. "Pandora," he hissed and reluctantly I pulled my phone out to call Precinct 12.

Within the hour, our home was swarmed by uniformed officers and a medical examiner—marking the onset of an unimaginable loss. "No, I got home and found her like this. I've been at the station all day on a case," my father said, sighing as he rubbed his temples. He sat on the couch surrounded by officers taking his statement, while I stood dumbfounded in the middle of our living room.

Everything I ever knew was gone.

The officer taking his statement nodded as he scribbled in his notepad. "When was the last time you saw Mrs. Vaughn?" he asked, pen poised above the paper. "I saw her this morning when I left for work—around 8 a.m." my father replied, pressing his elbows into his knees and resting his weary face in his hands. "How did she seem when you spoke to her?" the officer pressed.

Without lifting his head, my father murmured, "She seemed more despondent than usual. I should have asked what was troubling her. I should have stayed home." his voice was low and laced with regret.

The flashing red and blue lights danced off the walls,

momentarily clearing the haze from my vision. "She seemed normal when I left at 7," I interjected, still confused, "She said she was excited to try a new recipe for dinner."

Clarity had escaped me—she had always been so vibrant and full of life. My father lifted his head and stared at me for a long moment. "I'm grateful you didn't see her in the state she was this morning," He said softly before sinking back into his chair. My arms hung limply at my sides, and my jaw tightened with a mix of fury and anguish. Then the officer asked, "Has Mrs. Vaughn been suicidal in the past?"

"Dad?"

Hot tears streamed down my face, and I wiped them away with the back of my sleeve. He looked up at me, his expression unreadable. "Yes, she has been suicidal before," he admitted, then turned away.

My hand flew to my mouth as silent sobs overtook me. I had never known. My heart derailed and my breathing grew shallow. I needed some air.

Backpedaling, I rushed for the front door shoving past those in my path. As I swung the door open I collided with a tall, dark-haired officer who caught me by the shoulders as I staggered backward.

"I'm so sorry—I—" I stammered as he steadied me. "Detective Pandora Vaughn?" he asked, his piercing blue eyes locked on mine as he waited for my response. My breath caught in my throat, but after a moment I managed, "Yes. And who are you?" my eyes narrowed.

"I'm Detective Luke Nesnah. I've been assigned to your mother's case."

***

I woke with a start, my breath coming in short, panicked gasps. The nightmare still clung to me. The same one plagued me for weeks, ever since her death. Sweat gathered at the nape of my neck, and my sheets clung damply to my skin. I always woke from them disoriented, lost in the fog and unsure of where I was.

My eyes blinked once, twice, and I turned to check the clock—5 a.m. The weekend had slipped by in a blur of quiet hours and case files. I'd spent most of it buried in work at home. But now it was Monday, and I had no choice but to drag myself out of bed and head to the precinct.

I sank back into my bed, the blankets puffing up around me, reluctant to leave the warm cocoon. The gash along my arm throbbed beneath the tightly wrapped bandages, and I pressed my palm gently over the fabric, willing the discomfort to fade.

Aurelios' light began to filter into the room, casting a soft glow on the dark walls. Its golden rays danced playfully, but even their warmth couldn't lift the heavy weight anchoring my body to the mattress. Eventually, I accepted that it was time to get moving.

I rolled out of bed stiffly, yawning, and moved through my morning routine at a sluggish pace—pulling on clothes, fixing my hair, and brushing my teeth. A quick glance at my watch made me groan. Six a.m. already. There would be no time for breakfast. Hopefully, the station's break room had something quick to grab.

I stepped into my tan heels, then paused to inspect my reflection in the mirror. Navy slacks, crisp white blouse, and a light brown blazer. Not bad.

I gave a small nod and tucked a loose burgundy strand back into the tight, military-style bun at the nape of my neck. My heels clicked against the floor as I grabbed my leather bag, laptop inside, and headed for the front door. It slid open with a quiet hiss, and I stepped out toward my car.

Outside, Aurelios had climbed higher, casting a soft, pale light across the horizon. I stifled another yawn as I opened the door to my sedan. It's hinges groaned in protest, echoing my own reluctance to greet the early hour. Sliding into the driver's seat, I shifted into drive and rolled down the long gravel driveway leading from my cabin.

The car jolted slightly as I made a right turn at the end, heading toward the city. Quaint houses gave way to corporate structures, which soon evolved into towering skyscrapers. I turned on the radio and tuned in to an old station. Smooth jazz filled my ears while streaks of chrome flashed by in my peripheral vision. Massive bronze buildings glistened in the Aurelios light as I sped into the heart of the city—a sprawling, endless sea of metal and gold towering over its inhabitants. Finally, I pulled into Precinct 12.

My arm still throbbed beneath the hidden bandages as I swung open the glass doors to the police department lobby. At the front desk, Margaret glanced up at me over the rim of her ruby-red glasses.

"Long weekend?" she asked. "Something like that," I mumbled while scanning my badge. "I don't have any paperwork for you right now," she added, punching a staple into a stack of files. "Thanks," I nodded as I passed through the scanner. The AI chimed, and the glass doors slid open, ushering me into the lobby just like every other day. Colleagues calmly chatted as I made my way to my desk finding Ivy already deep in paperwork. Her blonde hair was perfectly curled and brushed gently over her shoulders.

"Morning," she hummed as I sat across from her. She bit into a blueberry muffin letting a few crumbs fall onto her lap. "Morning," I replied dryly. She gave me a questioning look, but continued, "Forensics on Amy came back this morning," Her words were slightly muffled by the muffin.

She pulled a paper from the stack and placed it in my hands. "You might want to look at it," she said with a sigh before leaning back, leaving me to read it on my own.

Name: Amy O'Rayne
Maternal Identifier: Gaythe
Paternal Identifier: Human

"Gaythe?" I asked, re-reading the paper. "Yep," she replied, finishing her muffin and crumpling the wrapper into a ball. "That can't be right," I repeated the word over and over in my mind—Gaythe. "As in, the species from Gayle, not here on Liarta," I added not necessarily as a question but more of a cautious statement. My eyes widened as I looked at her.

"They ran it twice. The lab said it's not wrong," she said with a shrug. My mouth gaped open as I blinked assessing the new information. "But she looked completely human," I protested, my mind racing.

"Well, she's *half* human and half Gaythe," she responded, tapping the paper in my hand. "I can read," I muttered, scanning the document again. She rolled her eyes. "Has there ever been a half-human, half-Gaythe?"

The paper felt warm in my hands, the words almost glowing before me. "Not that we know of," she said softly. "Why was she here?" I asked, rifling through the rest of the documents in the stack. "That's what I was about to mention," she said, pulling out a specific page from the edge of her desk stack. "Remember, she traveled here six months before she was killed. She didn't live here—she was here to *find* someone." she tapped the paper, revealing her register date through the Liarta border. Sure enough.

Registeree: Amy O' Rayne
Species: Human
Birth Date: May 7th 3017
Booth 447
Officer Meredith Jenkins
December 19th 3039 02:18

"Officer Jenkins tabbed her as human," I murmured to myself. "You would have too. You still can't believe she's half Gaythe—and you're holding her DNA transcript." she replied as she handed me the registry paper. "I never suspected anything. She appeared utterly human," I admitted, chewing on the inside of my lip. "She arrived at 2:18 a.m. in December," I continued, cocking my head. "That's strange. Hardly anyone travels through the border terminals at that time—the travel zone is practically a ghost town."

"Agreed," she said, glancing at me. A thought passed through my brain—dangerous and wild. "We need to go to Gayle and find her mom. She might be able to tell us who her father is and why she came to Liarta," I suggested excitedly. "This might save the case!"

Ivy's eyes widened, and she shook her head vigorously, "Whoa, calm down. They're in an active war with the Nephrians right now. They're threatening to seize Gayle and wipe the Gaythe clean out of the solar system. Do you *really* think risking a whole team for one case is wise?" She gripped the back of her swivel chair and leaned toward me. "You're crazy if you think your dad will give you that kind of clearance," she whispered, glancing around to ensure no one was listening. "And have you forgotten that setting foot on Gayle soil is a punishable offense by death because of that war? They don't want human involvement."

I bit my lip as I remembered exactly who we'd be facing if we dared to make that trip.

It all began billions of years ago when the Nephrians discovered their planet's iron core was cooling—a harbinger of its eventual demise. It was believed that Veneu—located much farther away than Feros and Gayle—had once been as lush and temperate as Liarta, providing sustainable food and abundant resources for its inhabitants. However, Veneu's days had been numbered.

Though the Nephrians shared a human-like stature, they were remarkably different in appearance. Their skin was milky white, stature was thin and spindly instead of muscular, and they possessed large, round black eyes. They moved with such ethereal grace that it seemed as if they simply *floated* anywhere they went.

Adapted to their world's endless night and biting cold, their vision had adjusted to the darkness while their skin blended with the wintry landscape.

Ancient Liarta texts hinted at a revolutionary conflict within the Nephrian species, dividing them into four sectors and each sector branded its people with a deep navy insignia along the center of their spine—a crescent for Anu, a circle for Wyn, a triangle for Saph, and wave for Lei.

Some human religious groups even worshiped the Nephrians, convinced that they were the progenitors of humanity and the creators of Liarta. As Veneu's crops withered and its water turned to ice dust, its numbers dwindled, and extinction loomed unless they found a new home.

Desperate, the Nephrians decided that Liarta was their only hope they had attacked. Their initial assault had been swift. They descended from the sky in overwhelming numbers as if shooting stars were raining down upon Liarta's surface.

They crashed into buildings and homes, engulfing areas in dark voids upon impact. Black holes seemed to open up, drawing humans into their wake, and from that darkness, the Nephrians emerged—skin gleaming in the Aurelios light as if reflecting off a mirror.

Clad only in garments as black as the depths of the soul billowing in great swaths off their shoulders, they were a remarkable sight—but despite their grace, they lacked strategic finesse. Their surprise initially had given them the upper hand, but the humans were scrappier and armed to the teeth.

In retaliation, Liarta launched a counterattack on Veneu. They deployed their best-trained fighters to the planet's surface and obliterated Kamai, the Nephrians' primary city. The Nephrians then doubled back and vanished as swiftly as they had appeared.

At the same time, Liarta's forces grew even more brutal—hunting down and flaying the remaining Nephrians in search of information. They hadn't been defeated, though, merely doubling back to rebuild forces.

Since then they had changed their sights to Gayle, the jungle planet home to the Gaythe, and with the active war between them and the Nephrians travel to Gayle would prove to be quite complicated to say the least.

I chewed my lip and asked, "What will we do then?" Lifting my eyes to hers, I waited for an answer. "Figure something else out," Ivy replied, snapping her laptop shut.

***

It was already 6 p.m., and most of the officers—including Ivy—had left for the evening. I munched on a protein bar while squinting my bleary eyes at my computer screen so tired the words were starting to blur together. I blinked trying to clear the haze when my phone suddenly buzzed, and a hologram flickered into view.

"Detective Vaughn," the voice announced. I closed my eyes in irritation, recognizing it immediately. "Why are you calling me Detective Nesnah?" I asked, my breath coming out in an irritated huff. In the background, muffled chatter hinted at activity—several car doors opening and closing and voices overlapping. I leaned closer to the hologram and asked sarcastically, "Who can I thank for this lovely chat we're about to have?"

"You can thank Lieutenant Smith," he replied gruffly and his hologram arms folded neatly over his chest. I pinched the bridge of my nose, "Out with it then." I said waving my free hand in the air. "Get to Fritz Co. You'll want to see this."

I opened my mouth to say something snarky, but the holo blipped off before the air had begun to leave my lungs. I gritted my teeth and closed my laptop with a snap. Gathering my papers I shoved them into my bag and made my way out to my car.

When I was assigned to this case, I had a burning feeling in my gut that something hadn't been right—the pieces never added up, and no apparent motive emerged. There was only a dead young woman, her life shrouded in inexplicable mystery. And now, Detective Nesnah was somehow involved.

Lost in thought, I drove to Fritz Corporation silently, letting my worries consume me.

Chapter 9

"You can't detain me again, Detective. I told you everything I knew during questioning last week," Adam snapped, his annoyed voice crackling. Detective Nesnah leaned casually against his squad car as Adam fired off half-assed insults in his direction. The two were so deep in conversation that they hadn't even noticed I arrived until I slammed my car door shut, forcing both of them to turn around.

"Boys," I drawled, rolling my eyes, "Can someone please explain what's going on? It's 7 p.m., and I have a hot shower waiting for me at home." My heels clicked on the pavement as I strode over to them. It had been a long day, I was worn thin by this case, and I just wanted to go home. That had been wishful thinking though.

Luke stepped forward blatantly ignoring Adam, who was throwing eye daggers into his back. "Amy's belongings were found this afternoon right where her car was parked, and Mr. Fritz was the only person on the property at the time. He dismissed his staff for the rest of the day." he gestured toward a flustered Adam, who raised his hands defensively.

"Now, Detective," Adam insisted suddenly refraining from the insults he had so haphazardly thrown towards Nesnah this entire time. My brows rose as I waited for him to speak. "I know how this looks, but I can assure you I wasn't the one who planted her belongings. How do you know *he* didn't plant this evidence to frame me?" he gestured frantically to Luke. I rolled my eyes.

"As much as I'd love to see Detective Nesnah behind bars," I shot a pointed glare at him, "You're the one who employed Mrs. O'Rayne. Based on the information my precinct has gathered so far, a jury could easily conclude that you killed her in retribution on behalf of your company."

Silence fell. He knew exactly how it looked—and I wasn't wrong. If he were innocent, he needed to play his cards very carefully to avoid further implicating himself.

"Mr. Fritz, I suggest you contact your attorney once you return to the station. Otherwise, one will be appointed to you." I waved to get the attention of an officer who promptly finished his conversation with the crime scene investigator and lumbered over to us.

Officer Charles Covet easily towered over Adam and his dark complexion was a stark contrast to Adam's fair skin. At 6'5" he was the tallest officer at Precinct 12 and his imposing presence often unnerved people, though his nature was incredibly kind. He kept his short buzz cut meticulously clean, and his white teeth glimmered against his ebony skin when he smiled.

"Officer Covet, please escort Mr. Fritz back to the station," I gestured to Adam. "Come with me, Mr. Fritz—we're gonna take a nice little ride to the station." He scanned Detective Nesnah up and down then asked, "Pandora, are you sure you'll be alright by yourself?" His gaze never left Detective Nesnah.

Nesnah scoffed and shook his head not offering further explanation. "I'm fine," I replied with a smile. "And if Nesnah here decides to get any bright ideas, he can answer to Commissioner Vaughn." Venom dripped from my smile as I glared at Luke, who did his best to ignore my jabs. "Yes, Detective," Officer Covet said as he cuffed Adam.

"*Detective.*" Adam curtly addressed me in farewell. "*Adam.*"

I responded coolly as Officer Covet directed him towards his SUV. I sighed watching them leave then straightened my shoulders and cleared my mind, entering detective mode. "Detective Nesnah, if you would," I said, turning to adjust the badge on my hip while motioning toward the crime scene. He nodded and proceeded toward the roped-off area behind Fritz Corporation.

True to Liarta's style, Fritz Corporation was a shiny, pristine building occupying grounds separate from other nearby companies. Because it was situated on ample land away from the dense city structures, Adam's office didn't need to be as tall or ornate as those deeper in the city.

It was a simple two-story building, its facade dominated by windows of one-way glass that gave the exterior a mirror-like finish. The structure was roughly L-shaped, with the entrance located in the inner corner, and overlooked a large parking lot dotted with plain street lamps.

I trailed behind Detective Nesnah, the soft scrape of his boots across the pavement, echoing faintly in the crisp spring evening. A shiver ran through me and I tugged my brown blazer tighter. I always seemed to forget a jacket.

The afternoon's warmth had vanished with Aurelios, leaving behind a sharp chill as dusk settled in. The sky had deepened into a rich violet, and the parking lot lamps flickered on reluctantly, casting tired pools of light. I silently wished for year-round warmth as the cold had never suited me. Nesnah, however, walked on, unaffected by the temperature—a quiet reminder of what he'd said the other night behind Lady Emerald. He was from *Cappurn*.

With Cappurn so far from this system's star, Aurelios, he was accustomed to frigid temperatures and constant snow. Not quite as frigid as Veneu, but still less than enjoyable. That was why he walked around the precinct with such a stiff demeanor I guessed—I'd be equally irritable if I'd grown up there too.

He swept aside the yellow police tape and I ducked underneath to approach the scene where Amy's belongings had been found. As described, a small black purse and a tan briefcase sat neatly upright where the car had sat. Eerily, whoever returned her items had placed them in the exact spot where she was found—down to the millimeter.

I donned a pair of nitrile gloves and made my way over. First, I carefully picked up the purse and opened it. The strap was neatly folded, with no sign of ripping or wear on the thick black leather. Searching inside, I hoped to find a wallet or other belongings, but the only item present was her license. I handed the purse and license to him and he accepted them without a word. "Let me check the briefcase," I muttered, bending down to retrieve it.

Unlike the purse, the briefcase bore signs of having been manhandled—the shoulder strap had been torn and caked in dirt. I raised my eyebrows and glanced at Nesnah, who shrugged. Lifting the top flap, I discovered a folded slip of paper peering back at me.

Carefully, I extracted it and unfolded its creases, angling it toward the light of a nearby streetlamp. I gripped its furled edges as my eyes scanned over the words.

She is not who you think she is.

That's all that had been written by hand in bold red ink. "What does it say?" he asked. "It says she's not who you think she is," I replied slowly, mulling the words over in my mind. "Does that mean anything to you?" he asked, cocking his head. "No, not yet," I responded, glancing around. He asked many questions for someone not assigned to the case.

"Do you want to explain why you're here?" I pressed. "I've been designated to assist in your case," he replied curtly. "And how exactly did that happen?" I asked, rubbing my forehead. "Strings," he said, arms crossed watching me. I glared at him. "So, no explanation it is then," I muttered. He simply shook his head.

It was dark now—Aurelios had set, and the parking lot lights glowed a somewhat brighter pale yellow. This was out in the wide open with no hiding spots. Who had placed these items here? When? Why?

The gears in my head churned as I reviewed every detail of the case. She had no family on the planet, hadn't been dating anyone, and her coworkers claimed they'd never seen her out and about. I folded the paper carefully and slid it into an evidence bag.

"That's the most important piece of evidence we have so far," I murmured, still dazed as my mind whirled with questions. "That's not all you need to see," Luke said quietly, as if lost in his thoughts, before starting toward the line of trees at the back of Fritz Corporation's property. I trailed silently behind him.

The parking lot's pavement ended, but he continued through the grass. I paused briefly at the edge of the asphalt. "I'm not exactly wearing hiking boots," I remarked. He paused and turned to look at me. I pointed at my heels and a shit eating grin formed up his face. "Seems like a you problem." he quipped and turned on his heel to continue through the trees. I scowled but removed my shoes and trudged barefoot through the ankle-high grass.

"How far are we going?" I asked, tilting my head to follow the path before us. "Not far," he said. I rolled my eyes for the hundredth time that day and shivered as the cold mud fused to my heels. Raising my chin, I gazed at the night sky, where stars glimmered overhead and distant planets pulsed with light.

Abruptly, my chest bumped into Detective Nesnah's muscled back. He had stopped nearly half a mile into the trees in the middle of the trail. I reeled back startled, then stood on my tiptoes, craning my neck over his shoulder to see what he had stopped for. In front of us, the grass was bent as if gently folded over in a perfect circle, still alive.

"All our magnetic devices are affected in this area," he said, glancing over his shoulder at me. "So... a crop circle." I said slowly trying to understand why this one in particular would be important. "Someone must have flashed here." I shrugged and looked at him, still not understanding.

He surveyed the surrounding woods before continuing, "It's rather dense around here, and flashing is risky with so many obstacles. If you flash in a cluttered location, you risk binding your molecules to those around you—and in the blink of an eye, your molecules could explode into pink mist. Humans have taken a long time to handle flashing physically. Many other species can flit through dimensions and time, but humans are considered fragile. Our cells are far more particular and susceptible to molecular changes and interruptions."

I stared at him, trying to keep a poker face. It was the most he had ever said in one go. Although this information might break the case, I couldn't bring myself to let him know that.

"And?" I asked, nervously picking at the skin under my thumbnail. "Flashing is usually only performed by highly trained humans who have undergone cellular conditioning to handle the force without their cells imploding. Typically, it's safer for us to travel by ship, from relay stations, or car rather than risk flashing somewhere. Nephrians are the only species that can inherently flash anywhere without technological assistance. But apparently, someone was so desperate that they flashed in a hazardous location, rather than a receiving relay station," he gestured around us.

My eyebrows furrowed, "It could have been someone non-human. A Nephrian." I suggested scanning the area for evidence and footprints. "Sure, I thought that too—except that humans are the only ones who leave these prints." he said as he pointed to a partial boot print on the very edge of the circle. "Whoever flashed here did it in a hurry. They were barely in the zone, and it nearly cost them their life."

He crouched down and pulled out his evidence scanner, which chimed to life. He angled the light over the partial print as it scanned slowly with it's pale blue light.

"Military boot model 657," The scanner dinged, identifying the shoe that left the print. "Fuck," I hissed sharply. "Military." He huffed and stared at the screen. "Cross-reference everything. Nothing can slip through on this case. If the killer is military, they probably already know everything up until now."

"Woah. Woah. Pump the brakes, Detective." I huffed pinching the bridge of my nose and placing my other hand on my hip. It was bad enough that he was keeping my mother's case open. He couldn't possibly expect me to comply with this buffoonery. "What makes you think you can just roll up on my crime scene, start talking about crop circles and military boots, and expect me to follow your lead blindly?" I stepped directly in front of him.

Even though I stood six feet tall, I still had to look up to meet his eyes. He ignored my question. "The information that Amy had must have been incredibly important—or extremely confidential," he continued blatantly ignoring my previous question and striding around me. I sucked my tongue against my teeth, forcing myself to remain professional.

"Detective Nesnah, I appreciate the work you've done to assist in my case," I said, emphasizing the 'T' in 'assist' as if it warranted its own punctuation. "However, I am fully capable of handling this case alone but thank you."

"That's not for us to decide." He turned and trekked back toward the parking lot without saying another word. I blinked, feeling my eyes roll back in their sockets once again—they might as well have been a pinball machine bouncing off the back of my head.

I trudged through the mud, following Detective Nesnah as he led the way. He slipped silently through the grass, his footsteps barely audible on the wet soil. "You can't just expect me to let you in on my case," I said, trailing behind him. "You don't have a choice," he replied without turning to face me.

This arrogant man—this arrogant man who was going to get me fired for workplace hostility if he kept it up.

"On whose orders?" I asked. "Again, if you have a problem with this arrangement," he said, turning abruptly and stopping me in my tracks. "You can talk to Lieutenant Smith." his minty breath washed over my face, and the hair on my arms stood on end. "I'd rather not," I clipped back. "Do you think I *asked* to be assigned to your case?" his chin angled toward my face, and my breath hitched in my throat.

Why did he make me feel so small?

I said nothing. "Well then, it seems we're at an impasse." He was uncomfortably close, and my heart quickened, but before I could muster a response, he turned swiftly on his heel and continued toward the parking lot.

We silently reached the lot, our mutual irritation smoldering like embers threatening to burst into flames. I popped the trunk of my vehicle and retrieved an old gym towel to wipe my mud caked feet.

He strode off without another word to his squad car. The muscles in his shoulders strained against his shirt as his arms swung with each step. The lump in my throat bobbed as I watched him slide into the driver's seat. He glared at me one last time before driving off down the Fritz Corporation's paved entrance.

Good *riddance*.

I pulled on a pair of chunky white sneakers from the back of my car and scanned my surroundings one last time. There had to be answers still here—just hidden. A blue light flashed in my peripheral vision and I whipped my head around to catch it, but whatever it was, it was gone.

Driving home, I listened to jazz on the radio my thumbs drumming on the steering wheel with the beat. The drive felt faster than it had that morning, and before I knew it, I pulled into my driveway.

Dust plumed behind my car as it bounced over the gravel, and soon, my cabin came into view. I dragged myself out of the car and into my front door, kicking off my shoes in the usual spot. Rounding the corner, I found a bag of takeout on the counter with a note attached.

"I heard about Detective Nesnah and thought you could use a pick-me-up. —Ivy"

I smiled as I reached into the bag and pulled out fried rice and orange chicken—my favorite. Ivy always knew the way to my heart. I took my time enjoying dinner alone at the kitchen counter.

With each bite, the day's exhaustion slowly lifted away. After finishing my meal and disposing of the trash, I headed to the bathroom for a much needed shower then sleep.

***

My eyes snapped open to the noise. Soft footsteps barely audible and indistinguishable to anyone who wasn't heavily trained. I couldn't tell how late it was but late enough that the moonlight no longer illuminated my bedroom. I strained my ear focusing and heard it again—the soft footsteps outside—and fear slithered up my spine.

I slid my hand under the covers toward the bedside table. A gentle click sounded as I opened the drawer and freed my pistol.

My father had warned me that living this far from the city alone was dangerous, but I hadn't listened. I craved solitude, away from the busybodies of the city. I had said if danger came to find me, I'd prove I would always be more savage than my assailants and I was hard pressed to let anyone prove me wrong, even tonight.

Sliding quietly out of the covers, I crept across the room. My bare feet hissed against the floor as I pressed myself against the wall. The door to my room was shut as I sidled up to it, not daring to take a breath.

Gingerly, I turned the doorknob, the air in my throat pausing as I willed it to be silent. The door swung open a couple of inches without a sound. Unable to exhale, I slipped into the hallway like a shadow retracing my steps from when I got home.

The noise had ceased moments ago, but I knew that if I stopped, I'd be as vulnerable as a fish in a barrel. Someone had entered my home, and either they'd fled or they knew I was awake and were searching for me.

I moved to the opposite side of the hallway and peered into the kitchen. There, a folded piece of paper was delicately placed on the counter. I paled. Slowly, I crept toward it, my eyes wide in horror.

I am not who you think I am.

The words were scrawled in bold, furious red ink. I cursed under my breath at the same time I heard the front door click shut.

I sprinted, my feet pounding against the floor, and flung the front door wide open with such force that it slammed against its hinges, protesting the abuse. My pajamas fluttered in the midnight draft as I panted, scanning the darkness outside with my pistol held tightly in my hand.

The cold night seeped into my fingers and toes as I stood on my doorstep, staring into the shadowed woods surrounding me. They were gone and I was left standing in the shadow of their wake.

Chapter 10

I sat in silence at the kitchen counter, eyes fixed on the folded piece of paper still resting precisely where it had been the night before. I hadn't dared to touch it—or even fully accept that it was real.

As dawn crept in, it bathed the house in a warm golden light, and the reality of Tuesday morning settled over me. I was supposed to be at the office. Still rattled from a sleepless night, I had decided to take the day off and texted Ivy to meet me here—fifteen minutes ago now. Since then, I hadn't moved, just sat here staring at the paper like it might suddenly ignite and reduce the house to ashes.

I took a small sip of coffee, the mug trembled slightly in my grip. I glanced down at my arm, at the streak of red where my arm was healing from the assault the other night. It had already started to close, and I had opted to not replace the bulky bandages. It was unlikely to open back up anyway since he hadn't struck anything vital, and thanks to some remarkably good genetics it seemed that I healed faster than most humans.

Mayra hadn't found any sign of an intruder, and if not for that paper's undeniable presence, I might have chalked it all up to a hallucination. In all my years as a Liarta detective, my home had never been breached—that is until now. And after the incident with Mr. Malone, a disturbing realization was beginning to form, piece by piece. Someone was targeting me, but *who?*

They had been far too close—someone had gained the upper hand once again. I took another sip of coffee and forced myself to stay calm. At this very moment, whoever was behind this was already two steps ahead, bold enough to send a message by sneaking into a detective's home in the dead of night.

Setting my mug back on the counter with a soft clink, I resolved to figuring out how they had gotten in.

I stepped outside, slipping into my chucks and tugging on a red hoodie. A light rain pattered against the roof and pooled under the porch overhang and I groaned as a blast of cool wet air hit my face. I despised the chill.

With my hood pulled up, I began my investigation at the front door, running my hand along the door frame's lip. Finding nothing amiss, I leaned over the railing to search for footprints in the grass and mud. Nothing.

My shoes crunched on the gravel as I strode to the back of the house, searching for any sign of tampering. All the windows appeared intact, with no disturbances in sight, but a chill ran down my spine as I rounded the corner to the window facing my bedroom.

What if they had been watching me? How long had they been here before making their move? I could feel the dark purple bags forming under my eyes after a sleepless night—hours spent staring out the windows, praying not to see an unfamiliar face peering back at me. Huddled on my bed with my knees drawn to my chest and pistol in hand, I had only risen when the Aurelios light began filtering through the canopy, revealing the silhouettes of trees.

I pressed myself against the shrubs beneath my window and ran my fingers along the pane. Something brushed against my fingertip. Peering beneath the window, I discovered a small scrambler chip wedged between the window frame and the house's stone. I cursed under my breath. "Okay, that's how they bypassed my AI," I muttered.

Using my fingernail, I lifted the lip of the chip and shimmed it free. By then, the rain had started to intensify, soaking my back through the hoodie. Clutching the scrambler in my fist, I trudged back inside, kicked off my shoes at the door without a second thought, and settled back into the kitchen. Flipping the chip over in my fingers, I narrowed my eyes—this one looked familiar.

"Mayra," I called. "Yes, Detective Vaughn," she replied as she appeared in the kitchen. As an AI, Mayra could tailor her appearance however she chose.

Often, AI presented themselves in humanoid forms to appeal to their users. Mayra preferred a slender, average-height figure with blunt, shoulder-cut silver hair.

Like many AI, she eschewed traditional clothes. Her body was a sleek chrome from the neck down, boasting subtle curves and distinctly feminine features. Her eyes glowed purple as she waited for my response. I pulled my hood down, letting it settle on my shoulders.

"Mayra, I found a scrambler chip wedged in my bedroom window frame—that's why you couldn't detect anyone here." I slid the chip to her side of the counter and sat on one of my bar stools. "Indeed," she replied, then added, "Scanning chip for identification number." Her eyes locked into place as she went quiet.

I sat, clasping my fingers together in anticipation. "Chip identified," she chirped, "Registered to Detective Pandora Vaughn, Precinct 12, issue date January 12, 3030."

I froze, "What?"

"Registered to Detective—"

"No, I heard you, Mayra. What do you mean it's registered to me?" I stood abruptly, snatching the chip from the counter.

"It appears to be the scrambler issued to you by the precinct, along with your badge, duty weapon, and atom scanner," she explained, her stature unwavering as she turned to look at me.

I stared at her incredulously. "Mayra, how could they have gotten my scrambler? It's always locked in the station." I flipped the chip around in my fingers, biting my lip in frustration. "That information is unavailable to me at this time," she said tilting her AI head at me. Her silver bob flittered with the unnatural motion.

"Run another malware sweep and manually override a factory reset of your software, Mayra. I don't want any chance they left spyware on your systems." I pinched the bridge of my nose and paced back and forth. "Confirmed. Running malware filter," Mayra responded before her hologram flitted away.

"Fuck me," I hissed to myself as a car door closing in my driveway tore me from my thoughts. I pocketed the scrambler and briskly walked to the door, swinging it open. There, Ivy stood, slightly damp, her arm raised halfway in a knock.

She had opted for casual attire over her usual business office look—a blue, long-sleeved waffle shirt paired with jeans and white sneakers. Her blonde hair was neatly pulled back into a ponytail.

"Come in," I said, leaning partially out the door to glance at the woods behind her. She stood alone, raising an inquisitive eyebrow. I pulled her into the house by her elbow without a word. "I got your text—you didn't elaborate. What's going on?" she asked, her eyes scanning the room as her expression grew more tense.

"Listen," I began, taking a deep breath. "Someone came broke into my house last night." My voice dropped to a whisper and Ivy's eyes widened. "Who? Was it someone involved with Mr.

Malone?" she whispered. "I'm not sure, but they left a scrambler in my bedroom window. Mayra didn't detect anyone in the house besides me," I explained. She paused, absorbing the information. "Did they leave anything else? How do you know someone was here?"

"I heard them," I replied, shivering. "They were in my kitchen. They left a note," I added, gesturing toward the curled-up paper still sitting where I had left it. "What does it say?" she asked, setting her things down on the couch and walking over to the paper. I stayed silent. "Pandora?" she queried as she picked up the note and began to unfurl its edges.

"It says, *I am not who you think I am*," I murmured, my arms hanging limply at my sides. "It's like the note we found at the Fritz Co. crime scene." I said and Ivy looked up from the paper. "Someone doesn't want you to solve this case," she said, setting it back down.

Outside, the rain picked up pounding the roof relentlessly. "I know," I replied, sinking onto the sofa. "So, what now?" she asked, plopping beside me. I pursed my lips in thought, "I've been considering Amy and her ties with the Gaythe on Gayle." She waved her hand, urging me to continue.

"There's a story my mom used to read to me about a woman named Odina." I watched her reaction closely. "A woman named Odina? Where have I heard that name before?" she murmured, glancing down at the floor as she pursed her lips. "I think I still have the book she used to read to me."

I stood up, crossing the living room to retrieve a worn book from the shelf. The spine read "The History of Gayle." I flipped through the pages until I landed in the middle, then handed it to her. She accepted it, puzzled, as her eyes drifted over the worn pages.

"Born at the peak of the tallest mountain on Gayle, a girl from the southern Gaythe tribe was born. Only a few lanterns glowed in the darkest of midnight. The elders whispered of the great war she would deliver their tribe from.

Wrapped in thick blankets the mother held her baby girl tightly, brushing her fingers against her tiny, scaled cheek. Tears streamed down her face as she beheld the small face gazing up at her, quiet and observing.

The baby was not afraid, for a warrior brought her into the world. The mother knew her time was close to an end as she clung to her daughter. Beads of sweat formed on her brow as her purple-scaled face slowly turned ash grey.

She was dying.

The healer held the young mother upright as she became too weak to hold herself. The mother's eyes glazed as the healer whispered ancient spells unlocking the gate to the afterlife. It was considered the highest honor in the Gaythe culture to die during childbirth. The Gaythe believed that it was the most selfless thing a person could do, and mothers who passed while bringing life into the world had a special place saved for them in the afterlife.

"A name, my dear?" One of the elders whispered placing a hand on her arm gently. It took every ounce of life for her to respond. The baby's eyes bore into her mother's soul, seeing her as she was.

Lifegiver.

"Odina." She whispered and let death sweep over her. Her beautiful iridescent scales turned to black coal and a whisp of silver light was released in her final breath. "The one born of the mountain." The elder nodded and gently eased the baby out of the woman's arms. She stared into the baby's face as her deep green eyes stared her back. "Welcome Odina, to the Southern

tribe." She greeted the baby.

Odina reached her tiny, webbed fingers out of the blanket toward the elder stretching them in the pale light. This little baby girl would be the strongest female Gaythe warrior ever born. Tales would be told of her incredible swimming speed, faster than the speed of sound and strength of a thousand human men. She would deliver her people to salvation—Queen of the Southern Gaythe Tribe."

Ivy blew out a sharp breath. "Pandora, you can't seriously think we will just fly to Gayle to meet this so-called Queen of the Gaythes—especially in the middle of interplanetary war. Do you?"

"It might be our best lead," I said, offering a hesitant smile.

"*Absolutely* not. Have you lost your mind?" she shook her head, her ponytail swishing behind her as she snapped the book shut with a loud thud. I crossed my arms. "Then tell me—how else are we supposed to figure out why she left Gayle without actually going there?"

Ivy shot me a glare, her fingers tapping impatiently against her knee. "And what exactly do you think Detective Nesnah will say about this?"

"Fuck Nesnah. This is *my* case." I scowled as I ground my molars together. Ivy's eyebrows lifted. "That's not what Lieutenant Smith told him at the precinct yesterday." I stiffened, "what did you hear?"

My voice came out sharper than I intended as my eyes narrowed. "Pandora—" she hesitated, shifting on her feet. "What did you hear?" I pressed, my tone firmer this time. Her expression faltered, and guilt hit me like a gut punch. It wasn't her fault my case had turned into a dumpster fire, tangled up with a detective we weren't sure we could trust.

"They were just talking about how he's been assigned to it and that you've been taken off." her voice was quiet, almost reluctant. "That's all I heard before I got called into a meeting."

My shoulders slumped. "Maybe he was planning on telling you himself this week," she added gently, giving my back a reassuring pat. I nodded, though it felt hollow. I'd never been *removed* from a case in my entire career, and the blow stung just a little.

"I'll meet you at the precinct." she pulled me into a quick hug before walking toward the front door. Just as she reached for the knob, she glanced back at me. "Oh, and don't get too absorbed in this case and forget—we still have the precinct ball to prepare for this weekend. Your dad is speaking, and he expects you to be there."

With that, she was gone. I groaned, dropping my head into my hands as if I needed one more thing on my plate.

The next few days blurred together, each as frustrating as the last. We made little progress on the case, training felt like a waste of time, and sleep was a gamble I kept losing.

Lieutenant Smith avoided me like the plague, even as I brazenly shot daggers at him through his glass office doors every time I walked by. Before I knew it, Saturday evening had arrived, and I stood in front of my mirror, dressed for the precinct ball.

The long purple gown draped over my frame in smooth, cascading silk, its two narrow straps resting delicately on my shoulders. The fabric hugged my hips before flowing all the way down to the floor, a far cry from my usual cargo pants and tactical boots.

I turned slightly, watching as the soft auburn waves of my hair tumbled over my shoulders framing the delicate gold jewelry I had opted to wear. I sighed as I noted the red streak on my arm already started to be less noticeable, but still there. It would have been much easier to cover it in anything other than this revealing dress, but formal attire was expected since it was indeed a formal ball.

With a final glance in the mirror, I grabbed my keys, bid my house farewell, and slipped into my car. Then, with a press of the gas, I sped off to the ball.

Chapter 11

The tallest building in existence, The Loft, loomed over the city of Liarta, an architectural marvel suspended high above the ground. Massive magnets held the structure aloft, defying the very laws of physics. Something so vast, so impossibly heavy, had no business floating as if it weighed nothing more than a swan feather.

I parked my car and slid out, taking a moment to survey my surroundings. The air had grown more humid since earlier in the week after the rain. It clung to my skin as I adjusted my black clutch under my arm.

Along the riverwalk, citizens strolled, their voices mingling with the gentle churn of the river flowing through the heart of the city. Ahead, impeccably dressed politicians funneled toward a grand elevator encrusted in smooth stone. It chimed softly before its doors slid open with a hiss, welcoming its passengers.

I followed the clusters of people inside, and with a near-silent hum, we ascended, floating effortlessly through the air toward the gravity defying Loft above. As the doors parted, we stepped out, now hundreds of feet higher than we had been moments ago. Floor-to-ceiling glass windows lined the walls, showcasing the golden cityscape below.

Aurelios had begun to set, its amber light washing over the buildings, making them twinkle like precious gemstones. My heels clicked against the pristine tiled floor, polished to a mirror finish. I glanced down, catching my reflection smiling back at me.

Fairy lights flickered along the dark walls, tiny pinpricks of brilliance against the black surface, giving the illusion that we were walking among the stars. My eyes snagged on a sleek wooden podium with a sign behind it that stood at the center of the vast space, positioned in front of the glowing skyline.

President Danny Fritz.

The bold black letters loomed over the room, a reminder of who this event really was for. Well, he certainly knew how to throw a precinct party. Across the room, Ivy waved, her other arm casually draped over Chance as he took a slow sip of what looked like whiskey. I maneuvered through the crowd, exchanging polite greetings as I passed.

"Whiskey?" Chance offered, holding out a crystal glass filled with amber liquid. His black suit shifted against his broad shoulders, the fabric rustling with his movement. His blonde hair was perfectly coiffed, not a strand out of place. I smirked, accepting the drink. "Do I look like I need it?"

"You said it, not me." he turned slightly, the corner of his mouth twitching with amusement. "You look amazing!" Ivy beamed, her eyes twinkling with delight.

Her black glittering gown hugged her curves, snaking up her chest before fastening at her throat, leaving her entire back exposed. Her blonde hair had been twisted into a flawless coiled roll, each wisp sleekly tucked into place.

"Thanks." I grinned, spinning for her. The draped purple silk of my gown flared dramatically around my feet. Chance clapped quietly, nodding in approval, while Ivy raised her arms theatrically, bowing as if I were royalty. I rolled my eyes. "You two are ridiculous." I muttered, but couldn't hide my grin.

"Pandora. Ivy. Chance." A gruff voice behind us cut through the moment. I turned, my gaze meeting his. Tall and broad-shouldered, my father stood before us, a drink in his hand. His salt-and-pepper hair was neatly combed, and his navy suit contrasted sharply against his tanned face, making his blue eyes gleam under the warm lights.

"Dad," I mused, smiling behind my drink. "Commissioner Vaughn." Chance jutted his chin in acknowledgment before waving down the bartender for another round. My father chuckled, "I trust you'll behave tonight and refrain from patronizing the guests?" His voice was deep and rumbling and made me feel at ease.

His eyes drifted to the mark along my arm, concern flickering through his face, but I quickly adjusted it hiding the red streak. "Eh." I shrugged insinuating that I would make no such promises. His eyes narrowed slightly, but amusement danced at the edges. "How's your case coming along?" he asked, swirling his drink. I peered over my glass my lips parting as I spoke, "We found more evidence yesterday at Fritz Corporation, and our DNA lab results returned earlier this week."

"Excellent. Keep anything regarding Fritz Corporation under wraps for tonight." his tone shifted into something more authoritative. "I have an announcement, and I need everything to go smoothly. No scandals." I nodded, scanning the room. "What did the lab work show?" he asked, leaning against the bar, casually nodding at passing guests who waved in our direction.

I scooted in slightly. The last thing I needed was someone overhearing classified information and blowing the case open before we could control it. I tapped the rim of my glass, the soft clink filling the space between us.

"Turns out she wasn't human." I swirled the amber liquid

in my glass. "Half Gaythe." I added quietly. My father stilled, his forehead creasing. "Half *Gaythe?*" he murmured, leaning in closer now. "That's what the lab report said." I downed the rest of my drink, letting the burn settle in my throat. The grip on his glass tightened, "That's not possible." His voice was low, measured. "There are no Gaythe-human hybrids."

"There is now," I said, my gaze unwavering from my father. "Er—was." I corrected myself. "Did she come here from Gayle? Why was she here then?" Harrison ran his free fingers through his speckled grey hair leaving creases through the gel. "I think that—"

"Ahem! May I direct your attention to the podium for Commissioner Vaughn," a speaker announced, their voice cutting through the chatter in the room. My father exhaled, setting his glass down. "We'll talk later." he excused himself, drifting toward the podium.

I glanced around, realizing how crowded the space had suddenly become. Women in tight satin gowns draped in pearls clung to their wealthy husbands watching the announcer—though they hardly paid them any mind.

Across the room, a group of men huddled in a hushed conversation, their expressions tense, smoke curling from cigars clutched between their fingers. I waved down the bartender for another drink before sliding into the crowd beside Ivy. Our shoulders brushed as I subtly leaned away from the curious eyes of a few men watching me from down the bar.

Ivy noticed and looped her arm through mine, resting our temples together in a silent show of female solidarity. Chance stood just behind us, one elbow propped casually against the bar, his gaze scanning the room. His expression remained unreadable, but for a brief moment, his eyes narrowed. I followed his line of sight, rising onto my tiptoes to see what had caught his attention.

Across the room, with one hand tucked casually into his pocket, stood Detective Luke Nesnah. His deep green suit clashed against the sharp intensity of his blazing blue eyes as he scanned the crowd—just as Chance had moments before.

Even through the layers of his suit, tension coiled in his frame, his broad shoulders rigid and arms unmistakably defined beneath the fabric. His dark brown curls rested in effortless disarray, barely shifting as he took a slow sip of his drink and I scowled at his deliberate choice. Whiskey.

Of *course* his taste in alcohol was the same as mine.

He blinked slowly, unfazed, his gaze drifting through the room with calculated ease. Shifting nervously from one leg to the other I watched as his eyes roamed over the guests making their way towards me—then finally, they locked onto mine.

A sharp breath caught in my throat, and suddenly, my mouth felt impossibly dry. A slow grin ghosted at the corner of his lips. He cocked his head slightly, raising his glass toward me in a silent toast. I bit my lower lip.

Why did he make me so *nervous*?

I was brought out of my thoughts as Harrison stepped onto the stage, his signature camera-ready smile firmly in place. "Good evening," he began, his voice smooth and authoritative. "I hope everyone is enjoying this magnificent night—and this breathtaking view." He gestured toward the massive windows behind him, showcasing the sparkling cityscape below. Applause rang through the room, and he paused, waiting for the excitement to settle before continuing.

"We chose this venue deliberately—to highlight the groundbreaking work that has gone into building this city and, more importantly, to express our gratitude to *you*, the citizens, who have supported it." Another round of applause rippled through the crowd. For a fleeting second, his gaze flicked to me. And in that moment, something flashed across his expression—regret, maybe? But just as quickly, his practiced media mask snapped back into place.

"Thanks to your generous donations," he continued smoothly, "We've allocated additional funding to Precinct 12, allowing for upgrades such as state-of-the-art scanners, new equipment for our deputies, and enhanced gear for our existing officers."

Soft murmurs stirred across the audience. Harrison let the moment hang before delivering the next announcement, "And I'm happy to share that, thanks to this funding, we will also be updating equipment on our sister planet, Feros, to reopen the mines." The response was immediate. The murmurs grew into loud, excited chatter as the news rippled through the crowd.

Reopen the mines?

The Feros mines had been abandoned years ago and deemed worthless after their resources were depleted. "I thought the resources ran out on Feros," a young, dark-haired man called out from across the room, "The last thing we were told was that the mines were empty." Several people around him nodded in agreement. Harrison remained unfazed.

"The iron and metal resources have indeed run dry," he replied smoothly, "but we have reason to believe a different resource—*Element X*—exists in abundance on Feros."

My stomach tightened. *Element X?* I'd never heard of it before. And how long had they planned to reopen the mines without anyone knowing? "That's strange," Ivy whispered beside me. "I've never heard of an Element X."

"Me either." I nodded, but my eyes never left the podium. A woman near the front—full-figured with sleek black hair and sharply lined red lips—spoke up next, "And who exactly do you expect to work in these mines?" Harrison's expression remained steady, "Mining will be voluntary. However, many miners who settled there when they were first opened still inhabit Feros." He paused before adding, "There will be some assigned personnel assisting with the reopening, but all Liarta citizens will have the choice of whether or not to go."

I swallowed hard, my throat dry. Something about this didn't sit right. "And what is the value of this *Element X*?" a short, red-haired man asked, narrowing his eyes skeptically. Harrison's fingers curled around the edges of the podium as he delivered his following words, "We believe this resource holds enough energy to power an *entire planet* for *millions of years*."

A chill ran through me as my father's gaze flicked to mine. That kind of *power*, in the wrong hands could be catastrophic. "Something's off," Chance murmured, his voice low. "Why haven't they told us about this resource before now?" Ivy mirrored his concern whispering in my ear and making me jump slightly. "I don't know," I admitted, keeping my tone just as quiet, "He didn't mention any of this to me." My brows knit together as unease slithered up my spine. "And he tells me *everything*."

I chewed on my bottom lip, trying to shake the creeping doubt. My father was a good man. If Element X was as powerful as he claimed, surely, it would be used for *good*—not hoarded by Liarta officials as some bargaining chip.

Harrison's voice rang through the room again, "The first team is preparing for departure to Feros to assess which mines can be restored. Humanity has endured dark times, but it is time for us—the Liarta government—to shed *light*." He smiled as the city lights flickered to life below, illuminating the sprawling metropolis.

Aurelios dipped past the horizon, casting the golden skyscrapers in a celestial glow, their gleaming spires reaching for the heavens. The crowd erupted into applause, but I barely heard it. My gaze stayed locked on my father as he stepped off the stage, his expression unreadable. Then, without hesitation, he turned and strode toward a back room secured with a padlock.

I rose onto my tiptoes, straining for a better view. He tapped in a code, and the lock clicked open. Just before he disappeared inside, I caught a fleeting glimpse of movement—someone already waiting for him. But before I could determine who, the door shut firmly behind him.

I felt lightheaded and turned to excuse myself but wobbled some. Chance caught my elbow. "Are you alright?" He asked. "I'm fine. I'll be right back." I mumbled and weaved my way through the crowd towards the bathroom.

I locked my sights on the door and quickened my pace. Before I could get close, something clamped around my wrist, yanking me sideways into an adjacent room. "Let go of me!" I hissed, twisting against the grip. I threw a fist out, but it met nothing but air. "Detective Pandora Vaughn," a familiar voice purred. My pulse spiked.

"Adam?" I snapped, my eyes adjusting to the dim light. "Cut the shit."

"I don't have much time, but you must listen to me." His voice was low, urgent. Now that I could see him clearly, I took in his appearance—dark navy suit not unlike my fathers. The top button of his satin chestnut shirt was undone with ease, but his brown eyes? They were sharp. Serious. My own narrowed, "And why exactly should I listen to you?" Everyone was acting incredibly strange tonight.

I crossed my arms. "Let me guess—you're one of the politicians bankrolling the mine reopening? Anything for the money, anything for the power. Or have you conveniently forgotten the stories of workers being *forced* to mine until they collapsed from exhaustion?" I stepped back, my bare skin brushing against the cool wall as I registered how *close* he was to me.

His jaw tightened, "I'm not. But my father is." He glanced toward the partially open door, as if checking for anyone who might have followed. "That's essentially the same thing." I scoffed. He ignored my comment.

"I overheard your conversation with Commissioner Vaughn," Adam murmured. "You need to get to Gayle and find Amy's mother—without your father knowing. He'll *never* allow you to set foot on Gayle's surface, not with the war between them and the Nephrians." He leaned in, his voice dropping even lower. "I have a private ship. It's unregistered. It's yours to take."

My eyes widened, "You were eavesdropping? Private ship?" My jaw tensed, but my detective instincts kicked in before my outrage could fully surface. What else did he know? I narrowed my gaze. "What do you *really* know about my case?" I murmured. "Not much," he admitted, "but I do know you need to close this case—fast." His voice barely carried between us and he raised a finger to his lips, a subtle warning.

A slow, uneasy feeling curled in my stomach as I lowered my voice, "Why do you want me to go to Gayle?" His eyes flicked past me, scanning the shadows, but we were alone. "I have my reasons, Detective." His gaze settled back on me, assessing. "I need you to trust me."

I scoffed in response, "Trust you?" My face heated with frustration. "If anyone overheard this conversation, you would be arrested for obstruction of justice, *Mr. Fritz*. And in case you need reminding, *you're still a suspect*." I turned sharply, ready to walk out—But his hand caught my wrist again, stopping me in my tracks.

He rotated my wrist over revealing the scar forming up

my forearm and stilled as if he was caught off guard. "What happened to your arm?" He whispered his eyes lingering on the red puckered skin before lifting to my face.

"Let go," I hissed. Adam's grip loosened and he blinked clearing his mind. We stood there for a moment in silence before he took a deep breath, "Detective, there is *so much more* at stake than you realize." His tone was low but insistent. "I know you think you have all the information, but listen to me very carefully." I yanked my wrist free. He didn't try to stop me again—his hand remaining suspended in midair for moment before he let it fall. "Listen to Detective Nesnah. *Go to Gayle.*"

He slid a small card into my palm with a subtle nod and stepped away. I turned it over in my fingers. A phone number was scrawled on the back in blue, looping handwriting. "What does Detective Nesnah have to do with—" I started, but when I looked up, Adam was already gone.

Biting my lip, I tucked the card into my clutch and smoothed out my dress, forcing myself to regain composure. The moment was over, but I couldn't afford to linger. I slid through the partially open door and pushed through the crowd, scanning for Ivy.

I spotted her mingled with a few officers from Precinct 12. Chance's arm was loosely draped over her shoulders as he animatedly gestured with his free hand, likely in the middle of telling some exaggerated story. She caught my eye and smiled, waving me over.

I maneuvered through the guests, careful not to bump into anyone. "Excuse me," I said to the group, forcing a polite smile. I gestured to Ivy, "I need to borrow her."

Before anyone could protest, I grabbed Ivy's arm and pulled her toward a secluded corner, away from prying eyes and ears. She eyed me carefully, her expression shifting when she looked closer at my face.

"What's wrong? You look shaken." Her brows knit together as she gently gripped my shoulders. "Adam just pulled me aside," I said, glancing around to ensure no one was listening. Her hands dropped from me. "*Adam Fritz?*" She blinked in surprise before quickly scanning the room, searching for him. "Yes." My voice dropped lower as I explained everything he had told me. Ivy's expression darkened, her eyes narrowing as she listened. "I thought Adam had nothing to do with your case," Ivy said, pausing as if trying to piece everything together. "I did, too." I murmured, absentmindedly rolling my necklace between my fingers.

In the center of the room, a game of pool was drawing most of the attention. Laughter echoed through the space as players leaned over the table, focused on their shots. Then—a flash of emerald green and navy caught my eye. Adam Fritz stood near the pool table, conversing deeply with none other than *Detective Luke Nesnah*.

They were speaking quietly, their exchange unnoticed by the distracted crowd. Luke leaned in a bit, nodding while Adam whispered something in his ear and passed him an item, hidden in a closed fist. A small flash of something dark flickered between their hands and Detective Nesnah quickly pocketed the item. Then—Adam looked at me.

Our eyes met across the room and his gaze softened. Almost apologetic. Beside him, Luke's attention flickered toward Harrison, who had at some point returned to the mingling crowd. He nodded once, then took a slow swig of his drink. My stomach twisted.

Why is he bringing Nesnah into this?

Something wasn't adding up. A piece was missing—one I should have seen by now. "He said to trust him," I whispered, pulling Ivy further into the shadows. "Trust *him?*" She arched a brow. "That's what he said," I replied, my gaze never leaving Luke. He set his glass on the table in front of him and his eyes locked onto mine. "Maybe you should just ask him," Ivy suggested, following my line of sight. "I'm going to have to," I muttered. "Good luck." She squeezed my arm before slipping back into the crowd. Luke and I remained locked in a silent stare across the dance floor.

One heartbeat.

Two.

The music pulsed louder, vibrating through the floor. Lights flashed against the mirrored tiles, fracturing into patterns that danced along the walls. The crowd moved in a chaotic rhythm—arms, heads, bodies weaving together between us, an entanglement of motion.

Three.

Luke stood still, hands in his pockets, his expression unreadable. My pulse quickened. His eyes—*why were they so blue?*

I bobbed my head and pushed my way through the dance floor. A woman's arm swung too close, forcing me to duck as she shot me a glare, clearly annoyed that I had been in her way. A couple brushed against my back, their laughter mixed with the pounding bass as I maneuvered past them. I quickened my pace, weaving between moving bodies, until—I broke free from the crowd, stumbling as my heel caught on the edge of the polished tiles. A hand shot out, catching my arm.

Luke.

His grip was firm and steady—his fingers brushed mine just long enough for a jolt to shoot up my arm, sharp and electric. He blinked startled, but quickly smoothed the expression over.

"Detective Vaughn," he said smoothly, his voice just audible over the music. I steadied myself, yanking my hand back as if burned. "Detective Nesnah." I huffed. "We have to stop meeting like this." He smirked and I chewed the inside of my cheek but didn't take the bait. "We need to talk," he said, his voice low but insistent.

My pulse thrummed, almost in sync with the beat. "I'll say," I snapped, irritation lacing my tone. "Not here," he added, glancing subtly around the room. "Too many eyes. Too many ears."

"What do you suggest?" I asked, narrowing my eyes at him. "Meet me downstairs by the riverside. I'll explain everything." he said and without another word he made his way through the crowd, then was gone. Why did all the men leave me like this, abruptly standing here gawking like an idiot.

I blinked readjusting my sight against the lights and settled my eyes on my father poised near the one way windows and deep in conversation with a grey-haired man. I might as well say my farewells for the night.

I wove through the partiers, offering polite smiles and handshakes as I went. Some asked about the case, while others simply greeted me in passing. My cheeks ached from keeping up the facade, but I played the part. Dutiful decorated detective. As I neared my father, the man he was speaking with came into sharper focus.

Danny Fritz.

He stood with one hand tucked casually into the pocket of his charcoal-gray pants, a cigar resting in the other. His dark hair bobbed slightly as he spoke, his posture relaxed but commanding. I placed a hand on my father's arm just as he turned toward me.

"Ah, *Pandora*," Danny greeted, flashing me a practiced smile. "Evening, *Mr. Fritz*." I returned the gesture, my smile just as theatrical. His brown eyes lingered, dark and piercing—much darker than Adam's, though their resemblance was undeniable. The sharp angles of his face remained chiseled, still striking despite age creeping in at the edges.

"How's that case of yours coming along, *honey?*" he asked smoothly, a sinister edge lacing his tone. I held his gaze, unflinching. "My name is *Detective Vaughn*, sir," I corrected, my tone polite but firm. "And we found a small lead this morning. Thank you for asking." I waited, hopeful he would slip—leaving a loose thread that would hint at his son's true intentions. But Danny Fritz only cocked his head, studying me with that ever-calculated gaze.

"Well, that's *wonderful*," he said smoothly. "Such a shame what happened to that poor Amy." He shook his head, feigning sympathy. I narrowed my eyes slightly. "It is," I replied, keeping my tone neutral. "I was just speaking with your father about the reopening of the Feros mines," he continued, watching my face intently. "With this newly discovered resource, I'm hopeful business on Feros can be reignited." His words were careful and measured. *Testing me.*

"It seems to me we've already drained that planet dry, *Mr. Fritz*," I countered. "I don't believe humans have any place there." The words left my mouth before I could stop them. A slow, knowing smile curled his lips. "You'll come around to it, darling," he said, fastening the button on his suit jacket. "In time, you'll see—humans will always crave power, by *whatever means necessary*." A chill crawled up my spine, my pulse quickening.

Power?

He turned sharply. "Harrison. *Detective Vaughn*." He nodded a curt farewell before striding off, cigar smoke trailing in his wake. "So *that's* what reopening the mines is about?" I hissed, my voice low but heated. "Not the potential to share the energy this new material could provide—but for strategic *power*?"

Harrison shot me a warning look, subtly gesturing for me to lower my voice. "Of course not. That's *not* what he meant," he assured me quickly. "He's just saying that humans will always seek discovery. We don't even *know* the full extent of Element X's power—only that it radiates immense energy." He said and I clenched my jaw. "And what kind of energy is that, exactly?" I pressed.

He exhaled, running a hand through his hair. "All we know is that when a miner first discovered the material on Feros, he could feed it into the grid and power *every* mine on the planet simultaneously with only *one gram* of the stone." He slid a hand into his pocket, his gaze steady. "Do you even understand what kind of power that is?" His voice softened, almost in awe. "What kind of things we could do with that?" I lifted my chin. "All I can think about is what it *shouldn't* be used for."

Silence stretched between us. "What have you gotten yourself wrapped up in?" I asked finally, my voice edged with something I wasn't sure was anger or fear. He stared at me for a long moment before shaking his head. "I haven't gotten myself wrapped up in anything, Pandora," he said evenly. "I'm just doing my job as Commissioner."

"You're commissioner here." I gestured around me, "Not on Feros. What are you doing getting involved with the mines there?" I asked and he paused to look at me. "I will tell you in time, Pandora. I have to be certain things are set in motion and have been completed. It's classified."

"I hope this *Element X* is worth it," I whispered. "Because I'm afraid no one should have that kind of power." Harrison licked his lips but didn't respond. "Goodnight," I said, stepping back. "I'll see you Monday at the precinct."

With that, I turned on my heel and wove back through

the crowd, searching for Ivy. She immediately spotted me and waved me over from the bar where she was ordering another drink. The bartender glanced his brown eyes at me expectantly. His white shirt, black vest, and black bow tie were dull compared to the surrounding glittering attire of the ball attendees. I shook my head and offered a dismissive wave. He shrugged his narrow shoulders and whisked away to retrieve Ivy's drink, his brown hair fading in the dimmed lighting.

"What did Nesnah say?" she asked, her hands clasping mine. "He said we need to talk and asked me to meet him downstairs." I said and she nodded, but concern flickered across her face, "Please be careful. We don't *know* him."

"I will." I gave her hand a reassuring squeeze, then glanced at Chance, who raised an arm in silent farewell. "Call me if you need anything," she added, giving my hand one last squeeze before drifting back into the crowd. I moved my way across the mirrored tile and stepped into the elevator pressing the ground-level button.

Before the doors could close, a drunken couple stumbled in, their hands locking onto the frame to hold it open. I shifted to the side to make room. The woman, wrapped in a tight turquoise dress, giggled as the man pressed her against the wall, his mouth already on hers, tongue pushing between her teeth. His buzzed brown hair was just a shadow over his scalp, obviously intentionally shaved for one reason or another.

From this angle I just barely made out his hazel eyes as his muscled shoulder dipped under his black suit jacket lifting the woman further up against his body. Her long blonde hair cascaded over her shoulder, but beneath it a faded jagged scar branched from her chin to her right temple. A very distinct marking, one that I didn't recognize. I swallowed and cleared my throat. They both turned to glare at me.

"Well, well. *Detective Pandora Vaughn*," the woman slurred, but her grey eyes were clear as they locked onto mine. I blinked. "Do I know you?" I asked slightly confused and she smirked causing the freckles dotting her nose to lift with the corners of her eyes. She waggled a surprisingly steady finger at me. "No, but *I* know *you*."

I frowned, about to respond, but she cut me off as the elevator came to a stop at ground level. "Have a good *evening*," she sneered. The elevator doors slid open, the cool night air rushing in. "Come on, Jade. Let it go," the man muttered, gripping her shoulders and steering her outside. I watched them disappear into the night before stepping out, shivering slightly as the breeze bit at my exposed skin.

I should have brought a jacket. I *always* forgot a jacket.

The riverwalk bridge came into view, its pale green metal structure forming a lattice above the rolling blue water below. The city lights twinkled around me, their glow reflecting off the waves. My heels clicked softly against the sidewalk nearing the bridge and my pulse quickening as I spotted Detective Nesnah.

He stood in the middle, one arm draped casually over the metal railing, waiting. I forced myself to steady my breathing as I stepped onto the glass-paned section. Hundreds of feet below, the water churned in restless, frothing waves. My stomach twisted and a wave of nausea rose in my throat. I *hated* walking over this bridge.

I swallowed hard and quickened my pace. Luke turned as I approached, his piercing blue eyes catching the city lights, unreadable.

"Tell me everything," I demanded, my eyes locked onto him. "I've been assigned to your case," he said. I didn't bother reacting— I just watched him. "I *know*," I said flatly. "Tell me everything I *don't* already know." He exhaled again, this time slower. "Lieutenant Smith wants me to take over your case. *However*—" he hesitated, glancing at me, "I need your help." I scoffed, rolling my eyes. "And *since when* have you ever asked for help?" I shot back. "Let alone *my* help?"

Frustration built up inside me, bubbling over, seeping through my words. "Actually," I continued, crossing my arms, "you've done everything in your power to keep me out of this investigation. So why—" I took a step closer, lowering my voice, "—should I *suddenly* help you now?" Luke licked his lips, shifting his gaze back to the water. "Listen," he said finally, his voice measured. "Things will start *happening*, and I *can't* tell you what until I *know* I can trust you."

For the first time, something flickered in his eyes—*worry*. A chill crept up my spine. "What do you mean?" I asked, stepping in closer, my pulse picking up. He hesitated. "I know things about people—things I can't tell you until I can prove I'm right. But to do that, I need your help." My stomach knotted as I spoke, "What do you know that you're not telling me?"

Luke rubbed the back of his neck, tension evident in the way his jaw clenched. As he moved, his suit jacket lifted just enough to reveal the service pistol tucked into his waistband. I waited. The night air started to feel *thicker* somehow. Finally, he exhaled, his voice barely above a whisper. "I need you to trust me."

"That's what *everyone* keeps telling me tonight," I hissed, stepping back. "This was a mistake," I muttered, turning to leave. Luke didn't follow. He only exhaled heavily, the sound carrying through the wind. "Your mother was murdered."

I froze.

The world around me seemed to be still, the only movement the wind whipping between us. "What?" My voice came out small, strangled. "It wasn't suicide." He said quietly, but firmly.

Silence stretched between us. He waited for me to respond. I couldn't. "Say *something*," he urged and I heard him step forward.

I spun around, eyes blazing, "Don't you *dare* come any closer." A flicker of surprise crossed his face, but he didn't move again. My pulse hammered against my ribs. "Is *that* why you've kept her case open all this time?" I spat.

He gave a slow nod, the only movement he made. "Do tell me, *Detective Nesnah*—" my words ground out through clenched teeth, "why do you think she was *murdered*?" His gaze locked onto mine. "She had vecuronium in her system when she died." He spoke and I let out a bitter laugh. "We *already knew that.*"

"Yes," he agreed, his voice steady. "But it had the *exact* same molecular tag as the vecuronium given to Amy." The anger inside me faltered then died as confusion took its place. My brows furrowed as his words settled over me. "The same tag," I repeated slowly. He nodded once. "And what they didn't tell you from her autopsy—" he took a step closer "—was that she also had an injection site at the back of her neck. *Just like Amy.*"

My breath caught and Ivy's voice echoed in my head. *Please be careful. We don't know him.* My eyes darted around as the dusty cogs in my brain worked overtime, clicking into place with terrifying slowness.

"You think..." My throat tightened. "Whoever killed Amy *also* killed my mom." A beat of silence. "Yes," he said. The wind surged, wild and unrelenting. My auburn hair lashed against my cheeks like a whip. I barely felt it as I shivered, but not from the cold.

"Take this." Luke slid off his green suit jacket and draped it over my shoulders, his touch featherlight. Warmth enveloped me instantly, chasing away the chill. "Please, *help me.*" His hands rested gently on my shoulders—not heavy enough to trap me, but steady enough that I couldn't tell if he was keeping me from running or holding me up so I wouldn't collapse.

I swallowed against the dryness in my throat, forcing myself to look up at him. His blue eyes practically *glowed* in the darkness, and for a fleeting moment, I felt myself getting lost in them. Then, slowly, he lifted a hand and tilted my chin upward with his thumb. My breath hitched. Blue on green. Searching. Reading.

His head tilted slightly. "Pandora?" his voice was soft, questioning. I blinked, shaking my head quickly. *Focus.*

"Yes." I cleared my throat, stepping back just enough to regain some air. "I'll help you." Relief flickered across his face. "Thank you." His arms dropped to his sides. "I should go," I murmured, licking my lips. He nodded, his brown curls bouncing slightly in the wind. "I'll see you Monday."

Without another word, I turned on my heel and hurried off the bridge, the weight of his jacket still clinging to my shoulders. "Pandora?" He called again after me. I turned slightly my eyes resting on him. "Keep this between us." He said, and I turn on my heel without saying another word. I didn't stop until I reached my car.

I slid into it, the green suit jacket brushing against the seat. *He gave me his jacket.* The thought lingered as I stared out the windshield, my mind a tangled mess of questions with far too few answers. I needed to get to Gayle, needed to find Odina, and needed to figure out what my mother had to do with Amy's death.

Reaching into my pocket, I pulled out the card Adam had given me, flipping it between my fingers. The ink shimmered under the dim light, teasing me with the weight of the decision it carried. My jaw tightened and I clenched the paper in my fist, the edges crumpling beneath my grip.

I *couldn't* trust him. He was playing games, and games like his got people *killed.* My hand shot toward the open window, ready to toss the damn thing into the night—But I *hesitated.*

What if he *was* my only way off Liarta? My only chance at the truth? Frustration clawed at me as I uncurled my fingers, smoothing the creased paper back open. *Choose.* I needed to make the choice. Right *now.*

I pulled out my phone and dialed the number, my fingers trembling. The hologram light pulsed as I waited. *Ten seconds. Twenty. Thirty.*

"Pick up!" I hissed in frustration. The screen flickered—then his face appeared. "*Detective,*" Adam cooed, his expression infuriatingly smooth. "Adam," I replied coolly. "Do you require departure assistance?" his voice was measured. I narrowed my eyes at his flickering hologram. "What's in it for you?" I asked, drumming my fingers against the car's dash. "Justice, Detective. Peace." He tilted his head slightly. "We are not as different as you think we are, *Pandora.*"

I clenched my jaw and we stared at each other in silence, the tension thick between us. "Can you get me off Liarta?" I asked finally. "I can," he confirmed with a slow nod. "Not easily, but I can."

I bit down aggressively on my bottom lip. *This was it. No turning back.* "When?" My fingers stopped tapping and my body tensed. If caught, my badge would be pulled. But there was so much more at stake than just my career. "Monday night." he said and the pressure in my throat tightened. I *had* to do the right thing, even knowing the risks. I inhaled sharply, "Get me off Liarta, Adam."

"Done," he replied, completely unfazed. "You'll need an identiscanner to confirm her mother's identity when you reach Gayle. If I'm correct, your department keeps one in the equipment locker."

I let out a slow, deep sigh. "I'll have to badge it out. Someone will notice." The lockers were in the back of the department—there was no way I could slip one out without raising suspicion. "Then I suggest you be *speedy* and *inconspicuous*, Detective." His voice was calm as if he were giving casual directions instead of instructing me on how to commit a felony theft. "Meet me at dock twelve tomorrow at midnight. *Good luck.*"

His hologram flickered—then vanished. I exhaled the breath I hadn't realized I was holding, my shoulders sagging slightly. Everything felt heavy. My pulse pounded as I put the car in drive, my chest rising and falling with slow, deliberate breaths. This *infernal* case.

Element X.

The pieces were stacking up, but nothing was *adding* up. Something strange was happening, and I was going to figure it out. I forced my body to relax, inhaling deep as I pressed the gas and sped home.

Chapter 12

I walked into *Precinct 12* Monday morning with a hammering headache. Sleep had been a lost cause—most of my night had been spent tossing and turning, haunted by nightmares of *Element X*. What kind of power did it hold? What type of control could it give us? The questions gnawed at my mind, offering no answers, thus leading to the headache.

The fabric of my green long-sleeve shirt bunched slightly at the waist of my grey slacks as I moved through the back of the precinct. The familiar rhythm of clacking keyboards provided a small, grounding comfort.

Sliding into my chair, I exhaled and smoothed the front seams of my pants. It took every fiber of my being not to adjust the badge on my hip out of habit. Across from me, as usual, Ivy was already at her desk heavily consumed with a stack of paperwork. Aurelios light caught the crisp white of her blouse and the soft beige of her trousers, making her look far more put together than I felt. She studied me in silence for a moment before quirking a brow.

"Well, *you* look bright and cheery this morning," she quipped. I shot her a glare and she smirked. "So, you wanna tell me how it went with that one Saturday night?" She jerked a thumb toward Detective Nesnah, who sat flipping through paperwork at his desk, completely unaware—or *choosing* to ignore us. To ignore *me*.

"He said the person who killed Amy also killed my mom," I said quietly. Ivy's head snapped toward me. "What?" she blurted out loud enough that a few neighboring officers glanced over. I shot her a look, "*Calm down.*" I hissed. She leaned in, her voice dropping to a sharp whisper. "You're telling me to calm down?" Her voice became a sharp shrill in my ears. "I thought your mom committed suicide!"

"That's what I—we thought," I murmured, glancing around before continuing. "Turns out Luke was withholding some *details* from her autopsy." Her eyebrows shot so high they practically touched her hairline. "*Oh?*" she drawled, tilting her head. "Are we on a first-name basis with Detective Nesnah now?" She looked at me like I'd grown a second head. I scowled, "Cut it out and *listen* to me." I raised a knife hand in her direction, my other gripping the armrest of my chair. "Someone killed Amy. That *same* person most likely killed my mom. I need to get to Gayle, find Odina, and figure out *how* the two cases are connected." The words spilled out in a rush, my pulse quickening from saying them out loud. Ivy just stared at me, her wide eyes blinking rapidly. "Have you *lost* your ever loving mind?" she finally asked.

"Ladies," Chance greeted as he strolled up to our desks. "Not now," We said in perfect sync. His face twisted in confusion. "Okaaay..." He said his eyes flickering to Ivy, then back to me. Without looking at him, Ivy waved a dismissive hand, swatting him away. Narrowing his eyes at us, he hesitated before slowly meandering back to his desk. He sipped his coffee as he watched us across the room.

I chose to ignore him.

"What else did Luke say the other night?" Ivy pressed. She was fully invested now. Good, maybe that meant she would be convinced to go along with the plan. "He asked me to help him,"

I admitted, glancing toward his desk—only to startle. He wasn't there anymore.

Where the hell did he go?

Ivy frowned, "He asked you to help him?" She sounded confused and rightfully so. "I thought you said he's spent this entire time telling you *not* to get involved." Her voice started to rise again. "Shh," I hissed. She pressed her lips together but leaned in, whispering, "Why is he asking for your help now?"

I swallowed, scanning the room for any sign of him. "He said he needs me to help him prove the cases are connected." Ivy opened her mouth to respond, but her eyes flickered to someone standing next to us. "*Detective Nesnah.*" She cooed his name, and my head whipped around. He was standing beside my desk. I hadn't even heard him walk over. His navy shirt pulled taut across his chest with every breath, and I caught myself watching as his fingers tapped idly against the badge at his hip.

"Detective Zephyr. Detective Vaughn." He nodded at us, his voice smooth and composed. "So we're *not* on a first-name basis, then?" Ivy muttered under her breath. "*Cut it out*," I scolded, smacking her shoulder over the desk. My face instantly turned a bright flaming red. Luke raised an eyebrow at her but didn't acknowledge the comment. Suddenly, everything I was going to say vanished entirely from my mind. He clicked his tongue against his teeth. "I was wondering if you could spare a moment, Detective Vaughn." His deep voice cascaded over the desks like a slow-moving current. I swallowed, nodding quickly, "Sure, give me a minute to collect my things."

His eyes scanned over me once, unreadable, before he turned and walked toward one of the briefing rooms. The door clicked shut behind him. I turned back to Ivy, who looked far too entertained. Her eyebrows were practically flying off her forehead. "I'm handling it," I muttered. "With the way he was looking at you, it seems like he's the one doing the *handling*," she quipped, biting back a grin. "*Stop it.*" I pointed at her, narrowing my eyes. She waggled her fingers at the briefing room door. "Well, go handle *whatever* it is you're handling."

Rolling my eyes, I scooped up my papers and let the steady click of my heels carry me to the door without so much as a glance behind me at Ivy, probably gaping at me from her desk. I stepped inside and closed the door behind me as he looked up. His blue eyes locked onto mine with unnerving precision. "All right," he said, straightening just enough to show he meant business. "If this is going to work, I need everything you've got on your case. No holding back." I stayed by the door, my papers clutched tight against my chest like a shield. "And you're going to give me everything on yours?" I asked, lifting my chin in defiance. His jaw tightened, lips drawing into a thin line. "I'll tell you everything I can."

I didn't move and watched him carefully, trying to decide if I could trust him—or if I'd regret even stepping through that door. I could still turn around, walk away, let this whole mess unravel on its own. But deep down, I knew this was the only shot I had to pull the pieces together. "That wasn't the deal." I murmured. "It will have to be," Luke stepped back and gestured toward the table. A chaotic spread of documents lay before him—some stamped *CLASSIFIED* in bold red, others so heavily redacted they were practically blacked out. "Start wherever you want," he said quietly. "But start."

Great. Super helpful.

I stepped forward, setting my papers down on the corner of the table across from him. "You better not be lying to me," I said, mirroring his stance. My palms pressed against the table as I leaned forward, the overhead light casting sharp shadows across our faces. "I'm not," he said firmly, standing upright. He moved around the room without another word, methodically closing the blinds to the windows facing the office. Through the slats I caught a quick glimpse of Ivy watching us from her desk. Then, just as quickly, Luke flicked the blinds shut. The room dimmed instantly. I hadn't realized how dark these briefing rooms could get. Now it felt like the walls were closing in and a quiet, uneasy tension settled between us.

"What do you know about Amy? Let's start there," Luke said, returning to his end of the table. I opened the manila folder before me, flicking through the pages. "Amy O'Rayne. Date of birth: May 17th, 3007. Age: 33. Female. Species: *Half Gaythe, half human.*" I glanced up. He didn't flinch—just met my gaze with unreadable calm and gave a slight nod, signaling me to continue. I narrowed my eyes but kept going. "Her last known employment was as a secretary for Adam Fritz at Fritz Co. She was discovered dead in her car in the company parking lot and reported missing by Adam Fritz himself on Sunday, April 20th. The estimated date of death is April 15th sometime between 7–10 p.m."

As I spoke, Luke paced slowly, one hand scrubbing at the stubble on his chin. He didn't interrupt—just circled, listening. "Cause of death," I added, pausing for emphasis, "Vecuronium injection to the base of the neck. Autopsy confirmed it." I stopped reading and watched as he completed his second lap around the room. "Who have you questioned?" he asked without stopping.

"Adam Fritz."

"Did he have an alibi?"

"He did. It checked out." I watched him closely for a reaction before continuing, "But I'm guessing you already knew that—since I saw you two deep in conversation at the precinct ball."

Luke halted mid-step. "He said you were in over your head," he replied, eyes locking with mine. "And that someone was trying to frame him." My jaw tightened, "So he told you I needed help?"

"Yes." He resumed pacing. "You said he claimed he was being framed?" I asked, my fingers tightening around the edges of the paper. "Did he perhaps mention by *who*?"

"His father. *Danny Fritz.*" He responded and I exhaled slowly, disbelief curling at the edge of my throat. "And why, exactly, would his own father want to frame him for Amy's murder?"

"That," Luke said, "I can't tell you." His boots made a soft scuffing sound as he circled behind me. I turned to follow his movement. "Do you think Danny Fritz killed Amy?"

He paused, hand grazing his chin in thought, "I think he was involved. No doubt about that." I didn't push him. The room fell into a quiet lull as I tracked his steady pace. "Do you always do that?" I asked, eyes trailing him. "Do what?" He muttered under his breath not looking at me. "The pacing?" I tilted my head in his direction. "It helps me think," he replied without slowing. Luke didn't meet my eyes. Instead, he reached for a sheet on the table and held it out to me. I took it, my fingers unsteady as they brushed his. My gaze dropped to the page—at the bold black lettering stamped across the top.

Esme Vaughn Autopsy

A lump rose in my throat. I swallowed hard and looked up at him. He was no longer pacing—just standing still, his gaze locked on mine, calm and unreadable. "I said I'd tell you everything I can," he murmured, nodding toward the document. My pulse thundered in my ears as I skimmed the page. Most of it was redacted and I let out a frustrated sigh. *Of course it was.*

Cause of death: Vecuronium injection.
Location: Back of neck.
Time of death: 3–5 p.m.

My eyebrows knitted together. "*Wait.*" My voice was barely above a whisper. "Time of death is almost the exact time my father got home." I looked up at Luke. He nodded urging me to go on. "If that's accurate," I continued, my grip tightening on the paper, "how did he not see anyone leave?"

"Good question, Detective." His voice was measured, almost hesitant as he spoke again, "I don't know."

My gaze dropped back to the report. The words swam in front of me. *That couldn't be right.* "I asked him," Luke said, leaning forward over the desk. "He swears up and down that no one else was there. That she was already like that when he got home." A wave of nausea rolled through me, but I forced myself to ask the question I didn't want the answer to. "Do you think my father had something to do with her death?" Silence. Then— "Yes."

A cold, weightless sensation washed over me. My vision blurred at the edges. Luke moved fast, coming around the table and scooting a chair under me before I realized I was swaying. I collapsed into it, my breaths shallow. "Is he being blackmailed?" I asked, focusing.

Inhale. Exhale. Inhale. Exhale. Anything to steady myself.

Luke crouched in front of me. "I don't know yet." He said and my fingers curled around the table's edge, gripping it like an anchor. "You said Amy was *half* Gaythe." Luke bent down so his head was level with mine. "Half Gaythe, half human," I confirmed. He was close—*too close.* I could *smell* him—eucalyptus and sandalwood. The scent curled around me, grounding and distracting all at once.

His neckline dipped slightly with the way he leaned forward, and the fabric cupped just enough to reveal a glimpse of his collarbone. My eyes flicked downward to his chest, and for a moment, my eyes caught the imprint of a pendant hanging beneath his shirt. It was small and circular, hanging dead center. I narrowed my eyes at it. I hadn't seen him wear one before.

"How are we going to confirm who her parents are?" His voice cut through my daze, pulling me back. I blinked. "We have a DNA scanner," I answered quickly focusing back to his face, not his neck. "A *DNA scanner*?" His brow lifted slightly. "Your precinct has funds for that?"

"We do." I replied, raising an eyebrow, "doesn't your precinct have one?" He shook his head, his expression unreadable. "No, my precinct barely had enough officers, let alone high-tech equipment. We're not exactly on the rich side of Liarta. We had to make do with whatever scraps we could get from this place." He gestured to the walls surrounding us and his words threw me off guard. "That can't be right," I murmured, my voice betraying my surprise. "We just increased funding. Every precinct should have more than enough to cover the basics."

Luke tilted his head, his eyes narrowing slightly as he studied me. "They increased funding to *this* precinct," he repeated, as if savoring the irony. Then he leaned in—just a few inches away now—and his voice dropped to a near whisper. "There's so much you *don't* know about the government you work for," he said, his words slow and deliberate.

A chill ran up my spine. I swallowed again, trying to push down the uneasy flutter in my chest. "Then tell me." I whispered. "I can't." His answer was sharp, clipped, and his jaw tightened. I narrowed my eyes, leaning forward, "Why not?"

He exhaled through his nose, frustration flickering across his features. "Because if I told you everything we—er—I know all

at once, it would tear the whole plan down by the hinges."
His deep voice wrapped around the words, low and precise, as
if each syllable was meant to settle inside me like a secret. I
inhaled sharply, something in my stomach shifting. A heat curled
through me, slow and simmering. Was I turned on? Was it the
way he spoke to me? The quiet authority in his tone? The way
he held himself—so controlled, so confident?

Pull yourself together, Pandora.

"What plan?" I asked blinking. He shook his head roughly,
the brown clump of curls swishing under the single dim
light, "Doesn't matter." He muttered. "You will have to tell
me eventually," I said as he leaned back on his heels and
straightened his spine. I exhaled the breath I hadn't realized I
was holding, letting my shoulders relax as I spread my trembling
fingers across the table to steady them. The dark wood gleamed
under the light, cutting through the mountain of scattered
papers between us. "Correct." He said lifting from his crouch and
turning to pace again, "But not today."

"If you won't tell me everything you know, then I have to
work with what little I do know," I said, my voice firm. "And that
is this—a woman was murdered, and she has family. Some of
whom live on an entirely different planet." Luke paced around
the room, his movements measured, but his gaze never left me.
"There's no way to track down her father here on Liarta. Too
many human men to even begin narrowing it down. But if I can
get to Gayle..." I paused, taking a slow breath. "I'd have a much
better shot at finding her mother."

I lifted my eyes from the table, meeting his with a steady
look. He had stopped pacing again, his focus now sharp as
he assessed me. "What do you know about a woman named
Odina?" he asked, his voice low, carefully controlled. I stiffened,
my stomach clenching. *How did he know that name?*

"Where did you hear that name?" My eyes became irritated slits. "Doesn't matter," he said again quickly, cutting me off, "What do you know about her?" I hesitated, biting my lip, my mind racing. His hands pressed flat against the table as he leaned in, his gaze intense and unyielding. "Whatever you tell me in this room stays between us," he said, his voice soft but firm. I exhaled slowly, then met his gaze. "I have a book." I watched him closely, searching for any flicker of reaction, but he didn't even flinch.

"It says Odina was—or is—the Queen of the Southern Gaythe Tribe. Born of power, destined to lead her people. She's dangerous, but..." I licked my lips, gauging his response. "If any of it is true, she's our best shot." Luke's expression sharpened, "Where did you get this book?"

"My mother gave it to me."

His expression finally cracked, his eyes widening for a fraction of a second. *Interesting.* This time, I caught *him* off guard. He nodded slowly, glancing down at the papers spread out on his side of the desk. Then, without looking up, he asked, "How do you plan on getting us to Gayle?" I blinked. Wait, what?

"What do you mean, *us?*" I demanded, rising from my chair so quickly that a few loose strands of auburn hair tumbled free from my bun. Luke barely spared me a glance, his expression unreadable. "You didn't think I'd let you go to Gayle alone, did you? Not for an investigation we're both wrapped up in."

My jaw clenched, my teeth grinding together so hard I thought they might crack. I felt my pulse quicken, but I didn't back down. His nonchalance only added fuel to the fire burning in my chest.

"Must you always insert yourself into my business?" I snapped, frustration bleeding into my voice. Luke's eyes lifted to mine, sharp and unwavering. "I thought we agreed—your business is my business now," he shot back. I opened my mouth, my finger already halfway to jabbing at his chest—then snapped it shut just as quickly. His jaw tightened, his brows raising slightly as if *daring* me to argue.

I groaned, throwing my hands in the air. Spinning around, I faced the closed blinds and crossed my arms tightly over my chest. I exhaled sharply, glaring past the slats at the desks beyond the wall. Luke's voice cut through my thoughts, "Well, since that's settled—do you have a plan?" I clenched my teeth. "Adam Fritz offered me a ship off Liarta," I muttered, barely loud enough to be heard.

"Excellent." His tone was infuriatingly smug. "About time he was *useful.*" I could already hear the but coming before he even said it. "Do you even know how to fly a ship?" His voice dripped with accusation. I turned back to face him, my jaw tightening.

Damn him.

"No," I admitted, letting out a sigh of defeat, "I hadn't gotten that far into the plan yet." Luke pinched the bridge of his nose, his sigh heavy with frustration. "Good thing I can." His voice was filled with attitude and I rolled my eyes, the annoyance rising in my chest. "Of course you can." I sniped.

"Getting off Liarta is one thing," he said steadily, "But have you figured out where we'll land once we reach Gayle?" I nodded in response, feeling the weight of the exhaustion in my bones. "I spent most of the night thinking it through. Not that I've been getting much sleep these days." I flicked a page across the desk, watching it land in front of him.

"The last known location of the Southern Gaythe Tribe was at the base of Mount Akasari." I leaned forward, pressing my finger onto a section of the map. The edge of the table dug into my hips, but I ignored the discomfort. "Our records show it's about fifteen miles out.

The Gaythe population has been dwindling for years—less than three million left. Even without the war with the

Nephrians, they're facing extinction." I paused, my gaze locked on the red dot marking Mount Akasari. A knot tightened in my stomach. "It's possible this Odina woman isn't even alive anymore," I said, my voice quieter now, as though the thought of it made it too real. Luke didn't speak for a moment, his eyes scanned the map as I traced the surrounding terrain.

Most of it was water, but a dense jungle pressed against the mountain's base. *Odina. Born of the mountain.* If she was still alive, that's where she'd be. "That's our best place to start," Luke finally said, his voice steady but with a sharp edge. "And right now, she's our only lead. If she's alive, she's the only one who can tell us why Amy left Gayle—and how." He looked up at me, his expression strained, as though he were seeing more than just the map in front of us.

"It's a day's travel at light speed," I said, the words tumbling out quicker than I meant. "This is the last confirmed map we have—over fifteen years old. So our best shot is to dock as close as possible to the base of Mount Akasari, then hike the rest of the way." I paused as he rubbed his palm along the base of his jaw, deep in thought. "I'm concerned we don't know exactly where their tribe is," he finally said, gesturing toward the landmass we had been studying. "We could end up landing right on top of them and not realize it until it's too late."

He wasn't wrong. Gayle didn't have much land, but the little it did have was a jungle—dense, nearly impenetrable. Thick trees, tangled vines, terrain so unforgiving that you'd be lost within minutes without experience. The Gaythe may not have had the technological advances of humans, but they were experts in stealth. You could walk straight into the heart of their tribe—hundreds of thousands of warriors—and not even realize it until you were already captured. They'd perfected the art of disappearing into the trees.

It was definitely a problem.

If they deemed us a threat before we could even explain ourselves, we might never return from this mission. I studied the map, but not in the way most people would. There were no large clearings, no apparent signs of settlement. But no matter how advanced, every species relied on *strategy*—on terrain, elevation, and natural defenses. If I wanted to find the Queen of the Southern Gaythe Tribe, I had to *think* like the Queen of the Southern Gaythe Tribe.

"There," I said, pointing to an outcrop at the entrance of a narrow trail leading up the mountain. "That has to be where they transport their women in childbirth. It leads straight to the peak—where they perform the birth ceremony." Luke leaned in, studying the area I indicated. "What birth ceremony?" He asked curiously.

There wasn't much recorded about the Gaythe species. Most texts theorized their customs, but very little had ever been confirmed. Most of what I knew came from my mother.

"My mother always spoke of their traditions with deep respect," I murmured, "every Gaythe baby born on Gayle is part of a birth ceremony. Pregnant mothers are carried up the mountain—from the water—to give birth in their most sacred place. Elders and healers accompany them, and they don't return until after the baby is born." Luke's eyes flicked over the rocky outcrop, the gouge in the mountainside. "How long are they up there?" he asked. "Sometimes days," I said. "And sometimes... the mothers don't return."

Silence stretched between us.

"Okay," he said finally, nodding as if he settled the decision on his own. I rolled my eyes. "We start there, then." I exhaled, pushing away from the desk. "They don't take kindly to outsiders," he warned, crossing his arms over his chest. I met his gaze. "Then we'll have to make them listen to us," I said, "And hope they don't decide to kill us first and ask questions later." His blue eyes echoed with something close to concern. "Meet me at Dock 10 at midnight tonight." I said gathering the papers and shoving them back into the manila folder. Luke studied me momentarily, then exhaled, shaking his head slightly. "I hope you know what you're doing."

I took one long, steady breath before responding, "Me too."

Chapter 13

I made my way to the back of the station, nervously chewing the inside of my cheek. I needed to be in and out fast—before anyone started poking around and asking questions I didn't want to answer. The lockers finally came into view as I rounded the corner.

The large room resembled a cage framed in thick metal and concrete. The only way in was if you were supposed to be there. Everything—equipment, weapons—was stored inside, and anything removed had to be badged out and assigned to an officer. The armed officer stood by the entrance, shifting lazily from one foot to the other, bored out of his mind. His ginger hair was meticulously styled—except for one rebellious strand sticking straight up at the back like a feather.

"Good morning, Detective Vaughn." He grinned when he spotted me. "Morning," I replied, forcing a polite smile. "I need to grab some equipment for my case."

"Sure!" he chirped, turning to enter the code into the lock. A bead of sweat formed on the back of my neck as the bolts clunked open. "You all right, Detective? You don't look like yourself this morning." He cocked his head, watching me curiously. "I'm fine," I lied, forcing another smile. "I didn't sleep well last night, but thanks for asking." He hesitated but finally stepped aside, allowing me to slip past him into the locker room. I pasted a polite smile on my face as I slid past him.

Inside, the air was cool and sterile and the harsh overhead lights gave the space an almost prison-like feel. Rows of secured metal lockers lined the walls, and at the back, lines of riot gear hung from hooks, helmets resting above them—waiting for the next deployment. I pressed my thumb to the fingerprint reader, unlocking the identiscanner compartment. The door popped open, revealing an array of police gadgets.

The scanner wasn't big—just small enough to fit in my pocket. Its green indicator blinked slowly, ready to configure. I preset the DNA code the lab had given me and waited for the beep of confirmation before shutting it off and sliding it into my pocket. That's when I heard the voices—officers or precinct personnel slowly heading this way. They echoed down the hallway, growing closer and my stomach clenched. If I got caught now, the entire plan would fall apart.

I hurried out, nodding quickly to the officer on my way past. "Thanks." I chirped quickly. "Have a good day, Detective!" he called after me. I didn't respond as I hurried my footsteps, but the voices were just around the corner now. My pulse hammered in my ears.

Shit. Shit. Shit. I scanned the hallway for an escape. Interrogation Room 6. I reached for the knob—"Pandora?"

My stomach plummeted to my feet and I froze. My father's voice laced the question. I turned, pasting a neutral expression on my face. "Good afternoon." I eased my shoulders down from my ears, forcing them to relax. The last thing I needed in a station full of police officers was to look suspicious.

My father stood beside Lieutenant Smith, both eyeing me like they knew I was up to something. "I was just retrieving some equipment for my case," I rushed out. Harrison narrowed his eyes. He knew I was investigating Amy's murder, but I hadn't updated him on why I needed new equipment—or any leads I was following. "I heard about your case," Smith said, shaking his head. "Unfortunate, isn't it, what happened to Mrs. O'Rayne."

"So everyone keeps saying," I murmured, my attention jerking back to my father. He stared, his jaw set like stone. "Have you spoken with Detective Nesnah?" Smith asked his tone even and unrushed. "I have." I responded. Harrison didn't move, didn't *blink*. Beside him, Smith's expression shifted—just for a second. *Worry.* Then it was gone. I frowned slightly.

"What is it?" I asked, but Smith ignored the question. "Did you bring in Danny Fritz? Luke had requested his presence for some questioning." he asked instead. A flicker of something crossed my father's face this time instead it was *surprise*. His gaze snapped to Smith, but he still said nothing. My frown deepened.

"No," I answered slowly. "I can't rule him out, but I—*we* don't have enough evidence to bring him in. Other than Amy working for him, there's nothing directly connecting him to her murder." I watched as my father's shoulders eased and again my stomach flopped over. Had I imagined that tension? The brief flash of relief in his posture?

"Interesting," Smith mused, rubbing his chin. "Well, I wouldn't rule him out just yet. I'm sure you'll make progress soon enough. You are your father's daughter, after all." He clapped Harrison firmly on the shoulder. "Best of luck, Detective." He smiled one last time before walking off, my father in tow beside him. "I'll see you this evening, Pandora," Harrison said smoothly, his eyes lingering on mine a moment longer before turning forward. I stood there, heart still pounding, as they disappeared around the corner. I forced myself to breathe evenly and walk back to my desk— despite the tiny voice in my head screaming to run.

Ivy's head lifted the moment I slid into my chair. "You've been gone a while," she observed. Her gaze snapped to Luke, who was typing something into his computer, then back to me. Her expression shifted as she finally saw my face, "What happened?" She asked. I hesitated for a heartbeat before I chose my words carefully, "I don't know how much I can tell you." Her eyes widened. "What do you mean you don't know how much you can tell me?" She whipped her head toward Luke. "What did he tell you?" Her brown eyes glistened with fear. "It's fine," I assured her quickly. "It's just... classified things." She chewed on her lip, clearly unconvinced. "Well, did you at least get anywhere on the case?" I nodded, leaning in, "We're going to Gayle."

"WHAT!?" Ivy's voice boomed loudly through the precinct and I nearly toppled out of my chair to slap my hand over her mouth. Luke's head snapped up at her outburst. Ivy glared at him like she could set him on fire with her eyeballs."I *told* you this was a bad idea," she hissed. "He's *dangerous*." She jabbed a finger in his direction." No, he's not," I shot back. "*Calm down.*"

"Stop telling me to calm down," she snapped, shaking her head with so much sass I suppressed a laugh. "Just listen to me," I pleaded. She clenched her jaw but finally tore her gaze from him.

Across the room, Luke raised an eyebrow at me as if silently asking, *everything good?* I waved a hand at him, signaling him to mind his business. Ivy was grumbling under her breath at me as several officers turned their heads toward us, curious. "You're making a scene again," I muttered under my breath. "Fine." She huffed, crossing her legs and leaning back in her chair. "I'm calm." She muttered and I had to bite my lip to keep the grin from curling up my face. "You still owe me," I reminded her and Ivy sighed rubbing her temples. "What am I supposed to tell Chance?"

"Nothing," I said quickly, "The fewer people who know, the better." She gave me a look. "You can't expect me to keep this from him." She sighed, but I held my ground, "You have to." Ivy's shoulders slumped, "You owe me now," she said, defeated. "I know," I said, giving her a small, tired smile.

Chapter 14

urelios had set hours ago when I tossed the last of my
things into a duffel. The evening had been spent preparing
for what was arguably the most dangerous mission I had ever
taken on as a detective. The weight of it pressed into my body,
exhaustion wrapping around me like a second skin. *Poor sleep,
too much stress—it was all catching up.* I clipped Mayra's chip
into my watch and locked my front door behind me. Pausing, I
turned, taking one last look at my cabin nestled in the woods.

Would I see it again?

Shaking off the thought, I headed to my car, parked in the
driveway. My body ached with fatigue, my brain overloaded
and still racing. And the night wasn't even close to being over.
We still had to get off-planet unnoticed. Something *pulled* at
me—something deep, insistent, beyond logic.

Odina.

The name whispered through my mind like an echo, tugging
at some unseen thread inside me. Was she the key to solving
Amy's murder? Maybe. The key to something *else?* Maybe. It
was a void I couldn't explain, a question I couldn't yet form
into words. I shoved the car into drive, tires crunching down
the gravel path. The city's lights reflected off my dashboard as
I sped beneath an overpass, pressing the pedal down. The car
hesitated—then purred to life, rocketing through the streets of
downtown. I rolled the window down and the wind caressed my

face, forcing me back into the moment. I was leaving Liarta. I was headed for Gayle.

***

When I pulled into Dock 10, the ship was already waiting. Sleek. Black. Almost invisible against the night sky, its smooth junctions molded together so seamlessly that it looked more like a gaping void than a physical vessel. The delicate, razor-thin wings folded outward, poised to slice through the atmosphere. She was glorious.

I slung my duffel over my shoulder and walked down the tarmac. Luke and Adam stood by the cargo hold deep in conversation, but both turned as they heard my shoes squeak against the asphalt. "You better make it quick if you want to hit hyperspeed," Adam warned, tossing the keys to Luke, who caught them midair. "You have a three-minute window before security ships pass back through this zone." He added and Luke nodded in acknowledgement. "Good luck." Adam's voice was quieter this time, more serious. Then, without another word, he disappeared into a sleek black sedan, tires screeching as he sped away.

Luke jostled the keys in his hand. "After you." He said waving a hand in the general direction of the ship. I hitched my duffel higher on my shoulder and climbed the rungs into the cargo hold. The metal groaned beneath me, but I ignored it, throwing the hatch open and stepping aboard. The floor vibrated faintly under my boots as Luke followed, both of us shoving our bags behind the cargo net before heading toward the cockpit. I slid into my seat and buckled in, the harness snapping tight across my chest with a sharp click. Behind me, Luke sealed the hatch with a hiss. No turning back now. He dropped into the pilot's chair and powered up the ship, the quiet hum beneath us building into a low, steady rumble.

"You sure about this?" he asked, glancing my way. I nodded, eyes fixed on the wide front window. Honestly, I'd never been more certain of anything. Around us, the flight instruments blinked to life. We pulled on our headsets, syncing frequencies just as Luke eased into launch mode. Beyond the glass, patrol ships skimmed the edge of Liarta's atmosphere, their white stripes slicing through the dark. "Wait for them to pass," Luke murmured, his voice steadier than I expected. I nodded again, watching the ships arc silently across the perimeter.

Three minutes.

That was all the time we had before the patrol ships looped back into our airspace. My pulse thundered in my ears. Luke flipped two switches, and the ship lifted off the ground, steady and controlled. "Adjust the wing flares," he ordered. I reached up, fingers trembling, and pulled the lever overhead. Stay calm. Breathe. Just like training—except this time, there was no margin for error. The wings reconfigured with a soft whine, and the ship angled upward, rising fast. Below us, the city shrank, its glow fading into the distance. We held our breath as the police cruisers dipped out of sight, swallowed by the curve of the horizon.

"Now." Luke slammed the steering column forward. The ship catapulted ahead, tearing through the night sky like a blade. My stomach lurched as acceleration pinned me to my seat. *Too fast. Too loud. If they hear this—*"Boosters," he snapped, his voice sharp and steady. I fumbled for the switch, found it, and flicked it. The boosters roared to life. The ship jolted, the sudden burst of speed hammering us back. My teeth clacked together as the turbulence hit. *Hold it together. We're not clear yet. We're not—*

Then I saw them—two police ships cutting across the dark sky, heading straight for us.

Shit. They were faster than we thought. Too soon.

Sweat trickled down my spine. "We're not gonna make it," I muttered under my breath. "Here they come," Luke said, yanking the controls to the side. The ship swerved, barely missing the peak of a golden skyscraper. "Almost there," he assured me. I ignored him as I was too focused on breathing. Then—The air smoothed. The turbulence vanished and we burst through the edge of the atmosphere into open space. I exhaled hard, watching the police ships in the distance. They swung wide over the sector, just missing us—mere *seconds* too late. We had *barely* made it. Luke's voice cut through the quiet. "We're through." He breathed.

The engines softened to a low hum beneath us, the tension bleeding out of the controls as the ship settled into weightless glide. The panic in my chest eased, but didn't disappear. Not completely. I stared through the viewport in awe. Liarta shimmered below, its golden surface soft and quiet now, like it had never known war or blood or the corruption we were running from. Funny how something could look so beautiful from a distance. "Take us to hyperspeed, Detective." He said and I hesitated—just for a moment before pressing the switch. The stars stretched, light fractured, and Liarta vanished behind us in a streak of gold and black. We were in it now. All the way.

I unbuckled my harness and eased myself out of the seat, my muscles aching from tension. Luke remained behind for a moment, tapping coordinates into the control panel before switching the system over to autopilot. Then he stood and followed me into the corridor.

The ship felt tighter than the department vessels I was used to—cramped, utilitarian, every inch of space accounted for.

The hallway barely allowed for one person, let alone two. We moved carefully, the narrow walls forcing us close, only a foot of space separating us. I caught his profile in the dim overhead light, studying him for a beat longer than I meant to. I probably looked like hell—exhaustion etched into my face, my shoulders slumped under the weight of too many sleepless nights. Luke braced his palms against the wall behind him, leaning back slightly. "We need to figure out what exactly we're willing to share with the Gaythe," he said, his voice low, thoughtful. "And what they might already know."

I nodded, letting my head rest against the cool metal behind me. "We should express interest in meeting with Odina," he went on, "but we proceed with caution. Until we're sure they won't kill us on sight, we don't assume anything." I swallowed as I listened to his voice, the reality of what we were walking into settling heavier than before. This wasn't just an off-world mission—it was diplomacy with people who had every reason not to trust us. Or worse, every reason to kill us.

"I'll speak to her," I offered. We leaned against opposite walls, the narrow corridor cocooning. Luke's lips tugged into a crooked grin. "That was kind of fun." He said and I rolled my eyes, though I felt the edges of a smirk pull at my mouth. "What? Almost getting caught?" I asked. He shook his head lightly. "Narrowly escaping," he corrected, his voice still carrying the echo of adrenaline. His blue eyes glinted under the soft overhead lights. "Mmm," I hummed, not giving him the satisfaction.

He cocked an eyebrow, mirroring me with an amused spark. "Mmm?" He mimicked the sound, letting it rumble low in his throat. I shook my head and was suddenly aware of the lack of distance between us. My mouth felt dry and my tongue stuck to the roof of my mouth as I searched for any words, but none came to mind. Silence hung between us. Luke finally cleared his throat and eased from the wall he had been leaning on. "We've got twenty-four hours until contact with Gayle," he said, "Get some rest. I'll keep an eye on the flight board."

For once, I didn't argue and dipped my chin in agreement before whisking myself down the hallway. The floor panels lit up faintly with each step as I made my way toward the sleeping quarters. As I approached, the door hissed open in a soft breath, revealing a row of compact bunks curtained in muted silver. I climbed into the closest one, barely managing to kick off my boots before collapsing into the narrow mattress the material cradling my shoulder and hip. The ship rocked gently beneath me—weightless, almost comforting. Somewhere out in the stars, a woman waited. Or a ghost. I wasn't quite sure yet.

Odina. Her name drifted through my mind like smoke. And then, everything went dark.

Chapter 15

*I*n the weeks following my mother's death, lines of police officers came and went from the Vaughn residence. Our front door had become a revolving one, a constant parade of investigators repeatedly rehashing the same questions. "Remind me again, Mr. Vaughn," Detective Nesnah started, tapping the back of his pen against the faded yellow notepad. "When you got home, nothing was overturned or out of place?"

My father exhaled sharply, his patience clearly worn thin, "As I've told every other officer investigating this case, nothing was out of place." He was seated in his usual spot—the old recliner in our family living room. I sat across from him on the couch, silent for most of the interview, watching as yet another detective poked at an already festering wound. This one being the newer Detective to precinct 12, Detective Luke Nesnah.

He had been transferred recently to our department. I didn't know much about him, but I had a feeling I soon would after his sudden involvement regarding the death of my mother. I wished they would all leave us to grieve in peace. But then Luke's next question snapped my focus back to him. "What can you tell me about the empty filing cabinet investigators found in your basement?"

I straightened lifting in my seat. None of the other detectives had bothered to ask about it. None of them had even mentioned one.

I opened my mouth to question his interest, but Luke raised a finger, silently telling me to wait—to let my father respond first. Anger flared in my chest, my teeth grinding together. For the first time during the entire interview, my father hesitated. No immediate response. He ran his fingers through his hair, a nervous habit I hadn't seen in years. Luke pressed forward, "What was inside the filing cabinet, Mr. Vaughn?"

My father sighed, rubbing a hand over his face. "They were old precinct case files I had stored in the basement. I took them to the precinct to be filed. Some of them were level-one classified." There was a weight to his words, something more profound than the simple statement suggested. "Dad," I said carefully, "if those files have anything to do with Mom's death, you need to tell Detective Nesnah now."

His shoulders sagged. "Pandora," he said, exasperated, "if I thought they had any connection to this, I would have mentioned it. But I personally went through those files—none of them have anything to do with your mother or her decision to end her own life." his words were clipped, but his exhaustion was unmistakable. He slumped back in his chair, looking worn and frayed. "That's enough for today," I said, rising from the couch. Luke didn't move. I clenched my fists at my sides. This was our house, our grief, and I wasn't about to let him keep dragging my father through the same endless cycle of questioning.

"You have one minute," I hissed, "before I kick you out of this house." He cocked his head at me but gave a slight nod of agreement. "One more thing, Mr. Vaughn," he said, voice steady. "You reported handing those files off to the precinct's filing department a week before your wife's death, but they have not been recorded in the precinct's inventory. If these files were truly classified, you should be certain they're not in the wrong hands."

He snapped his notepad shut and turned toward the door. I followed his confident strides with my heart pounding. It was unlike Cathy to not be meticulous with her organization. Missing files were not of the norm, and that was concerning. I waited until we were just out of earshot before I spoke. "What do you mean they're not in our inventory?" I demanded. A pit of worry settled deep in my stomach. Luke stopped at the threshold of our front door, tucking his notepad into his back pocket. "We don't have them, Detective Vaughn." He said with a sigh and I narrowed my eyes. "Then where are they?"

"That's what I'd like to know." He studied me for a moment before continuing, lowering his voice. "Those files had been in your basement so long that dust had settled around them—thick enough to show exactly how many were there and exactly how long they'd been untouched. Why, suddenly, did your father decide to move them back to the precinct? And one week before your mother's death?" His words settled heavily in my chest, but I bit my tongue.

"Could it be related?" He exhaled and paused for a beat before continuing, "I don't know. But your father hasn't been forthcoming about what was in those files, when exactly he moved them, or who he handed them to. If they were truly level-one classified, they would have been immediately recorded in our system." He hesitated, then leaned in slightly, voice just above a whisper. "We need to find those files, Detective."

My breath caught in my throat, but I forced myself to nod in response. He tilted his head spilling brown curls from one side to the other and I heated under his scrutinizing gaze. Wildly uncomfortable, I took a step back creating a pocket of space between us again. He blinked then straightened again as if he had been in a daze. "I will find the truth." He said then, just as *quickly, he opened the door and disappeared into the night. I stood there for a moment, rubbing my arms against the chill that had settled deep into my bones.*

I closed the front door, turning and forcing my feet to carry me back inside. The house felt eerily quiet. No smooth jazz played in the background like it usually did on weekends—just silence. I took a slow step toward the kitchen, careful not to disturb my father any more than he already had been today. A faint clink of glass drifted down the hallway to my ears. Peering around the corner, I found my father standing by the counter, pouring himself a glass of whiskey. He downed the first in one gulp, then refilled it—this time, for sipping. His free hand slipped into his pocket as he stared out the window, lost in thought. Was he stressed? Exhausted? Hiding something?

I watched him for a moment longer, torn between questions I wasn't ready to ask and answers I wasn't prepared to hear. Maybe my mother had been battling demons I never knew about. Or maybe, just maybe, there was something more to those files than my father wanted to admit. But that was a mystery for another day. I retreated silently, slipped out the front door as quietly as I could, and climbed into my car. Sinking into the worn leather of the driver's seat, I let out a slow, shaky breath. Nothing in my life felt real anymore. One of the people who had shaped me—who had made me—was gone. No warning. No chance to say goodbye.

Was that all life was? A collection of fleeting memories, just waiting to fade into the background of someone else's story? The thought sent a sharp pang through my chest. I leaned my head against the headrest, closing my eyes.

Would my mother's legacy become nothing more than a whisper in the minds of those who knew her? Would I, too, one day fade into nothingness, my existence reduced to a handful of memories before being forgotten altogether? Tears rolled down my cheeks. Angrily, I wiped them away. I had never faced these questions before—not until now. Not until the weight of existence pressed against me like an unbearable force. Is this all we were? Just temporary blips in time? A brief moment of awareness before being replaced, over and over, in an endless cycle?

A deep, aching sob tore from my throat before I could stop it. My hands clenched the steering wheel, knuckles turning white. And then—I screamed. The noise tumbling out of my throat until my lungs burned. Until my voice gave out. Until my vision blurred with so many tears that I couldn't even see the night sky above me. And as I wept in the silence of my car, Liarta plunged wholly into the darkness of another night.

***

I jolted awake to Luke's hand on my shoulder, instinct snapping my fingers around his wrist before I registered his face. Surprise flickered in his eyes. "It's just me," he said quietly. I released him, my hand falling limp on the mattress. "We're ten hours out." He sank into the chair beside my bunk rubbing his face, exhaustion ebbing on the edges of his expression. I stretched, muscles stiff and aching from restless sleep.

"You need rest," I murmured, voice thick. He didn't argue—just slid into the opposite bunk, staring at the ceiling. I hesitated, thoughts sluggish but persistent. "Why did you ask my father about the missing files in his basement?" I finally asked. Luke didn't answer right away. His thumb grazed his lip, eyes distant. "I don't think they were his." He said. I straightened up from the bunk, "What do you mean?" He looked at me, "I think they were hers."

Shock rolled through my like a tidal wave, "My mother's?" I whispered. He nodded, "And I think he destroyed them. Or at least stored them somewhere other than the precinct. Somewhere where no one but he could get ahold of them. They have to have been highly incriminating." The words landed hard in my chest. "Why else wouldn't he have brought them back to the precinct?" His tone was calm but deliberate. "He said he did," I insisted. "Well, forensics said he didn't." Luke replied steady and firm, but the underlying accusation stung. My thoughts tangled. He cut through them with another question— "Who was Malone?"

I blinked, caught off guard. "Malone was charged with murdering his wife. I led the case. Found the evidence that convicted him." I tapped my fingers against the mattress, trying to center myself. "It was personal—revenge." I muttered. Luke didn't look away. "He said he was paid to make you disappear. Doesn't sound like personal revenge to me." A chill tightened around my spine. "Look, I don't know who paid him." I said, jaw clenched. Luke studied me in silence. "Besides, why were you even there?" I asked, suspicion flaring. "Were you following me?"

He didn't respond. I stood to leave, but his hand caught my wrist—gentle, not restraining. "I was worried about your safety." His voice was soft, and his eyes searched mine like he was hoping to find something there. Heat rose to my face—anger, maybe, or something I didn't want to name. "I can take care of myself." I snapped, yanking my arm back. I felt exposed, stripped down in a way I hadn't expected from that admission. His gaze darkened. "Why are you so concerned about me?" I asked, my tone sharp.

Silence.

His jaw tightened. "Nothing to say?" I pushed. He opened his mouth, then—quietly—"I'm not your enemy." My pulse thudded. "And how would I know that? You don't tell me anything."

"I'm telling you everything I can." he said, frustration bleeding into his voice. "Everything you can, not everything you know." I shot back.

When he didn't respond, I took a step towards the door. "You will tell me everything. Even if I have to interrogate it out of you." I didn't turn my head to look at him as I took another step towards the door, then paused with my back still facing him. "Don't make the mistake of thinking we are all of a sudden allies. Not when you don't even know me." My fingers brushed the door controls. "I will find out what happened to my mother. And if you had anything to do with it.." I turned my head just enough for him to see my stone faced expression. "I'll bury you and anyone who stands in my way."

The door clicked behind me as I left him behind. The cockpit was dim, the soft glow of instrument lights casting pale reflections. I slid into the pilot's seat and pinched the bridge of my nose. What the hell was I doing? Trusting him—even for a second—was a mistake. A mistake that could get me killed just like my mom. I'd been a fool to think he was holding back for my benefit.

Get your shit together, Pandora.

I stared at the controls. Everything was stable. Auto-pilot was engaged. Outside, Gayle hovered on the edge of view—a pale, flowing blue sphere suspended in the dark. I scrubbed at my eyes. Ten hours to contact. Ten hours to figure out what the hell I was doing.

Chapter 16

The soft *click* of the bunk door startled me. I sat up quickly, my heart kicking against my ribs. I must have dozed off briefly. The flight log flickered on the screen—*30 minutes until atmospheric entry.* Beyond the thick glass shielding us from space, Gayle loomed much more prominent now. Her glowing blue surface radiated different hues across the water—deep, endless oceans swallowing most of what I could see, with lighter cerulean waters lapping against lush, green outcroppings of land. I scanned the terrain, searching for our contact point.

There—*Mount Akasari.* Its jagged peak pierced through the jungle, lifting high into the sky.

Unclipping my harness, I moved from the pilots seat and adjusted into the co-pilot position just as I heard Luke's footsteps in the hallway. Slow and almost hesitant. He slid into his seat without a word. I didn't look at him. I didn't want to address him. Not yet. Instead, I bit my tongue and followed his lead, my hands moving automatically through the docking protocol. If I spoke now, I'd say something I'd regret later. Pulling the lever slightly, I adjusted the wing flares, slowing our approach.

Below, the land masses scattered across Gayle's watery surface like dark freckles against the sea of blue. The ship's hull was eerily silent as we drifted forward. We had no idea how Gayle's atmosphere would affect the flight compared to Liarta.

The air density and the gravitational pull—both unknowns. We could only hope the ship's structure would hold.

Ten minutes out.

I tightened my harness, securing the chest clip. Then, I dared a glance at Luke. He held his composure, either unaware of my stare or deliberately ignoring me. I studied him, searching for cracks. His jaw was set—strong, unwavering. A shadow of stubble darkened his chin, marking the passage of time. His breathing was even. Controlled. His fingers moved over the steering column with precision, weaving us smoothly through space debris. I swallowed and cautiously let my gaze flicker to his eyes.

Blue. So blue.

The kind of blue that shouldn't *exist* outside of oceans or frozen tundras. Beautiful. But there—*at the threshold of his pupils*—was something else. A glimpse of his *soul*. Dark. *Twisted*. A double-edged sword. His eyes carried sorrow—*agony*. But also something else. Something I couldn't quite name. Something dangerously close to *light*.

"Five minutes."Luke's voice jolted me, and I jumped. I nodded, quickly turning my focus forward. We donned our flight headsets, syncing to the universal frequency. "Gayle, this is Detective Nesnah and Detective Vaughn requesting landing near Mount Akasari. Do you read me?"His voice came through my comms clear and steady. The signal beaconed outward. Then—*silence*.

We waited. Thirty seconds. Sixty. Luke's eyebrows furrowed as he glanced at me. "They should have comms towers. Why aren't they responding?" I shook my head, "I don't know. They've had comms towers for years... Something must have happened."

"Gayle, this is Detective Nesnah and Detective Vaughn. Do

you read me?" We stared out at the massive planet now looming impossibly close. Still—*nothing*. No static. No interference. No sign of a signal at all. A pit formed in my stomach and I blinked, processing. "Something must have happened to their comm towers," I said finally. "Should we still land? We're flying in blind now."

Luke exhaled sharply, "I've never docked blind, and we don't know the terrain. That's risky." He studied me for a moment as I met his gaze, "We don't have another option." I said firmly and the resolution slowly sank into his expression. He turned back to the controls, his jaw tightening. Thirty seconds to atmospheric entry. His grip on the steering column tightened and he pulled it back, pressing into his seat as we braced for impact.

Entering an atmosphere in a large ship usually felt smooth—Most department vessels had advanced stabilizers that absorbed turbulence, making it feel like slipping into warm water, but this *wasn't* a department vessel. No, this ship was small, had no stabilizers, and no atmospheric dampeners. Just raw physics and a prayer. I inhaled deeply, forcing my body to relax.

Ten seconds.

Nine.

Eight.

Luke clenched the controls his forearms flexed in the looming Gayle light.

Three.

Two.

One.

The ship *slammed* into the atmosphere. Everything lurched, and I felt the impact in my chest, the pressure rattling through my harness. My arms braced hard against my seat as we jolted violently. Luke gritted his teeth, his knuckles turning white on the controls. Outside, Mount Akasari loomed larger—closer—revealing its wicked, jagged features. The base of the mountain hurtled toward us at an alarming speed. A surge of panic shot through me. "Luke, we need to slow down—now. We're coming in too fast!"

His entire body pressed into the seat, fighting against the pull of the ship. "I miscalculated," he admitted, his voice tight with strain. "Gayle's atmosphere is thinner than Liarta's. I can't straighten out fast enough."

My stomach *plummeted*. If we didn't lose speed, we wouldn't land, we would *crash*. I yanked the lever for the wing flares—*SNAP*. The lever broke in my hand then went flying out of my grip. Metal clattered against the cockpit floor. I froze as our speed increased. A sharp curse flew from my lips. "I have to release the wing flares manually, or we'll crash."

Before Luke could protest, I unclipped my harness. "What the hell are you doing?!" Luke's voice was sharp, his eyes flashing in disbelief. "Get back in your seat! If we crash and you're not strapped in, you're dead!" The ship violently shook as I fought to stay upright. "If I don't manually release the wing flares, we're *both* dead!" I shouted over the chaos, already moving.

I pushed off the console, fighting the ship's rapid descent as I bolted for the back. The cockpit tilted, and my shoulder slammed into the wall. Luke cursed behind me, gripping the controls with every ounce of strength he had. I didn't stop. I ran. The metal corridors blurred as I fought toward the emergency release panel. We were seconds from disaster. And if I didn't act now—This mission would be over before it even began.

The emergency control panel at the back of the ship violently rattled as I scrambled to locate the manual release. "We're picking up speed!" Luke bellowed from the cockpit. Sweat dripped down my neck as my eyes darted over the controls.

"Come on, *come on*—Found it!" I gripped the lever and yanked it with all my strength. The ship lurched. A violent jerk sent me flying, my boots slipping out from under me as I hit the floor hard.

"You good?!" Luke's voice carried through the hallway, strained and urgent. "Yes!" I shouted back, though my ribs disagreed. But even with the flares deployed, we were still plummeting way too quickly. The ship groaned, metal straining against the sheer force of our descent. The steering column clattered wildly in the cockpit, and the deafening whistle of the wings cutting through the atmosphere sent goosebumps racing up my arms. I reached for the doorframe, trying to pull myself up, and *missed*. The ship tilted again, and suddenly—I was sliding. My boots squeaked uselessly against the floor as the force yanked me forward, accelerating toward the cockpit like a runaway projectile.

"I'm sliding!" I shouted, hands slapping against the floor in a desperate attempt to stop myself. Pain burned my palms as friction fought me, but it was no use—The windshield was getting closer. The surface of Gayle rushed up at us through the glass impossibly fast, and I braced myself to be thrown clear out of the ship. Then—we hit. The impact launched me airborne, my body hurtling toward the control panel. I squeezed my eyes shut, bracing for the inevitable crash—But it never came.

A strong arm snapped around my waist, stopping me inches from slamming into the console. I gasped, my heart hammering against my ribs. Luke's grip held firm, his chest rising and falling just as hard as mine. For a long moment, neither of us spoke. The ship groaned in relief, the landing gear settling into the soft Gayle soil beneath us. Luke powered the ship down, his fingers impossibly steady despite nearly being flattened like a pancake.

My breath still came in shaky gasps, my lungs burning. He

finally turned his head toward me, "Let's not do this again." His arm was still locked around my torso, voice flat. I swallowed, nodding slowly. "Yes, let's not do this again."

His grip loosened, and I felt my boots finally touch solid ground again. I wobbled slightly, steadying myself against his outstretched arm. Then, I looked out the windshield for the first time since we landed. I gasped. We had touched down exactly where we planned—at the base of Mount Akasari—But the environment was nothing like I expected. I stared in shock.

Ginormous kapok trees towered over our ship, their thick canopies stretching high above us like an emerald sky. A dense jungle brush engulfed the ground, a plush, living carpet of neon green. The color was almost too vivid, burned into my vision. I had never seen greenery this vibrant before. It was breathtaking.

"Do you see anyone?" I asked, suddenly remembering how close we had come to crash-landing. If anyone was nearby, they would surely come investigating. Luke scanned the jungle, his jaw tight. "I don't," he said, "but I don't want to wait around and find out." He unclipped from his harness and brushed past me, heading toward the cargo hold. I followed, the faint squeak of my boots against the floor the only sound filling the silence. "Only carry what you need," Luke instructed, slipping his black backpack over his shoulders. "I don't know how far we'll be trekking before we find anyone. If we find anyone."

"It's strange their comms towers didn't respond," I murmured, sliding my arms through the straps of my backpack. "Do you think the Nephrians destroyed them?" I asked, activating the DNA scanner. A soft beep resonated within the hull of the ship. It was only then that I noticed just how quiet it had become. No hum of flight electronics. No low whirr of the ship's systems. Just silence. The scanner's screen flickered to life.

Configured: Amy O'Rayne. Searching.

The scanner would alert us if we encountered anyone with a matching DNA profile. The green light blinked at the top indicating a match detected. My eyebrows furrowed. "That's strange." I smacked the edge of the scanner, half-expecting it to be a malfunction, but the alert remained. Luke zipped his pack and glanced at me. "What is it?"

"The scanner is picking up a partial match to Amy's DNA." His expression darkened. "Someone might already be nearby." I cleared the alert and shook my head. "Maybe it's a glitch."

"Or maybe," Luke said quietly, "someone matching is right outside the ship." A chill crawled up my spine. "We won't know until we step outside," he added. "The hull seals mute external noise."

I nodded, sliding the scanner back into my pocket. It felt heavy against my leg, a weight reminding me exactly why we were here and why this mission was so dangerous. Adjusting my communicator on my wrist, I woke Mayra up. "Detective Vaughn," her AI voice chimed through the device. "Be in standby mode, Mayra," I said, tightening the communicator snugly around my arm. "Standby confirmed, Detective Vaughn," she responded before powering back down. Luke gave me a questioning look, but I answered with a nod. I was ready. He pulled the lever for the door, and it opened with a heavy clunk.

A thick, humid sea breeze hit us at once, heavy with salt. It soaked into my skin, tingling as if the air itself were alive. The scent of brine and damp soil mingled in the wind, carried on the sound of waves crashing against a nearby shore. We climbed slowly down the ladder to the jungle floor, stepping into a world unlike any I had ever seen. The greenery was massive. Ferns the size of cars stretched their long limbs outward. My arm brushed against one as I turned from the ladder, and the branch recoiled instantly, furling in on itself to protect its delicate leaves.

Curious, I reached out and gently caressed another. It curled tightly in response. Amazed, I extended my fingers toward a third. "Be careful what you touch. We don't know the foliage here," Luke reminded me, nodding toward bright flowers and strangely shaped plants that were unlike anything we had seen before. I hesitated, my arm lingering in the air before I nodded and lowered it. "Anything could be dangerous here," he added, cautiously stepping toward Mount Akasari. I followed, conscious not to touch anything unless absolutely necessary.

The jungle was incredibly dense, vines coiling around thick trunks, massive leaves fanning overhead, filtering the Aurelios light into golden beams. My pack jostled against my back as Luke led the way, rifle in hand. His movements were quiet and calculated, leaving as little disturbance as possible on the jungle floor.

I listened intently, anticipating any sound, any sign of life. As we pushed through the thick underbrush, the light suddenly spilled through the trees. We emerged into an open space, the jungle retreating behind us. Underfoot, the sand was a deep shade of amethyst, crunching softly beneath our boots. I gasped as the grains reflected the Aurelios light, scattering tiny prisms of light in every direction. Ahead, a vast body of bottomless indigo water stretched toward the horizon, rolling in big, lazy waves over the shimmering sand. I was at a loss for words. Gayle was breathtaking.

"Have you ever seen sand like this? I mean I read about it, but to see it in person..." I trailed off bending down for a closer look. "I haven't. It's incredible," Luke said, picking up a handful and letting it flow lazily through his fingers. The grains cascaded in a river of purple, shifting colors as they tumbled back to the ground. He scanned the area, looking for a path forward, while

I turned my gaze toward the water. From here, the land beyond the beach wasn't visible, swallowed by the dark, endless waves stretching toward the horizon. "We should follow the shoreline but stay under the cover of the trees," Luke finally said, nodding toward a cove a couple of miles away near the mountain's base. "We can rendezvous there. It looks like that's where Mount Akasari begins."

I pocketed a smooth rock from the beach before trailing behind him into the jungle. The terrain grew thick again as we moved carefully through the brush, pausing every few minutes to listen. Aurelios was high overhead, but the canopy was so dense that only thin beams of light managed to filter through. I was grateful for the shade, though—the humidity felt like we were wading through thick pond water. The silence gnawed at my nerves, making my thoughts restless. "Do you think we'll find them?" I asked, watching the back of Luke's shoulders as he navigated the path ahead. "I'm not sure," he said evenly. "This is a big planet. Who knows how many survived after the Nephrians. They might be holed up somewhere else."

"The base of Mount Akasari was the last confirmed location of surviving Gaythes after the most recent Nephrian attack," I said, pushing aside a giant banana leaf that blocked the path. "If they're still here, that's where they'll be." I said and he nodded in agreement. "They're a strong species. I hope they held out,"

Each step made my boots feel heavier, and sweat trickled down the back of my neck. Luke grunted as he shoved a fallen log aside, his skin starting to shine with the heat. "It's so hot here," I muttered, adjusting the straps of my pack as sweat pooled beneath it, soaking into my shirt. The Gaythe had evolved to thrive in this climate, but it was quickly draining me. If we had to hike much longer, I would have to start shedding layers. As we moved forward, my thoughts wandered to the water, imagining how the cool, weightless embrace of deep blue waves would feel against my skin.

A huge pink flower came into view ahead. My eyes were immediately drawn to it, and I scurried quickly around Luke for a closer look. Its petals pulsed gently, almost as if it were *alive*. I leaned in, studying the velvet texture of each petal, their delicate fibers trembling lightly in the Aurelios light. "Be careful," Luke warned, striding up beside me. His eyes narrowed as he leaned forward. Beads of sweat formed on my forehead under a warm beam of Aurelios light filtering through the canopy. The flower smelled sweet, like honey and pecans.

"It smells incredible, doesn't it?" I said, grinning at him. He nodded, his expression distant, and slowly reached out his hand. I caught his wrist midair, my brows knitting together. "I thought we weren't supposed to touch anything." He didn't respond, his gaze fixed on the flower, almost entranced. "It looks so soft," he murmured. "Like I could just sink into it and take a nap in the petals." He leaned in closer, inhaling deeply. "It feels like it's calling to me."

The tiny hairs along the petals flickered in response. My eyes widened. It could *sense* us. "I wouldn't touch that if I were you," came a deep voice behind us. The accent was strange—English, but with an unfamiliar lilt. We froze, my hand still wrapped around Luke's wrist. I swallowed hard and turned my head slowly.

My eyes were drawn to his scales first—iridescent and vibrant, shifting in color like the winding ribbons of the Liarta northern lights. He practically glowed as if bathed in pure starlight. I knew immediately what he was, even if I had never met one. *Gaythe*.

A rush of cold washed over me, despite the jungle heat, as I took in his towering height and build. His face, framed by delicate lavender scales, was mesmerizing. They were much smaller than the ones covering his arms, so fine and intricate that they could almost be mistaken for human skin from a distance.

The Gaythe were known for their intimidating size and features, but standing this close to one was entirely different. His eyes caught the Aurelios light, reflecting an eerie pale-yellow hue beneath his vertically slatted pupils. The gills along his jawline opened and closed in slow, deliberate movements. He wore only tan canvas pants, his bare scaled chest gleaming under the light. Sharp, three-pointed fins jutted from his forearms, their webbing so thin it was nearly translucent. They looked as fragile as silk but held the lethal precision of a blade. A black scar curved across his right hand in the shape of a crescent moon, the scaled texture raised and ridged, as though it had been carved into his flesh rather than something he was born with.

He was beautiful.

Striking enough to make you forget—if only for a second—just how extraordinarily dangerous the Gaythe were. I forced myself to look down, and the blood drained from my face. His feet—not feet at all, but massive taloned fins, pointed in my direction. The edges gleamed like polished obsidian, curved and sharp enough to tear through muscle and bone with terrifying ease. My breath felt thick and hot in my throat as his gaze locked onto me.

"What are you humans doing here?" he hissed. The sound came from deep in his throat, guttural and unnatural, as though forcing himself to speak our language was an effort he barely tolerated. His posture, the tension in his shoulders, the way his gills flared—everything about him made it clear. He wanted nothing more than to tear us limb from limb. I took a slow, steady breath, forcing my legs to remain still as I turned to face him head-on.

"I'm Pandora Vaughn. We're from Liarta." My voice trembled, but I focused on speaking as clearly and calmly as possible. "I know where you're from." His lip curled in disgust, revealing rows of razor-sharp teeth. "Why are you here?" he repeated.

My eyes flicked to Luke, who had turned slightly but remained frozen. His body was tense and his mouth was closed. "We're here to find Odina," I whispered. The reaction was immediate. He took a threatening step toward me. "How do you know that name?" he spat through his teeth. My pulse thundered in my ears, drowning out the sounds of the jungle. "My mom told me about her," I managed. "I believe she is the key to solving a murder."

I didn't move. I barely breathed as he stared me down, unblinking. His gills flexed and then folded shut as if he, too, was steadying his breathing. "And why," he said slowly, "would you think she has anything to do with your murder?" A flicker of hope sparked inside me. "So she is alive," I whispered. "Answer my question," he growled. His voice rumbled deep in his chest, the vibration so powerful it seemed to shake the air between us. I flinched at the sound. "The woman who was murdered was half Gaythe, half human," I said quickly. The words rushed out before I could fully form them, "we think she came from here." My voice trailed to a mere whisper.

His slitted pupils widened, then narrowed, his body still and unreadable. The silence between us stretched thick with skepticism. He was measuring every detail of my presence, weighing my words against whatever knowledge he already had. "Gayle is in danger," Luke finally spoke. His voice was steady, calm. No tremble, no hesitation. He relaxed his posture slightly and took a step forward.

The Gaythe man's gills flared. "Gayle is *always* in danger," he hissed. He rose to his full height, his massive shoulders casting Luke in shadow. I tried to swallow, but my throat was completely dry. Luke stopped moving but kept his composure. The tension between them lingered, heavy in the humid air, but the Gaythe man's rigid stance eased slightly. "We have been fighting the Nephrians for years," he said, his tone edged with suspicion. "How could we possibly be in more danger now?"

Beneath the grating force of his words, there was something else—a smoother, quieter tone, like the distant purr of a predator before it struck. I turned to Luke, waiting for his response. "One of your people came to Liarta," he said firmly, "and now she is dead."

The Gaythe man's eyes widened—only briefly—but in recognition.

"We need to speak with Odina," I said gently. His eyes flicked to me, but he remained silent. Without a word, he gestured forward, and two more Gaythe men emerged from the dense ferns behind him. They looked nearly identical to him—the same iridescent scales, the same imposing size—but a few subtle differences set them apart. One had deeper orange irises instead of yellow, while the other was leaner, his facial complexion slightly lighter. Like the first, they wore only tan canvas trousers, their bare chests gleaming under the jungle-filtered light. A wave of nausea rolled over me. They had been watching us. *Following* us. And we hadn't noticed.

"Drop all your weapons at your feet," the first Gaythe commanded. Behind him, the two remained motionless, waiting. Luke hesitated, gripping the rifle with both hands. I exhaled slowly, then nodded, reaching for my pistol. I pulled it from my side and set it carefully on the ground. Luke reluctantly followed, lowering the rifle, his gaze never wavering from the Gaythe man staring intently at us. "Kick them toward me," he ordered, his stance unmoving. I nudged my pistol forward with my boot, watching it roll through the thick undergrowth, stopping just short of his taloned feet.

Using his heel, Luke nudged the rifle forward as close as he dared, then slowly backed away to where he had stood moments ago. The Gaythe man picked up our weapons, inspecting them briefly before waving the two others forward. They moved toward us, pulling small, glowing blue rings from their pockets. He spoke in a language unfamiliar to me, the sounds fluid yet sharp, layered with guttural tones. The two Gaythe hesitated, eyes shifting from me back to him. "What is on your wrist, human?" he asked suddenly.

Before I could answer, Mayra's voice chimed from my communicator. "Good afternoon." Her hologram flickered to life above my wrist. I swallowed hard. "It's my AI communicator," I said quietly, lowering my eyes. "Take it off and give it to me," he ordered, holding out his scaled hand. I hesitated. "Detective Vaughn, it is against code 112 to hand me off to unregistered personnel," Mayra protested. "Mayra, enter sleep mode," I commanded quickly.

"Entering sleep mode." She powered down without further argument, and I reluctantly removed the communicator, placing it in his open palm. "Packs too." He said, and we both exchanged glances but eased them off our backs, setting them with the weapons on the ground. I didn't mention the scanner in my pocket. That information I kept to myself. Without hesitation, he waved the others to continue. The blue rings softly hummed as they slid over our wrists. They felt weightless, like air itself, but the moment they cinched down, my arms were locked behind me. I strained against them instinctively, but there was no give. Luke remained unreadable, his expression betraying nothing as the Gaythe with the deep orange irises grasped my wrist. I hissed in pain as his grip tightened. He hissed back, his lips peeling apart, spit flying from between his rows of needle-like teeth.

"They will not harm you," the first man assured us. "But they do not know English. They understand body language only, so it would be in your best interest to behave." He slung Luke's rifle over his back and slid my pistol into his pocket. Only then did I notice the long spear strapped behind him. Its tip glinted dangerously as he shifted, so sharp that it caught the light with every movement. A ripple of unease settled in my chest. I adjusted my weight from one foot to the other, suddenly feeling far too exposed. "We will take you to our city, Kehel," he said, stepping closer. "However, your first lesson here on Gayle shall be this." He reached into his pocket and pulled out a small, silver-scaled fish. A pungent, briny scent filled the air. I scrunched my nose at the distasteful aroma but watched in growing confusion.

"These are called vipyrs," he said, gesturing to the massive pink flower behind us. "They emit an intoxicating scent to lure in their prey. The fibers on their petals detect disturbances in the air—movement, sound, even the slightest shift in temperature." He took a slow, deliberate step toward the plant. "But what they love most," he continued, his voice steady, "is human sweat."

A chill ran down my spine. My eyes flicked away from him and back to the flower, uncertainty creeping through me. "If a vipyr detects the sweat of a human nearby," he said, tilting his head slightly, "It draws them in and swallows them whole."

Before I could process his meaning, he flicked the small fish into the air. I barely had time to track its arc before the plant reacted. The petals shot upward, stretching impossibly fast, and snapped shut with a sickening *crack*.

I gasped, stumbling back as fear slammed into me. Luke went

rigid, his face draining of color as the realization struck—he had nearly been that flower's next meal. The two Gaythe men gripping our wrists grinned, their sharp teeth glinting in the light, then shoved us forward. The leader turned, disappearing into the dense foliage along a barely visible path. The one with the orange irises gave me a rough nudge, urging me onward. Begrudgingly, I followed. Luke's face was locked into a hardened expression. His jaw clenched tight as he trailed beside us. I risked one last glance over my shoulder, watching as the pink flower faded from view, still twitching as it devoured its midday snack. Regret settled deep in my chest.

Nothing was left to do but follow them—to whatever fate awaited us next.

Chapter 17

We walked for what felt like forever, the only sound was the rustling of the brush as we pushed through the dense foliage. Occasionally, the Gaythe would stop and listen. Part of me wanted to ask what—or who—they were looking out for. Part of me didn't want to know. My thoughts drifted to Liarta, my father, and everything unraveling in my absence. What was Ivy telling the precinct? Was it believable? Would she forgive me when we returned?

If we returned.

The Gaythe stopped again—for what felt like the hundredth time—but this time, the leader veered sharply to the right, disappearing into the undergrowth. I hurried after his footsteps, unwilling to lose sight of him in the thick jungle. "Where are we going?" I asked. "I told you I'm taking you to Kehel," he replied without looking back. "Yes, but we've been walking for ages, and I haven't seen any sign of a city. Is it hidden?"

"You could say that," he murmured, still moving forward. "Are we close?" I quickened my pace, trying to keep up. I was beginning to feel restless. He suddenly turned, tilting his head. "You have so many questions, human." His lips curled slightly. "There will be answers." His golden eyes flickered over me, assessing. "You're rather tall for a female human," he mused. "Tell me... are you afraid of heights?" His grin widened into something wilder, sharper. I narrowed my eyes as I spoke, "Maybe... why do you ask?"

"If you wish to meet Odina," he said, spreading his arms wide. His wingspan was impressive, and I gawked at the sheer size of him. "First, you must jump." he said and with that, he let himself fall backward—disappearing from sight. I barely had time to register what was happening before I heard it.

A long pause— Then a *splash*.

Luke shot me a sideways glance, and together, we edged forward peering over the ledge. Just beyond the grass disguising it, a massive crater gaped beneath us, cutting deep into the planet's surface. At the bottom, glowing fluorescent-green water rippled where the Gaythe man had landed. He chuckled, floating effortlessly. "Your turn," he called up.

The hair on my arms stood on end, and I swallowed hard. It was a long way down and I was, in fact, afraid of heights. "Why should we trust you?" Luke shouted. "Do you see another option?" the Gaythe called back. "There's always another option," Luke snapped. The two Gaythe men behind us nudged us forward, and my stomach lurched. "Jump or die," the leader shrugged. Luke looked at me, then at the man with the lighter complexion.

"Will you at least untie us?" he asked, lifting his bound hands. "Not a chance," came the flat reply. Well. They were undoubtedly serious about their hostages. I inched forward until my toes met empty air. The glowing water seemed impossibly far away. "How do you know humans can even survive in that?" I asked, squeezing my eyes shut. "We don't," the Gaythe replied, his voice laced with impatience. "Now hurry up. I don't have all day." I opened my mouth to argue, but before I could form a single word, I felt the unmistakable sensation of being shoved forward.

The ground beneath me vanished, and the air swallowed me

whole. My hair whipped around my face as I plummeted, the wind howling in my ears. I squeezed my eyes shut. Whether this was the end or not, I didn't want to see it coming. The impact was anything but graceful. I hit the water hard, its warmth unexpected as I plunged beneath the surface. My body twisted awkwardly, limbs flailing as I fought against the downward pull.

Kicking furiously, I clawed upward, my bound hands useless against the current. Breaking through the surface, I gasped for air. "You pushed me!" I seethed, whipping my head toward the ledge above. The Gaythe men were howling with laughter. The leader barked something in their native tongue, and they immediately stifled their amusement, straightening as if nothing had happened. I rolled my eyes.

"Let's go, pretty boy," the leader called to Luke. Luke stood at the edge, clearly unconvinced after witnessing my less-than-elegant landing. But with no other option, he took a few readying steps back, then leapt. Even with his hands bound, he cut through the air with the same grace as the Gaythe, plunging cleanly into the water. He surfaced a moment later, his dark hair slicked back, expression unreadable. Meanwhile, I was growing tired of treading water without the use of my arms. "I'm going to drown if we stay here all day," I snapped. My arms ached, and my legs were beginning to burn. "Hold your breath," the leader instructed.

Before my mind could catch up, strong fingers wrapped around my chest. A sharp inhale barely filled my lungs before the world became a blur of motion and I was yanked under. Water rushed around us at an impossible speed and his scaled body was cool against mine as he propelled us downward, cutting through the depths like a torpedo. The deeper we went, the colder it became, pressing against my skin like a vice. I didn't know how fast we were moving, but I knew one thing for certain— I had never traveled this fast in water before. My lungs burned. They practically screamed for air, but I gritted my teeth, forcing my body to hold on. I wasn't going to drown. Not when I was this close to finding Odina. Still, the pressure tightened, my body begging for oxygen. Maybe this was it. Maybe I was going to drown, pulled into the depths of the Gayle ocean.

Suddenly, we burst through an opening in the water, landing hard on dry sand. Hot air rushed into my lungs, burning like fire. I coughed, sputtering as I struggled to steady my breath. "I could have died! What were you—" But my words died in my throat as I pushed myself to my feet and took in my surroundings. We were at the base of the seafloor, encased in a *massive* air bubble. Above us, the deep blue ocean pressed against an invisible barrier, lapping against it as if teasing the edge of its prison. Schools of fish swam just beyond, utterly unaware of how close they were to a hidden city tucked beneath the depths.

And what a city it was.

White and blue coral structures sprawled across the seabed, their surfaces pulsing with bioluminescence. Roads wound effortlessly between the buildings, carved from gleaming stone and lined with vine-covered pillars bursting with bright, alien flowers. There was no Aurelios light this deep, yet the city seemed to generate an ethereal glow, casting shimmering waves of soft light over its inhabitants.

Breathtaking.

The sand beneath my boots was the same stunning amethyst as the beaches above, softly crunching as I stepped forward. Gaythe men and women moved through the streets, some pausing to glance at us with wary curiosity, others avoiding us entirely. Nearly all of them wore nothing, their iridescent scales shimmering as they shifted and flexed with every movement. My mouth opened, then closed. I had no words for what I was seeing.

"I apologize, human," the group leader said, his voice smoother now. "I didn't mean to throw you onto the sand. I'm not used to making a landing while carrying someone." I turned, about to fire off a sharp retort, but was interrupted as Luke and the other two Gaythe sliced through the water wall, landing effortlessly beside us. Luke's eyes widened, mirroring my awe as he took in the hidden world before us.

"Humans," our captor said, spreading his arms. "Welcome to Kehel." His voice carried over the sand towards the ethereal city beckoning to us. Luke and I exchanged a look. "How long has this been here?" I asked, my voice laced with disbelief. "There are no records—no texts, no history—nothing that even suggests this place exists." The Gaythe leader regarded me coolly. "No humans have ever been here before," he said. "You are the first." I swallowed hard, unsure how to process that information. But, why *now*?

"Why did you bring us here?" I asked, my confusion growing. If we were the first humans to step foot in Kehel, there had to be a reason and a significant one. "Because we need your help," he said. Then, without warning, he reached for my wrists and pulled off the glowing blue rings. I exhaled sharply as they released me, rubbing at the sore indentations they left behind. Luke flexed his fingers as the leader's companions freed him next. "Help with what?" Luke asked warily. The Gaythe leader didn't answer immediately. Instead, he turned, motioning for us to follow. "Come with me," he said, "I will show you."

We followed the man through the coral city, weaving through winding streets carved from smooth stone. Eyes turned toward us, more and more people pausing to watch our small procession. "Most of these Gaythe have never seen a human," our guide said as if reading my mind. "And most do not speak your language. They mean you no harm. I apologize for the stares though, few have ever left the city."

I nodded, absorbing the information. The stares weren't hostile—just curious. "They seem to find us interesting, at least," Luke smirked as two giggling Gaythe girls waved down at us from a balcony. I rolled my eyes. "They take interest in *you*," I muttered, the words sharper than I intended. Luke's gaze flicked to me, his head tilting slightly in question. I just shook my head and turned my focus back to the man leading us through the growing crowd.

"The Nephrians have slaughtered most of the women here on Gayle. We advised the remaining to stay hidden here in Kehel," our guide said, his voice heavy with grief. Sadness settled deep in my chest. "Why?" I asked, though I already knew the answer. The same reason the Gaythe were at war was likely the same reason the Nephrians had attacked Liarta before.

"The planet the Nephrians reside on is dying," he continued. "Their core has cooled, causing their world to freeze. They have no water or food, and their species is slowly ceasing to exist. They intend to take over Gayle, and it's quite possible they will attack soon to finish off the rest of us—taking our home as theirs. They killed as many women as they could attempting to stop us rebuilding our numbers."

Silence followed. Nothing I could say would remedy the sheer loss the Gaythe had suffered. "It's genocide," he added, his voice clipped with restrained emotion. My heart twisted. "Who did you lose?" The words slipped out before I could stop them. He stopped in his tracks, mulling over the question. I thought he might ignore me for a moment, but after a pause, he spoke. "My parents," he murmured, his voice distant. "And my sister."

He resumed walking, and we followed in silence, the sounds of the city around us a blur. Conversations in their language floated past, unfamiliar yet filled with emotion. I wished I could understand—even if it was just small talk. "The loss you've endured..." I trailed off, but he didn't respond. Instead, he shifted the subject.

"We had some doctors here," he said. "Doctors?" I asked, confused. "Human doctors." He confirmed and I nearly collided with a potted flower plant hanging from a decorative hook as we turned a corner, ducking just in time. "You had human doctors here on Gayle?" My forehead creased. Luke pressed his lips into a firm line and I glanced at him, narrowing my eyes at his expression. He knew something.

"Yes," our guide confirmed. "They were here to assist us. The Nephrians cursed us when they killed many of our women." He turned his head over his shoulder to look at me briefly before continuing. I nodded, listening carefully. "The Nephrians wield powerful, ancient magic," he said. "And with it, they placed a curse that prevents any of our women from being able to reproduce."

I gasped, my chest tightening at the weight of his words. Luke's expression became unreadable, his face a perfect mask of indifference. "They were here trying to lift the curse," our guide continued. "However, they were killed in the most recent Nephrian attack. From the journals they left behind, it seems they had been close."

Luke drifted closer to me, his posture tense, but his eyes remained locked ahead on the man leading us. Our footsteps filled the silence. I bit my lip, glancing at him from the corner of my eye. What was he not telling me now?

"Up until then, there was still hope for us," the Gaythe man said, his voice quieter now. "But after the attack, we lost the doctors and most of their research. Even our most skilled Gaythe haven't been able to replicate their studies." His words lingered in the air like a final, heavy note, thick with unspoken grief.

We continued through the twists and turns of the muted red-paved coral road. Shadows cast over us as we entered a tunnel, our footsteps echoing loudly against the walls. The light from the barrier above struggled to penetrate through the thick walls as we delved deeper into the city. The hustle and bustle from the outer edges of Kehel faded into a distant hum as we passed through several heavy copper gates, each clinking shut behind us.

The Gaythe man led us toward the most prominent structure we had seen yet. It was made entirely of coral as the rest of the city was. Its intricate surface polished to a smooth sheen lead to a towering spire reaching toward the peak of the underwater dome. I eyed it curiously, wondering if it might pierce through the veil above us.

"How does it work?" I asked as he closed the final gate behind us with a thud. "How does what work?" he asked, climbing the long slope of stairs leading to the building's entrance. "Your magic underwater air bubble," I said, gesturing to the shimmering barrier above. "Ah, our shield," he stated simply. But it wasn't simple at all. In fact, none of this was. "Yes, your *shield*," I repeated, the word taking on a heavier meaning in my mind. He remained silent for a moment as we were led inside to a vast waiting area. The space was grand, with smooth pillars lining the walls and delicate bioluminescent strands draped from the ceiling like a web of glowing veins.

"Our ancestors created the shield thousands of years ago when we were still being poached for our scales," he finally said. "Back then, the Gaythe primarily inhabited the ocean, only able to survive above water for short periods. Their adaptation to air was much weaker than ours now. They established cities throughout the sea, but none provided true protection from outside invaders. So, they built Kehel. It took years of magic and sorcery to create this sanctuary." His voice darkened. "Now, it is the only one on Gayle that remains."

I swallowed hard, the weight of his words settling deep in my chest. "Some of our northern sister tribe still survives, but they are nomads now. Their last remaining city, Amarith, was destroyed in the last Nephrian attack. We have some of their survivors seeking refuge here in Kehel, but most of them refuse to request aid."

I nodded slowly, absorbing the tragic history he shared. "Do you still possess this magic?" I asked cautiously. He finally stopped before two armed guards flanking a set of reinforced doors. The tension in the air thickened, his following words almost hushed. "Only one of us has enough power to even think of recreating our shield should it ever go down." He exhaled, a shadow passing over his expression. "To wield the witchcraft, you must be chosen by the stone. It is the source of our power, our magic." Luke stepped forward slightly. "Who has that kind of power?" The Gaythe man turned to face us directly, his golden eyes gleaming in the dim light. "Odina."

"Ragnai." One of the guards nodded to the man leading us, then stepped aside to allow us through. The name echoed in my mind, rattling around like a puzzle piece struggling to fit.

Ragnai. Why did that sound familiar? I couldn't help but glance again at the half moon imprinted on his right hand. It symbolized something important, as he was the only one who bore it. I chewed on my bottom lip, sifting through the archives of my memory. I had heard that name before—I was certain of it. Ragnai gave the guard a curt nod and guided us through the heavy door.

The air changed the moment we stepped inside. The

temperature plummeted, the chill settling into my bones and sending goosebumps up my arms. A solitary, dim lamp cast unsteady shadows throughout the enclosed space, its weak glow barely reaching the far corners. Before us stood a massive four-poster bed commanding the center of the room. Its thick wooden columns, as sturdy as tree trunks, rose to the ceiling, casting shadows over the heavy, woven blankets draped across the bedding—rich in deep reds and adorned with intricate tribal patterns. As my eyes adjusted to the gloom, I took in the full scope of the room. Then—I saw *her*.

Odina.

Chapter 18

S he lay motionless, her body unnaturally still, except for the slow, almost imperceptible rise and fall of her chest. Her eyes were open, but they were empty. A hollow void in her violet irises pulsed faintly in the dim light, an eerie glow that sent a shiver through me. I covered my mouth in shock.

"What's wrong with her?" I whispered, stepping forward cautiously. Odina, the Queen of the Gaythe, frozen in time as if straight out of a nightmare. Her long braids, woven thick and masterfully, rested limply around her head like a broken halo. The closer I got, the more I realized—the cold in the room radiated from her.

"She's been like this since the last Nephrian attack. Our healers say it's a curse laid by the Nephrians. There are remedy herbs close to the northern tribe, but none of us are of suitable health to make that trek, and I must remain here protecting the tribe. We only have a few surviving healers." Ragnai's voice was even toned as he spoke. I was unable to tear my eyes off her, wondering if she was aware of what was happening or just suspended in her mind. I hoped for the latter.

"This is our Queen. The final hope of my people." Ragnai's voice came almost as a whisper. It broke my gaze from her. "She was destined to deliver you." It wasn't a question, more of a statement. I already knew, as my mother had told me years ago, who she was destined to be. He nodded. I surveyed the rest of her, hoping for answers. Her arms were folded neatly over her chest, almost as if she was sleeping. "We think that's why she was targeted." He responded, his hand brushing the end of the blanket.

"Who cursed her?" I asked, gently taking Odina's hand in mine. The palm of her hand was still warm, but her fingertips were ice-cold. A creeping ashen gray spread up her arms like frostbite, as if the curse was slowly consuming her, devouring her from the inside out. "We believe Brykan did." Ragnai's voice was low, almost hesitant, as he stepped closer to the bed. "She was on a pilgrimage to Mount Akasari, escorting a woman in labor. Our sacred birthing temple was ransacked." He exhaled sharply, his eyes flicking to Odina's unmoving form. "She was the only one we found—left like this." My stomach tightened. "And the woman she was with?" His jaw clenched. "Our last woman with child," he murmured, "was never found."

"The last woman with child because of the curse," I murmured, thinking out loud. Ragnai nodded grimly. "There was no sign of the baby or the mother."

My stomach churned. The Nephrians didn't distinguish their victims—they slaughtered without mercy, even children. "Who is Brykan?" I asked, turning to him. Rage flickered in his eyes like a storm barely contained. "He is the most evil of them all," he said, voice tight. "The Nephrian frontrunner. It is rumored he lacks a soul."

I swallowed hard, "Lacks a soul?" Impossible, it had to be utterly impossible to be alive and not possess a soul. Ragnai's gaze darkened as he nodded, "They say he was an ancient dictator—one they raised from the dead." A chill rushed down my spine. "Raised from the dead?" Luke asked from behind me, his voice edged with skepticism as he leaned against the wall. "If anyone could do it, it would be the Nephrians," Ragnai said, his voice laced with pure hatred. "Their dark magic has run unchecked for thousands of years on Veneu. They have no limits. No boundaries. No morals. If they found a way to resurrect the dead, Brykan is proof." He shook his head as if trying to clear away his thoughts, then straightened and bowed slightly at the waist in Odina's direction, his movements precise and militant.

"Good afternoon, my Queen. I brought guests." His voice was respectful, almost reverent, as if he genuinely believed she could acknowledge him. But she didn't respond.

"Can she hear us?" Luke asked, his eyes drifting from Ragnai to Odina. "We believe so, but we are not sure. We have never seen a curse like this before," he admitted, his voice carrying the weight of uncertainty. Silence settled over the room. Then, a faint beeping broke through the stillness.

My head snapped up. "What's that noise?" I asked, scanning the space. Ragnai frowned. "We don't have any equipment that sounds like that." My heart pounded as I shoved a hand into my pocket, fingers brushing against the scanner. I pulled it out, watching as the screen flickered erratically, its green light flashing an alert.

87% match.

"There's no way," I murmured, my fingers scrolling through the data. The gears in my brain turned rapidly. Half human, half Gaythe. Amy wasn't just any hybrid—she came from someone powerful, someone extraordinary. Someone with not just physical strength but significant influence.

"Amy was Odina's daughter." The words left my mouth before I fully processed them. "What?" Luke pushed off the wall, crossing the space in two steps to peer at the scanner. His eyes flicked over the numbers, disbelief tightening his jaw. "She has to be," I insisted, the puzzle pieces clicking together too perfectly to ignore. My gaze shifted to Ragnai, who stood utterly still, watching us intently. "Unless she's your daughter."

His golden irises sharpened. "I have no children, but neither did she." He gestured to Odina. "How do you know?" Luke asked, eyeing him with suspicion. Ragnai's expression didn't waver. "Because Odina never had children," he said firmly. But the doubt in his voice betrayed him. Luke and I exchanged a glance. "She did," I whispered, glancing down at Odina's still form. "And now she's dead." We were all still for a moment, contemplating.

"Only one way to find out." I said reaching into the side compartment of the scanner and pulling out a small needle. Ragnai moved faster than I could blink. He leaped over Odina's still form in a single, fluid motion, shielding her body with his own. His gills flattened against the edges of his face and his golden irises narrowed to slits. The scales along his arms pulsed, shimmering under the dim light as his body tensed in warning.

"What are you doing?" he hissed, his voice laced with a deadly edge. Luke immediately stepped in front of me, creating a barrier between us. My heart slammed against my ribs as I froze, suddenly aware of how this must have looked—I was a complete outsider, standing over the Queen of the Gaythe, holding a needle. We were lucky he hadn't killed us on sight.

"I'm not going to harm her," I said quickly, leaning out from behind Luke, my palms raised in surrender. "I promise. I want to confirm the DNA match to Amy." Luke glanced at me, his posture rigid, but I nodded slightly, signaling that everything was under control. Ragnai's pupils contracted, sharpening as he studied me. A heavy silence filled the room, the tension thick enough to suffocate. "I just need one drop of blood," I said softly. "That's all."

His gills flared slightly, but he didn't move. Cautiously, I inched forward. Ragnai remained crouched at the edge of the bed, his body still coiled, but after a long moment, he—reluctantly—backed away. He remained close, hovering just inches from her, his every muscle primed to strike if I so much as breathed wrong. I swallowed hard and carefully reached for Odina's hand. Her long, scaled fingers were cool against my palm, her skin's deep violet hue contrasting against mine. *Please* let me be right.

The scales were impossibly smooth, tiny, and delicate, like snakeskin. I pricked the end of her finger as gently as I could, squeezing out a single drop of blood. It shimmered an iridescent light blue. Ragnai watched closely, his expression unreadable, as I guided the scanner toward her finger. The droplet slid into the receiving window, and after a moment, the scanner chimed.

Maternal match.

Luke released a slow, heavy breath, running a hand down his face. "This is a lot more complicated than we imagined." His voice was low as if the weight of the revelation had physically pressed down on him. Ragnai leaned in, his golden eyes fixed on the scanner, "What does it say?"

I swallowed, dread already pooling deep in my stomach. "She's Amy's mother." The words tasted bitter in my mouth. If Odina ever woke up, we would have to tell her that her daughter was dead. That the child she had once carried, the last hope for her people, had been murdered on a distant planet. Ragnai's brows furrowed as he took in the information, "Who is the father?"

"I don't know," I admitted. "But if she's half Gaythe, half human, her father must be from Liarta." Luke rubbed his chin in thought. "That means Odina left Gayle, or a human was here long enough to..." His voice trailed off, his gaze darkening. "Either way, it means someone has been keeping secrets." Ragnai turned to me, his expression sharp, "What happened to this, *Amy*?"

"She traveled to our planet and worked for Fritz Corporation. Someone used a drug called vecuronium to kill her." I hesitated, glancing between Luke and Ragnai before continuing. "A large sum of money was wired to her account from the company just hours before her death. We don't know if she sent it to herself, if it was a bribe, or if it was payment for something. But she never used it."

He absorbed the information silently, his fingers curling slightly against his knees. "Do you have any suspects?" He asked his eyes flickering with something I couldn't interpret. "We had two," Luke answered. "But their alibis cleared them." Frustration burned in my chest. I had nothing to give them. Nothing to offer these people—no justice, no resolution. One of their own had traveled to Liarta and was murdered, and I didn't even have a clear suspect. I pressed my palms to my temples, closing my eyes. Helpless. That's what I felt. Completely and utterly helpless. The silence stretched between us, heavy and suffocating. Ragnai didn't move, just stared quietly out the window, lost in his thoughts.

"We need to find those herbs," Luke said, breaking the heavy silence. Ragnai and I both turned to him. "Where are they exactly?" He asked. Ragnai stood up, rubbing the back of his neck. "I can take you to our senior healer. She should be able to tell you." He gestured for us to follow him.

"Are we going to go get them ourselves?" I asked as we moved through the door. "We're going to have to," Luke replied. "Odina isn't helpful to our investigation if she's in a coma and she's the only hope for these people. We're obligated to try." He shook his head.

The guards outside the room remained as still as statues, their eyes carefully tracking us as we passed. One of them inclined his head slightly in my direction. I hesitated before offering him a small, uncertain smile.

Following Ragnai, we descended a spiral staircase, our footsteps echoing off the stone walls. The deeper we went, the more humid the air became, carrying a faint herbal scent. "I don't have a choice but to trust you, humans," Ragnai said as we reached the bottom of the stairwell, stopping in front of a large wooden door. His hand lingered on the handle as he turned to face us. "I trust that what you say about Liarta is true and that you are here because of this woman, Amy." His jaw tensed as he ran his fingers through his smoky hair. "But," he added, his voice dropping to a low, dangerous tone, "if you so much as lay a hand on our healers, I will gut you myself."

The weight of his words hung thick in the air. His loyalty to his people was unwavering, and I didn't doubt that he meant every syllable of that threat. "We wouldn't dare harm your healers," I assured him, my voice firm with sincerity. "They are safe with us."

Ragnai studied me for a moment, then gave a single nod before pushing open the heavy wooden door. The scent of herbs, dried flowers, and something vaguely medicinal flooded my senses as we stepped inside the healing den. I took a deep breath, humming in quiet satisfaction. The air was thick, and Luke seemed to appreciate it as well. He closed his eyes briefly as his chest rose and fell steadily. "Manika," Ragnai called through the door without stepping inside, "I have guests."

There was some shuffling in the back room, followed by the appearance of a short Gaythe woman from behind a desk piled with assorted greenery. She was much older than the others we had seen in the city streets, her scales softer, her face marked with deep lines of age. Yet her pale blue eyes glittered with warmth, and when she smiled, ripples of creases formed along her cheeks. Her frame was small but sturdy, and as she moved toward us, the long, intricately woven braids cascading down her back brushed against her hips. She hummed softly under her breath, an unfamiliar and soothing tune, as she waved us inside.

This space was vastly different from the towering structures upstairs. Potted plants and tangled vines lined the deep brown walls and floor, their leaves spilling over the edges like cascading waterfalls. Large clusters of herbs dangled from the ceiling, their tips brushing against our scalps as we ducked through the narrow walkway. The air pulsed with an almost tangible energy, thick with the scent of soil and renewal.

"Manika, this is Pandora and Luke," Ragnai gestured toward us. "They're from Liarta. I'm hoping they can help." Her gaze met mine, and she smiled—a knowing, almost curious expression. There was wisdom in her eyes, the kind earned through decades of experience. "You're her." Her delicate voice was gentle to my ears. My eyes widened in surprise that she spoke our language. "I'm her?" I asked softly. She took my hands in her own. "I have been having visions of a tall red-haired woman." She said, her eyes traveling over my face, pausing to take in my eyes. "*The moon child.*" She said quietly. My eyes bulged with shock as she leaned forward, pressing her forehead to mine. Lights flashed, and everything went dark as my mind wound with hers spiraling into the vision.

We hid on the edge of the jungle, waiting in silence. My daggers were clutched tightly in my fists, their sharp, iridescent edges raised and ready. Sweat trickled down my back, but I didn't dare move. Here, in the shadows of the dense foliage, we were concealed—safe only as long as we remained still. An earsplitting crack opened a dark hole on the amethyst beach. I tensed, every muscle coiled in anticipation. From the corner of my eye, I caught a glimpse of Ragnai, his breathing slow and measured. He reminded me of a carved marble statue—utterly still, perfectly controlled. The hole pulsed, its edges curling and unfurling like something alive, swallowing any light that dared approach. My heart pounded against my ribs, my palms clammy despite the iron grip I maintained on my weapons. The roar from the void grew louder, deeper, reverberating within my chest. I swallowed hard, forcing my breath steady as the darkness stirred. And then, from the abyss, a figure emerged. His stark white skin gleamed unnaturally in the Aurelios light, a sharp contrast to the swirling void behind him. My breath caught in my throat as his dead, black eyes swept the tree line. He raised a scepter, its tip blazing with a light so intense I had to squint against its radiance. When he opened his mouth, his grey, rotting teeth bared, he released an earsplitting shriek that sent ice through my veins. Every hair on my scalp stood on end. Ragnai crouched low, leaving the cover of the trees, and I followed without hesitation. The ferns brushed against our ankles as we stepped onto the brilliant purple sand. The pale figure locked eyes with me. His clawed hand lifted in a slow, deliberate motion, and darkness exploded from the swirling void before I could react. Shadows writhed and shot toward us like living tendrils of night.

I felt dizzy as the room spun back into view, but the sensation quickly dissipated. My heart pounded in my chest, and I pressed a hand against it, willing it to slow down. Taking several deep breaths, I steadied myself. When I finally looked up, Luke and Ragnai watched me silently. This healer, it seemed, also possessed the gift of visions.

Luke's jaw was firmly locked in place, his expression unreadable, but the tension in his shoulders eased slightly as I met his gaze. I turned to Ragnai, whose sharp eyes were focused solely on me. "That's why you brought us here," I said, realization washing over me. His eyes flicked to Luke, lingering there before answering. "Yes," he admitted. I rubbed my temples, easing the pressure building. The vision was still fresh in my mind—the towering figure, the eerie glow of his scepter, the way the shadows slithered toward us.

I swallowed hard. "Who was that?" I asked, my voice quieter than I intended. "Brykan," Manika answered, and his name alone made my stomach twist. I clenched my hands into fists, trying to ground myself. "What can you tell me about that vision?" I asked, my voice betraying the fear still lingering in my chest.

In the vision, I had seemed ready, prepared to face whatever was coming. But if that man indeed was Brykan, he was far more terrifying than I had imagined. "I haven't been able to interpret it," Manika admitted, her hand resting gently on my arm as if to steady me. I nodded, absorbing her words. The weight of what we had just seen pressed down on me, but one thing was clear—whatever lay ahead, Brykan was waiting. "We need to find those remedy herbs," I said softly. "If that man is coming, we need Odina." Manika nodded, finally releasing my hands.

"What can you tell us about the herbs?" Luke asked, his curiosity piqued as he lifted a dried bunch of herbs from the ceiling. "The whistler herbs," she stated dragging a small step stool over to a bookcase. As she passed Luke, she slapped his wrist sharply, narrowing her eyes. Surprised, He blinked, quickly setting the dried bundle back on its hook. I shot him a look that clearly said *don't touch anything.* He only shrugged, his shirt bunching over his shoulders, emphasizing his broad frame.

Manika pulled a worn-out brown book from the shelf, flipping through the pages with practiced ease before stopping at a specific entry. "Whistler herbs," she repeated, placing the book on the table in front of us. Luke leaned forward, resting his palms on the table as he studied the ink-drawn picture. I stepped beside him, both of us scanning the details on the page, our minds already working on the next step.

The plant didn't appear too intricate—long, thin leaves spiraled into a tight corkscrew, stretching toward the edges of the page in delicate strokes, almost as if they were swaying in a breeze. The text scrawled across the page was written in an unfamiliar language, the letters forming small, elaborate curls. Though I couldn't read the details, one section stood out in bold, clearly more important than the rest. "What does this say?" I asked, tapping my finger lightly over the bold words. Manika leaned in, her eyes scanning the text before speaking, "It says *Caution: Imitation Herb—The Rambler.*"

I looked up at her, my eyes narrowing. "Imitation herb?" I repeated, my tone laced with suspicion. "The Rambler," she said again, this time with a hint of exasperation, "It's a look-alike herb, but it has toxic effects instead of healing." She traced the outline of the plant on the page with her finger. "If you pluck a leaf from its base, you can tell the difference—green is the whistler, red is the rambler. It's only toxic if ingested, but you'll need to be careful." Ragnai leaned over the table, his face shadowed with concern. "I have warriors on patrol near Mount Akasari. They've reported Nephrian sightings in the area."

The room suddenly felt colder. My gaze snapped to Luke, who nodded, his expression unreadable. "How many?" he asked. "So far, four," Ragnai answered. The two men stared at each other across the table momentarily, a silent exchange passing between them before Luke turned to me, "Then we shouldn't waste time."

"Where are these whistlers?" I asked, watching Manika as her eyes darted between the three of us. "They grow near the hot springs at the peak of Mount Akasari," she said, closing the book curtly and placing it back on the shelf. "How far of a trek is that?" I pressed, feeling the weight of time pressing down on us. The Nephrian sightings, the investigation, Odina's condition—every second mattered.

"It should take a day to hike up, and a day to hike down." she answered. "But it is quite a trek. I hope you are both prepared for some climbing. I will prepare a pack for each of you." She bowed slightly, then disappeared into the back room to gather supplies. Ragnai straightened, his expression unreadable as he gestured for us to follow him. "Give her time to prepare," he said. "Aurelios is setting on the surface. You should rest here for the night and head out at first light." Luke and I exchanged glances before nodding in agreement, following Ragnai out of the healing den and back up the winding stairs.

Exhaustion pressed down on me, and I realized my body did indeed need rest. The day had been relentless, and every muscle in me ached from the strain. We followed Ragnai down the hall until he stopped at a room lined with several bunks. The space was narrow but stretched deep, the wooden beds tucked neatly against the walls. Dim light from the city filtered through several small windows, casting shifting shadows against the dark walls. Each bed was made with dark blue woven blankets, tightly tucked over firm mattresses and small pillows wrapped in pale blue sheets.

"These are for our warriors during training," Ragnai said quietly. "They haven't been used in months; most of the ones left alive are above, currently patrolling the surface." He paused at the doorway, glancing back at us. "I will return in a few hours to escort you to the surface. Rest." With that, he slipped through the door, letting it click softly closed behind him.

I lay down on the bottom bunk, staring at the wooden slats above me. The dim light from the window cast shifting patterns on the ceiling, but my mind was too restless to appreciate the stillness. Luke settled onto the bed beside mine, moving slowly, his posture stiff as he turned to look at me. "We will find them," he said, his voice firm but quiet. "What if it's too late?" I murmured, closing my eyes. A dull ache had started to form at the base of my skull, and I pinched the bridge of my nose, trying to ease the pressure.

"It's our only option. It's *their* only option. If we don't at least try to get the herbs, this could be the Gaythes' death sentence—the end of their entire species." Luke exhaled, his voice measured. "And she's the only one who can tell us who Amy's father is," I muttered, and Luke leaned forward, resting his elbows on his knees. His gaze was steady on me. "We'll travel up to the hot springs, get the herbs, and return as quickly as possible." His voice was calm and deliberate as if saying it aloud made it so.

I sighed, my fingers tracing the fabric of the blanket beneath me. "Odina will know what to do," I whispered. Silence settled between us, thick with the weight of unspoken thoughts. My mind buzzed with questions I hadn't yet dared to ask him. "What do you know of Element X?" I asked, feeling him go still beside me. I didn't dare open my eyes, letting the question linger. "It's one hell of a resource," he muttered under his breath, but I heard the apprehension in his voice. "What else?" I asked. Silence stretched between us, broken only by the faint creak of the mattress as he leaned forward. "I know it holds enough power to start a *war*," he said, his voice dropping lower.

I finally opened my eyes to look at him.

"What power?" I whispered. His gaze moved to the pendant pressing against his shirt. Slowly, he pulled it free from under the collar, and my eyes widened at the sight. The stone was pitch-black. "Have you ever seen Element X?" he asked, watching my reaction. I shook my head, staring at it. Before the precinct ball I hadn't even heard of it, let alone seen the material. Something about it felt alive—like it was calling to me. "Adam handed this to me at the precinct ball," he explained, letting the pendant dangle in the space between us. I sat up, swinging my legs over the edge of the bed just as he did. "*That's* what he handed you?" I asked, my brows shooting up. He nodded, tilting his head slightly. "*This* is Element X." He shook the pendant a little, and a voice seemed to hum in my ear.

Touch me.

My eyes widened, and I leaned back slightly—maybe I'd imagined it. "Just this small stone is enough to power an entire *city*," Luke said, his eyes wild and glowing. "Can you imagine the power if thousands of tons are mined?" He shook his head again. "Where did Adam get this pendant?" I asked as I heard the stone humming once more. I tried to ignore it, keeping my focus on Luke. "Amy was wearing it when she was killed," he said evenly.

I sprang up from the bed, nearly smacking my head on the bunk above. "You're telling me you've been wearing evidence this whole time?" I hissed, pacing the length of the bunk room. My footsteps echoed off the walls as anger rose in my throat. Luke stayed where he was. "He gave it to me knowing I'd keep it hidden."

I spun on my heel to glare at him. "Oh, that makes it even better," I seethed. "One of my suspects casually hands you evidence, and you kept this hidden from me?" My fists balled at my sides. "I told you his father is framing him," Luke said, standing abruptly. "He found it in his father's study and recognized it because he saw her wearing it the day she died."

My face went pale. I stood there, arms hanging limply. "Why was she wearing it, and why did Danny have it in his study?" I asked quietly. Luke took a deep breath and began pacing while I remained still. "I think it comes from here—Maybe it's a Gaythe pendant. I think she brought it as a bargaining chip." His words tumbled out as he crossed the room back and forth. "A bargaining chip for what?" I asked, my brows furrowing. "That, I don't know yet." He said with a curious lilt. I blinked, my thoughts racing. If that pendant indeed came from here, it meant there was Element X somewhere on this planet—and if it genuinely harnessed that much power, it was exceedingly dangerous.

"How is the energy harnessed from the stone?" I asked. Luke turned to me. "I'm not sure. I haven't figured that part out yet." He lifted the pendant again, letting it dangle in front of him. The voice reached me again, and I felt the blood drain from my face. "Do you hear that?" I whispered. He seemed confused. "Hear what?" He asked. "The voice." I swallowed hard. "No," he said, his gaze flicking from the pendant to me. "You hear a voice?" I nodded, unable to tear my eyes away from the stone. "This stone *is* the war," I said, swallowing hard as I stared at it, feeling its pull. I leaned in for a closer look and realized it wasn't completely black—there were subtle, iridescent swirls beneath the surface. Luke tilted his head, watching me carefully.

Hesitantly, I lifted my hand and heard a faint whisper, "*Touch me*," a hazy female voice murmured in my ear. I bit my lip, my eyes flicking to Luke, who observed me with a hardened expression. "What happens when you touch it?" I asked quietly. "Nothing," he answered, his voice measured. "It's just a stone until some kind of conduit draws out its power."

I extended my fingers toward the stone. It seemed to lift into the air, drawn by some magnetic pull toward my hand. My heart pounded as it moved closer to my fingertips. The space between us felt charged, a strange static that made me furrow my brows. Warmth spread from my fingers down my arm as the stone's energy seeped into my skin. "It's warm," I murmured. Luke frowned. "Warm? It's never felt warm to me." He watched intently while I inched my hand closer. The heat intensified until it became uncomfortable, spreading across my ribs and down my torso as my heart hammered in my chest.

Suddenly, a sharp crack shattered the silence, and a jolt of electricity hurled me across the room. My back slammed against the door, pain searing up my spine. My head spun, and I reached for anything to steady myself. "Shit," Luke's voice rang through the haze. There was a shuffle of movement before I felt him touch my shoulder. "You alright?" he asked, helping me to my feet. His hand felt electrified against my skin.

"What was *that*?" I hissed, leaning against him despite the spark singing my skin at the contact. "It seems you have an innate affinity for the stone—or it has one for you," he said, keeping me upright. "What does that even mean?" I snapped, eyes clenched shut as the ringing in my ears gradually subsided. "I don't know," Luke admitted. "It's never happened before with me. It seems to discharge when we touch, though. It must be grounding itself to you through me."

I blinked hard, the two dizzy images of Luke merging into one. "In English," I muttered, waving my hand for him to cut to the point. "The stone holds power. When you touch it, that power directs itself into you," he explained, and I remembered the electric jolt I'd felt at the precinct ball. It must have been the pendant. "Keep that thing away from me," I hissed, stepping back. "We don't know what kind of effect it could have. It doesn't seem to affect you, so stay over there." I motioned for him to back away, but Luke's gaze only darkened as he looked at me.

"What?" I hissed, struggling to straighten my aching spine as I leaned against the door. His lips parted with a sharp intake of breath. "What are you staring at, Luke?" I demanded, then I felt it—a different sort of electricity. An undeniable pull toward *him*. My pulse quickened as we watched each other in silence. A sudden warmth crept up my neck as he took a single step forward, our faces only inches apart. Confusion flickered in his gaze as though he couldn't quite understand what drew him to me.

"What are you doing?" I whispered, fighting the urge to close the distance. A powerful force within me ached to touch him, to feel his skin against mine. My heart thundered in my chest, but Luke remained silent. He lifted his hand, pinching my chin between his thumb and forefinger. Heat flared where his skin met mine, and a small gasp escaped my lips—just before his covered mine.

A searing jolt surged through my body, every nerve alight. His mouth was hot and charged, as he used his grip on my chin to pull me away from the door. I grasped for anything solid, but I was held firmly against him. A fierce fire ignited deep in my gut, and I struggled to extinguish it. I wouldn't let my reaction bind me to him. I couldn't breathe, couldn't run. He was in control. My heart beat faster than hummingbird wings until, as suddenly as he'd seized me, he wrenched himself backward, leaving me windmilling my arms to stay upright.

"I'm sorry," he whispered, licking his lips. His hands trembled slightly, and I blinked, pressing my palm against my racing heart. "I'm so sorry. I don't know what—" His voice broke off, his gaze flicking to mine as he tried to steady his breathing. We stared at each other for what felt like minutes before he cleared his throat and lied back down on his bunk. "We should get some sleep," he said quietly. "We have a long hike tomorrow." Then he turned to face the wall, offering no further explanation.

I remained at the door until my skin cooled and the lingering heat faded. Minutes. I stood there for minutes waiting for the tingling to reside. Finally, I returned to my bed, fingers still shaking as I pulled the covers over me. That wasn't supposed to happen. The moment replayed over and over in my mind as I brushed my thumb across my swollen lower lip. I had never felt a jolt like that from a kiss before. Eventually, the static under my skin settled, and my pulse slowed. Drowsiness washed over me my body growing heavy against the mattress and I reluctantly let sleep take me, slowly drifting into my dreams.

Chapter 19

I woke the next morning just as tired as I had been the night before—or at least what I guessed was morning since the city looked no different than it usually did. Rolling over in my bunk, the mattress sagged beneath me as I spotted Luke already up and dressed in his usual T-shirt and black cargo pants. I scrubbed the sleep from my eyes with a rough hand.

"You're awake." He muttered tossing me my bag from off the floor. It landed roughly on top of the blanket I was still tucked beneath. I blinked again as I sat all the way up my head nearly bumping the bed above mine. "Ragnai stopped by earlier before you were awake. He mentioned a briefing with Manika before our departure and handed me a map." He said casually as he stood to gather his other things. Reluctantly I groaned but eased myself out of bed. I lifted my arms in a long stretch, a yawn escaping my lips as I suddenly realized I needed to change, "Where am I supposed to—"

Luke pointed toward a doorway at the far end of the room that led to the bathroom. "Thanks," I muttered, grabbing my spare clothes from my bag and trudging in. I changed into a black tank top and a pair of hiking pants, tucking the hem into my boots before lacing them tightly. Running my fingers through my tangled hair, I gathered it into a braided bun at the nape of my neck. True to stubborn redhead fashion, a few wisps had already escaped to frame my face, and though I sighed in frustration, I let them be. When I stepped back into the bunk room, Luke was holding out a heavy jacket. I took it, brows drawing together. "What are these for?"

"Ragnai brought them for once we reach the mountain's peak. He warned me that the weather changes quickly at high altitudes, and we'd freeze to death without proper layers." He responded. "Oh." I said quietly.

I lifted the heavy coat Luke had handed me studying it. It was a deep navy, lined with plush insulation so thick it barely flexed in my hands. The moment I slid it on, sweat prickled at my skin. The cuffs met my wrists, leaving my hands exposed, while the high collar brushed my jawline. I tied the front laces closed, feeling the soft, almost suede-like fabric beneath my fingers. Then I stepped into the matching thick pants, tucking them into my boots—no room for cold air to creep in. I looked like a walking snowman.

"These should keep us warm once we hit the peak of Mount Akasari," Luke said, his voice cutting through the quiet and making me jump slightly. I turned to see him shrug out of a matching green coat, rolling his shoulders before folding it neatly into his pack. "Hopefully. Freezing to death doesn't sound appealing," I muttered, and silence settled between us once more.

The thin fabric of his shirt clung to the defined lines of his broad shoulders, while the grip of his pistol jutted from his waistband, lifting the hem just enough to expose the deep V of his solid abdominal muscles. My eyes traced the lines lazily. The metal of his pistol glinted sharply in the light, a stark contrast against his skin, and the sudden flash snapped me out of it—I'd been staring again. *Damn it.*

I turned away quickly, biting my lip, hoping he hadn't noticed. He didn't seem to—just continued lacing up his boots, lost in thought. How was it so easy for him to ignore what had happened last night? I clenched my jaw, shoving the insulated clothes into my pack. Nothing, I was nothing and no on to him I reminded myself as I grabbed my pistol and slid it into the front of my waistband. It clicked into it's holster and sat snug against my abs, the grip just above my navel. Secure.

A knock at the door made us both look up. Ragnai leaned against the frame, scanning us both. "Humans," he greeted us. I slid my pack over my shoulders, testing its weight. Manageable, though I doubted I'd feel the same after hauling it up a mountain. "Come with me." He said turning and retreating down the hallway. Luke swung his over his shoulder and followed Ragnai out the door and with a deep sigh, I too, fell in line.

As we walked through the halls, I paused, looking for anything that might tell me more about the Gaythe. Their history, their *people*. My gaze snagged on a pair of daggers displayed on the wall. They shimmered and I stepped closer, drawn to them. The hilts were wrapped in worn black leather, the grips polished from years of handling. But the blades—jet black, sleek, and ominous—glowing with an iridescence along their edges drew me in, almost like the scales of the Gaythe themselves.

"They are hers," Ragnai said, and I jumped, suddenly realizing I had fallen behind. Luke and Ragnai had turned back to retrieve me. "The blades?" I asked. "Yes." Ragnai nodded. He lifted them from the hooks, thumbing the sharp edge. I hesitated, "Whose scales are those?" His yellow eyes met mine. "Hers. She pulled them off herself." Shock rolled through me. *Odina*. She had ripped her scales from her body to forge these blades. The Gaythe had long been poached for their scales, their natural armor stronger than any metal. But this—this was different. This was sacrifice.

"She made these as a gift for her mate," Ragnai continued.

"But he was killed in battle before she could give them to him."
I swallowed hard. "Or so she says," He concluded. "Why would
she tear off her scales for him?"

"Because no blade was sharp enough. No metal would be
good enough for him." His voice was quiet, reverent. I stared
at the daggers in his hands, feeling the weight of that statement
settle over me like a stone. He continued, "Gaythe scales are the
sharpest material known to exist. That's why humans hunted us
for armor." He turned the daggers in his palms. "These were an
indescribable gift—one she never got to give." A knot formed in
my stomach, "He was killed in battle?"

"That's what she told me."

It didn't make sense. If Odina had a mate—another Gaythe
himself— if she had loved him enough to endure such pain for
these weapons, then how did Amy exist? Gaythe only ever took
one mate for life. The timelines didn't add up.

"They're worn on the grips like they've been used for years," I
murmured, eyeing the faded leather. "She uses them. They are
the only weapons she carries." Ragnai turned toward me, his
towering frame imposing, "Have you ever wielded a blade?" I
opened my mouth, probably to say something bureaucratic, but
Luke beat me to it, "It's forbidden for officers to carry one. She's
one hell of a shot with a pistol though."

I glared eye daggers at him before returning my gaze to
Ragnai. He scowled, upturning his lips over his fangs, "You
humans and your nonsensical laws." He shook his head,
muttering something under his breath before lifting the daggers
toward me, "She would choose you to carry these. To keep
you safe on your journey." I blinked, stunned, "Me?" He nodded
solemnly, "Honor these, and they will honor you."

Slowly, I reached out and took the daggers from
his outstretched hands. The weight was perfect—balanced,

precise. The iridescent edges glowed as I turned them over, careful not to cut myself. Sliding them into the pockets of my pants, I dipped my head in silent thanks. Ragnai returned the gesture, then turned and continued down the hall. I followed, my fingers brushing the hilts of the new blades. They rested snug against my leg, concealed by my jeans but close enough to reach in an instant. As my stomach growled, I realized I had another reason to hurry to the briefing. Hopefully, it involved breakfast.

Chapter 20

We walked past the edge of the city escorted by Ragnai and another Gaythe warrior. My pack pressed roughly into my shoulders and as we drew closer to the shield, a slow, aching tension coiled in my chest—part fear, part hope, and something unnamed that tightened with every step.

"It will get better with time," Ragnai said, his head tilting towards me reading my body language. I rolled my shoulders and willed the tension to spool out of my body. They sank a fraction of a millimeter and I forced a small smile on my face with the intention of reassuring him I was fine. He quirked an eyebrow up at me, but thankfully didn't press. Finally, our group reached the edge of the veil and stopped as the warriors waited instruction.

Ragnai turned to face me, "Ready?" He asked his pupils flickering in the ethereal city glow. I nodded, though I wasn't sure if the gesture was in response to him, or in attempts to reassure myself. The bag on my shoulders lifted slightly as his arms wrapped around me, and I felt my weight shift into him. My pulse thundered in my ears. I wanted to say something—anything—but the words stuck in my throat.

Before I could second-guess myself or speak my fears aloud, one of the other Gaythe warriors seized Luke, and in one smooth, seamless motion, the group shot skyward, slicing through the misty veil that clung to the city's edge. The invisible shield shimmered faintly in the city's ethereal glow, a wavering curtain of refracted light. It bent beneath us as we hit, stretching thin like pulled glass. For one heart-stopping second, I thought it might push us back—but then it gave with a silent ripple, and I sucked in a breath just as the wall of water swallowed us whole.

The world turned blue. I clenched my jaw as the cold hit me, shocking and sharp. My thoughts were scattered as the surface of the city disappeared beneath us, replaced by rushing darkness between shafts of light. We were moving fast—too fast—and I fought the urge to struggle, to push away from the crushing pressure around me. Then, just as quickly, the water began to warm—unnaturally so. I couldn't tell if it was comforting or suffocating. My lungs screamed for air, my vision starting to fuzz at the edges. I needed to hold on. Just a little longer. I had done harder things than this.

Ragnai's grip tightened as his body tensed, every muscle working with focused precision. His feet kicked in sharp bursts, propelling us forward like a living engine. I couldn't see where we were going—only the blurry movement of water around us and the ache in my chest that grew with every second. Then we broke the surface. The world exploded into light and the sounds of the Gayle jungle filtered down to us.

I choked and gasped, air tearing into my lungs like fire. I held it together, chest heaving, and for a moment I just existed—floating, breathing, alive. Ragnai spread himself flat against the water, scanning the horizon. The water around us shimmered under a pale sky streaked with pink and silver clouds indicating dawn. Everything felt too wide, too quiet, despite the jungle sounds. Like we'd stepped into a world we weren't meant to be in.

Luke and his escort burst through the surface, their arc graceful, practiced. He emerged with the kind of ease that irritated me. I watched him breathe—calm, measured—and rolled my eyes, unable to help the quiet scoff that slipped into my mind. Of course he looks composed. He always did. Even now. But beneath that flicker of annoyance, something deeper twisted in my chest—uncertainty, *desire*. I squandered the thought just as quickly as it rose.

Ragnai waved his hands, signaling us to stay low, and we obeyed without a word, eyes scanning the surroundings. We had resurfaced through the same crater we'd used to enter the water the day before—the soil wall towering over twenty feet high, its rim seeming to rise and fall with the waves. With another silent gesture, Ragnai directed us toward the shore, and we swam to the edge, hauling ourselves out, remarkably dry despite having crossed the sea floor. Manika's spell had shielded us from the water entirely, leaving only the damp heat of sweat pooling at the small of my back as we adjusted our packs.

"Listen, humans," Ragnai said, seemingly convinced there was no immediate threat. "Head north along the tree line. There's a cove outlet at the base of the mountain. Once you find it, follow the marked trail that ascends to the peak, where you'll find the herbs. Move swiftly—and never let your guard down." He warned. "Good luck."

I opened my mouth to ask a clarifying question, but before I could speak, both of the Gaythe men slipped beneath the surface, vanishing into the water without a sound—not even a splash or ripple. I blinked, my question still hanging uselessly on the tip of my tongue. The moment felt abruptly colder, the stillness around us heavy and strange. I was still staring at the spot where they had disappeared when quiet footsteps to my left drew my attention. Luke was already moving, eyes scanning the steep, curved walls of the crater that cradled the hidden pool. His expression was unreadable, focused. Like this was just another day for him. I took a breath and looked around. The water lapped gently at the rocky edges of the basin, deceptively calm. No clear paths. No ropes. No handholds. Just soil and water and sky.

"Do you see anything?" I asked, my voice came out quieter than I intended. Luke didn't respond at first. His brow furrowed as he turned in a slow circle, scanning every contour of the crater. I followed his gaze, heart thudding. We were alone again—truly alone this time—in the unknown Gayle jungle and I couldn't help but wonder if this was a mistake.

"What do you think they meant by 'never let your guard down'?" I asked, pointing to a dirt tunnel to our right—roughly ten feet in diameter—that appeared to lead upward. "It means they've been at war with the Nephrians for several years—and it seems they're not winning. It's the same warning he gave us last night about the Nephrian sightings," Luke replied as we moved toward the entrance.

"I'm not worried about the Nephrians right now. I'm more concerned about the stone dangling from your neck." I didn't look at him, but I could feel his gaze on my back. "You should be worried about *both*," he retorted.

I gritted my teeth holding back from firing my instinctual response to tell him to go fuck himself and rested my hand against the soil—it held firm—and peered into the tunnel. Though shrouded in shadows, a distant light beckoned from beyond the crater. My fingers dug into the dirt as we crawled upward. The passage was damp as if it had just rained, with water occasionally dripping from above.

We emerged and stood upright, taking in our surroundings. The sound of waves from the sea drifted in from far to our left. "We head this way toward the tree line," I instructed, pointing to the sound. Allowing my feet to guide me, we began our journey.

For several long minutes, the only sounds were the soft rustle of our packs against the foliage and the crunch of our feet on the ground.

"You know they are inevitably going to come for us," Luke broke the silence. Alright, I'll bite. "Who?" I asked without looking up, too focused on not tripping over the enormous vines sprawled across the jungle floor. "The Nephrians," he replied. Their name sent chills down my spine, but I remained silent. He was right and we both knew that if the Nephrians claimed Gayle as they hoped, it would only be a matter of time before they boldly attempted to seize Liarta.

In comparison, Gayle was much smaller than their home planet, Veneu—roughly half the size—which meant that once their numbers recovered, expansion would be inevitable. I chewed my lower lip, knowing their fate would be sealed by victory or death—and I hoped it wouldn't be the latter. Yet the idea of wiping out an entire species, no matter how aggressive, did not sit well with me.

"I know, but where does that leave us?" I asked, using my arm to brace against a tree as I hopped over a fallen log. The log lay split in two as if it had been forcefully shoved aside in anger. "It's kill or be killed," he responded, effortlessly stepping over it. "Are you really okay with wiping out an entire species?" I asked, raising my eyebrows.

He paused, searching for the right words. "If it means saving the remaining ones, I have to be." he said. He wasn't wrong again—and that made my frustration grow. They would stop at nothing to seize complete power, annihilating anyone who dared stand in their way. The only check was that they hadn't yet amassed the numbers for large-scale damage—until now when no one suspected they had been secretly mass breeding to boost their forces into an undeniable threat.

"If we exterminate them completely, does that not make us just as abysmal as they are?" I asked, hoping he'd offer a reasonable response. "Probably," he replied, not countering my theoretical question. "But are you willing to risk several other species on the morality of not killing one?"

I opened my mouth again but I had no solid answer. I snapped it closed. Both sides tugged at me. I understood what it would take to save a larger number of people, yet I wasn't sure I could ever accept—or live with—that decision. "You don't have to like it," he said, as if reading my mind. "You just have to accept that it is how it must be—for the greater good."

I stopped in my tracks. "For the greater *good*?" I echoed just as he bumped the back of my pack. His eyes met mine when I turned around. "You sound like you're playing a god. You cannot possibly think that murdering an entire species is good," I countered, my voice laced with distaste. Unfazed, he replied, "I didn't say it was good, but it is necessary. For the better outcome. We don't get the luxury of being a god, of seeing and knowing all the different outcomes of every weighted decision. We can only make decisions based on the information given to us at the time."

I searched his face for any trace of emotion but found none. "The only other outcome is the death of *everyone*," he continued, his jaw set firmly. "And if you knew what I know, you wouldn't prefer that alternative." He brushed past me, bumping my shoulder. I ground my teeth and turned on my heel to follow him, seething. The death of anyone was never acceptable.

"So, what do you suggest? A mass killing spree of all the Nephrians?" I demanded, my voice rising as frustration took hold. He stopped and turned to face me. Grasping my shoulders firmly, he leaned in close. I tilted my head back, pressing my lips into a thin line.

"War is inevitable," he hissed. "They will come for us, and if you do not fight back, they will murder anyone and *everyone*. Men, women, and *children*. And not just the Gaythe, they're just the start. Their widespread destruction will not end with them, no it will continue until it reaches the humans." He paused, his breath washing over my face. "Things are far more complicated than you can imagine. You can't even begin to understand the complexities unfolding around us." My heart raced at his proximity, and the charged air between us crackled like static electricity.

"The human government on Liarta won the war against the Nephrians years ago. What is going on that I'm not aware of? What do you know of them that I don't?" I asked, watching as his expression shifted from irritation to a sudden awareness of the space between us—or the lack thereof.

We both froze, unable to move. I sucked in my bottom lip, struggling to breathe. His eyes drifted down to my face, focusing on my lip as I nervously chewed it. My arms burned from the contact with his fingers before he released one hand, gently taking my chin between his thumb and forefinger. He tugged my bottom lip, dragging it from side to side with a deliberate touch. Hot, my skin felt unbearably hot beneath his finger. His breathing was shallow and forced, as though he struggled to maintain control. I closed my eyes, blocking him out and inhaling a deep breath. His scent surrounded me—eucalyptus and sandalwood.

A sharp pop broke the tension, and we both jumped, instinctively looking to the sky. A bright light streaked across the blue expanse, disappearing over the horizon. "What was *that*?" I asked, breathless, as he let go of me. We both watched the streaking light above us. "Let's go," he said quickly, spinning on his heels and jogging away. I finally forced air into my lungs, cursing under my breath as I willed my legs to move. "Luke?" I called after him, but the brush around us was too thick, and I couldn't see him. He didn't answer. "Luke!" I shouted again, pushing myself harder to catch up.

I burst through the tree line, swatting leaves from my face. Ahead, he stood on the amethyst sand, one hand shielding his eyes as he gazed into the distance where the streak of light had vanished—though nothing else was visible. "Let's go," he said briskly, clipping a pace that made me blink as he strode past me toward the far end of the beach. I didn't bother to respond, my irritation still simmering from our argument.

Aurelios was now high overhead as we followed the same stretch of beach where we had been abducted by Ragnai and taken to Kehel just the day before. Aurelios' location promised most of the afternoon still ahead—a small mercy, as we were at least making decent time. However, a full day's journey meant we would have to camp at the mountain peak before descending tomorrow morning. I sighed. It felt as if we were racing against time.

After an hour of trudging through the sand, we finally reached the cove at the mountain's base. Aurelios had crested past its zenith, so we paused for a water break and to shake the sand from our boots.

I dropped my pack onto a rock with a heavy thud and sat down to unlace my shoes. Our shirts stuck to us, damp with sweat but at least keeping us cool. The boots, though—those traitors—were clearly not designed for sand. Every step felt like I was dragging half the desert with me. I finally gave in, pulled one off, and watched a small avalanche of sand pour out like it had been storing it for winter.

Luke, sitting across from me, did the same. "I'm doomed to have sand in these forever," I complained, peeling off the other boot to empty it. "Just a reminder we were here once we leave this planet," he quipped as he emptied his own. Yanking my shoe back on, I took a long swig from my flask. "You think we're going to make it off this planet?" I asked, watching his reaction carefully. He shrugged, his shirt bunching and then stretching back out. "I sure hope so—I'd like to go home," he replied, leaning back against the rock with a heavy sigh. "Liarta isn't even your home," the words tumbled out before I could filter them. He blinked a few times, his gaze fixed on me, "It's a home of sorts,"

I looked down at my feet as I slid my boots back on, lost for further words. He sat in silence, his eyes dazzling a mesmerizing blue. A stray curl puckered on his forehead, which he casually brushed aside, and with that gesture came the familiar electric tension. "You haven't been honest about anything," I said irritated as I lifted my eyes to him again. "If you listen carefully, I am being honest, just *selective*," he replied, narrowing his eyes in my direction.

"What, your weirdly worded, cryptic messages?" I retorted, my arms flailing in frustration. He merely nodded as he shoved his feet back in his boots. "You're wearing a stone that could single-handedly spark a mass war, given to you by someone I don't fully trust, and you want me to blindly follow your lead, ignoring all the evidence stacked against you?" I scoffed, noting the detached, emotionless set of his expression.

"I'm not going to start a war. I'm trying to *stop* one," he said, inclining his chin toward me and I couldn't help but roll my eyes. "I don't even know what that means," I said, hefting my pack back on as I stood and walked toward the marked base of the trail promptly ending the conversation. I heard the rustle of his pack and his footsteps trailing behind me, but I didn't look back—anger fueling my confidence.

Blue swirls adorned the rock face that formed the jagged stairs. Although some chunks were missing, the structure mainly appeared intact. "Ragnai said they weren't sure about the condition of the entire trail, but hopefully, most of it is accessible," Luke called behind me. I stared up the stairs; off in the distance, the stone steps faded into a misty fog that, if not for our safety concerns, might have seemed enchanted. "This way," I said, and together we hoisted ourselves up the steps.

Chapter 21

After two hours of climbing, Aurelios began to dip behind the rocky cliffs, and we reached the point where the weather noticeably shifted. We paused to change into our winter gear before continuing the ascent. The jacket and pants I wore were mercifully warm, and I found myself thankful the Gaythe had supplied us with proper clothing—our own wouldn't have stood a chance. The lined cuffs brushed against my wrists as I curled my hands into fists inside my pockets for warmth, and our hoods fit snugly around our heads, trapping heat while still leaving our faces exposed.

For most of the past few hours, the only sounds were our puffs of warm breath billowing into the cold air as we pressed on. I clambered up a rock clumsily, nearly losing my footing when Luke reached out to catch me. I yanked my arm away, and the hurt on his face made me falter, but not give in. We continued on, the trek growing increasingly complex. The rocks that had once formed relatively easy steps now became boulders to scale. I sensed we were close as even the air felt thinner. After hours of silence he spoke first.

"Turn around," Luke said sharply. I turned and gasped. I had been so focused on not falling that I hadn't noticed we had finally emerged above the clouds. Foamy white puffs dotted the skyline, Aurelios gleaming off them like mirrors. The quiet was eerie—every sound was swallowed by the vast, low-hanging clouds. Few flora and fauna could survive at this altitude; only a handful of silver, spiky plants clung to the rocks. It was no wonder why the Gaythe chose such a reclusive place for their birth rituals. As Aurelios began to set behind the clouds painting the sky in deep oranges and yellows, it seemed almost enchanted. As if the very air itself shimmered with magic.

My pack rustled as I shifted to take in the view. Luke lowered his hood, revealing a crown of brown curls, and blew a low whistle. "Incredible," he murmured, voicing what I had been thinking. We stood there for several heartbeats before I broke the silence. "Soon, we'll be in the dark," I said, lowering my hood. The wind chilled the tops of my ears and my nose scrunched against its bite.

"We should keep moving," he said, taking one last look at the horizon before following me. I pointed toward the ruined remains of what once served as their birthing temple. "Let's camp there tonight." The rocks crunched under our feet as we walked. "Something doesn't sit right with me," Luke remarked. "The Nephrians are the ones who took out that temple. They might still be in the area."

"Well, we're so high up that we'd probably see anyone coming, and I just happen to be with a man who knows how to *wield* Element X. So, I think we're alright," I gestured expansively, my tone dripping with sass. "I can't wield it and even if I could that doesn't mean we're protected. We don't even know what it's capable of." he countered, his face tense as he scanned our surroundings—unconvinced by my bravado. "We should get to the temple and set up camp for the night—the hot springs should be nearby." He led the way but I looked up longingly at the sky.

It was finally fading into a deep navy blue, the stars beginning to twinkle in the distance. Yet the planet I saw was Liarta, my home, patiently mirroring the light of our star, Aurelios. Its greens and blues swirled together in perfect harmony. I closed my eyes for a deep breath, then opened them again as I hurried to catch up to him.

After another thirty minutes of walking and we stood before the birthing temple—or rather, what remained of it. Chunks of once-intricate brown stone pillars lay scattered haphazardly, and the stone roof was shattered into three pieces, smashed atop the debris. "My goodness," I breathed. "They leveled the place."

We glanced around, searching for a safe spot to set up camp for the night. "And left no survivors except Odina," he added in a ghostly tone. I shivered at the thought of her being alone up here in that state. Luke dropped his pack in a corner formed by the scattered pillars and a fragment of what looked like a wall. I slid mine off my shoulders, the ache of carrying the heavy bag for hours settling into my bones.

Rubbing my thumb against my shoulder, I winced as it pressed into the mark left by the straps. "Help me unroll these sleeping bags," Luke said, handing me a bundle of fabric. I unrolled it, shook it out, and turned to him. "Do you think we're actually safe here for the night?" I spread the sleeping bag neatly across the ground, tucking it securely into the corner. "We should be, but I'm not lighting a fire—just in case," he replied. I chewed on the inside of my cheek and looked around.

The peak of the mountain was dead silent; we hadn't seen a single sign of life for hours, and as darkness fell, the quiet only deepened. I moved over to sit on a piece of fallen building debris that served as a makeshift seat. Luke busied himself retrieving our packed dinner. Even through his thick jacket, I could see his biceps curl as he moved. I tried to ignore the inexplicable pull I felt toward him—I willed it away.

"Here, this is what Manika packed us for dinner," he said, handing me the container. I accepted it without a word. The lid popped off easily, and I felt its warmth in my fingers. Somehow, she had managed to pack it so that the food remained warm after our long day's hike. I was grateful, as it smelled delicious—flaky fish resting atop a bed of fried rice. A hum of contentment rose in my chest as I took a bite.

Luke leaned against a pillar that still stood across from me, quietly eating his food. The wind nipped at our necks, nearly drowning out the scraping of our forks against the containers. He chewed slowly, his eyes fixed on me. "What?" I asked, feeling his gaze bore into me. "Nothing," he replied, though his eyes never left mine as he finished his meal. The pull was so strong—was it toward him or the stone? I wasn't sure anymore.

"If this Element X has enough power to start a war, do you think it could have enough power to *end* one if placed in the right hands?" I asked chewing the last bite of my dinner and setting aside it aside. He cocked his head to the side in contemplation as if he hadn't thought of that before. "Maybe in the right hands—but those would be rare and exceptional," he said quietly. "It would have to be in the hands of someone selfless enough to want to end the war for everyone, not just win it." his voice was even toned. I nodded. His eyes searched me as he took a deep breath, and my pulse quickened at the sight of him taking me in. I wondered what he was thinking. He pulled himself off the pillar and stepped toward me. "Sometimes there's a pull for me," he said softly, gazing at me. "It's much stronger up here on this mountain."

"A pull?" I asked, my voice thinner than I intended. So he had felt it too. He nodded once, almost reluctantly. "Towards what?" I pressed, though part of me wasn't sure I wanted the answer. He shook his head, a small, frustrated gesture, and took a step closer. I slid off the stone I'd been sitting on, but before I could move away, he closed the space between us. His fingers wrapped around my arm, firm but not rough, holding me there. His touch sent a jolt up my spine—whether from fear, anticipation, or something else entirely, I couldn't tell.

His eyes burned into mine, fierce and searching. My breath caught. Then, slowly, he lifted his hands to my face. I froze, torn between stepping back and leaning in. He inched closer, until there was barely a sliver of space between us. Our breaths tangled, warm against the cold air, and the world around us seemed to shrink to nothing but this moment. I leaned into his palms without thinking, desperate for the comfort of his warmth—and hating how much I needed it. A part of me whispered to pull away, to ask what we were doing, but I stayed there, suspended between the ache of wanting and the fear of what it might mean. "Luke?" I whispered, "A pull to—?"

Before I could finish, I felt his lips on mine, and a fire spread from my gut to my toes. My hands reached up, fumbling through his curly hair as he pressed me against the wall. His fingers trailed past my earlobe, tangling in the loosened bun at the nape of my neck. He kissed me with desperate need, our tongues wildly imploring each other. Tugging my hair gently, he pulled my head back and kissed along my jawline before returning to my face. His teeth scraped my bottom lip, and I moaned into his mouth. I wasn't sure if I ever wanted this to end—or if I did. Even now, he smelled delicious—of eucalyptus and sandalwood.

Then, as abruptly as he had drawn me in, he pulled back several feet, his eyes dark and shadowed. I took several deep breaths, placing a hand over my chest as I felt my heart pounding wildly beneath my puffy jacket. "This is a mistake," he said, his voice ragged as he panted for breath. He stood with his arms out as if afraid that even a touch might set him ablaze. "What part?" I asked incredulously, still catching my breath as I stepped toward him. He remained motionless. "I can't be with you." His words were clipped and cold. "What is that even supposed to mean?" I demanded, the heat in my chest fizzing like ice on a hot stove. Hurt flashed in his eyes—and almost panic—before his mask slid firmly over his face.

"I was told to protect you." His jaw twitched. I leveled my gaze with his. "What do you mean, protect me? Protect me from who?" I hissed, taking another step closer. He shook his head. "You do not want me, Pandora. When you find out—" He raised his hands, palms open in submission. "When I find out *what?*" I hissed.

His eyes widened, and though a small part of me regretted it, most of me felt nothing but burning disdain. "Pandora, I—" he began, but I cut him off by jabbing my finger into his chest. "Do not follow me." I stomped away, leaving Luke standing like a stone statue. I didn't look back as I kicked rocks angrily out of my path. The anger simmered beneath my skin, seeping into my bones. Only when he was out of sight did I lean forward against a rock, bracing myself as ragged breaths escaped my chest. I fought for control but lost, whipping my head back and screaming into the sky.

Chapter 22

My body felt heavy as I trudged the rest of the way to the hot springs. I was stuck atop a mountain with a man who was sending me mixed signals, who was claiming to protect me—but he wouldn't even say from whom. What a giant nightmare. I grunted to myself in frustration.

It was dark, and I held my hands out, searching for the path ahead. In my heated, angry departure, I had forgotten to grab anything to light my way. My lips were still puffy from his kiss and when I took a deep breath, I realized, I reeked of eucalyptus and sandalwood. How incredibly irritating. Even as I craved as much distance from him as possible at the mountain's peak, his scent clung to me. Still felt electric.

The gravel crunched under my feet as I continued toward the hot springs. I could smell the salt in the air, and the temperature gradually rose. Ahead, a thin veil of silver light shimmered through the rock formations. Clambering toward it, I kept my arms out for balance in the semi dark. Up here, even Gayle's gravitational pull felt different. I agreed with him—whatever it was, the pull from him and the stone was stronger at this altitude.

I fumbled awkwardly through the darkness until the hot springs came into view, revealed as I brushed past a pair of massive, shadowy boulders, their soft silver glow drawing me in. A thick fog clung to the springs, and the air grew noticeably warmer the closer I got. The rocks seemed to form a natural bowl, gently cradling the still water, its surface hazy with steam that curled into the air. The water itself glowed with a pale silver light, softly illuminating the small, hidden space.

I shrugged off my winter jacket, grateful that the peak breeze had died down somewhat behind the rock face—it crumpled into a pile at the base of one of the few trees high up on the mountain. Next, I tugged off my boots and glanced around. Luke was just back at the temple ruins, but I was still alone. With confirmed Nephrian sightings nearby, I needed to be extra careful not to be caught off guard. I set my boots beside my jacket and peeled off the rest of my clothes and weapons. Metal met stone with a muted clatter as I placed the blades and pistol on the ground. There I stood, naked in the near-darkness, illuminated only by the silvery glow of the water. I was secretly relieved that Luke hadn't followed me—I didn't need protection, especially not from him.

I dipped my toes into the milky water, feeling its warmth spread slowly up my leg. I swished my feet around, ensuring I wouldn't slip as I eased my body into the inviting pool. After such a long hike, it felt incredible. Tiny beads of steam clung to my hair as I waded deeper letting the water cleanse me. My thoughts raced the further out into the pool I went.

Nothing made sense. Why would Danny and my father want to mine Element X if it was as dangerous as Luke claimed? They wouldn't want that kind of heat smothering his campaign. And Ivy—she'd kill me if she knew I was getting involved with a detective like Luke. A tall, handsome, blue-eyed— I cringed at the thought, slapping my palm to my forehead. I was exceptionally screwed if I couldn't get him out of my head. What did he mean by *a pull?*

Swimming through the water, I found the edge of a rock to

sit against, submerging myself until I reached my collarbone, the heat welcoming the stinging sensation. I stretched my neck against the rock and gazed into the night sky, where stars blinked intermittently against a vast black backdrop. Why would someone be after me—to the point that a man I didn't know was instructed to protect me at all costs? I sat there for a long time, bathing in my own thoughts.

Eventually, my skin started to grow numb from the heat, and with that I decided it was best to dry off and return to camp. Gliding through the water, I reached the shore where I'd left my clothes. As I stepped into the colder air, it nipped at my reddened, puffy skin. I pulled my clothes back on one by one, forcing the shivering to subside. Reaching for the worn pistol and blades my gaze caught something across the glowing water and I froze in horror.

Across the pond stood a figure in a dark black robe. His shoulders seemed to rise off his body in sharp peaks, the fabric cascading like waterfalls of shadow. Although I had just been soaking in warm water, a cold shiver swept up my neck, and sweat began to form at its base. I didn't dare breathe. His black eyes locked onto mine, unblinking—cold, relentless. I knew exactly who he was. I'd seen him in the vision Manika shared with me back in the healer's den. But standing here, face to face, he was even more terrifying than he had been then

Brykan.

My heart pounded in my chest, urging me to move—to run—but I remained frozen, my feet cemented to the ground. He smiled, revealing razor-sharp teeth that gleamed like white needles. I wondered if the dark blood dripping from them was real or a figment of my imagination he willed me to see. His skin was ghostly, a colorless, waxy pallor that heightened my unease. My vision began to blur at the edges—was it his doing or merely the rush of adrenaline? His only movement was a subtle furrowing of his deep, shadowy hood, his bent nose tilting slightly as he watched me.

Without a sound, he glided across the pond toward me, his legs unmoving propelled by dark magic. Shadowy tendrils flowed from him, snaking along the ground at my feet, climbing up my legs and encircling my neck, binding me in place. I struggled against them, but they were as unyielding as wrought iron, completely immovable as he came within a foot of me. "*We meet*," he hissed, each word deliberate. His tongue slid through his teeth—long and sinuous, like that of a snake. I didn't respond. My eyes widened in shock as I realized he hadn't moved his mouth at all. His voice resonated within me, and paralyzing fear surged through my veins.

The tendrils lifted me off the ground, clasped around my neck like thick ropes. Even as I forced myself to breathe, the constriction made every gasp agonizingly difficult. "What do you want?" I managed to hiss, snapping my teeth in defiance. A tendril yanked the back of my hair, forcing my head back so I could see him more clearly. "*You have caused me quite the trouble*," he spat—though his words echoed only in my mind. I forced as much air into my lungs as possible and replied, "I have done nothing." My neck burned from the strain of speaking in such an unnatural position. "*Oh, but you will*," he said, his teeth clicking together as the sunken, black pits of his eyes narrowed on me. Looking into them, I saw nothing of my reflection—a void devouring any light in its wake. My feet dangled only an inch off the ground, yet the pressure of the noose-like tendrils was beginning to cut off my blood flow. Darkness crept into the edges of my vision.

"*I should kill you now*," he declared, his voice like radio static flooding my brain. "If you were going to, you already would have," I shot back, my vocal cords straining against the shadows constricting them. He raised a knobby, contorted hand—fingers that looked like they'd been dismembered and haphazardly reassembled. "*I have use for you,*" he said as the black edges of my vision pressed in. "What use for me?" I croaked. "*You will be my Queen,*" he whispered, his words flowing through my mind, overtaking everything. It felt as though ants crawled under my skin and in my thoughts. "I will never be your Queen," I whispered as the cords around my neck tightened with every passing second. "*We will see,*" he spat, black droplets dripping from his teeth and spraying across my face. Tears streamed down as I reached for the bands binding me. I tore at them, clawing at my neck in a frantic bid for escape. Darkness nearly flooded my vision, leaving only a tiny pinhole of light. Then he slammed me down on my back.

I groaned as pain radiated from my spine to my neck, and soon, my vision went completely black. "*Now, now, my dear,*" he hissed, "*I will find everyone you love and murder them all if you do not come with me when I call for you. I will send for you—be ready.*" With an earsplitting crack, I felt his presence vanish. The flood of shadows in my mind receded, along with the ropes that had held me suspended in the air.

I gasped for air, each breath ragged and shallow, my lungs burning like they'd been scraped raw. But the darkness clung to my vision, thick and unrelenting. Pebbles dug into my palms as I shoved my feet against the jagged rocks beneath me, the cold bite of stone scraping my skin as I twisted onto my back. My spine scraped against the uneven gravel as I scrambled, scooting blindly toward the rough bark of the nearest tree.

Branches overhead creaked in the wind, whispering like voices just out of reach. I whipped my hands through the air, wild and frantic, half-expecting to strike flesh—but there was nothing. Only the empty, still darkness around me as I fumbled for cover. My chest rose and fell in sharp jolts. The coppery taste of blood—mine, maybe—lingered on my tongue. I clenched my jaw, squeezing my eyes shut even tighter, and forced myself to inhale slowly.

In. Out.

My heart thundered in my ears, but I stayed frozen, listening. Waiting. Seconds passed, then minutes. Why was my vision still dark? I patted the ground around me—only rocks and dirt—and realized I would have to feel my way back to camp. I hadn't kept track of how far I had wandered; was there any way Luke could hear me from camp?

"Luke?" I called out nervously. Silence. "LUKE!" I yelled louder, my voice echoing off the rocks as goosebumps rose along my neck. What if Brykan was still here, watching me? I pressed my back against the tree, waiting for his voice to creep into my mind again—the worst sensation I had ever experienced, a complete violation. How could he invade my thoughts as if he were a part of me? Still, there was no response. "So much for that," I huffed under my breath. I was indeed alone.

I eased away from the tree, shuffling my feet forward. I felt around for my boots left near the springs and pulled them on. Then, gingerly, I started scooting through the gravel. My hands grasped large rocks for support as I made my slow progress. Rounding a rocky corner, a sudden gust caught my hood and flung it off my head. The cold air whipped around my ears, and I grumbled as I pulled it back on—this cold was seeping into my bones, a stark contrast to the warmth I'd felt hiking all day. I stopped and listened. All I could hear was the wind. My thoughts raced as I reached out, searching for anything around me. My hands came up empty, so I continued to scoot forward as slowly as possible. What if I were blind forever? Had he cursed me, or was this loss of sight simply the result of nearly being strangled to death? My ears rang slightly as I stretched my fingers as far as they would go, leaning forward in search of a guide.

Finally, my hand brushed against a tree on my right. I dug my fingers into its bark and pulled myself up against it, uncertain if I was even heading in the right direction. As my toes began to tingle, I attempted to wiggle them—they didn't budge. Strange, but I couldn't afford to worry about that now. I reached forward again, finding a rock face to cling to, and kept moving.

Over and over, I reached for anything to steady myself. I was moving, but so slowly—it would take forever to find my way back at this rate. Minutes passed as I trudged onward; my legs began to tire and stiffen. I massaged my ice-cold calves, which had grown numb. I could no longer move my toes and could barely feel my legs. My fingers finally started to tingle, so I shoved them into my pockets, clenching them into fists. Using the toes of my boots like a blind person's cane, I tapped against the smaller rock surfaces as I walked. At least this way, I knew I wasn't about to walk off a cliff—even if I wasn't sure I was headed in the right direction.

It seemed it had been at least an hour since I stormed away from camp. Surely, Luke must have noticed something was off by now. Maybe he was hoping I'd wander off and accidentally get myself killed so he wouldn't have to deal with me anymore. The thought made me grind my teeth in anger. I tried to pull my hands out of my coat, hoping they wouldn't feel as cold, but they remained stubbornly clenched. I used all my strength to unfurl them, yet they stayed cemented closed. Excellent. "Luke!" I called out again, holding my breath, hoping to hear any sign that I wasn't alone.

Silence.

Fear washed over me, and my knees buckled under my

weight. I pushed my hands forward, only to land on my clenched fingers. I braced for pain to radiate up my arms, but whether fortunate or not, I couldn't feel them anymore. If I survived this, they would hurt like hell later. My thighs cramped, begging me to stop moving. What on Liarta was happening to me? Then it registered—Brykan must have cursed me, just like he did Odina. The wind in my ears began to die down, reduced to a small whistle, yet it still assaulted my face. My hearing was failing.

Frantic, I tried to stand up, using one arm to push my weight up while the other gripped a nearby rock. My knees wobbled and buckled again, forcing me onto my hands and knees as I inched forward. "LUKE!" My voice cracked, coming out hoarse. "Now would be a great time to—" But it was as if my voice had been muted. I opened and closed my mouth repeatedly, forcing air through, yet no sound emerged. My wrists buckled, and my shoulder slammed into Gayle's surface. Rocks bit into the arm that lay on the ground, but my body was too far gone to do anything but wait for the end. My head rested against a rock as the wind howled around me—though I could barely hear it—and my heartbeat slowed to an unnatural pace. What if this curse wasn't the same as before, and it would simply kill me outright? A strange sense of calm washed over me.

Maybe I would close my eyes and rest here. My eyelids fluttered shut, and my arms stiffened until I could no longer move them. At least, I thought, if no one finds me out here, I won't be in pain.

"Pandora?" A faint voice echoed in my ears. I wondered if I was imagining it—there was no one else out here with me. "Fucking hell, what happened to you?" The voice sounded closer this time, yet still incredibly faint, then fell silent. Suddenly, I felt my body lifted off the ground, and I snapped my eyes open, only to be met by total darkness. I couldn't move, but

I could sense that I was being draped against someone's chest.

We moved quickly, and I jostled against the unseen figure. The familiar scent of eucalyptus and sandalwood filled the air as my head bobbed with every movement. I felt delirious—my mind spun like I was at the end of a rope being swung through the air, my brain rolling inside my skull as my weight shifted from side to side. It felt as though we were moving forever.

At last, I was set down on something incredibly soft and warm. I could feel my mind teetering on the brink of shutting down. This was it—this was what it felt like to die. Without warning, the person shoved something sour into my mouth. I couldn't move to spit it out; they forced my mouth open and closed it repeatedly, mimicking the motion of chewing. The foul, burning taste spread from my mouth over my tongue and down my throat, like I was drinking liquid fire. *Holy hell,* it *burned*—searing its way into the base of my stomach and spreading like molten lava.

Suddenly, I felt as if I were burning alive: my thighs, arms, and face stung, and I begged for it to stop. "Pandora, can you hear me?" The voice was calm yet urgent as my hearing gradually returned. I tried to speak, but my face was completely stiff. I was on fire—my pulse quickened, and a sluggish feeling began creeping back into my legs and arms.

Moving as best as I could, I clenched my arms and rolled onto my hands and knees. I needed this blaze to leave my body, and I struggled to crawl forward. A pair of hands grasped my shoulders. "Pandora, wait for it to ease," he said, helping me lean against a rock. I furrowed and unfurled my fingers; the burning sensation had now reached my fingertips and toes. Sweat poured down my face and arms in giant beads. Desperately, I worked to strip my clothes off—one layer at a time. I threw off my jacket as hard as I could. "Are you hot?" he asked, taking it from me.

A tiny pinhole of light appeared in my vision, and I blinked wildly. Was the curse reversing? I stripped another layer, tossing my top and bottoms toward his voice. "If you keep going, you're going to be completely naked," he murmured. "Then don't look," I hissed, my voice finally returning. "There she is." I could almost hear the arrogant smirk in his tone. The pinhole of light widened as I shook my head to clear it. I was drenched in sweat as if I were a human faucet. Finally, I removed the last of my clothes, waving my arms and breathing deeply in an attempt to cool myself down. I felt as if I were burning at over a thousand degrees. I rubbed my eyes as the burning subsided, and finally, my vision cleared.

It was mostly dark, just a dim torchlight nearby illuminating our figures. I looked up and met the shoulders of Luke Nesnah, who stood turned away from me, shifting from one foot to the other. "Will you at least say you're okay?" he asked without turning around. "You think I'm okay right now?" I hissed as the heat began to evaporate from me. I paced behind him—naked and vulnerable. "Can I turn around?" he asked. "No," I snapped. The burning sensation eased slightly, and I stretched my limbs, testing their strength. My hands didn't hurt as much as I'd feared after that fall. "What happened?" he asked. "Brykan." That was all I could say.

I could feel my body returning to normal temperature as I slid back into my undergarments. "*Brykan?*" he repeated, tilting his head as his gaze swept over me. "You better turn your head back around before you find yourself dead on top of this mountain," I growled. He sighed and turned his head forward again.

Men.

I gathered my scattered clothes and began dressing, trying to shake off the lingering disorientation. Once I was decent,

I turned to him. "Alright. I'm clothed again." He turned and his eyes darkened slightly as they passed over me. He reached toward my shoulder, but I instinctively pulled back. "Sorry," he muttered, letting his arms fall. Tension ebbed between us and a heartbeat passed before I spoke. "I think I'm *fine*," I said softly, still catching my breath. I glanced around the area—items were strewn in every direction, a mess of supplies and broken twigs, "What did you give me?"

"When you ran off," he said, gesturing to the chaos around us, "I went to look for whistler herbs so we wouldn't have to search for them tomorrow. It's a good thing I did, but when we got back, I couldn't find them right away." I followed his gaze to the scattered fragments on the ground—greenish remnants that must've been the herbs. "You gave me the whistler herbs?" I asked, lowering myself back onto the rock, my hands resting on my knees. "How did you know that would help?" I asked and he hesitated, then met my eyes. "I didn't know for sure," his voice was quiet, "But the way I found you... I had to try something."

"The way you found me?" I asked. "You were stone grey. I thought you were dead." His eyes furrowed as he shoved his hands into his pockets and stared at me. I glanced down at my arms and hands—they seemed paler than usual but otherwise customary. "Grey?" I asked. "Grey as death." He whispered.

I looked around, licking my lips. After a beat of silence I realized he was waiting for an explanation. I swallowed and continued, "He appeared at the hot springs just as I was getting ready to return." He settled on the rock beside me saying nothing. "He said I caused him a lot of trouble and that when the time comes, I'd have to answer as his *Queen*—or everyone I loved would pay the price." Luke's eyes widened as he stared at me. "His *Queen*?" he asked for clarification. I nodded, burying my head in my hands. "Did he say anything else?"

I felt his hand rest on my knee, but I didn't shove it away. "He said to be ready when he comes for me," I whispered shivering some as I felt the heat slowly being replaced with mountain cold. His hand left my knee and he offered up my jacket. I slid my arms into it silently. "You were gone for hours before I found you. You need sleep." He murmured.

"I don't know if I can sleep after that." I said as I stood up and shivered again rubbing my hands along my arms. "You have to try." He tilted his head and his blue eyes bore into me. "I thought I was going to die." My voice was small, yet it carried no fear. "I thought I was going to die—and I was okay with it." He nodded, dipping his head forward as if he understood what I meant, and I stared blankly back at him.

"Who murdered my mom?" I asked promptly changing the subject. He shook his head, his eyes averting mine. "By all means, tell me when you're ready then. It's not like one of us might die before I find out what happened to her or anything." I glowered at him. His gaze lifted again, "No use in telling you until I can prove it," he said. I blinked, my jaw firmly set as I stared at him. "You need to *trust* me," he said, his eyes searching mine. "Have you forgotten—I'm also a detective?" I gestured to myself with an open hand. He sighed, "I haven't forgotten."

"Then why won't you tell me?" I asked, leaning forward on the balls of my feet. "I'm trying to protect you."

"I don't need a protector," I muttered, not quite meeting his eyes. He gave a faint smile, more thoughtful than amused, and ran his tongue across his teeth as if weighing his next words. "What was in the documents in the basement?" he asked, his voice quiet but firm. "I don't know." My voice barely rose above a whisper. "You really don't," he said, and there was something in his tone—relief, maybe. Not judgment.

"Why would I?" I replied, trying for sarcasm but falling

short. My voice came out tired instead. "I believe you," he said gently. The words caught me off guard. Not because they were dramatic, but because they were simple—and sincere. Some of the tension in my chest loosened, just a little. He watched me for a moment, his expression unreadable in the low light. I studied him back, something stirring beneath the suspicion. "You don't know what was in those files either, do you?" I asked, softer now. He shook his head. "I've been looking for them for a long time. If they're what I think they are... they're vital." I hesitated, something close to empathy flickering through me, "But you're not going to tell me?"

"I want to," he admitted. "But I can't. Not yet." There was no defensiveness in his voice, no stone wall—just something guarded. Careful. He stood slowly, picking up the small torchlight and walking over to where our sleeping bags were bunched together in the corner. He sat down, then turned to me with a weary smile. "Look, you can stay up all night pacing, or you can rest. We've got a long hike when Aurelios rises and that's not far off." He lay back, clicked the light off, and the world fell into darkness aside for the stars overhead.

For a moment, all I heard was the soft rustle of fabric as he shifted, settling in. I lingered there, my thoughts a tangled thread, then finally moved to my sleeping bag. The zipper slid up with a low whisper. Beside me, his breathing was slow and steady, grounding in its rhythm. I lay still for a while, eyes open to the dark, just watching the distant planets in the sky flicker with light. The silence between us wasn't heavy anymore. It was something else—tentative, but real. And as the weight of the day began to fade, so did my resistance. Sleep crept in gently, even as my mind clung to the questions still unanswered. The mystery of those files intwined in my dreams.

Chapter 23

"Can anyone tell me about the protocol for an armed assailant when responding to the scene?" Professor Weld asked the class. I sat in my crisp, navy-blue cop uniform, tapping the back of my pen irritably—it was nearly lunchtime, and I was starving. In the front row, Jayne Mikay raised her hand, but before she could speak, the shrill sound of raid alarms interrupted us all.

My heart jumped into my throat, and I sprang from my seat. Instantly, everyone around me began forming orderly lines to file out the door. There was no screaming or talking—just the quiet, practiced urgency of a drill we had rehearsed countless times. The looming threat of a Nephrian attack had hung over us for months since we learned that their planet's core had cooled and come to a complete stop. I could feel Anna Jones's heavy breathing behind me as we rushed out of the lecture hall. My heart pounded, and my palms grew sweaty—this time it was not a drill.

We moved down the hallway in tight formation, our heads bowed and shoulders brushing against each other. My eyes widened as the emergency lights flashed in my peripheral vision. Suddenly, a nearby explosion shook the entire building. I shielded my eyes as debris rained from the ceiling, dusting our pristine uniforms with a fine layer of drywall. Bursting through the exterior doors, we were greeted by an absolute horror show.

Chaos.

Bright lights streaked across the sky in crisscross formations. Explosion after explosion pierced my ears, and the ground rumbled beneath us. In the distance, I watched in horror as the largest building in Liarta crumbled to ash. "Pandora!" someone screamed from behind me. "Pandora!"

***

I jolted awake, my breath coming in panicked gasped. Lurching upward I looked around frantically. Darkness, rocks, and Luke laying in his sleeping bag beside me. I steadied my breathing reminding myself I was safe. Instinctually I reached out towards him. He startled awake at my touch, his blue eyes lazily roaming over me.

"Nightmare?" He asked quietly. Unsure of what I should even say in response, I just nodded slowly. He rolled over to face me, scooting his sleeping bag a little closer. My heart rate started to slow and I laid back down, my eyes lifting to the night sky above us. To Liarta looming in the distance. Quietly I heard his sleeping bag unzip and without a word he offered me his hand. I blinked as I looked at it outstretched towards me, palm open.

I hesitated my hand poised in the air as if the moment our fingers touched I'd ignite into flames. He didn't say a word, just held his hand out for me a steady anchoring calm. I slid my fingers slowly into his, the touch instantly calming me. His hand was strong and rough, the callouses of training gently scraping against my matching ones. He squeezed gently, the pressure grounding me in here in reality. His blue eyes blinked in my direction, no judgement, just quiet assessing. I didn't dare look at him, not when I felt this raw, this vulnerable. Eventually that too eased from my chest, and my body relaxed into my sleeping bag.

Seemingly content, Luke closed his eyes again and very quickly fell back asleep. I wasn't sure how long I laid like that, our hands intertwined, but eventually I too, fell back asleep.

****

We packed in silence the next morning, my fingers moving stiffly, still aching from the night before as I rolled my sleeping bag and tucked it into the side of my pack. The chill in the air hadn't let up—it clung to the rocks and bit at any exposed skin, slipping beneath my jacket as I bent to gather the scattered supplies Luke hadn't yet touched. My stomach twisted sharply from the lingering effects of the whistler herbs. When Luke offered our packed breakfast, I shook my head. Just the smell of the food made my throat tighten. He didn't press. Instead, he turned away, quietly securing the straps on his bag. He hadn't mentioned the nightmare I had last night, and I for one wasn't going to be the one to bring it up.

Around us, Aurelios cast over the clouds, its light refracting into a soft, silvery haze. At this altitude, everything felt muted and surreal, like the world hadn't fully woken yet. A gnawing tension had settled low in my gut, steady and insistent. I drew a slow breath, then another, trying to hold the nausea at bay as I retrieved the weapons I thought I had lost last night, but somehow Luke had managed to track down.

My hair had come loose during the night, strands clinging to my cheek and neck. I swept it back with numb fingers, quickly twisting it into a French braid that fell neatly between my shoulder blades. The bright red shimmer of it caught the morning light like a flame—one of the only warm colors up here in a world made of grey stone and pale flora. Luke hoisted his pack over his shoulder, tightening the strap with practiced ease. I followed suit, wincing slightly as the weight settled across my back. Together, we turned to face the temple one last time.

In the soft light, it looked eerie—haunted. Shadows pooled beneath the collapsed columns, stretching like fingers across the cracked floor. The carvings that had once felt sacred now looked worn and hollow, half-swallowed by the creeping weeds and windblown dust. A lone silver tumbleweed bounced past the threshold, carried by a breeze that whispered through the broken stone like a fading memory. Luke gave a quiet nod, his eyes meeting mine for a brief moment. It was enough to say it's time. I looked around once more, the silence of the place settling deep in my bones, and then turned away. My boots crunched softly against gravel as I stepped onto the path, beginning the long descent down the mountain—into the unknown that waited below.

It was much windier this morning—the breeze weaving between the rocks, carrying with it the kind of cold that felt personal. I pulled the collar of my jacket up over my chin, trying to shield myself from the bite of it. The gravel beneath our boots slowly gave way to patches of grass that pushed up stubbornly through the dirt. With each step, the air grew less sharp, less dry—but no easier to breathe. Luke's footsteps matched mine in rhythm, his presence just behind me like a shadow I couldn't shake.

We hadn't spoken in hours. I glanced over my shoulder. He'd pushed back his hood, and the wind played with the loose curls on top of his head. His eyes were locked ahead, unreadable, jaw clenched tight. His hands were tucked into his jacket pockets, but I noticed how the fabric pulled taut across his biceps with each step, his body tense beneath the surface. I wanted to speak. Ask something. *Anything.* But the words caught somewhere in my throat, stuck behind the ache of last night's unspoken words.

Suddenly, he looked at me. Blue eyes met green—sharp, unblinking. Like he'd been waiting for me to turn around. My breath caught, too quick, and in that split second of distraction, the toe of my boot clipped a loose rock. I pitched forward with a sharp gasp, catching myself against the rough bark of a tree. The jolt snapped me back to the moment. "You good?" Luke asked, his voice low—almost gentle. Heat surged to my face. I straightened, brushing bark dust from my palms, avoiding his gaze. "Yeah, fine." I muttered, embarrassed. He didn't laugh or tease, just watched me with that same unreadable look that somehow made it worse. I turned away quickly, my heart thudding far too loud in my chest. Why couldn't I keep my eyes off him? And why did it feel like he noticed everything I didn't want him to see?

I quickened my pace to put more distance between us. As we continued, the trees thickened, and the once nothing but stone path softened to loose dirt. Warmth spread from my face down my arms as the temperature started to change along with the scenery. I pulled my hood back up and hopped off a large rock onto the damp soil. The rocky gravel had started wearing my feet out, but the soil was much softer under my boots in comparison. I paused as Luke hopped down after me.

"Let's put our coats in the packs—it should just get warmer the further down we go," I suggested, setting my pack on the ground. He nodded and removed his coat, revealing his muscles through the tight t-shirt beneath. I felt a flush of heat in my stomach as I stared at him, then shook my head, clearing my racing thoughts, and shoved my cold gear into my pack. My arms felt bare in just the black tank top after I removed the jacket and I shivered as I rubbed my hands down the exposed skin.

I quickly checked my pistol and daggers at my side—both still in place. Luke hefted his bag back onto his shoulder and turned toward me. I reached for mine, halfway to sliding my arms through the straps, when something brushed against my senses and rooted me in place.

A voice—feminine, distant, and not quite real—drifted through the wind. It was soft at first, almost like the sigh of leaves. But there were words beneath it. My name. Whispered with impossible clarity.

"Pandora."

The sound curled into my ear like a breath that didn't belong to this world. My skin prickled. Goosebumps sprang up along my arms, and something cold and ancient slid down my spine like an invisible thread. I blinked and turned sharply to Luke. "Do you hear that?" I asked, trying to keep the panic from bleeding into my tone. "Hear what?" he said a little too loudly, the wind catching his words and flinging them back at us. "Shhh!" I hissed, jabbing a finger against his lips. He recoiled slightly, brows pulling together in silent confusion, but I didn't have time to explain. I closed my eyes and held still, every nerve stretched taut. Then it came again—closer now.

"Pandora... come..."

The voice was unmistakable this time. Silky and smooth, but hollow around the edges, like it echoed from somewhere far too deep. Somewhere that didn't belong on any map. My heart pounded against my ribs. It sounded like it was coming from everywhere—above, behind, beneath the soil. "I don't hear—"

"Shut up," I snapped under my breath, waving a hand in Luke's face as if brushing away smoke. He surprisingly obeyed, falling silent, though his posture had shifted—alert now, sensing something was wrong even if he couldn't hear it. His eyes scanned the trees, muscles tensed beneath his jacket. I turned in a slow circle, my eyes flicking from tree to stone to shadow. The forest around us was too still, too quiet. The kind of quiet that made you feel watched. Haunted. I heard her again, and this time, clear words emerged instead of a distant murmur—

"Come to me, my child."

She spoke calmly, and a sense of warmth washed over me. The voice vibrated deep in my bones. Something in me—something buried and instinctive—told me to answer. Whatever it was, it knew me. And it was calling me *home*.

Luke cocked his head as I took a deep breath. My heart rate slowed and my hearing became fuzzy except for her voice.

"Come to me. Through the forest."

I felt an irresistible tug, and my body began to move. Whether of free will or not, I wasn't sure—But one thing was clear, I needed to find this woman, to follow her voice. I dropped my pack against a rock, leaving it behind as my feet carried me forward.

"That's it, not much further," her voice cooed, now so clear it almost sounded like... my mother.

I quickened my pace, launching myself over a fallen tree that groaned in protest under my weight but held firm. Soon, I was running through the forest—my braid whipping around as my feet pounded the soft soil. All I could hear was my heavy breathing and the rustle of leaves as I sprinted. Sweat rolled down my back soaking my shirt that clung to my chest as I panted for air. I ran and ran for what felt like ages. Branches scratched my face and arms, but I didn't care—I had to reach that voice.

Warmth tingled in my fingertips as I pumped my legs faster. The dull thud in my calves confirmed I was still pounding the ground, yet my head felt light as if I were floating. Where was she? She had to be here.

I erupted through a wall of branches, skidding to a halt. In front of me lay enormous black stones, *identical* to the one sitting around Luke's neck. I tilted my head back, my eyes tracing their massive surfaces—at least a hundred feet high. They whispered in a cacophony of voices, almost as if they were singing. As I stepped forward, the voice continued.

"Here, my dear. Come to us."

A tug pulled me into the center of the stone arrangement, where my reflection danced on each surface as if there were hundreds of me. My body shook, and the sounds in my head blended into a low, whining ring.

"Touch us," The voices called.

I raised my arms toward the stones, eyes wide with awe. There was immense power here—a force I could feel surging as I paced in circles, the power built inside me.

"Touch us," the voices coaxed again, almost demanded. My arms trembled as I was drawn back and forth within the circle.

Yanking myself to one side, I slammed my palms onto the nearest stone and roared as my body ignited with what felt like fire. Black streaks surged up my fingers and along my arms, pulsing with need. I clenched my eyes shut, a cry catching in my throat as the stone's power tore through me like fire in my veins. My entire body trembled, muscles locking up as my heart pounded violently, threatening to shatter my ribs from the inside. Then, suddenly, silence.

Everything stopped—no sound, no wind, not even my breathing. My eyes flared open as I gasped for air. *"You are chosen,"* the voice declared—and in the same instant, a deafening crack erupted from the stone, like lightning splintering Gayle itself.

The force slammed into me. I was airborne before I could

scream, limbs flailing uselessly as the world spun around me. I hit the ground hard, my shoulder smashing into the dirt with bone-jarring force. The impact ripped the breath from my lungs, and grit filled my mouth and eyes as I skidded across the forest floor. I finally came to a halt—right at the toes of Luke's boots. He was frozen, looming above me like a statue cracked by fear. His face was pale, lips parted, chest rising and falling in ragged gasps. He must have been running—hard—to catch up with me.

I blinked up at him, dazed and unmoving, the ringing in my ears almost drowning out the pounding of my own heart. His eyes locked onto mine, wide with something I'd never seen before. Not just fear. *Dread.*

"You just took off," he said, alarm cutting through his tone. "Then I heard the loudest crack I've ever heard and saw your body flying through the air." His mouth was slightly agape as he eyed me. He offered me his hand, but I ignored it, choosing instead to sit up and face the stones. His arm dropped to his side silently. I looked down at my arms, stretching my fingers out. Dark, winding streaks—glittering in the light—ran from my fingertips to my elbows. Rotating my arms, I saw that they covered most of my lower forearms, including the scar that Raj Malone had so graciously given me weeks ago.

"What is on your arms?" Luke asked from behind me. "I have no idea," I responded, mesmerized by the marks. They weren't painful as the power surging through me had been moments ago, but I could feel them writhing beneath my skin. I glanced back at the stones—they felt alive like they were a part of me now.

Luke stepped forward, slowly circling to the center of the ancient stone ring. His boots crunched over dry leaves and brittle moss, the only sound in the breathless silence that had fallen. His broad back was to me now, but even from where I lay, I could see the tension in his frame—his shoulders tight, fists curled at his sides, jaw clenched so hard the muscle twitched beneath his skin. I didn't bother trying to stand. My limbs still trembled from the fall, the impact reverberating in my bones. The cold soil pressed against my spine as I stayed partially propped on one elbow, watching him through strands of tangled hair and dust. The wind shifted, stirring the long grass that had grown wild between the stones.

A low hum thrummed faintly through the air—like the circle itself was alive, pulsing with ancient energy. Luke turned his head slightly, just enough to glance back at me over his shoulder. His eyes were dark, unreadable, but I didn't miss the flicker of worry—or was it recognition? Something had changed. He turned slowly, studying the stones. "Do you feel them too?" I asked quietly. "No. Can you feel them?" he replied, narrowing his eyes. "Yes," I murmured, choosing my following words carefully, licking my lip. "They called to me."

"Is that what sent you sprinting into the trees without warning?" he pressed. "They told me to come to them."

He raised an eyebrow, his eyes shifting in the light. "Do you listen to everything anyone says to you? Or just strange voices in the middle of a jungle on a planet you're unfamiliar with?" he quipped. I rolled my eyes. "I didn't feel malice from them—I just felt a tug and followed it here."

Luke rubbed the back of his neck, stretching it from side to side. "I'd say it was more than just a tug, considering you sprinted as if your life depended on it, but alright," he said, walking over to one of the larger stones. His fingers traced its surface, and I heard a hissing sound in my ears. The hair on my neck stood on end and I cringed at the noise. It was worse than nails on a chalkboard. "Stop whatever you're doing," I said my voice sounding like it had been dragged over gravel.

He lifted his fingers and turned to stare at me. "Why?" he

asked curiously. "Because they don't like whatever you're doing," I replied, irritated. "They don't like what I'm doing?" His voice shifted, pitching an octave, and his eyebrows shot up again. "Yes," I hissed, shaking my head. He removed his hand and the hissing ceased. I exhaled gratefully. Luke narrowed his eyes again. "Are you fucking with me right now?" he asked, arms at his sides, taking a step toward me. "Why would I do that?" I retorted, wrapping my arms around my knees and lifting my chin to meet his gaze. His eyes flickered between mine and the stones. "Are they talking to you now?"

"No." I muttered. "What did they say before?" He pressed as I braced a hand against my thigh and slowly pushed myself upright. The moment I rose, the ground seemed to tilt beneath me. A wave of nausea surged in my gut, and for a heartbeat, the trees around us blurred into watercolor smears. I squeezed my eyes shut, breathing shallowly through my nose as I waited for the spinning to stop. It passed but a strange pressure lingered in my skull, like the air itself had thickened.

"They just told me to come to them," I said, my voice felt distant and distorted—as if filtered through water. "And to touch them." I added and my stomach twisted at the word *touch*, a cold ripple running along the back of my neck. I blinked hard, forcing the world back into focus. Luke's silhouette was still in the center of the stone circle, slightly distorted by the wavering heat of the power that still lingered there. The wind whispered again, curling around my ankles like invisible fingers. Something about this place was warping more than just space.

"To touch them?" Luke's nose crinkled as he scrunched his face. "Not like *that*," I hissed. "It just seemed like they wanted to be with me," I murmured. He watched as I approached one of the stones and caressed a single finger over its cool surface. It didn't hiss—instead, it resonated like a single female voice singing. I closed my eyes and smiled at the beautiful sound. "What is—"

"Shh," I hushed him, pointing a finger in his direction. I heard his mouth close forcefully. A pleasant tingling spread through my arms—no pulse of power, no burning, just warmth. I stood there, lost in thought. Why would these stones be talking to me? My eyes snapped open. "The stones," I said, wide-eyed. "Yes, the stones?" Luke tilted his head, confused. "Ragnai said something about the stones. What was it?" I tapped my forehead, mumbling as I started pacing around the circle. Luke watched me curiously, his eyes following my every move.

The world was still faintly bobbing, but my steps were more sure now. "He said whoever could wield the Gaythe witchcraft had to be chosen by the stone," I recalled, gesturing around me. "This must be the stone," I said excitedly, a smile forming. "Sure, but if that were the case, wouldn't any Gaythe be able to come up here and obtain power from these stones? He said Odina was the only one with that power. Also, last time I checked, you were human. Why are they talking to you?" he asked skeptically.

I chewed on my bottom lip as a line formed between my brows. "Good point. I'm not sure—they didn't exactly tell me. They just called for me," I murmured quietly. We stood silently for a moment before Luke glanced at the boulder nearest him. "I've only ever heard of one kind of stone that holds the kind of power to send you sprawling through the air like that," he said, intently examining the large formations around us. My eyes widened.

"Element X," I whispered. He nodded, confirming my suspicions. "*Holy shit*," I breathed. Luke pulled the relic from under his shirt—a small piece that seemed to pull toward the larger stones as if magnetized. "These are freaking huge," I gasped. "What kind of power can they contain if that little piece around your neck is enough to power an entire city?"

A sick feeling churned in the pit of my stomach. "Too much," he echoed my worry. I chewed my lip again, the nervous habit impossible to break as my eyes drifted up his body—broad shoulders, lean lines, the subtle rise and fall of his chest. Even after everything—the brutal fall, the chaos still humming in the air—I still wanted him to touch me. To *feel* me. That need clung to my skin like heat.

"Would you stop doing that?" he muttered, his voice rougher than usual. I blinked, caught off guard, just as I noticed him watching me—his jaw tight, eyes darker than before. "What?" I asked, startled. He exhaled sharply and pinched the bridge of his nose. "Chewing on your lip. And looking at me like that." My face flushed, the warmth rushing up my neck in a hot, humiliating wave. I snapped my gaze away, tongue clicking in a stammered attempt to mask my discomfort.

"I wasn't—" I began, but the words evaporated, unconvincing even to me. The air between us crackled, silent but charged, like flint waiting for a spark. He shifted his weight, muscles taut beneath his jacket as if holding himself back. Neither of us said a word. But something unspoken pulsed there—just beneath the surface.

"We should head back," I said, my voice betraying the unease still curling in my stomach. "After you," Luke replied, his voice so close it felt like a whisper against my ear. The words brushed against my skin, and my breath hitched instinctively. I moved ahead quickly, pushing the air from my lungs as I tried to ignore the sharp, magnetic pull between us.

The forest felt quieter now, as if the trees themselves were finally eased from holding their breath. Broken branches crunched underfoot, and the trail I had blazed was littered with evidence of my hasty movements—the bruised soil, the tangle of disturbed leaves—but something else lingered too. The air had thickened, weighed down by more than just the humidity. And then I noticed it—the trees, the foliage, the very soil beneath my boots had darkened. The leaves near the stones had gone black, a deep, unnatural color. As if the power of the stones was leeching into everything around them—corrupting it. Just like the markings on my skin.

I glanced down again. The streaks were still there—etched into my arms like some dark, living thing. They shone faintly in the half-light, the strange warmth beneath my fingertips drawing me in despite my better judgment. "Did the stone do that to you?" Luke's voice was soft, just loud enough to break the silence between us. I didn't turn to look at him. I couldn't. Instead, I whispered, "I think so. It happened when I touched them."

"Does it hurt?" he asked, his tone lower now, tinged with something I couldn't quite place. Was it concern? I shook my head, but even as I said, "No," I wasn't so sure. The warmth under my skin felt like it was growing—too much, too fast. Luke's gaze was heavy on my back, his silence settling between us like a weight. I heard his footsteps behind me, the rhythm of them like a drumbeat—steady but somehow pressing. We kept walking in tense silence until he pointed out my pack that had been discarded in the soil. "There's your bag,"

I bent down to grab it, and as I straightened, my eyes caught his. He wasn't looking at my face anymore. His eyes were drawn to my marred hands as I adjusted the strap, and a flicker of something passed through his gaze. "Alright," I muttered, trying to push my thoughts away, and gestured ahead. "Onward." I could feel the electricity of his presence as he stepped forward. I didn't move until he glanced over his shoulder at me, his expression unreadable, though there was a touch of something raw in his eyes.

"Next time you decide to tear through a cursed forest, maybe give me a little warning," he said, but his tone wasn't just teasing. There was an edge to it, something unspoken in the way his lips parted, just enough for me to notice the tension in his jaw. Something more than frustration. His eyes met mine as he passed by, and for a heartbeat, time seemed to stretch. The air felt heavier, thick with unspoken words, with everything left hanging between us. I could feel the heat radiating off his body—closer now, dangerously close. I could smell him, too. Eucalyptus and sandalwood and something sharper, something raw—like lightning.

My breath caught in my throat, my pulse racing. I couldn't tell if it was the forest around us or the pull between us that made my skin prickle. Luke held my gaze for a long beat, his expression unreadable. But his lips pressed tight, and I knew then—*he felt it too*. He finally tore his gaze away, turning back to the path, but the space between us was charged with a tension I couldn't shake. I released a breath I hadn't realized I was holding and followed him, my steps slower now. The words we weren't speaking hung between us, unanswered as we continued down the mountain.

Chapter 24

Aurelios was just past its zenith when we finally returned to the cavern. We scrambled through the soil tunnel, our packs scraping against the dirt. A creeping sense of irritation rose in my chest, but I couldn't explain why. Something new ebbed within me—something that hadn't been there before I touched the stones. I straightened up at the opening, heading to the water's edge and dropping my pack beside a rock. My shoulders rolled, easing the tension of the long hike, while Luke set his bag beside mine.

"Are you going to explain to me what that voice said when it called through the forest to you?" he asked. I lowered myself onto the rock. Aurelios beat down on us, sweat pooling at the base of my spine. "I can't really describe it," I murmured, staring into the depths of the water. "It sounded like my mother's voice, but that's *impossible.*"

He tilted his head, crossing his arms. "Like your mother?" He asked and I turned to face him. "I mean, it wasn't actually her. But the voice—it reminded me of her." My earlier irritation ebbed away, replaced by curiosity, as he narrowed his eyes. "Did Ragnai mention any spirits here on Gayle?" he asked, leaning against a large rock slightly shorter than him. "No," I said slowly, working through my thoughts. "He mentioned that magic comes from the stones but didn't say anything about spirits or voices."

Just then, the glowing water before us began to bubble, and

a Gaythe face rose above the surface. I straightened, watching Ragnai come into view. "Humans. You are alive," he noted, his gills opening and closing as he spoke. "Yes, it seems that way," I retorted. His gaze traveled over me, landing on the marks winding around my arms. My shoulders tensed under his scrutiny. He narrowed his slit-like pupils, his yellow irises pulsing in the light.

"The stones have chosen you," he said, voice low as his eyes flicked to Luke. "Chosen me?" I licked my lips and stood up from the rock. "Did you hear their voice?" he asked. I looked down, twisting my arms to display the black stripes circling them. "Yes," I said softly, "What do you mean by 'chose me'?"

He drifted in the water, faint ripples gliding away from his fins. "The stones only bestow power upon those they deem worthy. It appears they judged you deserving of receiving their power." He sank a little, his neck bobbing amid the fluorescent waves. "I advise you to proceed cautiously, as I'm unsure how this power will affect... *humans*."

Chosen. That's what the voice had said too. I had been chosen. The hair on my neck prickled. "Why would they choose me?"

"The stones bestow power for a purpose," he explained. "Once it's determined what sort of power you were granted, it will reveal what purpose you must fulfill." He turned to eye Luke, who had gone silent beside me. "Why would the stones choose a human to give powers to?" He questioned, shaking his head. "Humans are much more *fragile* than Gaythe."

"I do not know," Ragnai replied, straightening his posture. "That is for her to discover." He gestured with a webbed hand toward me. My shoulders slumped. Another puzzle, another burden. That's exactly what I needed. Bubbles began forming on the green water's surface, and soon, another Gaythe face emerged—this one significantly larger than Ragnai's. "This is Haggik," he said, gesturing toward the slightly bluer companion with yellow-tinged gills. He hadn't been with Ragnai when we first encountered him; otherwise, I would have remembered.

Haggik was enormous, built like a tank. He wasn't carrying weapons but with massive muscles like his, it seemed he most likely didn't need any. He must have been at least twice Ragnai's size, floating effortlessly in the water as if he were made of air. He looked me up and down before furrowing his brows. I braced for his scrutiny, but he merely tilted his head, eyes assessing me with quiet curiosity.

"Humans," he said in the strange Gaythe English accent. I sighed with relief—thank goodness he spoke our language. "Haggik," I addressed him, uncertain whether to bow, nod, or display some sign of deference. I settled on a curt nod. He chuckled, low and harmonious, the sound bouncing against the cavern walls. The noise echoed in his eyes as they crinkled slightly at the edges. Every movement he made was calculated, deliberate, yet there was an air of ease to him—like he owned the very space they stood in.

"Throw me your packs," Ragnai said quickly. He raised his arm as Luke flung both my pack and his into the water. He caught them swiftly, handing mine to Haggik and tossing Luke's over his shoulder. "Any day now, humans," he muttered.

We stepped carefully into the glowing water, the warmth of it curling around my ankles like silk. Bioluminescent ripples shimmered with every movement, casting dancing reflections across the jagged walls of the crater. As we waded deeper, the heat soaked into my skin, soothing and strange. Like the pool itself pulsed with a slow, deliberate heartbeat. The crater's natural walls formed a cathedral of stone, echoing faintly with the sound of water dripping from the trees arched above. The air smelled of minerals and something ancient, something wild. Luke swam ahead beside Ragnai, their figures cutting through the shimmering surface with practiced ease. I followed, strokes quiet and smooth, until we reached the deep center where the light glowed brightest beneath us.

"Haggik is taking you, Pandora," Ragnai said, gesturing toward the looming figure waiting silently just beyond a veil of steam. Haggik swam half-submerged in the center of the pool, his massive form seemingly weightless, his scaled chest rising with slow, deliberate breaths. The surface of the water lapped gently at his waist, reflecting the faint glint of his blue-tinged iridescent scales like stars caught beneath his skin. He blinked once—calm, unreadable. I blinked back and exhaled softly, offering a tentative smile.

"Well," I said quietly, "I suppose it's nice to meet you." A low grunt escaped him—more vibration than sound—before he closed the space between us in a single, swift movement. His arms wrapped around me with surprising gentleness, and I froze, caught off guard by the contact. His skin was cool, smooth, and strangely soft despite the armor-like texture of his scales. A tremor ran through me as his chest pressed against mine, his heart thudding slowly and calmly in contrast to my quickening pulse. I tilted my head back, craning to see his face. His eyes—wide and inhuman, yet somehow still expressive—locked onto mine. His slatted pupils dilated suddenly, the dark ovals expanding like ripples across a lake.

Behind us, Ragnai and Luke slipped beneath the water without a sound, disappearing into the glowing depths. But Haggik and I remained still—locked in some strange moment that hummed with energy. His eyes, I knew his eyes and face. He seemed so familiar. His gills flared once, and he leaned down, bringing his face close enough for his breath to warm the shell of my ear. He inhaled deeply, slowly, and I felt it as much as heard it. My skin tingled with the electric buzz of being studied—of being *known*. The fine hairs along my neck stood up. Then, without warning, he pulled back sharply. His eyes widened further, his grip tightening. I opened my mouth to speak—*What is it?*—but before I could speak, he yanked me downward, and I barely managed a sharp gasp of air before the water closed over us.

The surface shattered above us, glowing bubbles racing upward as we plunged into the heat and pressure below. The water rushed past my ears in a deafening roar, and yet I could still feel his arms around me—anchoring me as everything else dissolved into light and sensation.

My lungs burned as we raced through the water, each wave folding over us, yet my face remained gently cradled against Haggik's enormous, scaled chest. The rushing sea enveloped us as he propelled us forward, and for a moment, it seemed as if he could part the water at will. His body angled to a precise point, slicing elegantly through the current despite his brute size. I held my breath—ten seconds, thirty seconds—as fire seared my throat, and my body cried out for oxygen. I knew I wouldn't make it. Kehel was so deep in the ocean that I was doomed to drown. My heart began to slow, and darkness fuzzed the edges of my vision, but I forced myself to hold on. Then suddenly, we burst through the barrier, stretching it before it snapped back into place, and we landed abruptly on amethyst sand.

I gulped in the air as my heart raced, trying to boost circulation. No matter how many times we did it, I doubted I'd ever get used to holding my breath that long. I started to slow my breathing then noticed Haggik was still standing, cradling me in his arms. He observed me with quiet curiosity, his pupils contracting and dilating in the light. "Are you alright?"

he asked. I glanced around and saw Ragnai and Luke staring at us—Luke's brows furrowed in silent inquiry as he watched Haggik. I blushed and replied, "Yes, sorry. You can put me down."

Haggik gently set me on the sand and straightened up; I basked in the cool shadow of the gigantic man standing motionless beside me. I paused for a moment, then gestured towards the bag, "My pack?" I asked softly. He slid it off his arm and handed it to me. "Thank you," I said, offering him an awkward nod. "Yes, my—"

"Ahem!" Ragnai cleared his throat, and we both turned to him. "We should get those herbs to Manika and have her inspect your arms," he said, then shot Haggik a pointed *keep your mouth shut* glare. Haggik merely shrugged and ambled toward the city. I blinked and glanced at Luke, whose narrowed eyes followed Haggik as he passed. Casting one final glance over his shoulder at Luke, Haggik continued on his path as we gathered our bearings and followed.

Chapter 25

We sat at the edge of a wooden table in the healer's den. Luke and Ragnai pored over a map while Haggik perched on a stool near the door, his back pressed against the wall—one arm draped over his chest and the other clutching what looked like a purple fruit of sorts. It crunched under his sharp teeth, and clear juice trickled from a hole he had made with his fangs. The room still carried its delightful aroma, with an assortment of herbs arranged on the table beside us. Manika was preparing tonics when we entered. Upon our interruption, she gave me a quick once-over before ushering me onto a stool to examine my arms.

With gentle care, her hands glided over them as I turned to face her, deliberately ignoring the towering behemoth in the corner who couldn't seem to take his eyes off me. "Is it painful, my dear?" she asked, flipping my arm over to examine it. I shook my head. "No, but sometimes they tingle and feel warm," I murmured as her dainty, scaled fingers brushed against my skin. "Strange," she hummed. "I've never seen anything like it before." She continued gazing at them, and I cleared my throat. "Ragnai said that the stones had chosen me. What does that mean?" I asked quietly, lowering my voice as my eyes shifted toward the two men at the far end of the table. Luke was pointing at what appeared to be Mount Akasari on the map as Ragnai bobbed his head in response. "It means you were chosen for a purpose greater than yourself," she explained, a gentle warmth softening her features. "It is the highest honor of Gaythe to be chosen."

"Were you chosen?" I asked, and she nodded. "I was chosen as a healer. My powers allow me to create medicine." I glanced around at the assortment of glass vials and jars filled with various liquids and plants. "What is my power?" I pressed. She clasped my hands as she leaned forward. "That is for Hanwi to decide," she replied.

"Who is Hanwi?" I asked my brows furrowing together in confusion. No one had mentioned that name before. "You will speak to them soon, my dear," she said, pressing her forehead to mine before releasing my hands and gliding to the other end of the room. I let my hands fall limply into my lap as Ragnai lifted his gaze toward me, but I continued to watch Manika, who was quietly humming as she mixed a batch of tonics.

"Luke told me you encountered Brykan by the temple. What happened?" He asked. I swallowed hard as a knot formed in my throat, and my mouth suddenly dried from the memory. Easing off the stool, I turned to face them. "He told me that I was to be his *Queen*."

Ragnai watched me, his expression stern, while Luke stood with his arms crossed beside the table, his gaze fixed on my face. A loud crunch filled the silence, and Ragnai hissed, his gills flaring. He glared at Haggik, who shrugged and continued munching before he returned his gaze to me. I couldn't bring myself to meet their eyes.

The assault at the peak had felt so personal, and recounting it was like pulling teeth. "He started strangling me and lifting me off the ground. Then he disappeared—I couldn't see anything, and my body began to shut down—" My voice died in my throat. Though my eyes remained on my hands, I could sense Luke's unwavering gaze as he spoke, "I found her grey as ash and forced some of the whistler herbs into her mouth. It was the only thing I could think to do—I thought she was going to die."

I looked up at him, a tiny sliver of fear creeping into my chest. My fear? Or was it his? An uneasy feeling returned that seemed to flow through my brain, consuming the most intimate parts of my conscience. "You did the right thing. She probably would have died otherwise," he admitted, running his scaled hand along the back of his head. "As for what he said, I'm not sure what he meant, but after your trek, you two should rest. Thank you for briefing me." He said easing from the table before adding curtly, "The bunks are still open—you know where they are. Forgive me, but I must report to my team."

Ragnai gripped Haggik by the shoulder and dragged him up off the stool. Though Haggik was much taller than Ragnai when standing fully upright, I watched as he was pulled by his ear out the door, the purple fruit still clutched in his hand.

"What did he say?" I asked quietly, my voice laced with fear as Luke moved over from the far end of the table. He stood just a foot away, casually leaning against the surface. "He's worried that the Nephrians are closing in and planning another attack soon," he explained. "The sightings keep getting closer together, and some of his warriors have gone missing on patrol." I furrowed my brows, "What can we do?"

"Nothing right now. We need to hope that the herbs heal Odina so she can form a plan," he replied. His face looked grim in the light as Manika's gentle humming drifted over. I turned to her. "Thank you, Manika," I said, and she smiled at me over her boiling vat of herbs. "Anytime, dear," her voice chimed before she returned to her work. "We should go rest," I said, heading toward the door, with Luke following close behind. We wound up the spiraled staircase leading to the den and down the hallway toward the bunk room.

The last time we walked these steps, I wasn't sure what the future held—and now, retracing them, I felt even more uncertain. The streaks on my arms shimmered in the shadowy evening light. Though we didn't know why they were there, I couldn't help but find them beautiful.

Finally, we reached the door to the sleeping quarters, and I pushed it open. Everything looked the same as when we'd left, except our packs had been neatly placed beside the bunks. The light from the city filtered through the open windows as I stepped aside so Luke could enter before closing the door behind us. I crossed the room to lie on one of the beds, not bothering to remove my shoes. Luke settled on the bed beside me, casually kicking his off. My eyes drifted to the bunk above, my thoughts racing.

"Ragnai mentioned that Odina had a sister," he said quietly. My face scrunched with confusion as I looked at him. "*Had* a sister? I thought she didn't have any siblings—her mom died giving birth to her." Luke sighed, "Manika said they don't speak of her sister but that she might be important in what's happening right now. She rarely mentioned her, but Ragnai says she hadn't mentioned a daughter either."

I blinked, processing, "Why don't they speak of her?" I asked. "There's no written evidence of Odina having a sister in any Gaythe text back on Liarta." Luke rubbed the back of his neck with his palm. "Ragnai said she caused her great pain—that's all he would tell me. It seems the texts we have on Liarta are missing some crucial information, considering they didn't mention Kehel either, and yet here we are." He gestured to the room around us as I pressed my lips into a thin line, "Trust me, I tried to learn as much about her as possible."

He laid down, shifting his gaze upward toward the bunk above. I propped my head on my elbow, and he watched with his peripheral vision but remained still. Several long minutes passed in silence as I stared at him, noting each breath—his chest rising and falling—while an underlying tension clung to his shoulders. "You said you felt a pull..." I said quietly. His eyes darkened, but he said nothing, waiting for me to continue. "What did you mean by that?" I asked, running my marred fingers along the blanket beneath me. They were pitch black, like the midnight sky—no normal skin visible below my elbows. His chest rose again as he took a deep, measured breath as if calculating his response. "I can't describe it—just an urge," he muttered.

My eyes drifted along the curve of his enormous biceps. "Well, try because I can't read your mind," I murmured. He sat up on the mattress, his legs swinging over the edge of the bed. Placing his head in his hands, he shook his head slowly. "It's not—it's nothing. I think I just imagined it," he said softly. "Was the pull toward me?" I whispered. His eyes lifted to meet mine—blue against green—blinking slowly as his gaze darkened and an unreadable emotion flickered within them. Was it confusion or desire? I couldn't quite tell.

I sat up slowly, swinging my legs until our knees were mere inches apart. A feeling built in my chest—a burning desire to reach for him. Swallowing hard, I lifted my hand toward him. He stiffened, watching my hand with wide eyes, yet he neither recoiled or ordered me to stop. With shaking fingers, I carefully cupped his cheek. The moment our skin made contact, Luke took a sharp breath.

"You should stop," he said quietly, his eyes never leaving mine. "Why?" I asked, dragging my thumb down his jaw and over his bottom lip. His eyes transformed into molten pits as his jaw flexed under my touch. Then, faster than I could blink, he grasped my wrist firmly. "If you do not stop, I will not be able to control myself," he said in a breathy tone as his eyes bore into mine. "Control yourself?" I asked, his fingers still locked around my wrist. "Yes," he growled. "Control yourself from what?"

"From taking you as mine, right here, right now." His voice was so low I could barely hear him. "What if I *want* you to?" I whispered. He growled again, still refusing to release my arm. "I'd say you have no idea *what* you want and because I can't," he said, his tone laced with anger. I tilted my head in confusion. "And why not?" I asked, narrowing my eyes on him. "Because when you know everything, you will never want to be with me."

"So, tell me now," I demanded, my voice rising as I looked at him. He released my wrist and, in one swift motion, stood up—forcing my hand away. "I can't, not yet." he said abruptly as he strode toward the door. I shifted on the mattress, following his movement as his shadow danced on the floor behind him. "You can't just say something like that and then refuse to tell me what is going on." I said, jabbing my marred pointer finger at him. His jaw spasmed with restraint. "It's not my place to choose your path for you." He closed his eyes again, pinching the bridge of his nose. My face flushed eight shades of red as I trembled with fury. "Then whose is it?" I half-yelled in his direction. "Yours?" his voice pitched incredulously, then he stomped toward the door. "Where are you going?" I called in his direction. "Somewhere where you aren't."

With that, he slammed the door closed behind him.

Chapter 26

I tossed and turned in my bed, anger building within me. The room was oppressively hot. sweat pooled at the base of my neck, and I patted it away with my palm. I couldn't stay here, tossing about sleepless all night.

What had he meant by if *I knew everything*. Irritation simmered beneath my skin as I swung my legs over the side of the bed and sat up straight. I ground my teeth, tension knotting in my temples. Since sleep eluded me, I decided to make myself accustomed to the city where we might be stuck for a while. I yanked my boots back on and padded to the door. Pressing my ear against it, I listened. It didn't sound like anyone was stirring at this hour. Everything was quiet and peaceful—everything and everyone except me.

I cracked the door open just enough to peek through. The hallway beyond was silent and empty, no sounds stirring in response. Slowly, I eased my face out, then my shoulders—still no one. Slipping fully into the corridor, I closed the door behind me with a quiet click. I held my breath, hoping my movement hadn't disturbed anyone. If someone was asleep nearby, I doubted they'd appreciate being woken.

Despite the building's ornate exterior, the interior was remarkably plain—mostly white coral walls and floors, occasionally decorated with red woven rugs bearing tribal patterns. Three unmarked wooden doors stood in the hallway—two on the right and one at the very end. I bit my lip, wondering whether I should investigate or avoid possibly stumbling into someone's bedroom. Perhaps it was best to explore them in the daytime, though here in Kehel, you couldn't tell when it was day, as the ambient glow remained constant regardless of surface time.

I turned right and headed away from the doors, thinking I might ask Ragnai for a tour of the building if he was awake. My footsteps echoed softly off the walls. I thumbed at the hilts of the blades pressed against my leg, their weight was comfortable, easy. As if they were simply an extension of my body.

An arched doorway appeared as I passed the stairs we had climbed earlier to my left. I walked through and found myself in a large banquet hall. Massive windows stretched from the floor to the ceiling—at least twenty feet high—letting in a generous amount of light from the outer city. The room felt welcoming. A long wooden table sat at its center, surrounded by about thirty chairs, while a large fireplace occupied one side, accompanied by a red rug and several woven chairs. Whatever this room was used for, it must be imperative as it was one of the most decorated rooms in the building.

My feet shuffled toward the windows, and I looked out onto the city. Few Gaythe were visible, most either resting or indoors. Those who roamed carried large spears, likely guards on duty. Two nearby conversed quietly before the taller one left his post and walked inside—perhaps switching guard shifts. I looked further out. Most of the smaller buildings—what appeared to be homes—were tucked together on one side of the city, while the larger, taller structures dominated the other. I wondered if we were in the capital building of Kehel. I'd have to ask Ragnai later.

My hand brushed against the large, deep-green canvas

curtains beside me. Their rough texture tickled my skin. The fabrics here, all seemingly woven by hand, were unlike anything on Liarta. I ran my fingers along the stitched edging of the curtains, marveling at how the intricately hemmed curls glided through my touch. I stood there for a while, basking in the view, then turned and headed for the door furthest from the one I had entered. It led to another hallway, and I proceeded cautiously down it, careful not to make too much noise.

Almost inaudible voices reached my ears, and I paused. Where were they coming from? It was so quiet I had nearly missed it. I continued a few feet forward, and the murmurs grew louder. Ahead, a couple of closed doors lined the corridor—one of them slightly cracked open. I tiptoed closer and recognized Ragnai's voice. Why was he up this late? I edged along the wall until I was right by the door, leaning in to listen.

"She needs to be told. She's a liability in the dark, Ragnai," a male voice said. I furrowed my brows—who could he be referring to? "She's not a liability. Don't be dramatic, Haggik," Ragnai replied. So, the other voice belonged to Haggik—the huge Gaythe man who had brought us back after our trek to the peak. I risked a peek through the cracked door and saw Ragnai sitting at a table with his head in his hands. I couldn't see Haggik, but his enormous shadow loomed on the wall behind Ragnai. "I'm not being dramatic. We don't know her power, don't know what she is capable of, and now that she's a *chosen*— " Haggik hissed. "*Enough*," Ragnai growled.

A *chosen*. I furrowed my eyebrows. There was that word again. Part of me felt it was much more deep, more pivotal than what had been explained to me. There was some shuffling, and Ragnai looked up. I pulled myself further back into the shadows while keeping my gaze fixed on him, hoping he couldn't see me. "If she were dangerous, something would have already happened, Haggik," he sighed, tension furrowing his brows as he pinched the bridge of his nose in discomfort. "There is no telling how the power affects her! Does she even *know* who she is!?" he demanded, his tone turning angry as I saw the shadowy figures on the walls gesturing.

Know who I am?

"No, Odina will speak with her when she wakes," came the final, somber reply.

Know who I am. Know who I am. Know who I am.

The sentence repeated in my skull, bouncing around like a pinball machine. I could barely hear the rest of their conversation, my mind so focused on those four words. "*If* she wakes." He corrects him and walks around the table to stand next to Ragnai. I could see his figure now through the sliver of the open door. His eyes were worried as he laid a hand on Ragnai's shoulder. "She will wake. The healers say that the curse is already lifting." He doesn't look at Haggik.

"The healers don't know anything about the curse. They sit confined in their den, unaware of what we've seen and heard on the surface. Come, Ragnai—you can't possibly think they understand what fighting is like on the surface, what's happening inside Odina's body. For all we know, she could never be the same as she was before Brykan laid his hands on her." his voice trembled with stress as he leaned closer to Ragnai. Ragnai shook his head in response. "I know, Haggik, but we're out of options." his tone was resigned as wariness filled his eyes. He removed his hand from his face and looked directly at Haggik. "We'll just have to wait and see what happens."

"All I can do is follow your lead, Ragnai, but if the prophecy is right, you won't be leading much longer. Don't disappoint us," Haggik added, then stood up abruptly, his eyes darting toward the door. I flattened myself against the wall as quickly as possible, snapping my eyes shut. *Prophecy?* What prophecy?

I held my breath, listening to Haggik's footsteps drawing nearer. The door clicked shut, and their muffled voices started back up behind it. I exhaled with relief and slunk away from the door easing further down the hall. When I felt I was no longer at risk of being caught, I straightened up and resumed a more casual pace. Haggik must be Ragnai's right hand—if they were talking like that about Odina and their people. He had insisted that all he could do was follow Ragnai's lead. Was Ragnai in charge without Odina? He hadn't explicitly told me his role among the Gaythe, but everyone seemed to listen to him. I couldn't imagine he wouldn't be essential or highly trusted if everyone followed his orders.

The hallway turned to the right and then ended at a door. I hesitated, then knocked quietly. After waiting for a breath or two without any response, I turned the handle and stepped into the largest armory I had ever seen. Spears, crossbows, clubs, axes—every weapon you could think of, aside from firearms—lined the room. Quivers filled with arrows hung on the wall to my right, and spiked mallets were neatly arranged beneath them. My eyes widened at the sight of whips dangling from the ceiling. They had managed to survive this long alongside such rudimentary weapons, but now I understood why.

These weren't just basic tribal implements—they were handcrafted and honed to perfection. I had never seen such sophisticated, intricately carved bows in my life. I reached out and brushed my hand over one. It's light, sand-colored wood was smooth to the touch.

"Why are you up this late?" Ragnai's voice broke the silence, and I jumped out of my skin. Gaythe were stealthy creatures, and I hadn't heard him approach the room. "Sorry, I didn't mean to startle you," he chuckled, "Might have to work on your situational awareness, Detective." I turned to see him leaning against the doorframe, arms crossed over his chest as he watched me. "I don't mean to intrude. I couldn't sleep," I said quietly, retracting my hand from the weapon. His head dipped as he looked at me. "Feel free to examine whatever you want. You are welcome here." he stood there untroubled. I offered a small, curt smile and returned to the bow that had captured my interest a moment before.

"Who makes these?" I asked, my finger sliding slowly along its surface. "Our weapons experts," he replied, his head cocking to the side. I glanced over my shoulder at him. He hadn't moved, his yellow eyes fixed on mine. The fins on his arms flared slightly—the only movement he made. "How many are there?" I pressed. "How many bows or how many weapons experts?"

"How many experts," I clarified, turning toward him. "Right now, three," he answered. I eyed him but walked to the opposite side of the room to pick up an ax. He didn't budge. "That doesn't seem like a lot of weapons experts for the entire species," I said, concerned. "It's not. Most of them were sent to the frontlines during the last Nephrian wave. We lost a lot of our people." his body language shifted as if a weight had settled on his shoulders. "You keep saying that," I murmured. "Exactly how many people did you lose?" I asked, testing the weight of the ax in my hand. It was cumbersome, and I struggled to hold it. Ragnai sighed and took a few steps toward me, gently taking the ax out of my hand. "Several thousand," he said, then effortlessly lifted the ax and flung it across the room at a target about 15 feet away with a flick of his wrist. I gawked at him, my mouth opening and closing in disbelief. "How did you—"

"Gaythe strength," he replied, picking up a smaller blade shaped like an elongated triangle and testing the edge for sharpness, "We're stronger than humans."

"*Right*," I murmured, my gaze drifting to the ax in the middle of the target across the room. "Hanwi seems to have chosen power to give to you." he said, his eyes drifting down to my marked arms, then back to my face. "What does this power do to me?" I asked him, and he tilted his head to one side, observing me. "It depends on what kind of power Hanwi bestowed to you." he set the blade back in it's place gently. "How do I know what power I was given?" I returned my eyes to his face. Even though he was quite terrifying to look at, his features softened as he looked at me, and his eyes danced with a lightness that made me feel safe. "You will have to complete the ritual with Kirro, our warrior trainer. Every Gaythe bestowed power must complete it."

I rubbed my hands over my bare arms, suddenly feeling somewhat cold. "It will test every strength and weakness you have." He warned, "You have to listen carefully to what Hanwi has to say to you," I contemplated his words, tilting my head and changing topics, "What does the scar across your hand represent?"

He looked down, lifting it up some to see it in the light. "It's the Queen's marking. It symbolizes me as her shadow. To know all her secrets, all her enemies. I can see what others cannot, it marks me as her watcher, her protector." He said with pride, with purpose. I took a small breath and opened my mouth to ask another question, but I was interrupted by Haggik at the door.

"Ragnai—" Haggik started, but his eyes land on me. He furrowed his brows and then turned his gaze back to Ragnai, "you need to see this," Ragnai nodded and followed him into the hallway. I stood awkwardly in the middle of the weapons room, my arms slack at my sides unsure of where I was supposed to go now. Thankfully I didn't have to decide as Ragnai turned to glance at me. "Are you coming?" His voice echoed through the open door. "Yep!" I called back, taking one last look at the ax poised on the target before running after him.

The three of us dashed through the hallways back to the stairs leading up to Odina's room. None of us bothered to be quiet as we rushed upward. We ran past a door that suddenly flung open, and I briefly recognized Luke as we flew by. I turned to see him extending his arm in silent question, but I didn't stop as I followed Ragnai and Haggik. My focus shifted as I continued forward, careful not to bump into anything. I heard a door slam closed, and footsteps followed behind me. The halls wound endlessly, but we didn't slow as our feet carried us up and up following Haggik. At last, we reached Odina's door, where guards moved to let us through. "Haggik. Ragnai."

In perfect synchrony, the guards turned their heads toward me—their eyes landing on the markings snaking down my arms. Their gazes didn't waver, blank and unreadable, as if puppeted by a single mind. I swallowed hard, the weight of their attention prickling against my skin like static. Luke was close behind, his presence solid and grounding, though the unease curling in my gut only deepened as we crossed the threshold together. I wasn't sure what to expect as we rushed to her room, but I hadn't anticipated the temperature swinging from the bone-chilling cold of our last visit to boiling hot. Immediately, we all began sweating.

"What's happening, Manika?" Ragnai asked as he stood beside her. I fanned myself, still panting from the sprint up here. Luke stood closest to me, his eyes glued on Odina. I pulled my gaze away from him and focused on her—she was soaked in sweat. "I can't bring her temperature down," Manika said, worry evident in her voice. "Her body temperature?" I asked between huffs of air. "Yes—she's been burning up ever since I gave her the whistler herbs," she explained, gesturing to remnants of the herbs on the bedside table. "If we don't cool her down, her brain will fry."

Ragnai looked from the herbs to Odina and then back to Manika. "Are they the wrong herbs?" he asked. "They shouldn't be," she replied, her eyes wide with fear as she met his gaze. It took several seconds, but finally my mind caught up to my body. "I had the same experience when Luke fed them to me on Mount Akasari." I said and everyone turned their head to me. "We just need to cool her down until it subsides,"

Ragnai exchanged a glance with Manika, who merely shrugged. "And how do you suppose we do that?" he asked. "We could place her in water," Luke offered, glancing sideways at me. I shook my head, "That won't work—she'll just heat the water around her with a thermal layer."

"Then what do you propose we do?" Ragnai asked, and suddenly for some reason everyone was looking to me for advice. My mouth went dry, but I cleared my throat settling my shoulders and turned to him. "Is there any way we can have running water coursing over her?" His eyes darted around the room as if he were deep in thought, "We need Acotus." He then turned to Manika, "Where is she?" Manika's eyes flew wide. "She's with her sister in the outer city on leave," she replied, wringing her hands. "Haggik, please fetch Acotus for me and tell her it's an emergency," Ragnai commanded. Haggik nodded tersely and ran out of the room.

The air felt thick with humidity as I gazed at her. Her once dead, pallid complexion was now a deep, beet red, though the grey that had spread from her fingertips past her elbows was now confined only to her wrists. Her eyes were wide open, and I could almost see the turmoil roaring within her. I hoped with all my heart that she wasn't aware—if that burning had continued on the mountain, I couldn't have borne it much longer. Although

I had only been cursed briefly, there was no telling how long the herbs would take to reverse the effects on her.

"Who is Acotus?" Luke asked, crossing his arms toward Ragnai. "She is one of our most valuable healers," He said as he placed a reassuring hand on Manika, who visibly calmed at his touch. I wondered whether Ragnai's gentle gesture was meant to comfort her or if it was simply his natural presence. "Besides Manika, of course," he added with a smile. Manika mirrored his expression, looking up at him. "Manika is our eldest healer. Acotus is one of the younger, newer healers." he nodded, and his fingers curled slightly on her shoulder as she placed her hand over his and patted it gently.

Their interaction reminded me of a grandson with his grandmother. I couldn't help but wonder about their ages—Ragnai seemed middle-aged while Manika appeared much older—but I knew that among the Gaythe, outward age often didn't match the inner age, as they lived far longer than humans. *Hundreds* of years longer.

We waited for nearly fifteen minutes before loud footsteps echoed down the hall. They must have been truly sprinting for it to take so little time. The door burst open, and we all turned to greet them. Haggik was breathing deeply but didn't seem winded, while the petite Gaythe woman beside him was gasping for air. She quickly composed herself and straightened her back. "Ragnai," she said, nodding to him. He returned the nod.

"My Queen," she added, taking a deep bow toward the bed. Her English was astonishingly good, and her voice was as bright as fairy bells. I noticed that as she moved, her scales did not shimmer with the usual iridescence of the Gaythe but instead glowed with a pale, white-silver hue. She was very young—her face still soft with adolescence—yet incredibly beautiful beyond her years. Her yellow eyes, framed by long, delicate lashes, flicked daintily against her scaled face.

Her only clothing was a thin, satin-like fabric draped over her shoulder, covering most of her torso yet remaining virtually translucent. When her chest lifted as she recomposed herself, the fabric revealed subtle hints of her form. I blushed, realizing I was staring, and averted my eyes. While the Gaythe were unbothered by nudity—many of them wandered the city nearly naked—it felt wrong to gawk at her.

"Acotus, thank you for coming on short notice," Ragnai said, his voice clearing my muddled thoughts. I watched his body language shift—his spine stiffened in her presence. She must be incredibly powerful, critical, or just incredibly attractive to command such respect from the leader of the warriors. I rolled my eyes; even the most formidable Gaythe wasn't above being impressed by a beautiful woman. "Of course," she replied, her breath soft as she glanced around the room surveying us, "Anything for my Queen. How can I help?"

"This is Pandora," Ragnai announced as he gestured toward me. I bristled at the sound of my name before managing a small smile and a respectful nod in her direction. I wasn't entirely sure how Gaythe of different ranks greeted each other, but I wanted to show proper respect. She smiled warmly at me. "Nice to meet you," she said, nodding in my direction. "This is Luke." Ragnai swung his arm out, indicating Luke, who leaned casually against the wall with his arms crossed. I shot him a *make yourself at home, why don't you* glare, but he didn't seem to notice.

"Nice to meet you too," she chimed, her voice musical as her head rotated back to fixate on Ragnai, awaiting further instructions. "Pandora?" Ragnai called my name, and I cleared my throat, stepping toward her. She waited patiently, her smile never faltering. "I believe the curse is being purged from Odina much like it was for me on Mount Akasari," I began, licking my lips as I glanced around the room. Everyone intently watched the two of us—no one objected or interrupted—so I continued, "It's causing her body temperature to spike. If we don't cool her down soon, she'll suffer brain damage." Acotus blinked as I spoke and shifted her gaze toward Odina. "I think if we run water over her, it could cool her down enough to keep her from overheating," I finished quickly and waited for her response. She clasped her hands together before replying, "I will do my best."

I moved out of her way and we all watched as her assessing gaze swept over Odina's body. Quiet and calculating. The yellow veins in her irises flickered in the dim light as she blinked one second, another. Then, without warning, Acotus spread her arms wide, and I gasped as tiny water droplets formed in midair. Her silver hair whipped back from her face, and her eyes pulsed with power as she guided every droplet into a cohesive stream, moving gracefully back and forth before her. She swayed gently—the fabric draped from her shoulder seeming almost liquid as the small muscles in her arms tensed.

My arms tingled beneath me in response, and I shook them to dispel the uncomfortable sensation. Whoever this woman was, she was incredibly *powerful*. The water built into swirling, deep blue coils in the air, veering in every direction as she directed it around the bed. I shoved aside a flicker of jealousy and watched in awe as she closed her eyes and began humming. With expert precision, she wove the stream around the bed posts and underneath the mattress so that the water now flowed just above Odina's skin. I leaned forward in anticipation, crossing my fingers that it would work.

Gently, she lowered the stream, and the water hissed against her skin like hot metal being cooled. Immediately, the room's temperature dropped several degrees. "It's working," I whispered. Acotus then opened her eyes and slowly lowered her arms, but the water continued to cascade over Odina. "I think it worked," she said, smiling at Ragnai. We all collectively sighed with relief. The tingling in my fingers finally subsided, and I anxiously patted them against my thighs. The sweat that had once poured off Odina was gone, and the redness was beginning to fade.

"What now?" Luke asked, his chin directed toward Ragnai. "Now we wait again," Ragnai replied. "Manika, go rest. I will stay with Odina. I'll alert you if there are any changes," Ragnai ordered. Manika nodded and quickly excused herself from the room. Acotus then curved her neck toward Ragnai and spoke in their language. Despite having just displayed an astronomical amount of power, she didn't seem drained—only concern for Ragnai was evident. "I am fine, young one," Ragnai replied kindly in English, and she nodded curtly before turning to address us. "If you'll excuse me, I must return to my sister," she said, bowing her head before slipping out the door.

"She is incredible," I breathed while Haggik glowered at Ragnai from across the room. What had I missed? "She is. She is also my sister," Haggik stated, narrowing his eyes as I observed their interaction. "Remember that, Ragnai," he added before he too walked out the door. I raised my eyebrows in his direction, and he sighed with resignation. "She is my fated mate," he murmured, causing my eyebrows to shoot up further.

Luke adjusted uncomfortably beside me. "You have fated mates? I thought those were myths." I said, staring at him. "The stones decide them," he replied. I scrunched my face. "Does everyone have a mate like that?" My voice rose and I cleared my throat to expel the pressure. "Only those to whom the stones bestow power," his gaze fixated on me, his pupils silently scrutinizing my reaction.

"*Everyone* the stones bestow power upon?" I asked, my voice rising an octave with nervousness again. "I don't know if that includes you. You're an anomaly compared to what we thought we knew about them," he said, his eyes dipping to the floor. "Only you will be able to tell," he added quietly.

I glanced at Luke, but his expression remained fixed, revealing nothing of his inner thoughts. I ran my fingers through my scalp, snagging them in the auburn plait I still wore from this morning. "What else do I not know about this power the stones gave me?" I asked, wetting my lips. "So much," Ragnai replied, and I pinched my eyes together in disbelief.

Well, *fuck*.

Chapter 27

We stood in the courtyard of the largest building at first light, the air still cool with morning dew. The training field sprawled before us, not unlike the dome back on Liarta, though this one was entirely open to the glowing shield above. The grass beneath our boots was a vivid neon green, almost unnaturally bright, and cushioned each step with a velvety softness. Low stone walls, each brick perfectly aligned as if placed by obsessive hands, bordered the perimeter—standing about four feet high and worn smooth from years of use. Beyond them, the city veil cast a shimmering light over the grounds, refracting through the mist in a way that made everything feel slightly surreal.

Hundreds of warriors moved in tandem across the field, sparring in coordinated pairs. Blades flashed and bodies twisted with practiced grace, the sharp thwacks and dull thuds of impact echoing across the courtyard. We watched in silence, none of us having managed sleep after what had happened the night before. The tension clung to our shoulders like a second skin, and the rhythmic clash of the warriors only seemed to stir our restlessness further.

Odina was still in a coma. However, her body was not currently overheating thanks to Acotus, and the tension that had built in her room the previous night seemed to have dissipated some since. Ragnai had decided that until we knew exactly how long Luke and I would be staying with them, it was best to attend warrior training as well, so there we were, bright and early—or whatever passed for bright and early in Kehel—watching training commence.

I tugged on the hem of my long-sleeved shirt, the dark green contrasting the auburn braids trailing down my back. My pistol sat flush against my abdomen just as it always did, the grip just barely noticeable above the waist of the black cargo pants I had donned this morning. I hardly ever just stood there watching training and my very skin was itching to do something, anything. Back in the precinct, I was always running through drills. It's what kept my thoughts at bay.

Clashing of spears rang through the air as Luke and I watched Haggik repeatedly charge at a poor young Gaythe man with deep blue fins. He was obviously losing the sparring match, and with Haggik taunting him with every other attack, the distraught young man looked like he wanted to crawl under a rock and cease to exist. Barbaric if you ask me.

"Do you think you could take a break?" I called sarcastically from where we stood. Haggik and the man both turned to look at me. Sweat poured down his face, but Haggik looked cool as a cucumber. "Break?" He asked, gesturing the tip of his spear in our direction. "Whatever I would need a break for?" He grinned as he waggled his eyebrows. I gestured to the man across from him, "I wasn't really referring to *you.*"

The man's shoulders slumped some, and he retreated off the grassy field. Haggik ignored me and gestured his arms out to the man in a *where are you going* silent question. "I don't think this is what Ragnai meant when he said we should join them for training. Maybe you should keep your thoughts to yourself." Luke murmured quietly beside me. "He's wearing that poor man out." I turned to face him.

A brown curl puckered on his forehead and he ran his fingers through his hair, locking it back in place. His grey t-shirt seemed to make his blue eyes glow brazenly as his hands tucked into his nearly identical-to-mine black cargo pockets. The only thing missing were our detective badges. Although it didn't seem there was a need for that here, I did feel quite naked without it. "It seems that is how they do things here." He responded, crossing his arms over his chest. I snorted, but said nothing further.

Haggik found his next opponent several feet away—a more imposing figure I recognized from our first encounter with Ragnai. He was the man with the striking orange irises. I watched him bend and sway in perfect counterpoint to Haggik, deftly blocking the spear attacks. He was far faster than Haggik, but a single misstep would mean being skewered like a shish kebab. They danced around each other for several minutes as we watched. Haggik jumped to avoid the spear's sharp tip, barely grazing his opponent, then twisted to dodge the man's needle-shaped daggers narrowly. A huge grin spread across his face—this was a *real* challenge.

"Oh, come now, Ramus. Is that all you've got?" Haggik taunted his friend. Ramus grinned just as broadly. "No, I'm just wearing you out before delivering the final cut," he sneered. Haggik let out a booming laugh. "Do your best!" he challenged. Luke, who had been watching Haggik most of the morning, glanced from the match to where Ragnai stood with another man. This newcomer was more muscular than the last and had gills tinged green instead of yellow. At first, most of the Gaythe had looked similar to me, but after several days among them, the differences became more pronounced.

"Their banter is strange," I said, shifting my weight from one foot to the other. He merely nodded but didn't make to respond further, stiff as a board. It was military humor, a kind I wasn't accustomed to.

I shifted from one foot to the other, trying to ease the tension building in my legs. The muscles in my calves twinged with every movement, stiff from standing in place for so long. We had been here for nearly an hour, and the dull ache in the soles of my feet was growing into a persistent throb, radiating up through my ankles. Across the field, I noticed Ragnai watching us. Assessing.

Clashes still echoed from Haggik and Ramus as I caught sight of two different Gaythe men slamming into the ground further across the field, grappling for a sword one of them had dropped moments ago. "He can't possibly think we can spar with them, can he?" I muttered under my breath. I turned just in time to see Haggik fling Ramus through the air, sending him crashing down onto his back. Their sparring was unlike any human hand-to-hand combat—brutal and unrestrained. I cringed, imagining the pain. That had to hurt.

Haggik barely batted an eye as he moved on to his next opponent. Ragnai's voice rang out across the field, "Luke, are you warmed up?" My eyes widened, and I glanced at Luke. "I've been warm," he called back, a corner of his mouth twisting into a sinister grin. "What are you *doing*?" I whispered. "Training," he said, stepping onto the field. I cursed under my breath and folded my arms over my chest again. This was a *horrible* idea.

There was a loud smack and Ramus landed near my boots, his back sliding to a stop about a foot away. I looked down at him, and he glanced up at me. After blinking several times as if shaking off a daze, he sprang to his feet and jogged back to the field.

"Hey, do me a favor and stop throwing my warriors, Haggik," Ragnai called from across the field. Haggik only shrugged and threw a wink over his shoulder. Clearly, human male confidence wasn't so different from Gaythe male confidence. "Your turn, pretty boy!" he laughed, pointing a scaled finger at Luke. Luke didn't need to speak to talk trash. He simply raised his hand and beckoned Haggik to bring it on. I rubbed my palm over my forehead, certain this was a terrible idea. Haggik grinned in response to the taunt, razor-sharp teeth glinting as he strode to where Luke stood. They shook hands, and it felt like all the air had been sucked out of my lungs.

Game on.

Dropping into ready stances, they began circling each other. My nails dug so deeply into my palms that I almost didn't notice the sting. In the daylight, the Gaythe scales looked more mesmerizing than ever. Every twist and shift Haggik made caused the purple ridges to catch and reflect the light, especially against the blur of Luke's gray and black attire. Haggik stood several inches taller than Luke—a hulking figure compared to Luke's lean but muscular frame—and the contrast made my stomach tighten with worry. This was hardly a fair fight.

A bead of sweat formed at the base of Luke's neck. He waited, biding his time until Haggik finally revealed his first move. When Haggik swiped at him, the motion was so quick that all I registered was a streak of scales whipping through the air. He might have been huge, but he was alarmingly fast.

Luke slipped left and easily dodged before straightening up, both returning to their slow circle. Haggik's eyes narrowed, and he inched forward, talons digging into the grass for traction. He lashed out again, this time aiming for Luke's shoulder. Luke twisted, barely avoiding the blow by an inch. My pulse thundered in my ears, and I bit my lip as they continued circling.

Suddenly, Haggik struck again—just as Luke relaxed, thinking he had a moment to catch his breath. The same fist that had narrowly missed him moments before slammed into his shoulder with a jarring thud. Luke stumbled back on his heels, and I gasped, certain he would drop. But before I could even blink, Luke launched his fist straight up, smashing it into Haggik's chin with a sickening crunch.

Haggik's head snapped backward from the impact, and I clamped my hand over my mouth to keep from crying out. Luke didn't hesitate to use the advantage, springing forward onto Haggik. His spear and blades went flying as Luke effectively disarmed him.

A low growl rumbled from Haggik—so powerful it made the hair at the base of my skull stand on end. A primal reaction to the noise, like my body was answering to his warning call. I glanced around, and most of the other Gaythe seemed to hunker in response, watching with wide eyes. He bucked his hips, rolling Luke onto his back. Scrambling upright, Haggik lunged for his weapons. My heart seized. He wouldn't actually use them, would he? This was supposed to be sparring.

Panicked, I tore my gaze from their fight and scanned the onlookers circling the field. Ragnai stood at the edge, the fins on his arms held stiff. I gulped and started forward to interrupt, but a firm hand clamped down on my shoulder. Whipping around, I found a young Gaythe warrior behind me, the slitted pupil of his eye locking onto mine. His sharply defined muscles shifted beneath scaled skin, a simple waistband resting against taut abs. "Watch only," he said curtly in English, "no interfere."

He let go of my shoulder and I snapped back in time to see Luke latch onto Haggik's ankle. Haggik went down hard, his chin smashing into the grass and hand outwardly splayed just shy of his spear. Luke lunged for it but wasn't quick enough as Haggik seized him by the ankles and wrenched him onto his back. Luke's fingers just barely brushed the hilt of his weapon before Haggik pounced, slamming a fist into his chin. My stomach twisted as blow after blow landed. Luke's feet thrashed on the slick grass, searching desperately for traction.

Wham. Wham. Wham.

Haggik pounded his balled fist against Luke's face, again and again, until blood trickled down from a gash on his brow. Finally, Haggik ceased his blows and clamped his webbed hands around Luke's neck, his face flushing a furious red. Luke's fingers scrabbled across the grass until they finally closed around the spear's hilt. With a quick thrust, he slammed the spear's end against Haggik's nose, knocking him aside.

Both men scrambled upright, panting hard. Haggik snatched up a blade, blood dripping from his nose. He wiped it away with his forearm, his scales glimmering under a sheen of sweat. Luke was equally battered, blood running down from the cut on his brow. "So...You're not just a useless pretty boy." Haggik sneered, voice thick with derision. A rumbling chuckle escaped him as he sized Luke up, "I figured you were all bark, no bite—"

His taunt was cut off by Luke swinging the spear in a wide arc, the steel clashing against Haggik's blade. In return, Haggik swiped with his weapon, nearly grazing Luke's waist as Luke sprang back onto the balls of his feet. Wasting no time, Luke surged forward again, bringing the butt of the spear up to crack against Haggik's chin. Staggering back two steps, Haggik slashed out wildly but hit nothing but air at the same time Luke planted his boot squarely in his chest, sending him flying onto his back with a resounding thud.

A hushed gasp swept through the crowd as Luke leveled the spear's tip at Haggik's throat, the blade gleaming ominously. Luke had won—he had actually *won*. Relief flooded me, then bewilderment as I bent over, bracing my hands on my knees and released a shaky breath.

Applause rippled across the field and Luke extended a hand, helping Haggik to his feet with a firm pat on the shoulder. A low chuckle behind me made me turn. It was the same Gaythe warrior who'd held me back, grinning before walking away in the opposite direction of the onlookers. I recalled my initial impression when I first stepped onto this field. These creatures were indeed barbaric and brutal. The thought flickered through my mind again before I could stop it. Soon, I was supposed to train with them—to learn to fight with them. Squeezing my eyes shut, I took a slow, steady breath. What had I gotten myself into?

"Pandora!" Ragnai's voice rang out over the noisy crowd. I straightened, opening my eyes to see him waving me over to where he stood by the front gate with Luke and another man I didn't recognize.

Navigating around the field, I took care not to cut across anyone in the midst of training as I migrated over to the group. Luke swiped the drying blood from his face with the heel of his palm—somehow, it had even managed to coat his teeth. He ran his tongue over them, then spat the blood mixed with saliva onto the grass and flashed me a grin. I rolled my eyes.

Men.

"This is Kirro," Ragnai said gesturing toward the man with green gills. The man leveled a scrutinizing look at Luke who shrugged with minimal effort in response. He resembled the other warriors, wearing baggy canvas pants tied at the waist, barefoot and shirtless. A thick leather strap lay across his bare chest, pressing against well-defined muscles. Like Ragnai and Haggik, he carried a large, needle-like spear, its tip protruding just behind the coiled braids crowning his scalp. Although he looked young, the keen light in his yellow eyes suggested a wisdom beyond his years. He nodded politely to both Luke and me.

"He is in charge of all our warrior training," Ragnai continued, and Kirro fixed his gaze on us, his braided hair clinging tightly to his scalp. I dipped my head in greeting, and he returned the gesture. Turning to Luke again, he inclined his head. "For a human, your fighting style is remarkable," he said, slightly accented—one of the few among the Gaythe who could speak English although his dialect had a strange lilt to it. Luke seemed as surprised as I was but merely replied gruffly, "I was trained by the best." Kirro smiled before responding, "It would seem so if you can take down our best warrior in only a few minutes."

Best warrior? I bit the inside of my cheek, realizing I'd vastly underestimated Detective Nesnah. He might have hinted at more experience than an ordinary detective, but he'd never shared details about his training. What background did he have that I still didn't know about?

"Ragnai told me about the power the stones have given you," Kirro told me. "He's asked me to train you." I stiffened at his words, feeling Luke's sidelong glance though he remained silent. "Do you even know *how* to train me?" I asked, my voice edging with uncertainty. Kirro shook his head, "I'll be honest. When he first suggested I train a human, I scoffed. In our Gaythe combat, the idea seemed inconceivable. Humans are more fragile, but he explained that you share some of the same traits as our leader—similar power, similar spark. He believes you have potential and wants me to shape it."

My gaze flicked to Ragnai, who was watching me closely. He tilted his head, pausing before he spoke, "All I'm asking is that you try."

I returned my gaze to Kirro.

"I have never trained a human before," Kirro said, glancing at Luke who suddenly seemed tense. He stood so motionless that if I hadn't noticed the slight rise and fall of his chest, I'd have assumed he'd stopped breathing entirely. "However, I am willing to give you my best." He concluded with a curt nod.

"Do you even understand the risks of trying to train her without knowing her limits or power?" Luke finally spoke, his tone short, almost irritated, "She's *human*." I turned to him, confused, "Even if they don't, it's not your place to decide that, is it? I thought it was my place to choose my path, or is it now conveniently yours?" My eyes narrowed. "Look, all I'm saying," Luke grit out, turning to me, "Is that the power from the stones could be dangerous in the form of a human conduit. Who knows what might happen if you try to use it?"

"I have to try," I said quietly. "Otherwise, we'll never know and isn't that more dangerous?"

His gaze traced my features, lingering on my lips as I stopped speaking. Nervousness crept through me, and I chewed on my bottom lip. Realizing, his eyes widened slightly, and he turned away. They both nodded in tandem, glancing my way before returning their focus to Luke.

"I have no intention of harming her." Kirro said then shifting his gaze to me, he added, "And I have no intention of letting you harm anyone *else*, either." I swallowed around the sudden lump in my throat. "When do we start?" I asked, and everyone's eyes settled on me. "Tomorrow," Kirro replied. "I have some preparations to make. I'll fetch you when I'm ready. We will start with your ritual. Until then, please excuse me. I have training to lead today." He walked past us and headed straight for the field, where the waiting warriors snapped to attention as he addressed them.

"You can't possibly believe training her is a good idea," Luke hissed at Ragnai, causing me to spin around and face them. Ragnai's gills flared before snapping closed. "She will be trained as Odina was—and as every Gaythe granted the power of the stones. That is not your decision to make. It is only hers and Odina's. Learning to control her *potentially* dangerous power is in her best interest." He bared his teeth at Luke before adding, "And if I were you, I'd watch how you speak to me, *especially* in front of my warriors."

Luke ran his tongue over his still slightly crimson stained teeth, weighing whether it was worth challenging Ragnai further. "Besides," Ragnai added in a low, rumbling tone, "she's far more dangerous without *control.*"

I rolled my eyes in response. "Well, boys, if you're done with your dick-measuring contest..." They both spun around to face me. I tugged Luke back by his arm. "It wasn't a *dick-measuring contest,*" Ragnai grumbled, still glaring at Luke. "Sure," I said with an exaggerated eye roll, angling my shoulders toward him.

I needed to change the subject before the tension cracked wide open. "Do you still have my communicator—the one you took when we first got to Kehel?" I asked. It took him a moment to tear his gaze away from Luke, who was watching him like he half-expected him to sprout a third head. "It's locked in the weapons room," he finally said. "Why do you need it?"

"I need to contact my friend at the precinct back on our planet," I replied. His eyes darted between us before he answered, a hint of something unreadable in his voice. "Well, that's going to be a problem." Luke narrowed his eyes. "And why is that?" He muttered. "All our comm towers are down. They were destroyed the same night Odina was found," Ragnai explained. I pursed my lips. "All of them?" He nodded, "Every single one."

"That explains why you didn't respond to our radio call when we landed," I said. He gave another nod. "We saw you coming—knew it was a human ship—but we had no way to reach you."

Out of the corner of my eye, a lean Gaythe man swung his weapon in a high arc, narrowly missing his opponent's collarbone. "Where's the nearest tower?" I asked, curiosity piqued. "There's one here in the city," he said, his gaze drifting toward a nearby sparring pair. Kirro barked out the occasional correction, guiding their form. "It works down here?" I asked, surprised. "It did," Ragnai replied. "But after Brykan fried the surface towers, the surge overloaded the lines and shorted it out."

I chewed the inside of my cheek, my attention drifting as Kirro stepped in to demonstrate a new move for one of the few Gaythe women in training. Her powerful, scaled legs swept in a graceful crescent kick, catching her much larger partner at the temple. The grin that lit up her face was contagious, and I found myself smiling too as the man blinked in disbelief, rubbing the side of his head.

"I could look at it," Luke said, prompting both of us to turn his way. Ragnai blinked as if Luke had just spoken in a completely foreign tongue. "I worked on Cappurn as a radio tech for a while," Luke explained with a shrug. "What *can't* you do?" I muttered under my breath. "Control myself, apparently." Luke shot back so softly that I almost missed it. My eyes snapped to him, but he kept his gaze locked on Ragnai, who appeared lost in thought.

"Haggik will take you," Ragnai offered after a moment, his eyes landing on mine, "He'd be offended if I offered anyone else as your escort." It felt like he was talking to just me, but Luke didn't catch it as he nodded and said, "Might as well be useful while we're here."

"He'll take you once the morning's training is finished," Ragnai said, waving Haggik over. He jogged toward us, muscles bunching with each step. Given his sheer size, the sight of him jogging was almost comical—like watching a massive boulder bounce along on a pogo stick. I grinned but kept that thought to myself. "Ragnai," Haggik greeted the warrior. "When you're done here, take Luke and Pandora to Tower Seven on the east side," Ragnai instructed. "It seems we have a radio mechanic who might be able to help."

Haggik's body angled toward Ragnai, skepticism clear in his stance. "Sure," he replied shrugging, "Give me a few minutes, and we'll be on our way." He brushed against my shoulder as he walked off. "Is there anything he can't do?" he muttered under his breath. "That's exactly what I'm saying!" I called after him. Haggik glanced back and winked, a mischievous grin spreading across his face.

Despite his rough edges, there was something undeniably likable about him. He reminded me of Detective Kamar, and I couldn't help but feel a small connection forming between us. The reminder had me wondering what was happening back on Liarta. Had Chance believed Ivy, or had she broken down and told him the truth? We needed this tower fixed so I could give her an update.

The sparring sounds died as several male Gaythe turned to gape at the entrance. We all turned to see what everyone was looking at. Acotus slipped through the open gate, moving as weightlessly as a feather at dawn. Ragnai stiffened, and I bit my lip to hide a grin. Luke shot me a puzzled look, but I avoided his gaze. The girl was so obviously unaware of how captivated Ragnai was by her—adorable. He cleared his throat as she reached us.

"Acotus," he said softly, taking her hand. She accepted it shyly, her eyes sparkling in the light. The tension in his shoulders melted as soon as her fingers slid into his. Noticing the onlookers, Ragnai hissed and flattened his gills. Embarrassed, they quickly returned to their training, backs turned so they wouldn't catch his eye. He raked a hand through his smoky hair, then focused on Acotus again.

"I don't mean to intrude," she said in a delicate voice, "but I was wondering if I could speak with you alone about the Queen." If I hadn't witnessed her powers the night before, I might have believed she was as fragile as she sounded. "Of course." Ragnai gently squeezed her hand as she turned to Luke and me, "It's good to see both of you at training. Don't let them wear you out too much." She flashed us a bright smile. "If you'll excuse us." Ragnai murmured with a dip of his brow. They both turned as Acotus led him away, their hands gently folded together. "Good luck," He called over his shoulder without so much as another backward glance. I chuckled softly, watching the muscles in his arms flex as his hand moved to guide her forward by the waist.

"The two of them are something else," I remarked, and Luke nodded. "I didn't realize Gaythe had mates," he murmured. "Me either," I admitted. "I always assumed they all married like we do."

I let his comment hang, and we stood silently, waiting for Haggik. He was deeply conversing with Kirro, gesturing at a few warriors lined up in rigid formation. It reminded me of human military drills—everyone stood stiffly, arms at their sides, waiting for orders. Kirro dismissed them with a wave, and they scattered. Haggik finally strode our way, his spear slung over his back, the tip visible above his colossal shoulders.

"Shall we?" he asked, bowing slightly as he offered me his arm. I snickered at the sight of Luke glowering. He was so serious that one—probably never allowed himself to have any fun. Ironically, that was what Ivy always thought of me. I guess now I understood.

I slipped my arm through Haggik's. The contact felt odd, but familiar and he didn't seem bothered. He didn't even flinch when the black markings on my arms brushed against his scales.

"Tell me, human," Haggik said, gazing down at me as we walked. "Are all female humans as tall as you?"

His curiosity made me smile. "Not usually. I'm taller than most human women. Why do you ask?" He turned his attention forward, pushing open the gate so we could step onto the coral paved street beyond the training field. Luke shut the gate behind us and followed in silence. I glanced back, meeting his steady blue eyes. He said nothing, just kept scanning the surroundings. Always observing.

"Gaythe women are much taller than most other species," Haggik explained, patting my hand where it rested in the crook of his elbow. "We were told human women are small and delicate. You're the first I've met. I was curious." He flashed a gleaming smile. Oddly enough, walking arm in arm with him felt comfortable, like we'd known each other far longer than a few days—almost like family. We strolled that way for a few minutes before I spoke again. "Is Acotus your only sibling?" I asked, watching a warm smile spread across Haggik's face. "I have two younger sisters," he beamed with pride. "She's the youngest." The youngest and *that* powerful?

"Who is the other?" I asked my curiosity getting the better of me. "Monarch," he replied as we continued down the path. "That's quite a name," I remarked. "My mother gave it to her,"

I inclined my chin with inquisition. The ease of his walk with my arm in his, as if this was his only purpose in life. And it felt *safe*. "Do you have powers like Acotus?" My voice echoed down down that path as he steered us to the right, passing an open window filled with red flowers that smelled faintly of cinnamon. I closed my eyes briefly to savor the scent. Without missing a stride, he spoke, "She's the only one of the three of us."

I frowned, "How is it decided who receives these powers and who doesn't?"

Behind us, Luke walked in silence but angled his ear towards us. "We don't decide," Haggik explained. "The stones do. They choose whoever they believe to be a worthy conduit for their power."

"Well," I said, my gaze drifting to a nearby cluster of pale blue blooms, "it seems they chose wisely with her."

"I would be inclined to agree, as they chose wisely with you." Haggik said and I blinked in surprise. He merely patted my hand and chuckled, glancing at Luke behind us. Their eyes locked for a moment and his face returned to a more serious expression. "He's a strange one," he remarked. I snorted, "That's an understatement,"

Luke only narrowed his eyes but made no indication he would respond to the taunt. Haggik smirked, his lips parting to reveal sharp teeth. "His fighting style is familiar," he added, quietly enough that Luke wouldn't hear. I frowned, "What do you mean?" My voice was just as hushed as he had been.

"He's more advanced than most of our warriors. I'd keep an eye on him—he could become *problematic*." Haggik turned back to the path ahead. His words sank into my mind as I risked another quick look at Luke. His blue eyes blazed, his jaw set, and he met my gaze without flinching. My heart thumped. I whipped my head forward, searching for a new topic.

"Does everyone who is chosen have the same powers?" I asked. Haggik chuckled. "You ask a lot of questions, human." Heat crept into my cheeks, and I shifted my gaze away. "Sorry," I mumbled, snapping my mouth shut. "I didn't say it bothered me," he said with a shrug, "just an observation."

We continued along the street, which began a slight incline. A tall metal tower loomed in the distance—unmistakable against the coral architecture. It was the first metal structure I'd seen in Kehel, and it stuck out like a sore thumb among the white and reddish-pink coral buildings. Most rooftops were tiled with red clay, many covered in climbing vines. The Gaythe seemed to favor organic style and materials, starkly contrasting Liarta's gleaming metal skyline.

"No, the stones grant each wielder a unique power," Haggik went on. "Still, some abilities are common: strength, eyesight, scent, and hearing are all enhanced. They're amplified far beyond that of other Gaythe—or humans, in your case. Though I've never heard of a human inheriting power from the stones, so who knows how it will manifest for you."

I nodded as we approached another gate, locked with a heavy padlock. Haggik released my arm and fished out a key. After some fumbling, he got it open, pushing the door wide. We stepped through, and he locked it behind us. All three of us tilted our heads back. The tower soared nearly as high as the one Odina was in, but instead of a gradual ascent, this metal framework shot straight up from the ground. I hadn't seen a comm tower like it since I was a child—it reminded me of the old power lines we'd dismantled on Liarta.

"The power box is over there." Haggik pointed to a small metal unit attached to the fence at the far corner of the enclosure. Thick cords snaked from it up the tower. "The control panel is in that shed." he gestured to a small, windowless structure. "And the danger is up there." he jabbed a clawed finger at the top of the tower. It groaned slightly in the wind, and I felt my stomach tighten. "How old is this thing?" I asked. "Old," Luke answered before Haggik could, the first thing he had said in several minutes. His gaze was fixed on the tower's summit—a makeshift lookout station perched at the top. Haggik glanced between us, his eyes lingering on Luke. "I'll be back soon. I have other business nearby. Good luck, and try not to break anything further." He slipped back through the gate, shutting it with a click. Luke and I exchanged looks.

"All right," Luke said, rolling his shoulders, "Let's give it a go."

I gave the tower's peak one last glance before trailing after Luke as he headed to the shed. The doorknob groaned as Luke twisted it. He pushed, but the door wouldn't budge. He tried again, harder, and it finally gave with a cracking protest. "Yeah," he muttered, stepping inside, "it's definitely old."

"Do you think you can repair it?" I asked as my eyes adjusted to the dim interior. Luke didn't answer. When I could finally see, I understood why he was quiet—the shed was *packed* with wires. They covered every inch of the walls, rafters, and floor. "Well, I was more optimistic before this," he sighed but kept going. "How hard can it be?" I asked, lifting a coiled green wire in the corner that wove through the rafters. "Don't touch anything," he snapped, swatting my hand away. I clamped my lips shut, frowning. "So why am I here, then?" I planted a hand on my hip, "to stand around and look pretty?"

"Sure, why not," he said, his shoulders buried in a tangle of wires without glancing in my direction. I pursed my lips, trying to think of a snarky response, but heat crept up my neck so I quickly turned away. "What were you two talking about?" he asked.

"He has two younger sisters—Acotus and one named Monarch," I explained. "I was asking about Acotus's powers and if he thinks I'll ever be able to do what she can."

"What was his response?" Luke inquired. "The short answer is no." I sighed with a heavy breath, "He said it's different for everyone given power by the stones." A beat of silence passed between us. "What do you think is wrong with it?" I asked, changing the subject and trailing a blue wire from the control panel through the knot of cables to see where it led. "Not sure," Luke said, voice strained as he hefted a heavy box out of the way. Cords rattled against the shed floor.

My breath hitched at the sight of the muscles in his back flexing, but I quickly darted my eyes elsewhere, pretending to examine another wire. He plugged in a few connections on the wall, then yanked down a worn red lever on the control panel. It shuddered as it powered up, the old screens flickering and spitting out endless error codes. "This might take a while," he murmured, scanning them. "Well, at least you have me for company," I said with forced cheer. "Mmm, lucky me," he answered, swiping a layer of dust from the closest screen. The stale air in the shed pressed down, so I propped the door open wider to let in a little breeze and leaned against the frame. It dug between my shoulder blades as I idly picked at my nails.

"What was it like on Cappurn?" I asked. I noticed him pause, shoulders going tense. "It was cold," he said flatly, typing away on the keyboard attached to the control panel. The archaic device clacked loudly, and some error messages vanished. "That's not what I meant," I muttered, "I already knew it was cold." He tapped the keys a bit harder, "It was cold *and* snowy."

I rolled my eyes at his so-called explanation, which offered nothing of substance. "Go on," I prompted dryly, fiddling with the end of one of my scarlet braids. He cast a sidelong look over his shoulder—one that spoke volumes—then turned back to the console. "I lived up in the mountains with my parents and my older brother. Because of the weather, most of what we did was hunt. It was too cold to farm much of anything." He ducked under the control table, rummaging for something as he wiped dust from another monitor.

"Is your family still alive?" I asked. "As far as I know," he said, voice muffled under the desk. "Were you close with them?" I pressed, watching his silhouette contort among the wires. Suddenly, sparks flared in the corner, spitting tiny embers.

I yelped and jumped back, my heart thudding in my chest. "Careful," Luke warned, popping up from under the table. He crossed over to the sparking wire, gently bending it away from the metal it touched. "I'll need to fix that." His gaze swept the cramped shed, "There must be a toolbox somewhere."

I helped him search, shoving aside some empty boxes until I found a blue-and-black kit in the corner. Our fingers brushed as I handed it over, and my eyes caught his—a flash of blue meeting green. "Very close," he finally said in response to my earlier question, returning to the damaged wire. He dragged over a wobbly stool and started snipping and splicing. "When was the last time you saw them?" I asked gently, leaning on the doorframe again, watching him work. "Right before we left Liarta." He groaned as he moved another set of wires out of his way. "They're on Liarta?" I asked, my voice pitching an octave higher in surprise. "My brother is," Luke replied, lifting an eyebrow at my reaction. I smoothed down the front of my shirt and gave a casual shrug. I hadn't thought he had family on Liarta. "Who is your brother?"

His eyes flicked to mine—assessing. "No one you know," he said curtly, returning to the wiring. I decided to let the topic drop—for now. He shut off the control panel before touching the exposed cords, stripping away the plastic coating from one wire and splicing it with another. "All right, let's see how that does," he muttered, flipping the power back on. This time, the screens lit up without sparking at the corners. "Great. It's got power," he said. "Now let's see if it's functional." He tapped a few keys, but giant red error messages burst across the monitors, he sighed furrowing his brow.

"What about your parents?" I asked unable to let it go. I leaned against the shed's back wall causally. "What about them?" He quipped not looking up from his fingers typing quickly on the keyboard. "Are they on Liarta too?" I asked. "No." His response was short, and I rolled my eyes—it felt like talking to a brick wall. "Are they on Cappurn?"

"Yes," he said tersely. I blinked, formulating my next question. "When was the last time you saw them?"

"Right before I left for Liarta." His tone was gruff as he brushed past me and leaned out the shed door, looking straight up the tower. "I'm gonna have to go up there," he announced, looking at me. "Up that death trap?" I tilted my eyebrows at him. "Yep," he said, walking toward the metal ladder. "What am I supposed to do?" I asked, trailing after him. "Make sure I don't die." He responded. "Well, that's comforting," I muttered. "I wasn't trying to comfort you," Luke replied with a chuckle. I rolled my eyes at him again.

"Pull the power lever beside the door when I tell you to." he gestured toward a large metal device protruding from the wall. It was longer than my forearm, roughly two inches wide. Before I could fire back with something snarky, he was already ascending the rungs of the tower. "What do your parents do?" I called, craning my neck. The metal ladder creaked under his weight. It was startlingly tall, and my palms went clammy just imagining myself that high off the ground. I wasn't even the one climbing the rickety structure, but my nerves still flared as the tower seemed to stretch ever higher. Feeling lightheaded, I kept my eyes glued to him as though my gaze could somehow prevent him from falling. He was easily a hundred feet above me now.

"So, you're not afraid of heights, I take it?" I shouted up. "Not at all," his low voice echoed back, bouncing along the metal framework. I held my breath as he swung onto a small platform at the top, the tower groaning ominously. It held firm, though, and Luke leaned over the banister, grinning down at me. "Nervous yet?" he asked. I scoffed but flipped him off.

He laughed, then disappeared from view again ."What do your parents do?" I repeated, hoping he could still hear me. "Help people," he called back, his voice fainter at this distance. "How do they help people?" There was a brief pause. "They run a nonprofit for the sick."

"What kind of nonprofit?" I ask curiously. "You sure do like to ask a lot of questions." He bickered down at me. "So, I've been told. But you never answered," I called again, waiting through a longer pause. "It's an organization that assists people with biological DNA fragmentation," he finally replied. "So...cancer?" I ventured. "Sure." He quipped.

I leaned against the doorframe, gazing up at Luke on the platform. From this distance, I could see his arms moving back and forth, though I had no idea what he was doing. "What do you mean, *sure*?" I called up, only for a frustrated sigh to float down. "Are you going to let me fix this?" he retorted. I huffed but didn't respond, letting him work in silence.

Several minutes later, he leaned over the banister again. "I think I've got it. Go flip the lever." Pushing off the wall, I walked over to the power switch, grabbed it with both hands and yanked. It gave a protesting creak but finally snapped over. A sharp crack echoed, and a deep hum rippled through the control panel, surging up the tower like a living pulse. The entire structure shuddered under the sudden rush of power. "Watch out!" I shouted, cupping my hands around my mouth as Luke clung to the railing. The tower swayed violently, and before I could blink, he pitched forward over the banister and my breath seized in my throat.

Luke managed to snatch a metal rung with one arm, slamming into the side with a loud clang. He grunted, then grabbed hold with his other hand. Relief flooded me as I watched his feet find purchase and he cautiously descended. Jumping off the last rung, he landed in front of me with a breathless grin. "Well, that was exciting," he said with a short laugh. He lifted the hem of his shirt. A dark bruise had already begun to form along the edge of his ribcage where he'd hit the metal. I reached out instinctively, but his grin vanished the moment my fingertips grazed his skin. A zing shot up my fingertips at the contact. He shoved the shirt back down.

"Don't touch me," he growled, eyes darkening. I recoiled, the blood draining from my face, but said nothing. "Sorry," he murmured, smoothing his hair back with one hand. I tucked my arms behind my back. "I'm not going to hurt you," I whispered. He leaned in, leaving only an inch between our faces. His warm breath washed over me. "You have *no idea* what you're capable of."

Goosebumps prickled along my neck, and I licked my lips. "I know I'm not going to hurt anyone," I insisted. He took a deep breath, his gaze flaring. "How do you know you're not going to hurt me?" The deep rumble of his voice coiled in my ear, and I found it strangely pleasant. "I don't *want* to hurt you," I said softly. "You will," he said, straightening up. "Why would I want to hurt you?" I asked, my eyebrows drawing together. "It doesn't matter." He shook his head abruptly, curls brushing across his forehead. "It does matter," I pressed. I could feel anger blossoming in my chest as I stared at him. He just blinked at me as I fisted my hands at my sides.

From this distance, I could see every fleck of color in his blue irises, but my anger kept me from getting lost in them. He was playing an unfair game, keeping me in the dark. He pressed his lips into a thin line and leaned back. He was just tall enough that I had to tilt my head to meet his gaze, my braids slipping further down my shoulders. "I will tell you everything," he murmured. "Soon."

"Not soon enough," I snapped, tearing my gaze away. He cleared his throat just as Haggik pushed through the gate. "Well, this looks promising," Haggik said, eyes lingering on the tower, which now hummed with power. "Hopefully, it's enough for your communicator to reach Liarta." I brushed past them both, annoyance burning beneath my skin. Haggik glanced at Luke, who only shrugged, but I kept walking. "I guess we're leaving," Haggik called after me.

The gate clinked closed behind us, but I didn't turn around. My anger mounted with every step I took. Finally, I whirled on them. "I am not going to hurt *anyone*," I hissed. Haggik started to speak, but I held up a hand, and he snapped his mouth shut. "Stop treating me like I'm a bomb about to go off. I can control myself. Yes, maybe the stones gave me powers we don't fully understand, but they didn't change who I am inside."

They both went rigid, staring at me. I stalked a few steps away before spinning around again. "And another thing," I said, pointing a finger at Luke. "If I find out the information you keep hiding has any impact on the people in my life because you kept it from me, I meant what I said. I'll bury you." He just blinked, starting to speak, but I jabbed my finger at him again. "Save it," I growled, then stormed off into the city, leaving them both in my dust.

Chapter 28

I spent the next few hours perched on my bed in the sleeping quarters, my thoughts in turmoil. I picked a fuzz out of the end of my braid, flicking it into the floor lost in my thoughts. Fear enveloped me as I worried about Ivy, Chance, and my father on Liarta. We'd been away for days now—who knew what might be happening in our absence? My father had mentioned mining on Feros. What was he planning to do with the power of those stones—or, as he called them, Element X? And even more alarming, what did Danny Fritz intend to do with that kind of power? His ominous words at the Precinct ball still echoed in my mind, and I couldn't shake the feeling that something critical had already been set into motion. Every fiber of my being insisted I was missing a clue right before me. I was a detective—so why couldn't I piece it together?

Anxiety twisted in my gut like a tightly wound spring, growing worse by the minute. I closed my eyes, resting my head on the pillow, and wondered if something more sinister was unfolding behind my back.

A sudden knock on the door interrupted my spiraling thoughts. Ragnai stood there, his face grim. I pushed myself up on my elbows, waiting for him to speak. "You're going to want to see this," he murmured, and I scrambled off the bed, following him into the hallway. "What's going on?" I asked, my heart pounding. He didn't answer, striding straight toward Odina's room. A wave of dread slithered down my spine. "Is something wrong with Odina?" I asked, wringing my fingers as we navigated the winding corridors. "Something like that," he muttered, and I hurried to keep up, tension thickening the air.

We passed several doors in silence before he finally spoke again. "It seems she's coming out of her coma," he began, turning left and climbing a spiral staircase. "That's good, right?" I asked, searching his face for reassurance. He clicked his tongue against the roof of his mouth, revealing pointed teeth as he hesitated. "Yes, but something's off. She isn't entirely herself."

"What's that supposed to mean?" I demanded as we reached the door to her room. The two guards stepped aside, greeting Ragnai by name—something they did every time, no matter how recently they had seen him. I acknowledged them with a brief nod, then followed Ragnai through the doorway. "See for yourself," he said, stopping just inside. He let me move past him for a clearer view.

Everyone was there—Haggik, Acotus, Luke, Manika, Ragnai—everyone except me. Irritation flickered in my gut, but it vanished the instant I took in the scene before me. The blood drained from my face, and my chest constricted painfully. Because the woman in the bed, who had once looked like Odina, now looked *identical* to my mother.

I stood there, speechless. No one made a sound; I was almost sure no one was even breathing. I took one shaky step backward, pressing into Ragnai's chest. "No," I whispered.

Across the room, Luke licked his lips and stepped forward as if to say something. "No," I repeated, my legs threatening to give out. Luke closed the distance between us, his hands gripping my arms. "No, no, no. It's impossible!" I screamed, my voice breaking. He flinched at the outburst but held firm. Desperate to prove I was imagining things, I twisted around him, praying

I'd been mistaken about what I saw. But there she was, lying in the bed, still as stone, staring at the ceiling with wide, unblinking eyes.

A terrible, grating scream filled the room. Her auburn hair fanned over her shoulders in soft waves—a red sea. It was *identical* to my mother's hair. *Identical* to her face. Tears streamed down my cheeks, and I realized the awful screaming was coming from me. Time felt frozen as my anguish echoed in the silence.

Luke wrapped his arms around me, a protective cocoon against the horror. I pounded weakly on his chest, sobbing uncontrollably, and he held steady, letting me release the pain. I couldn't say how long we stayed that way—long enough for my grief to hollow me out completely. When I finally sagged in exhaustion, he loosened his hold and gently lifted my chin. His gaze locked on mine, and something in his expression shifted—like a mask slipping away. "I need you to listen to us." He said softly. I nodded, and he released me from his hold.

I moved closer, my gaze never leaving her. Every detail matched my mother down to the slightest nuance. Luke's arms fell to his sides as he watched me. She was breathtaking—so much so that it felt like I was looking at a ghost. My mouth opened and closed a few times, but no sound emerged. Nobody moved; nobody spoke. They all watched.

At the edge of the bed, I reached out and touched her hand. It was no longer gray; instead, it had become ivory-toned—just like my mother's soft, flawless skin. Tears blurred my vision as I turned to face the others. "Someone, please tell me what's going on," I whispered, my voice cracking.

Ragnai cleared his throat. "I've never seen her like this," he began, clearly unsettled. "But Odina is one of the rare Gaythe who can shape shift." His words made little sense, considering

I was literally staring at my mother's likeness. "It's still Odina," Luke said gently. "She's just taken on your mother's human form."

I turned back, studying the face more closely. Everything was identical—except for the eyes. Purple irises gleamed where my mother's green ones should have been. So it was Odina, after all. An unidentifiable torrent of sorrow, relief, and confusion twisted in my chest. "What do you mean human form?" I asked in a quavering voice. Luke spoke carefully as if trying not to frighten me, "We think Odina's twin sister was your mother."

My head snapped up. "Excuse me?" I demanded. He stood rooted in place, slipping a hand into his pocket to pull out the identiscanner. "No," I breathed, shaking my head fiercely. "There's no way my mother was her twin sister," I hissed. "I would have known."

"Not unless knowing would have gotten you killed," he said, still holding the scanner in my direction. It blinked wildly, indicating nearby matches. I bit my lip, unsure of what to believe. There was no possible way. "You all have lost your minds," I said bitterly. "Arguably, I never had mine." Luke stepped closer, setting the scanner in my hand and covering it gently with his own. "Please," he urged, voice low.

Our eyes locked—green meeting blue—and I hesitated. As impossible as this seemed, part of me dreaded it might be true. I wanted to believe my mother would never keep something so immense from me that she wouldn't hide our family's truth my entire life. But deep down, I'd always known something was amiss. That I had been *different*.

Carefully, I took the scanner and glanced at its display. Two sets of DNA were already loaded. Odina's and Amy's. All that was left was for me to add mine.

The room felt stifling, my lungs tight with every breath.

Luke lingered just a foot away, empathy flickering in his gaze. Tears slipped down my cheeks. "It's your choice," he murmured. Dragging my eyes from his, I looked back at the scanner. Raising my marred hand to the tiny needle he offered, I barely felt the prick—numbness taking over. A bead of red appeared on my blackened fingertip, and I pressed it against the reader, watching as my blood vanished into the machine. The identiscanner chimed, and my name appeared on the screen. Pandora Vaughn. I held my breath, time stretching unbearably. This was it—this was the clue that could unravel everything. The scanner blinked, processing the results.

Match

It felt as though all the air had been sucked from my lungs. I shoved the scanner back into Luke's hand, and as he turned the screen toward himself, I watched realization drain the color from his face. Odina was my aunt. Amy was my cousin. I had just discovered two relatives I never knew existed—and one of them was already dead. Luke's eyes met mine, filled with sorrow. "I'm sorry," he whispered, "I had hoped I wasn't right."

Whatever fight remained in me dissolved. I felt utterly numb as I turned to Odina on the bed. "My Queen," I rasped, my voice raw with emotion. I bowed slightly, unsure how else to acknowledge her. "It seems I have come home."

A hush fell over the room. Manika and Acotus exchanged a glance I couldn't read while I slipped past them, moving closer to the head of the bed. Odina no longer radiated heat. "What happened to the water?" I asked, unable to tear my eyes from her. I took in every detail of her altered form, memorizing it all. "She was no longer overheating," Acotus replied, her silver scales catching faint light in the dimness. She wore almost nothing—her slender form mostly veiled in shadows. "Then why hasn't she woken yet?" I asked, my voice trembling at the last word. "We aren't sure," Manika said from the small stool where she perched. She wore primarily black—a healer's cloak draped over her shoulders—but a flowing green skirt spilled from her waist, nearly grazing her ankles. It was probably the most clothing I'd ever seen on a Gaythe. "All her vital signs are normal," she continued. "There's no clear reason for her to be still unconscious."

I narrowed my eyes and leaned over the bed. "Odina," I called softly. There was no reply, but her slitted pupils flickered. I inched closer, my face hovering over hers—green eyes meeting purple. "Odina. Wake up." Raising a hand toward her cheek, my black-tipped fingers hovered just over her skin—my mother's skin. I hesitated, glancing at Luke a few feet away, still clutching the scanner. His eyes were wide. Carefully, I pressed my fingertips to Odina's cheek, feeling warmth seep from her into me. "Odina," I murmured again, but before I could say more, her hand snapped up and clamped around my wrist.

She lurched upright, wrenching my hand away from her face and shoving me back. Several people in the room gasped as I stumbled. The brown leather chest piece she wore strained against skin that looked so much like my mother's and the tan undershirt wrinkled at her elbows. Without a word, she dropped my wrist and latched onto my neck, rising from the bed. My boots scraped the floor as I backpedaled under her pressure.

"Odina," Ragnai's pleading voice came from behind her, but she whipped her head in his direction, not loosening her grip. He went silent as her fingers tightened around my throat. My airway constricted, and I struggled to breathe, my larynx growing more compressed by the second. "You're going to kill her," Ragnai pleaded again. Odina raised her free arm in his direction, and an unseen force slammed him against the wall. He clamped his mouth shut, clearly fearing to provoke her further.

Luke went pale, frozen in horror. Odina forced me backward until my feet left the floor.

This is fantastic, I thought grimly—*my new relative is trying to choke me out.* My back hit the wall, and I dangled in midair, my face a mottled red and purple. I could barely rasp a breath. Her gaze raked over me as if trying to piece together who—or what—I was.

"Pandora Vaughn," she hissed, spittle flying from her teeth and spraying my face. I watched in horror as her skin began to bubble, scales rippling up her arms, shifting from silky ivory to an iridescent sheen. Her features twisted, and her teeth elongated into needlelike points. I blinked as she leaned in, her face mere inches from mine, and the rest of her body finished transforming into her Gaythe form. "*Welcome home*," she said in a low, eerie voice that washed over me. Then she dropped me like a sack of potatoes, and behind her, I heard Luke take a slow, steadying breath.

Her gaze swept the room, and Manika leapt off her stool, spine rigid. No one else dared to move. I braced a hand on my knee, wheezing as I tried to breathe normally again. "What is your deal?" I snarled, rubbing the finger-shaped bruises forming around my neck. "What is my deal?" she spat, angling forward as if ready to pounce. "Why are you *here*?" Anger coated every syllable while she stalked around me. Straightening my back, I caught Ragnai's eye—he shook his head, warning me to back down. Her shoulders lifted like a cat's hackles. "How dare you come to my home and lay a finger on me." She circled behind me. I couldn't see her, but I felt her presence looming. She was like death, elegant and lethal, confined to a sleek, beautiful body. I caught the glimmer of her scales in my peripheral vision as she rounded to face me again.

She turned to Luke. "Who are you?" she snapped. He

swallowed, then gave a slight bow—something that surprised me. "Detective Luke Nesnah, Queen," he said. I rolled my eyes. Of course, he'd be formal and polite with her. Her pupils flicked back to me. Her leather pants creaked in protest as she stood straighter, arms slackening at her sides. "*Niece*," she breathed, and my heart twisted. She already knew who I was. "You have a backbone, I see." She prodded my shoulder, testing my balance, "You weren't afraid of me."

I pressed my lips into a thin line. "Don't worry, it's just hidden," I muttered. Her mouth twitched at the corners, and I hoped it signaled humor rather than anger. I drew a shaky breath steadying my nerves before I spoke. I had to tell her, *now*. "Your sister is dead." She narrowed her eyes.

"Your daughter is dead," I added softly, more cautious this time. Her eyes went wide, and she whipped her head toward Ragnai. He gave a subtle nod, revealing he already knew. My teeth clenched. She kept her gaze on me, though her body remained angled toward him. "Ragnai," she commanded, her voice suddenly cold. "Yes, my Queen," he answered. "No use for formalities." She crooned. "Yes, Odina," Ragnai answered, his tone softer now. "Is it true?" she demanded, her gaze drilling into mine. "We have no reason not to believe them," he said quietly, glancing between us.

I shifted my focus from Ragnai back to Odina's anguished eyes. They were filled with the same agony that had haunted me for months after the death of my mother. "My Kimi." She whispered as her body pitched forward, hands gripping her knees, and she gasped for air. Unsure how to help, I searched the room in a panic. Manika moved swiftly, placing a hand on Odina's shoulder. "My Queen," she murmured.

Ragged growls churned in Odina's chest, growing louder as she straightened. Something knowing flashed in Haggik's eyes and he quickly closed the gap between us. Sliding an arm around my waist, he urged us to step back in sync. Fury and heartbreak glowed in Odina's eyes, and then a rush of power exploded from her, tearing through the room like a hurricane.

The bed splintered and slammed against the wall, and Haggik hunched over, shielding me, as shards of wood pelted his back. Odina's wail ripped through the air, so deafening that I clapped my hands over my ears beneath him. Acotus braced at our side while Ragnai threw himself in front of her.

Splintered wood battered him, gouging into his outstretched arm, and blood trickled from the wound. Still, he stood firm, blocking debris from striking her. The wind whipped my braids against my cheeks, and I felt Haggik's temple pressed against mine. He kept one arm braced against the wall, pinning me close, while the other curled protectively around my shoulders. I could feel my pistol digging into his hip on my right side, but I held my ground, eyes clenched shut, arms tucked in tight.

It lasted for what felt a lifetime, the roaring wind. Then at last, it subsided, and silence expanded in the room, broken only by gentle sobbing. We turned to see Manika kneeling on the floor, cradling Odina. Her face was buried in the curve of Manika's neck and her shoulders trembled with each ragged breath of *agony.*

This was why no detective ever wanted to deliver the news of a child's death. Amy might not have been young when she passed, but she was forever Odina's child—and as I watched Odina mourn her daughter, grief twisted through my own heart.

Chapter 29

I sat across from Odina in the banquet hall, slowly chewing a piece of bread. Just this morning, my long-sleeve shirt and cargo pants had felt perfectly comfortable—but now, under the weight of the thickening tension, they clung to me like a second skin. Neither of us had said a word since sitting down. My jaw tightened with every bite, each movement as sharp as the silence between us.

It was evening, but you wouldn't know it from the ethereal glow of the city at the base of the sea floor. Light streamed through tall, open windows, illuminating the long wooden table. Emerald curtains swayed slightly as the guards standing beside them shifted their weight. My gaze moved from Odina to the guards, who never met my eyes. Instead, their biceps tensed whenever I adjusted—nerves on edge for reasons I could only guess. Whoever prepared this meal was an excellent cook. The flatbread tasted sweet, almost like honey with a hint of pecans, an unexpected mirage of flavors.

Odina sat across from me, working on a bite of her fish. Her violet eyes never left my face, and her fork was raised like a poised dart as if waiting for the perfect moment to strike. She wore the same tan shirt and pants, along with the leather corset she'd had on since waking from her weeks-long coma. But the frail figure I'd first seen was gone—and now she was armed to the teeth.

Daggers filled nearly every pocket, and a massive spear loomed behind her, its triangular tip nearly the size of her skull. I couldn't understand how she had the strength to carry so many weapons, especially after so much time unconscious, nevertheless she seemed to carry them with elegant ease. If she meant to kill me, she would've done it by now, but the way her glare pinned me still made my skin crawl. If her muscles were stiff or tired, she didn't show it.

"Any day now," I muttered. She lifted an eyebrow in my direction. "I was letting you enjoy your meal," she retorted without pause. Her pupils swirled with light as she blinked in my direction waiting for my response. I narrowed my eyes. "Hard to ruin something I'm already struggling to enjoy."

She set her fork down with a loud clatter and stood. The chair scraped against the floor as she walked to the window. I took another bite, slower this time, letting the silence stretch. Aside from the two of us, only her small cadre of guards filled the room—rigid silhouettes standing beside the gently billowing curtains. Unlike the ones who had stood watch at her bedroom door, these guards barely acknowledged my presence, focusing entirely on keeping their Queen—who they believed had died—safe.

"I guess I should tell you how it started," she said, voice cold and tense. I could feel the raw power radiating off her in rippling waves. Whatever force I'd been granted responded instinctively, humming in my fingertips. Her power didn't just call to mine—it echoed it, like our souls were meant to align in this exact moment. The thought sent a chill through me and I curled my fingers into my palms, trying to silence the sensation.

"I guess you should," I replied, letting the sarcasm drip from my words. She hissed through her spiny teeth—a reaction I couldn't blame her for—but I'd grown too used to the Gaythe for it to truly rattle me. Still, when a wave of raw power crashed over me, my skin prickled and my hair stood on end. I swallowed hard, the sound audible in the silence. Her eyes locked onto mine, sharp and unrelenting, pinning me in place like a blade to the throat. "The only reason you're still breathing is because of who you are to me," she said, "otherwise I would have skinned you alive for the pestiferous display of attitude and disrespect you've shown me." Her lips thinned, and I stiffened, instinctively ready to defend myself—but I stopped.

She was right. I'd crossed light-years from my home world to hers, wandered her city freely and without respect, and greeted her return from a coma with nothing but grim news. Yes, she had delivered hard truths too, but not out of spite or malice. The truth was undeniable, I hadn't shown her the respect she deserved. "I'm sorry," I said quietly. A flicker of surprise passed over her face. For a moment, I thought she might reject it—but instead, she gave a slow, measured nod. Not forgiveness, exactly, but something close. A start.

"Let's start over," she said, pushing away from the massive window. The sharp tap of her leather boots echoed through the room as she moved. The power that had been so palpable around her receded, folding back in on itself, and the air felt lighter—easier to breathe. I lifted my fork and took a bite of fish—warm, flaky, and buttery enough to make me close my eyes in quiet satisfaction. How was the food here always so perfect?

The banquet hall seemed to stretch around us with high ceilings that echoed even the faintest of whispers. The walls, adorned with intricate carvings of long-forgotten Gayle sea creatures, shimmered with the soft glow of the bioluminescent lights embedded in the coral. The vast window she'd been standing near framed the endless, dark expanse of the sea above the veil, a deep, almost unnatural blue that swallowed the city glow. A gentle, rhythmic hum seemed to emanate from the buildings below, the heartbeat of a place that never truly slept.

Odina paced along the table, her hand gesturing as if she were weaving the air itself into a tapestry of thoughts. The faintest breeze stirred the curtains, and outside, the sea paused, as if listening in on our conversation. "When I was born, I was the second of a pair." I blinked, motionless, my gaze fixed on her as she spoke. She seemed to hesitate for a moment, a flicker of sadness passing through her eyes before she carried on, her voice softer. "My older sister was your mother. She beat me by two minutes."

I'd already suspected as much from the story of their mother's death shortly after childbirth, but I said nothing, continuing to eat in silence. "She was older," Odina went on, her tone steady now, "but I was the prophesied one. From the moment we were born, they knew she would be a traitor, and I, a redeemer—yin and yang, if you will." I swallowed a mouthful of fish, the weight of her words settling in the air between us. "What do you mean by a traitor?"

Odina sighed and stopped a few chairs away from me. "Your mom left our people here to be with your father on Liarta," she said quietly. "That makes her a traitor?" I asked, my tone shifting. "No," Odina replied, her voice softer now. "But when you add everything that happened before she left, it was enough to permanently brand her as one."

Odina resumed her pacing, drifting past me as I set down my fork, having finished my meal. "Your father came here, claiming to study our culture. We didn't know he was really here on Liarta's orders, doing recon for their government. My sister fell in love with him. He proposed to her, but only on the condition that she leave Gayle and return to Liarta."

I nodded, hoping she would get to the point. "She agreed,"

Odina went on, her tone quiet, almost reluctant. "But she didn't know that I had also fallen in love with him. When I realized our fated bond existed, I rejected him, because I knew how she felt about him. I couldn't do that to her." Her eyes met mine, and for the first time since awakening, there was a glimmer of real emotion there—vulnerable, raw. "He slept with me, weeks before they left," she said, the words barely a whisper. "My daughter was his."

A cold pressure gripped my chest as if my heart had stopped beating. Not only was this woman my mother's twin sister, but the woman murdered on Liarta—Amy—was *my* sister. The room seemed to tilt, the walls closing in. "Amy was my sister?" I choked out, struggling to keep my voice steady. "Half-sister, I suppose," Odina answered softly, standing still in the center of the room, her gaze distant. "Amy O'Rayne was her cover name. Her birth name here on Gayle was Kimi."

My entire world shattered. Everything I thought I knew—about my family, my past—crumbled away, revealing a lie so carefully constructed it had spanned decades. "Did he know?" I managed, my voice trembling with the weight of the truth. She pressed her palms flat against the table, her head shaking slowly, the weight of her words thick with emotion. "No," she said, her voice breaking slightly. "No one knew about Kimi."

I swallowed hard, fighting to steady myself, trying to find the right words. "Did she know he slept with you?" I asked, the question hanging in the air. Odina met my gaze, her eyes quiet but intense. "Yes," she replied, her voice soft but clear. "I told her the truth the night they left."

"Did you know you were pregnant when you told her?" I asked my throat feeling raw and scratchy. "No." She said softly. I drew in a sharp breath. She'd known her sister had betrayed her but had never realized there was a child involved. A better question bubbled up as my detective instincts kicked in again. "Who else knows?" I asked.

A guard coughed in the corner, drawing our attention. He flushed scarlet and avoided meeting my gaze. "Only my guards, Ragnai, and now you," Odina replied. I narrowed my eyes. "Ragnai knew this whole time and never told me?" I hissed. "He swore not to," she countered, crossing her arms. "I'd be disappointed if he had. Any personal guard worth their salt would've taken a secret like that to their grave." My mouth snapped shut, though I continued to glare. She was right—again.

I wet my lips, trying to order my thoughts. This wasn't a formal interrogation, but if I was going to discover who killed her daughter—my sister—I needed all the facts. Odina watched me intently, her braids slipping forward over her shoulders. "How was she able to pass through our terminals as a human?" I finally asked, pushing my plate away and flattening my palms on the table like she had. "She can shape shift," Odina said. "As you've seen, she inherited that power from our bloodline." She paused, watching me closely, waiting to see what connections I would make, how my detective mind would fit together the broken fragments of the story. "Even as half-human?" I questioned further. She tilted her head, a subtle nod of approval, before speaking. "It seems half-human Gaythe are just as powerful as we full-bloods."

My eyes widened in disbelief. "What do you mean?" I asked, my voice tight with confusion. "In some accounts, she was *more* powerful than even me." Her gaze drifted, and she spoke softly—almost as if thinking aloud. "I always wondered why the stones chose who they did. It was never the strongest, never the one with the most potential. It was always... strategic. As if the power was given to the right person, at the exact moment they were needed, chosen by forces beyond our understanding." She paused, then added, even quieter, "Kimi was no different."

I pursed my lips, wondering how someone so powerful could have been killed on Liarta—and, more importantly, who had done it. That question was what brought me to Gayle in the first place. "Why was she on Liarta?" I asked. Odina let out a long, steady breath, as if bracing herself for something difficult. "I sent her," she said. I tilted my head, frowning, "You sent her? Why?"

Her eyes darkened. Without answering right away, she turned from the table and walked slowly toward the open window, her silence stretching tight between us. When she finally spoke, her voice was low. "I sent her to find your mother."

A knot twisted in my stomach. I stood from my chair, the legs scraping softly against the floor. "Why?" I asked, my voice sharper than I meant it to be. I snapped my mouth shut, tension buzzing in the space between us. "We're losing the war against the Nephrians," she explained, her gaze drifting over the buildings outside. "I had hoped that if she could find your mother—and convince her to sway Harrison to our side—we might actually have a chance," her voice was laced with both resolve and regret. "Your mother had influence, history with him. If anyone could reach him, it was her. And Harrison... he's not just some government leader. He's a strategist, a power broker. If we could've brought him over—just him, not even the whole government—it might've shifted the entire balance. We needed someone who could think like them. Someone who could act as a bridge." She turned to face me, her expression unreadable but her eyes clouded with the weight of what hadn't come to pass. "I didn't send Kimi lightly. She was young, but she believed in the cause. And she believed in your mother. I thought maybe if we stood together, we could avoid what's coming." She paused, voice softening. "I never intended to send her to her death."

My heart ached at the admission. Of course, she hadn't—no mother would knowingly sacrifice her child. She fell silent, letting me absorb her words, and one of the guards shifted in my peripheral vision. I tilted my head back, eyes closed, piecing everything together. "Do you know if she ever found my mom?" I asked finally. Odina turned her head to glance over her shoulder. "I don't. We lost contact during the last Nephrian attack—our towers are all down." Folding her hands behind her back, she added, "It seems Detective Nesnah repaired the one here in Kehel, though."

I nodded, feeling as though the walls of the banquet hall were pressing in on me. "Why are you losing to the Nephrians?" I asked, opening my eyes and turning my gaze back to her. She didn't answer right away. Her eyes remained fixed on the horizon, staring past the shimmering veil that shielded the city—out into the endless dark of the ocean beyond, as if watching something just beyond reach. "They outnumber us," she said finally, her voice quiet. "And they out power us."

"But what about the power from the stones?" I asked, taking a step toward her. She shot me a sharp look that made me freeze in place. After a moment, her features softened, almost apologetic. She clearly wasn't used to people speaking to her as I did, so I decided not to push my luck and stayed where I was. "Despite our best efforts, the stones have not bestowed power since Kimi. You're the first in twenty years." She paused, then continued, "The Nephrians can also use the power."

I glanced at my hands—the black coils curling up from my fingertips. At the power dwelling within them. She continued, "I knew what happened the first moment I laid eyes on you. I knew you'd touched them," I stretched my fingers in the light, watching the dark patterns seem to swallow any hint of brightness. "So, what happens now?" I asked. She shook her head. "That's what we need to figure out, why Hanwi bestowed power to *you*, of all people."

My jaw tightened as her words stung, and I paced behind her. Although she respected my place on Liarta, she didn't believe that the power the stones bestowed on me, was warranted or justified. Her gaze followed me, the purple of her irises vibrant and sharp. "No one ever told me about the stones. How was I supposed to know that touching them would cause this?" I threw my arms in the air, frustration blazing through me. She turned back to the window, and my hands fell, balling into fists at my sides. "Most sane people wouldn't go around touching glowing black stones they find in the middle of a forest," she muttered. "But you seem determined to do whatever you please." I clenched my jaw with her revelation, the words spilling out before I could stop them, "Sorry we can't all be as unshakable as you."

She turned sharply, eyes narrowing. "I don't think you understand who you are," she said, her voice suddenly cool and commanding. "You're the daughter of the second-most powerful Gaythe woman who ever lived. Your lineage is more storied than any human bloodline you could begin to comprehend. Your mother was a warrior—brilliant, breathtaking, and deadly. A blade disguised in silk."

I swallowed hard as she stepped closer, the air between us taut with rising energy. "She wasn't you—" I began, but she lifted a single finger in warning, silencing me. In that instant, the vulnerability she'd shown vanished. The softness fell away like a mask. The Queen of the Gaythe stood in her place.

"You're a spoiled child, speaking whatever comes to your mind the moment it crosses it," Odina snapped. "You need to learn to think before you speak. No, she wasn't the prophesied Queen, but she was still a part of me." Her voice softened for just a moment, but the weight of her words lingered. "I wouldn't be who I am without her. Iron sharpens iron, and she sharpened me. It's a damn tragedy she isn't here anymore." She stepped closer, her gaze hardening again. "So if you want to have any purpose in this broken world, start acting like you belong—and keep your mouth shut."

Her words slashed through my ego, paper-thin as it was, and I sucked in a sharp breath. The temperature in the room felt like it had plummeted as her power roared around us and the hair on my neck again stood on end. "Understood," I forced out through clenched teeth.

"Now then," she said, running her palms down her pants, smoothing out invisible creases. The vibrating in my fingertips eased once more. "Ragnai informed me that he's introduced you to Kirro," Odina said, her tone serious. "It's crucial that you trust him and allow him to train you. We don't know what power you're capable of yet, so let him test your limits. He's our best warrior trainer, and I need you to listen to his guidance. Your ritual will be first." I nodded, but wisely remained silent. She studied me for a moment before shifting gears. "Now, tell me what you know about who killed our family."

My gaze dropped to the floor. I had so much to learn about these people—*my* people—but that would have to wait until we uncovered what happened to them. "Kimi went to Liarta and found a job as a secretary," I began. "She was found dead in her car at the company parking lot, killed with a paralytic drug—the same one used on my mother. Initially, the attending officers ruled my mother's death a suicide, but Detective Nesnah took over the case and pushed for a second autopsy. That's when they confirmed she was murdered. There's no way she could have injected a paralytic into the back of her neck at that angle. And the lab confirmed it was the same agent used on Kimi. I interrogated the only suspect I had, but he turned out to be clean, and my gut tells me he's not our guy. His father raises my suspicion, but I haven't questioned him yet. He's going to be more *challenging*." I raised my eyes to Odina.

She stood perfectly still, absorbing every word. Then she turned on her heel and paced back and forth. "Who was she in contact with while there?" she asked. "We don't know," I admitted. "Aside from her car and a torn-up purse, we found no belongings. We don't even know where she stayed during those few months on Liarta."

Odina pursed her lips. "I sent her to find your mother. Could she have made contact?" The question roiled through my and I pondered it for a moment. "Maybe," I said, "My mother never mentioned anything to me, but I wouldn't be surprised if she did. It would've been quite the scandal for anyone to learn my father had a child with a Gaythe woman." My words tasted bitter in my mouth, "They would have wanted to keep that under wraps—especially now that he's the commissioner on Liarta."

Her brows lifted in surprise, "So, he's the commissioner now," she murmured, more statement than question. I nodded. "Done well for himself, then," she added, her voice trailing off as she seemed to weigh the thought but didn't elaborate further.

I pressed on, "There were some documents that went missing from their basement around the time of her murder. People assumed they were related to my father's precinct work, but Detective Nesnah suspects they might have belonged to my mother. Do you know anything about them?" She shook her head slowly, her braids shifting with the movement. "I don't," she replied quietly.

A heavy silence fell between us. "Did you love him?" I finally asked. Her eyes begged me not to force her into an answer. We both knew what it would be—what she felt—but speaking it aloud was another matter entirely. "I did," she admitted softly. "When he walked away, it felt as though Aurelios itself had withered—its warmth stolen, its light extinguished. I was left hollow, a barren shell echoing with loss. For a Gaythe, finding your mate means forever. It's not just love; it's a soul-deep tether, unbreakable and eternal. The moment I gave myself to him, I knew I had sealed my fate. He became my universe, the center of every breath I took. But I was only a passing shadow in his sky. He was my entire world, but I was never his." Her words tugged at my heart, filling it with deep sorrow. The one person in the universe no one should ever have to lose—their mate.

"He loved your mother, and she loved him in return—but not with the kind of love that binds souls. He was never her destined mate. She gave her heart to someone who was never truly hers to keep, and in doing so, she lived a life woven with quiet ache, always reaching for a bond that was never fated to hold." Odina said, closing her eyes briefly as though lost in a distant memory. I had no comfort to offer, so I just nodded.

Coming to Gayle had revealed so much I never knew, yet all it gave me was more heartbreak than answers. I cleared my throat, "I suppose I should give these back to you," I said, pulling the iridescent daggers from their sheaths on my thigh. I'd secured them there this morning, but after everything that had happened, I realized they belonged with the one who made them. I held them out toward her. She regarded them with a look of haunting emotion—memories I couldn't possibly delve deep enough to understand. "Those were my favorite daggers," she murmured, turning away. "It seems more poetic for you to have them. The sorrow they bring me doesn't outweigh their usefulness."

Careful not to cut myself, I ran my fingers along the razor-sharp edges. I recalled what Ragnai told me. Odina had pulled off her scales to forge the blades. The pain she must have endured was unimaginable. And the irony was just as sharp—giving these daggers, once meant only for her mate, to me instead. The daughter of the sister who betrayed her and the fated mate that left her.

I slid them back into their sheaths. They felt almost natural against my skin, as though they'd been crafted for me—though we both knew they weren't. They were a lost dedication, a symbol of a prophetic love that had died before it truly began. And now, that burden was mine to bear.

"Tell me about this, Detective Nesnah." She pointedly changed the subject. "Can we trust him?" Her gazed drifted over her soldiers still as statues. The one closest to me shifted from one foot to the other, but made no other movement. "We?" I lifted my brows.

"*Our people,*"

"Right," I said, thumbing at my pant pocket. "He hasn't *necessarily* given me any reason not to trust him. He's selective with his information, but given what he was hiding, I can't really fault him." I admitted. She tilted her head, "What do you think of him?" I mulled her question over, but not as long as I should have before I spoke. "I think he's arrogant." The words slipped out before I could stop them. One of her eyebrows arched. "Oh?" Her voice lilted. My face grew hot, and I closed my eyes. "I mean—he's—it's just—" I sputtered, searching for the right words. "He gets under my skin," I finally managed. A guard in the corner coughed, reminding me again that we weren't alone. Odina grinned, "Is that so?"

Amusement sparked in her eyes, and I felt my cheeks burn hotter. "The last time I heard anyone stutter about a man, it was your mom talking about your dad." Her smile sharpened with memory. "In my experience, only the best ones get under our skin. Hell, they practically build a house and settle right in there." She chuckled, then shook her head, "I know you're hurting, but you need to find clarity—because right now, that man is breaking under the weight of your confusion. He won't wait forever for you to make a decision."

"Come again?" I blinked. "Gaythe, adorned with the stone's power, get a fated mate bestowed to them. It isn't always our choice, but sometimes it aligns to be exactly who we're supposed to *need*." she said. "I'm not sure I understand," I said quietly. "Mmm." She mumbled quietly, "Go to him."

With that, she quickly rounded up her guards and headed out of the banquet hall. They filed out in silence, Odina taking up the rear. But just before she closed the door, she turned back, a glimmer in her eye. "Your mother would be proud." A tear slipped free as I watched her go. The door clicked shut, and the tension in my body melted away.

Go to him.

"What does she know?" I muttered, smoothing the auburn flyaways framing my face. Probably more than I gave her credit for, if I was honest. So why did it feel so unsettling? Was I refusing to admit I had feelings for Luke? Or was I terrified that he might feel the same way? Worse yet, what if he didn't? What if he rejected me the same way Odina had been rejected? He'd already told me he couldn't be with me—that his duty was more important than any feelings he might have. What exactly did he mean by that—that I wouldn't *want* to be with him if I knew the truth.

Hugging my arms across my chest, I considered the possibility that I might be afraid—afraid he'd hurt me or that I wouldn't live up to the expectations. The fear that I'd never be enough. Did it stem from facts or merely my assumptions about his feelings? I didn't know. Was it better to never open that box, to save myself the heartbreak, but always wonder what could have been? Or to open it, knowing I could never close it again?

I bit my lip, recalling the story of Pandora's box—how opening it unleashed sorrow, disease, violence, greed, madness, and death. Paradise lost, all from a small, insignificant container. Yet the very last thing released was a single silvery thread of hope. I closed my eyes. *Hope.* I needed to cling to hope. So I took a deep breath, steadied myself, and held on to hope.

Chapter 30

I raised my hand to knock but froze with my knuckles just inches from the door. I'd spent too long in the banquet hall, pacing for what felt like hours but was likely only minutes. Everything had changed in a matter of days, and now my life felt like some looming tragedy. I held my arm there, trembling slightly from the effort. Thoughts spun in my head—every possible outcome that, good or bad, might come from knocking. Why was I here, hovering in this hallway? Scoffing inwardly, I dropped my hand, deciding to walk away. But then the door swung open, sucking in a rush of air that rustled my shoulder. And there he was. The most incredible-looking man I'd ever met.

His eyes locked onto mine—blue on green. His curls were still damp from a shower, and he wore a gray T-shirt with dark jeans. His feet were bare, toes peeking out from beneath the denim. My breath caught as the scent of eucalyptus and sandalwood enveloped me, warming my cheeks. My mouth went dry.

"Pandora," he said quietly, his voice like silk. I tried to respond, but nothing came out, so I just blinked. He tilted his head in question. "Is everything alright?" He asked. "I don't know," I managed, my voice strangely robotic and foreign. It echoed through the hall, returning to me foreign and fuzzy. My hand rose to rub my shoulder as I struggled to compose myself—to formulate any words that were coherent. He stepped closer, his toes nearly touching my boots.

Even though I was tall, he still towered over me by several inches. Tilting my chin up, I met his gaze. Gently, he lifted one hand to cup my cheek, his thumb grazing my skin. It left a sparking tingling sensation in it's wake that traveled all the way down to my toes. I swallowed, my throat bobbing beneath his hand. "Tell me what happened," he murmured.

Tears welled at the corners of my eyes, and I fought hard not to unravel, to contain those twisted emotions clogging my throat. I wanted to tell him everything I felt and all that had happened. But I couldn't form the words. His attention flicked past me, scanning the hallway. His damp curls brushed his forehead. Then his focus returned to me, unwavering. No one else was up here. Everyone had left. Odina had summoned Ragnai immediately after leaving the banquet hall. Together, they called an emergency meeting about a Nephrian sighting on Mount Akasari, leaving me alone to stew in my turmoil and agony. Luke's hand slid into mine, guiding me through the doorway and letting the door click shut behind us.

There were no windows—only a small circular orb of light hovering in one corner, unattached to anything, glowing on its own. It gave just enough light to illuminate us, but cast long shadows behind me as I dragged my feet across the floor. Luke sat on a large wooden chest at the foot of the bed, his bare feet peeking out from beneath his jeans. He watched me silently as I took in my surroundings. The temperature of the room was warm, and the bed behind him was recently slept in. The crimson covers folded over themselves as if thrown aside in haste. The space was much smaller than the bunk room lined with rows of beds. It seemed like a guest room for one person rather than the entire Gaythe front line.

As I moved closer to him, my boots sank into the thickly

woven rug beneath me. He propped his hands on the chest's edge, shoulders tight with apprehension, eyes never leaving mine. In the corner, that flickering light mirrored the quick dilation of his pupils, and for a moment, I swore the stone hanging under his shirt gave off a pale glow.

My weapons felt heavy in their holsters, so I carefully removed my pistol and daggers, setting them on a wooden table against the wall. I already felt exposed without them, and when Luke's gaze traced over me, it was as if every layer of clothing I still wore suddenly evaporated. His jaw tensed, but he didn't otherwise move.

"He had been her mate," I finally found my voice. The words sounded distant like they didn't belong to me. "Whose?" he asked, sounding a bit puzzled. I assumed he thought I meant my mother. "Odina's," I said, my voice raw. He stood instantly without me saying another word and closed the space between us, folding me into his arms. My tears slipped free as I pressed my face to his chest, feeling his chin rest gently on the top of my head.

"Go on," he murmured, his voice vibrating through my ribs. "She rejected him to spare my mother the pain of seeing them together," I managed to whisper, struggling against sobs. "She loved him, too. But my mother left Gayle with him instead of honoring her sister's heartbreaking choice. She stabbed her twin in the back." A surge of anger flared inside me—an anger I'd never felt toward my mother before. How could she have done that to Odina? How could she betray her sister like that? I focused on Luke's breathing, each slow inhale and exhale bringing my fury down another notch. "She was a traitor," I whispered at last. "Everything I thought I knew about my mother—from the moment I was born—was wrong. Fabricated. It was all lies."

Luke tugged gently at the tie, securing my hair in a long braid, and threaded his fingers through to loosen the strands. I closed my eyes, savoring the feel of his touch against my scalp. This was the closest we had ever been physically, yet it felt natural—comfortable, even. Then reality hit me, and I pulled back, eyes going wide. The auburn strands he'd freed fell around my shoulders like curtains. His arms dropped to his sides, and he tucked his hands into his pockets.

"Everyone has reasons for doing what they do," he said quietly, "as different people, we may never fully understand the emotions or motivations that drive others to make certain choices. Sometimes those choices are bad, but they can still come from good intentions—if only for themselves." He paused for a breath, "Just like I've had to make decisions without telling you everything. I didn't mean them to harm you."

My heartbeat quickened as he circled me, and I followed his movements with my eyes. "I'm not from Liarta, as you already know," he said. "I'm from Cappurn—an ice planet where very few humans live because of the brutal weather." It felt like he could hear the thunderous pulse in my chest, but he didn't mention it. The rug muffled his steps as he paced across the room.

"There are things you need to know about the Liarta government you work for," he said, his voice echoing off the smooth coral walls. "Right now, they're trying to steal every scrap of Element X they can from other planets. That's part of why I was sent to Liarta—to find the humans in charge of the operation and shut it down."

I swallowed hard. "Humans in charge—like my father?" He nodded, "Your father has been a prime suspect in Element X overreach for years. He and Danny Fritz have lied to Liarta's citizens about where their funding goes." My face drained of color, "What do you mean?"

He ran a hand through his damp curls as he sighed deeply, "Precinct 12's funding has been diverted. Part of it is for the precinct's legitimate expenses, but the rest goes into training soldiers and miners—people sent to other planets to strip them of Element X for Liarta's use."

One piece after another clicked into place, though not how I'd hoped. My head shook in denial. "My father is a good man," I said, my voice trembling. "There's no way he's orchestrating the largest theft of planetary resources in human history."

"That's where you're wrong," he said, shaking his head slowly. "I'm not," I replied, lifting my chin in forced confidence. "Are you sure?" his eyes darkened as he stepped closer, "I'm not telling you anything you can't already confirm with the information you have. I'm just putting together the pieces you didn't realize fit."

I bit my tongue, studying him. He was *right*. Just like with Odina, I'd been a complete fool—blind to the truth right before me ever since I took on this case. At the precinct ball, Danny had practically spelled out everything I needed to know about the motives behind his and my father's Element X mining. A growl of frustration escaped as I clenched my fists and pressed them to my temples. "How could I have been so blind to what was right before me?"

"It's called the detective funnel," he said softly. "We get so absorbed in the details that we forget to step back and see the bigger picture. It's easy to do—especially when you're good at your job and hyper-focused on every little clue."

Frustration roiled inside me, and I pressed my fists against my temples, face scrunching in exasperation. I felt like I'd failed Precinct 12 completely. "I don't deserve the badge," I muttered through clenched teeth. He sighed heavily again, "That's not what I'm saying."

"You didn't have to. I did," I snapped back. "Sit down." He gripped my shoulders, guiding me until the edge of the wooden chest he'd been sitting on pressed against the back of my thighs. My knees locked in defiance. I refused to relax. "Sit," he repeated, more firmly this time. I let my gaze rise to meet his as he leaned in. Eventually, I stopped resisting and lowered myself onto the chest, sitting as he had been moments before. "Now then," he said quietly, "Would you like me to tell you what I know?"

Fear tightened in my chest, but I nodded for him to continue. "There's an organized movement on Cappurn called the Protectorate," he explained. "We're a small group of trained soldiers—only a couple hundred—who've sworn to eliminate anyone involved in the Element X mining operations. Most of us live on Cappurn, including my brother and parents, but some are on Liarta." His brother and parents. The last time I asked, he'd been evasive. Would he finally tell me now?

"My parents are doctors," he went on. "They came to Gayle to try to reverse the Nephrian curse that makes Gaythe women infertile." I gasped softly, but he didn't notice. Now that he had started talking, I wasn't sure he'd stop. "They haven't been successful so far, and during the last Nephrian attack, they were out in the field when we lost contact. We had to organize a rescue mission from Cappurn to bring them home." He paced in front of me, his feet just inches from mine. I wrapped my arms around myself, listening. "They're back on Cappurn now." He paused, looking at the bed as though lost in thought, then resumed pacing, "The man you know as Lieutenant Smith—he's my older brother."

Surprise flickered across my face, and my brows knotted. That's who his brother was? It made sense now—Smith's aloofness, mystery, and how he carried himself like a man on a mission. He'd been trained well. Before I could ask any questions, Luke pressed on, "He's a plant for the Protectorate, gathering intelligence on the officials behind the mining operation. He finally uncovered enough evidence to bring me in to shut it down. What he hadn't anticipated was your mother's death." His gaze flicked my way, and I clutched at the wooden chest as my heart pounded in my fingertips. He lowered his eyes to the floor, "With the investigation into your mother, he couldn't risk exposing the entire mission. It would have looked too suspicious to bring them in right then, so he had me take the case. He told me from the start that something seemed off about her death. Turns out his instincts were right."

All the puzzle pieces slotted together at last—Luke's sudden presence at the precinct, Smith's cryptic remarks about Danny and my father, the guarded way he acted around me. It all made sense now, though the bigger picture felt more ominous than reassuring. "He's the only one who knows we're on Gayle," Luke finished. "He told me to protect you with my life."

"I've known Smith for years," I said, "He should know I can handle myself. Why would he tell you to protect me with your life?" Luke shook his head. "He didn't say. Just that it's critical you stay alive and that people are coming for you."

The words settled in my mind like maggots feasting on rotting flesh. For Lieutenant Smith to bind his brother to my protection yet still withhold the reason why—it felt as if every answer I needed was being kept just out of reach. My heart pounded hard enough to make me dizzy. I pressed a hand over my chest, trying to steady it. "It all leads back to who killed your mom and Odina's daughter," Luke said quietly, drawing my gaze from the floor back to his. Blue eyes locked with green, silently begging me to draw closer. "What are you thinking?" he asked. "Do you want the real answer?"

"If I didn't, I wouldn't have asked," he murmured. At that moment, all I felt was fear—fear that everything I'd believed in was crumbling, exposed as a lie so entrenched it felt truer than the reality unfolding around me. "I can't put into words the sense of loss inside me today," I began, voice trembling. Luke stood patiently, shoulders rising and falling in a steady rhythm, waiting for me to continue. "I don't know what to make of my ancestry," I confessed, "Or my future. I don't even know what to do about either one. Odina said a Gaythe who's given a fated mate is bound to them forever. But what if I'm wrong about who mine is? What if they reject me because of who I am?"

"Who are you?" he asked, not maliciously, but as an open invitation for self-exploration. "You know..." An uncomfortable laugh bubbled up my throat, "I don't even know anymore."

"You do," he said.

"How can you be so sure?" I asked, grinding my teeth.

"Because who we truly *are* never changes." He leaned down, palms braced on either side of me. My pulse stuttered. "Some people think we're born one way or another, but that's bullshit. We get to choose who we are. Choose who to love, choose who to fight, choose what story to tell. Sure, the people around us shape us, but they don't live our lives for us—you have to do that. You have to decide to do the right thing and be the right person, and no one will know how to do that better than you. We might stray, but we always find our true north eventually." His face hovered an inch from mine, and I caught the flicker of his gaze to my lips.

"What if I'm *wrong*?" I whispered, tilting my chin up. "What if you're *right*?"

Neither of us seemed to breathe as time stretched thin between us. "I get to choose too, you know," he added softly.

"Choose what?" I bit my bottom lip, and his eyes flared at mine.

"My future."

With that, he pressed his lips to mine. I inhaled sharply, his freshly showered scent overwhelming my senses like a waterfall rushing over rocks. His kiss was soft, tentative, as though he wasn't sure how I'd respond. But he deepened it when I tilted my head back, letting my hair cascade over my shoulders in ruby waves. His tongue brushed my bottom lip, silently asking for more, and I granted it. A tingling spread from my fingertips, trailing up my arms, as a slow burn ignited in my core. My heartbeat thundered in my ears. One of his hands slid around to the back of my head, fingers tangling in my hair with a gentle tug. My mouth fell open, a soft moan escaping. His lips traveled beyond mine, leaving tiny firecracker kisses along my jaw. His breath, warm against my skin, made every hair on my body stand on end.

"I've been pulled to you from the moment I met you," he murmured, grazing my earlobe with his teeth. His voice was deliciously low, slipping into my ear. "I couldn't figure it out, but I'm done fighting it." He tugged my hair slightly, exposing the vulnerable curve of my neck and I gasped as his tongue ghosted over the sensitive skin above my collarbone.

"Do you believe in fated mates?" I whispered. He paused, lips hovering at my shoulder. "If you'd asked me a week ago, I'd have said no." his words vibrated softly against my skin, "But now, there isn't a thing in this universe that would keep me from claiming mine."

Before I could respond, his hand drifted from my hair, skimming the back of my neck before settling on my breast. My breath caught at the heat of his touch. The shirt I wore felt impossibly thin under his fingertips, and when his thumb grazed my hardened nipple, a jolt of electricity shot through me. I bit my lip to stifle a moan. How did he make me feel so utterly exposed and yet so safe?

He pinched gently, teasing through the fabric, and an ache flared low in my belly. My fingers clenched the edge of the wooden chest I was perched on, the wood creaking in protest. He chuckled, the rumble sending another wave of heat through my body. My heart pounded in my rib cage, anticipation flooding my veins. "I can't wait," he murmured, his gaze dark with promise, "to do filthy and wonderful things to you." A tremor of longing ran through me as I stared back, every nerve alive with the possibility of what might happen next.

Heat flared low in my core, and my breaths came in shallow bursts. His fingers traveled along my ribs, then over my lower abdomen. I clung to the wooden chest beneath me, my knuckles turning white as though it were the only thing anchoring me to this moment. His hand paused at the waistband of my pants, his mouth still hovering near my shoulder. Then he lifted the hem of my shirt, exposing the bare skin of my stomach. My eyes snapped shut when his hand slipped underneath, and his palm met my skin. He continued upward, tugging my bra aside until he could cup my breast. They felt tender and swollen, and instinct drove me to arch my chest into his hand. The contact scorched through my nerves, pulling a sharp breath from him. He toyed with my nipple, rolling it between his fingers, and my gaze locked on his.

Abruptly, he withdrew his hand from beneath my shirt, instead taking hold of my chin with both hands. His next kiss was anything but gentle—urgent, hungry. Our tongues tangled in a heady dance, teeth grazing one another. My hands fisted in his shirt, pulling him closer. He lifted me by my face, pulling me against his chest without breaking the kiss, then took three deliberate steps to the left, then pushed me until my back pressed against the wall. My fingers curled into his shirt, and I tugged it over his head, gasping at the sight of his bare torso. Muscles rippled in his arms and shoulders as he tossed the shirt aside and turned his attention back to me. He yanked my long-sleeve shirt all the way off, flinging it across the room, then unclasped my bra with one hand.

Before I could react, his mouth crashed into mine again, and I moaned softly against his lips. He captured both my hands in his, tangling our fingers before placing them above my head. Lowering his head, he hovered just above my breast, catching my eye. Slowly, he exhaled over my nipple, and the sensation sent a wave of electricity from my chest to my core. He enclosed it with his mouth, his tongue tracing lazy circles, and I whimpered, pressing my legs together. He growled softly, sliding his knee between my thighs and nudging them apart. His tongue's slow swirl wound that coil of need tighter in my gut.

"Ahh," I murmured, and he rose, pinning me firmly to the wall with his chest. In the dim light, his eyes seemed to glow an otherworldly blue. My gaze dropped, drawn to the hard length straining against his jeans. My breath caught.

"Do you feel me?" he asked, baring his teeth wickedly. "I'm so hard for you." The low rasp of his voice sent a shiver through me. I was acutely aware of his thigh rubbing against me, imagining how much better it would feel with no barriers between us. As if reading my mind, he reached for my pants, intent on ridding me of every last layer.

"Oh, Pandora," he murmured, sliding a free hand into my underwear. I gasped as his fingers found my throbbing clit. "How glorious you feel beneath my hands," he breathed, working agonizingly slow circles that made my legs twitch with pleasure. Over and over, his fingers moved, the spot growing more sensitive until pressure swelled inside me, consuming my every thought. My breath came in ragged bursts, and when his mouth closed over mine, the heat pooling between my thighs erupted. It felt like fireworks going off, lightning shooting through every nerve as I climaxed.

"*Holy fuck*," I whispered into him, still trembling. He didn't give me time to recover, scooping me up by the ass and laying me across the bed, his bare feet leaving warm prints on the floor. "I'm going to make you come completely undone for me," he hissed, tearing his jeans off and tossing them aside with the rest of our clothes. His cock sprang free—rock hard against his stomach—and I licked my lips at the sight, hunger flaring inside me. I wanted him in my mouth right now. He prowled up the bed until his face hovered above mine—blue eyes locking onto green.

"What do you want, Pandora?" he asked. Instead of answering, I reached down and wrapped my hand around his length. He sucked in a sharp breath through his teeth but didn't stop me. His weight in my palm felt like I was holding raw power, and I never wanted to let go. As I stroked him, he closed his eyes, his chest expanding with a deep intake of air, and I felt him twitch in my grasp. "Switch," I croaked. His eyes flashed open. "What—?"

I shifted my hips, rocking him onto his back—my turn. My legs slid over his, straddling him. His jaw tensed as he watched my breasts bounce with the movement, and I leaned in until the tip of my nose brushed his. "If it were life and death, fighting the pull I feel toward you, I'd be dead already," I murmured.

He opened his mouth to reply, but I didn't give him the chance. I shimmied down the mattress and lowered my head taking him entirely into my mouth, lips closing around the head of his cock. His hips jerked in response, a deep groan spilling from his throat. The taste of him flooded my senses as I moved up and down his length, cupping his balls with one hand while my tongue traced along the underside. He was delicious, and I savored every second, his skin glistening with my attention.

"Pandora," he warned, voice low, lifting his head to watch me. I glanced up, meeting his gaze as I kept going. His hand twisted into my red hair, pulling me farther down until he was buried in my mouth. My hands fisted in the sheets beside him, and I took him deeper. He shuddered, breath escaping in tight gasps that spurred me on.

As I pulled back ready to take him again he shot upright from the bed with a low growl, moving too quickly for me to resist as he lifted me into his arms. He stood from the bed and his eyes darkened as he pressed me against the wall again. "I'm going to take you right here, right now." I swallowed hard as he tore my panties away, discarding them in the floor and returning his thumb to my aching clit. The hard length of him slid against my drenched center, and his mouth found mine. I threw my arms around his shoulders, fingers tangling into his brown curls as he pushed inside. I gasped against his lips at the sudden, exquisite pressure. He felt so incredibly good.

Bracing himself with a hand on the wall, he pulled back, then thrust in again. I moaned, clinging to his upper arms. He let out a rough groan, steadying himself, then fell into a rhythm—out and in, over and over. The heat simmering inside me flared, tightening with each stroke. "Luke," I begged, and his nostrils flared in response. Every motion felt magnified, each wave of desire rolling through me almost too intense to bear. He drove into me again, pressing me more firmly against the wall. My thigh burned where his fingers gripped it, as though seared by his touch. If anyone were nearby, they would definitely hear us by now. My head tipped back against the wall as his thrusts continued, unrelenting. His strength held me aloft, and I felt weightless under his onslaught.

The coil of tension between us finally gave, and I cried his name to the ceiling, my climax tearing through me. He slammed into me one last time, his release following in a shuddering wave. At that moment—like a taut rubber band—I felt the bond *snap* into place. Everything, I could feel *everything*. His emotions and thoughts crashed into me as if I'd run headlong into a brick wall.

"How beautiful she is, coming undone around me. I could do this all night." I gasped, my eyes going wide. "I can hear your thoughts," I whispered, staring at him in shock. *"Oh shit, can he hear mine?"* His mouth tilted up into a grin. *"It would seem that way."*

Holy fuck.

Chapter 31

My back slid down the wall as he eased out of me, the ache between my legs already beginning to wane. His arms were still wrapped around me as he stared, his blue eyes felt as though they were blazing into my soul. My hands rested on his muscular forearms as I waited for my breathing to even out. "What did you say?" I gasped. He tilted his head in amusement.

"Oh, this will be fun." His lips never parted, yet his voice rang clear in my mind, as if whispered straight into my thoughts. *"I must be losing my mind,"* I told myself, heart pounding, as he lowered me with care. Relief washed over me the moment my feet met the ground—cool and solid beneath me, the chill creeping up through my toes, grounding me in a reality that felt anything but real. *"Welcome to the insanity,"* he chuckled in my head. I pushed at his chest, panic rising in my throat, but Luke didn't seem the least bit fazed.

His arms loosened at his sides, his expression amused. "What?" he asked, still grinning like an idiot. "You can read my thoughts," I wheezed, realizing that was precisely what was happening. "It appears you and I are *tethered* now," he said, "whether you like it or not. But based on the way you were screaming my name, I'll assume you like it."

I shoved his shoulder again. "Be *quiet*!" I hissed, glancing around as it dawned on me how loud we must have been just moments ago. *"Oh shit, what if everyone heard us?"* The thought caused heat to creep up my neck ."*Let them hear,*" he murmured in my mind and a blush crept up my neck, *"even if they are, I doubt anyone will need to ask what we've been up to."*

He lay down on the crimson sheets, unconcerned about covering his naked body. My eyes traced over him, remembering every detail of what he'd just done to me. I closed them for a moment. "We need to talk," I said quietly. "Funny you're saying that now," he quipped.

I shot him a smoldering glare before reaching down to pick up a discarded shirt from the floor. It wasn't mine—the scent clung to it, eucalyptus and sandalwood, warm and unmistakably him. Still, I slipped it over my bare skin, the fabric brushing lightly against me. It hung short, the hem skimming just beneath my hips. His gaze followed every movement, slow and hungry, tracing the curves it couldn't hide. Then his eyes dropped to my hands—my marred fingertips exposed.

Heat flushed through me, and I tucked them behind my back, suddenly self-conscious. When our eyes met again, his expression softened with something unspoken. He patted the mattress beside him, invitation lingering in the space between us. "Are you going to put your clothes back on?" I asked, one brow raised. He chuckled, "Why bother? It's not like I wasn't just fucking you."

The crimson sheets couldn't compare to the color on my cheeks as my face heated. He smirked but did lean over the bed to grab his jeans. His back flexed as he stood to pull them on, and before I could stop myself, a sigh escaped my lips. I clapped a hand over my mouth. "Oh, *Pandora*," he murmured. "I could listen to you sigh all day, my cock buried deep inside you."

I gulped.

"But you're right," he added, "we do need to talk."

I pouted as he jumped back onto the mattress, settling where he'd been lying before. His jeans hung low on his hips, and my eyes trailed to that defined V disappearing beneath the front zipper. I bit my lip because I didn't need to imagine what lay just beneath. He raised his eyebrows in question, and I shook my head, trying to clear my thoughts.

Right—he could hear them all now.

Goodness, I was going to lose my mind with this man. I crawled onto the mattress, sitting cross-legged beside him. He rested one hand on my knee but stared up at the ceiling. "This isn't how I pictured our trip to Gayle going," he murmured. "Me neither," I snorted. His white teeth flashed in a grin. My post-sex bliss started fading as my mind turned over everything that had happened that day. Odina's hand around my neck, the agony she felt revealing the truth about my father, the memories she kept burying. My lips pressed together as my heart rate slowed. His thumb drew circles on my knee. "You're *half* Gaythe, *half* human," he said, more statement than a question. "It would seem so," I replied quietly, "just like Amy—er, Kimi—had been."

"Kimi?" he asked, tilting his head. "That's Amy's real Gaythe name," I replied quietly, thinking of my cousin—killed before I could meet her. I closed my eyes. "We'll figure it out," he said softly. I swallowed. "From the moment I took this case, I knew it was different. I should've listened to my gut," I murmured.

"I've felt the same way about many things lately." He lifted an arm to rest behind his head. I couldn't stop my gaze from roaming over his bare chest, lingering on the patch of coiled hair between his pecs. "My father rejected her," I said quietly. "Odina?" he asked. I nodded, "They were fated mates. He slept with her the night before she left—they were *tethered*, too."

My voice was small as I became aware of that same tether between us. Suddenly, in my mind, I stood in a dark room with four walls and a single door. I took a few steps toward it, raising my hand to the dark wood. Faint whispers floated behind it as I turned the knob, inching it open. A burst of bright, multicolored tendrils of light slipped through the crack. I slid my finger along a vivid mauve strand and felt him shiver. "*Pandora*," he coaxed in my head. A pale green tendril flowed over me in another wave. I opened my eyes to look at him. His were closed, and he appeared completely relaxed, sinking into the sheets. I shut my eyes again and dipped my hand, caressing a deep blue tendril, and felt a sudden rush of emotion. Heated desire spread up my arm, and this time, I was the one who shivered.

A low rumble came from his chest as he took a deep breath. The green streaks of color overhead moved closer as he guided the blue one toward me. It wove through my hair, snuggling into the nape of my neck, and I felt a pull—as though he was siphoning my emotions. Goosebumps prickled my skin, and the sensation of him buried inside me rippled through my bones. He hummed in response. "*I could get used to this*," he thought, and I blushed.

The colors gradually faded, and I opened my eyes to find him staring back at me, his blue irises dancing in the light. "What are we going to do about the cases now that we know it was my mother's niece who was killed, just like she was?" I asked out loud. He pursed his lips, thinking. I could sense his thoughts weaving through mine, but unless I focused, they remained distant—fuzzy and closed off behind that wooden door.

"Did Odina say why she was there?" he asked, sitting up against the headboard. I remained cross-legged beside him. "She said she sent her to ask my mom for aid on Gayle against the Nephrians." My voice dropped to a whisper. "She had no idea she was sending her to die." Darkness threatened to overwhelm me. Learning terrible things about a family I hadn't even known existed until yesterday was too much.

"There have been no others bestowed powers from the stone since Kimi," I said, "That is until I was the other day." I flipped my hands over in my lap. The marks were so dark, spiraling up my skin. I gazed at them, failing to find the words for the fear coursing through me. "What did she say about your hands?" he asked, following my stare. I rubbed my thumb into my palm, wishing the dark color would wipe away. "They have no clue how the magic will behave inside me," I felt the bed shift as he stood, "We need to speak with Kirro,"

"What if they're right, and something's wrong with my magic?" I wrapped my arms around myself fear tightening my voice. "Then we'll figure it out." He turned, eyes blazing, "I just got you. I'm not about to let anything happen to you. I swore I wouldn't, and that means something to me."

I blinked at him, but the fear in my chest refused to subside. Deep in my bones, something felt off that I couldn't quite place. It felt like thousands of years of ancestry caught up to me, igniting beneath my skin. My fingers tingled with the thought, and I glanced down, watching the inky color seep further up my arms. My eyes went wide as I held out my arms in front of me. "It's creeping up my arms," I whispered. He watched me as I scrambled off the bed in a panic.

"Seems we should start training sooner rather than later," he said in a clipped tone. "Let's go find Kirro—now." With that, he tossed me my pants.

Chapter 32

This wasn't quite how I had pictured the so-called ritual going. As soon as Kirro had been alerted, they rounded up every Gaythe to breach the surface and perform the ceremony. Luke and I walked silently, trailing behind a crowd of Gaythe headed for the city's perimeter. I wasn't sure what to expect, and my nerves started to rise in my chest. Sensing my growing anxiety, Luke offered his hand, and I slipped mine into it, our skin melding together. As we went along, I tucked myself closer to his side, nearly everyone else remaining silent.

A steady rhythm of footsteps echoed around us, almost trance-like. We were in the middle of the procession—almost eight Gaythe wide—parading down the coral tiled streets. Even when standing on my tiptoes, I couldn't see past the tall, scaled shoulders at the front of the line, where Ragnai and Kirro were leading. Neither of them looked back, eyes fixed on the path ahead.

We had been walking for several minutes, and I felt my heart race, my breath hitching against my tight chest. I watched as citizens of Kehel leaned out of their windows to glimpse the throng moving through the streets, then quickly ran down to join it. What had started as just Ragnai and Kirro, followed by Odina, then Haggik, Luke, and me, suddenly became hundreds of iridescent, vibrant bodies flowing through Kehel. I could just make out Odina's firmly set shoulders in front of Haggik,

whose massive frame nearly blocked my entire view. He had
insisted that we walk behind him, citing tradition or some such.
Whatever *that* meant.

I glanced down at my black combat boots scuffing against the
tiled roads, wondering if I should have worn something else.
They felt too *human*.

Ahead, the neon-green grass at the city's edge suddenly
appeared. The parade slowed, then stopped, as everyone
clustered around Ragnai and Kirro, who stood facing us with
watchful eyes. The veil was only a few feet away, glistening
iridescent against the dark blue water beyond. Up close, it
looked like a bubble's surface, arching and flowing with the
currents. I couldn't tear my gaze away, feeling a pull toward the
water on the other side. Its whispers echoed in my mind as I
closed my eyes, slowing my breathing and feeling the tightness
in my chest gradually ease.

Because Kirro was only a training officer, he'd asked Ragnai
for help—apparently, it required two people to manage a
Gaythe with uncontrolled power. Though I knew Ragnai
typically attended rituals, something about this one seemed
different and more crucial—like more was at stake. I'd stopped
listening after Kirro's first few sentences of explanation—he
tended to be loquacious, and my nerves were too frayed to focus
on every word.

I heard footsteps but didn't bother looking—I had already
sensed who it was. I opened my eyes, and Odina stood before
me, her purple irises refracting the light and sending it skittering
across her wide pupils. She watched me with open curiosity.

She wore her ceremonial attire to befit a Queen. A beige linen
tunic bound tightly by a leather corset that covered her chest.
Bands of fabric were tied around her biceps, flowing gently
along her arms until they nearly touched the billowing beige

pants covering her legs. But her clothing wasn't what caught my attention.

No, what caught my attention was the coiled, inky-black body paint swirling in delicate arcs across her arms, back, and face. The tribal markings wound over her bright scales, framing her features and leading up to a massive headpiece fashioned from what looked like antlers. They perched atop her head, each point strung with small black *stones*—four in total. They whispered delectably dangerous, powerful things, and my eyes widened as Odina dipped her head to lift the headpiece from her scalp.

Around us, the Gaythe—dressed in matching clothing and black tribal paint—began a deep, guttural song. The sound echoed in my chest, yet it wasn't fear I felt—it was a sense of home. They sang in their native tongue, and although I couldn't understand the words, something about it comforted me, sending a tingle over my skin. Odina nodded at Luke, and his arm slipped from mine as he stepped back, leaving me alone before my Queen. I turned slightly, catching his gaze—blue on green.

"If anything seems off, say something," Luke murmured in my mind. His arms hung slack at his sides, the navy shirt tight across his tense chest, making his bright eyes seem a deeper blue than usual. He bowed silently to the Queen, then straightened his gaze back to mine. I took a shaky breath, returning my gaze to Odina, who held the headpiece before her—the black stones slightly shifting as if in anticipation.

"Pandora Vaughn," Odina's voice boomed as she eyed me. The surrounding Gaythe voices fell silent as they began pounding on leather drums bound taut with string. The rhythmic thud steadied me, and I clenched my hands to keep them from trembling. "Niece to Odina Hyran, Queen of the Gaythe," she declared. Her voice echoed among the crowd, though her gaze remained fixed on mine. "Daughter of Esme Vaughn and Harrison Vaughn," she continued. The pounding of the drums swelled, growing louder and louder. A wave of dizziness hit me, and I felt the skin at the nape of my neck cool with a breeze, raising tiny hairs. "Receiver of the stones and returner of life," I could barely hear the last of her words as I forced myself to breathe and focus. "Do you accept Hanwi's power and the responsibility they have bestowed upon you?" she asked. The noise ceased, complete utter silence as they watched. I waited a full breath before answering. "Yes, I accept responsibility for the power bestowed to me." A slight grin tilted her lips. "You will be afraid of *nothing* and *no one*. Rise to the life you were given, rise to the power within." she whispered.

The crowd erupted into chaotic shouts and tribal screams, fueling my energy until my arms tingled with fierce pleasure. Odina stepped closer, and I dropped to one knee, my auburn braids swishing with the movement. She set the headpiece, surprisingly weightless, on my head, and I lifted my gaze as she dipped her fingers into black paint, smearing markings across my forehead and chin.

"Stand, child," she said, and I rose. Cheers exploded around us as her eyes danced with light. She inclined her head in acknowledgment before turning to address the crowd. "We have finally been returned *life*," she roared and the Gaythe roared back, their needle-like fangs glinting in the light. "Free your power! Let everyone know who the Gaythe truly are!" her voice rolled in waves, and before I could blink, every Gaythe around me burst into a sprint for the shield. I felt my body rise as Haggik's enormous arms hoisted me onto his back. Clinging to his neck for dear life, we sprinted toward the veil. My fingers fumbled with the hilts of the daggers tucked into the pockets of my pants, ensuring they were secure.

The truth was, I was terrified. But something my mother had told me when I was just a little girl replayed in my mind like a broken record. *To be brave, you must first be afraid. To be strong, you must first be weak. To be a leader, you must first be led.* How I wished I could hear her voice just one more time.

Haggik's webbed feet pounded first on grass, then on sand, and suddenly, we were hurtling through the air toward the shield, just as everyone else was flinging themselves into the dark water beyond. "Open your eyes and trust your body knows what to do," he said as his eyes dropped to mine and for a moment we were suspended midair frozen in time. Just the two of us. It was the last thing I heard before water engulfed me, overwhelming all my senses. I fought the water as it threatened to flood my mouth and sting my eyes, struggling against the surge propelling us even faster than before. I fought the growing sense of suffocation, the water pressing tighter and tighter around me.

Then, in a sudden rush, I *gasped*—water flooding my lungs and eyes—and everything became crystal clear. I could see everything around us, the Gaythe scales reflecting the light even in these depths. Hundreds of them surrounded us as we rushed for the surface. I gulped down breath after breath of water, yet my chest felt like I was breathing *air*. Light as a feather.

Haggik swerved to the right, zipping past two smaller Gaythe women with their hands clasped as they darted after us. The water warmed as we neared the surface, and the Gaythe tightened their formation, weaving deftly among underwater rock caverns and coral taller than any building I'd ever seen on Liarta. All of Gayle was breathtaking and uncannily *familiar*.

We burst through the surface as Haggik leaped onto the shoreline, landing in the dirt. He paused only for a heartbeat before bunching his legs and springing to the crater's rim in a single, swift motion. My stomach lurched at the distance, but he didn't hesitate, and the whoops of the Gaythe rang out around us as we all charged into the jungle.

Spears and daggers belonging to the surrounding Gaythe glinted in the moonlight as dark trees whipped past my face. I clung to his neck as we hurtled through the dense foliage at impressive speed, with no sign of stopping anytime soon. From my perch on Haggik's back, I could see the Gaythe ahead, leaping over logs and shrubs with the grace of mountain cats. Their voices echoed off every tree, surrounding us in a cacophony that made my ears ring with exhilaration. I glanced around, searching for Luke, and spotted him behind us. Ragnai sprinted effortlessly with Luke perched on his back, the pair moving far too fast for any human to match. His blue eyes met my green, a grin spread across his face, and I felt my own match his. Alive, I finally felt truly *alive*.

We came to a sudden halt, my body pressing against Haggik as we stopped before an enormous stone dome—blacker than the night sky. I gasped, eyes trailing across its surface as we entered. Gaythe clustered inside, roaring, their fangs sharper than any blades they wielded, points threatening to slice the air rushing from their throats.

Haggik set me gently on my feet, then dropped to his knees. I advanced toward Odina, standing in the center of the crowded dome, the noise of the Gaythe echoing all around me. Ragnai and Luke took a seat at the edge of the crowd, where everyone knelt and screamed, their voices drowning out the boom of my heart. Odina's eyes flared as she watched me advance.

I finally stopped before her, standing in front of a black pit at the dome's heart. She raised one hand, and the room fell completely silent. Kirro stood adjacent to her, his jaw set firmly, while the swirling paint patterns danced along his scales.

"It is time to see what Hanwi granted you," Odina declared, her voice just loud enough to reach me. I dipped my head in acceptance, the black stones dangling from the bone crown. Odina stepped back a few paces to let Kirro take the lead. I could feel Luke's presence behind me, but I didn't dare turn to look at him. My eyes stayed glued to Kirro in front of me.

"Let us begin," he said, gesturing toward the pit before us. Everyone watched with anticipation as Kirro took a seat, legs crisscrossed in front of the black pit, while I sat to his left, mirroring his position. "The first thing we must do is learn the nature of the power the stones have given you. The power follows the pattern of natural law—you can have power bestowed as stones, air, fire, or water. There are branches from each, but these are the most common. It's possible we won't discover which subset you have today, only the amount of raw force you contain within yourself."

I blinked, absorbing the information as he continued, "The Gaythe with stone powers are most often our warriors. They are the strongest among us and work best as frontline fighters. Our water Gaythe, though the rarest of the three main power signs are often our healers. Air Gaythe tend to be our weapons experts. Their nimble hands work with impressive speed and dexterity and are suited to many tasks beyond weaponry. Fire is the most dangerous of all the signs—it's the hardest to control. Those with fire powers can serve as warriors or power grid workers. It's the most versatile of the four."

I nodded indicating I understood as he continued, "You are the first to take power in two decades." I blanched, but he didn't seem to notice. "Those are the four domains. However, I am not certain that is how your power will manifest. Only Hanwi will tell."

Odina watched me, her gaze unmoving as she stood nearby.

Kirro then pulled a vial of black liquid from the pocket of his canvas pants and poured its contents into the black stone bowl before us. A collective gasp rippled through the room, the only sound breaking the silence. The liquid swirled in the bowl momentarily, then evened into a mirror-like finish. It didn't even resemble a liquid—so still, so calm. My eyes widened in awe.

"The liquid in this bowl is what you *humans* call Element X. It is the most concentrated form of the power of Hanwi, they who live within the stones," Kirro explained in his distinctive accent. I leaned forward over the bowl's edge, my reflection staring back at me. "It can take liquid form? I thought it was just contained in the stones," I murmured, speaking more to myself than anyone else. "They can assume any natural form—smoke, water, stone, or fire. It transforms into the form that best channels the power it bestows upon you, depending on what is needed at the time." He leaned forward, and I watched his reflection merge with the silvery surface of the bowl as he continued his explanation.

"You mustn't touch the purest form of Element X—it is known to consume those who contact it in its most concentrated state." The liquid pulsed once, then twice, and a small drop rose from the bowl, drawing the rest of the fluid with it. It resembled a finger reaching from the bowl toward my face. I pulled back in startled shock, and the drop vanished back into the mirror-like surface.

"It seems it has more affinity to you than most," Kirro said, glancing at Odina. Her eyes met his, but neither spoke further on the matter. The hair on the back of my neck again stood on end, and I licked my lips in anticipation. Kirro lifted his webbed fingers and placed just the pads on the lip of the bowl. Everyone stared at me, yet my gaze was fixed on the fluid. Part of me feared the ominous black void it created, while another part yearned for it—and *that* conflict was the scariest part. I forced my eyes away.

"When you're ready, place your fingers on the edge of the bowl just as I have. Close your eyes and call to the power within you." He withdrew his fingers from the bowl and set them on his knees. Taking a deep breath, I lifted my hands from my lap. The pads of my fingers hovered over the edge of the bowl, just an inch away. He nodded, coaxing me onward. As cautiously as I could, I touched the rim. The cool stone brushed against my fingers, and slowly, I felt the warmth from my skin transfer to it.

At first, nothing happened. We sat in silence, staring into the mirrored pool before us. The eyes of all the Gaythe surrounding me were fixed on me. I frowned—was it not working? I opened my mouth to speak, but Kirro lifted a finger in my direction. I turned back to see the liquid slowly beginning to swirl. His gaze never wavered. I closed my eyes trying to focus.

Call to my power.

I found myself in the dark recesses of my mind—a black room where a door I identified as Luke stood nearby, completely shut. Then, I noticed a different door before me. Unlike the ebony wood of Luke's, this door seemed to be made of pure *moonlight*.

With my eyes still closed, I crept through the dark room, the door silent and unmoving, waiting for me to unlock it. Wisps of silvery steam trailed from the doorframe, coiling like ribbons in an otherwise stagnant space. I inched closer and reached for the handle. It turned easily, barely whispering as it swung on its hinges, revealing a dark hallway that ended in a black void.

My eyes fluttered open in the tangible realm, yet I could no longer see. It seemed I was trapped in the dimension of my mind. Fear crept up my neck, but I stifled it, taking a deep breath and focusing—I was here to discover the extent of my power.

To be brave, you must first be afraid.

Squinting, I turned my attention down the dark hall. Silvery light strands began floating from it, creeping along the walls and heading straight for me. I froze, waiting. They made no noise, only whirled around me, filling the room with bright radiance.

"You have come to us," said an echoey and distant voice. It didn't belong to one person but to a chorus of voices layered atop one another. My heart raced, but I forced myself to remain calm. "Come to who?" I responded, scanning the room for the source of the sound. *"We are not one person, but a collection of ancient ancestors—descendants of the Gaythe who came before you,"* the voice intoned, its sound bouncing off invisible walls in the dark room but honing into a singular female voice that took precedence over the others. Hanwi had chosen the voice of the one who brought me the most comfort.

My mother.

"What do you want with me? What is my power?" I asked. A low hum resonated as if the voice were contemplating its response, *"The power we bestow upon you is unlike any we have given before,"* I watched as the silvery strands wove around my feet like a snake coiling around its prey, and my heart pounded in my chest. *"The power we grant you is not of choice but of necessity. We are at war, moon child."*

"At war with who?" I asked, daring to tilt my head as the silver strands wound around my legs. *"With the Dark One,"* the voice replied. "Who is the Dark One?" I pressed, growing more confused with every word. Everyone was at war with someone, yet how could the stone power be at war with anyone when it seemed more in control than in danger?

The voice ignored my question, *"The Dark One wants to use us—to weaponize us against his enemies. You mustn't let him. Pandora, you are THE chosen one. The LAST chosen one. You embody us to your core; do not disappoint us."*

"How can I be the last chosen one? What do you mean?"

I asked, but the voice offered no reply. The silver strands descended back down my legs, retreating toward the door. "Wait!" I called, stepping toward the door as the strands slinked away. "I don't understand!" I cried, reaching out to catch the strand closest to me.

My fingers wrapped around it yet sank through nothing—as if it were made of smoke and didn't truly exist in the natural realm. Faster than a heartbeat, the silver threads spiraled together, whipping wind into my face as they twisted faster and faster. I raised my arms to shield my eyes, and they coalesced into a gigantic floating face before me. I couldn't tell if it was a woman or a man—just a face made of silvery light, its eyes gazing down on me.

Yet I was not afraid.

Somehow, I knew this face. I'd seen it before in a past life—or maybe in another time—but it was undeniably familiar. "*Pandora*," the voice intoned, and the silver lips of the face parted with each breath. "*You must protect our ways, our power. Do not let it end with you.*" Before I could ask what that meant, the face was gone—shooting down the hallway in a flash of light. The door slammed shut, and my eyes burst open.

The liquid had risen from the stone, bathing my hands and climbing up my arms, covering only the black, marred skin beneath. I gasped and jerked my hands away. The liquid pulsed with the abrupt motion before falling back into the bowl, which tipped slightly—nearly spilling its contents—until Kirro steadied it, careful not to disturb the Element X.

Everyone stared and Luke looked as pale as a ghost which was exactly how I felt considering I had just seen one. He rushed to us from the crowd.

"Tell us what happened," Kirro began as Odina approached, her eyes also wide. I stood up abruptly, my hands trembling at my sides. This was all too much, too soon. I had only just learned that my mother was Gaythe, and now I was expected to be the last chosen one, with all this spiritual power resting on my shoulders. The silence of the surrounding Gaythe watching us roared within my skull.

"Pandora," Kirro said as he rose from his seat, raising his hands to show he meant no harm. I blinked slowly, and with each breath, the fog in my mind cleared until everything around me came back into sharp, undeniable focus. Kirro lowered his hands taking a cautious step towards me. "You look shaken. Why don't you sit back down and tell us what they told you?" My eyes shifted from him as he spoke to Odina, who was now standing still observing us, and then to Luke, who was now only a few feet away but hadn't continued to advance toward me.

"Sit down," Odina said firmly but not meekly, gesturing to the ground. I complied reluctantly while Luke remained at a comfortable distance. I could sense what he was feeling—not fear, but uncertainty. It barreled into me with no hinderance, a welcome distraction from the distorted feeling the element X had given me. His hands were crossed tightly over his chest as I forced myself to relax, slowly lowering my tense shoulders.

"Now, tell me everything that happened," Kirro said as the tension that mirrored mine also started to ease. I bit my lip as I looked at him. "I saw something," I said chewing on my lower lip, a nervous habit I needed to break. "What did you see?" he asked, narrowing his eyes. They flicked to Odina, who didn't respond, then back to me. "I saw strands of moonlight that formed a face."

"Hanwi." He nodded with resolution, "what did they tell you?"

"That I was *the* chosen one," I breathed. His eyes widened at that statement. I took a deep breath, collecting my thoughts. "They told me they were at war with a 'Dark One' who wanted to weaponize them. They said the power it gave me was unlike any power bestowed before—that I was *the* chosen one, the *last* chosen one—and that I somehow embodied them. What does that mean, Kirro? Who is the 'Dark One'? How can I embody the power of the Hanwi?" The questions tumbled out of my mouth one after another as panic rose in my chest. "I don't know what that means. This has never happened before. Are you sure it said you were the *last* chosen one?" he asked. "I'm sure." I said softly as I nodded.

At last, Haggik moved, rising slowly from his knees. From the edge of my vision, I saw his eyes lock onto Ragnai, tracking his every step as he advanced toward me. A low snarl rumbled from Haggik's throat, his needle-like fangs glinting beneath a curled lip. But before he could act, Odina raised a hand—calm but commanding. Haggik froze, his shoulders tight with restraint, every muscle coiled, yet he obeyed. He stayed. For his Queen. Then both their gazes turned to me, and in that moment, I felt the weight of every eye in the room—every breath, every silence—pressing in around me.

Luke turned to Ragnai, who stood silently, rubbing his chin, his face drawn tight with strain. I turned to him, desperation in my eyes. "Ragnai, do you know what this means? What power I have?" I asked, my voice barely above a whisper. He exhaled slowly, shaking his head, "I don't know. Usually, when a chosen one completes the ritual, it reveals their gift—and with it, a duty. A calling. They're shown how they're meant to protect the Gaythe and the force held within the stones. But the stones themselves, they aren't the true source of power." He paused, as if searching for the right words. "The power comes from something older—something sacred. It's a gathering of ancestral spirits, not unlike the 'God' some humans believe in. These spirits gave everything in life, and even more in death. They watch, protect, and guide those still walking in the living

realm. We call them *Hanwi*. It's not a being—not a man or
a woman—but a collective of countless guardian souls who
existed before us. And now it seems they've chosen you." He
looked at me, the weight of his words settling between us.
"Though why—or for what purpose—we've yet to understand."

My brows knit together trying to absorb his words. "I tried to
ask what they meant, but I couldn't understand them. I didn't
understand what they were saying." My voice cracked, and the
tears welled before I could stop them, blurring the edges of the
dome, "I don't know what Hanwi wants from me. I don't know
how I'm supposed to help. What am I supposed to do?"

Ragnai didn't answer me. Instead, he turned toward Kirro,
who had knelt again before the stone bowl. With steady hands,
Kirro tipped it carefully, pouring the shimmering liquid back
into its vial. He sealed it tightly with a cork, then slipped it
into his pocket before rising, and stepping toward me. "You'll
know when the time comes what Hanwi asks of you," he said
gently, "The future isn't fixed. Hanwi can see the paths ahead,
but even they cannot command what will be. They are guides,
not gods. They offer their wisdom, their presence, to help you
shape what's still unwritten."

"Some wisdom and guidance," I muttered under my breath.
"Hanwi knows what they are doing. Trust them," he said, his
hand resting briefly on my shoulder—steady, grounding, "If
Hanwi trusts you, then you're not a danger—to us or to yourself.
Your focus now must be on training the power that stirs within
you and discovering the gift Hanwi has placed in your hands."
He withdrew his hand and gave a subtle nod to Ragnai and
Luke, both of whom had silently stepped to my side. Luke,
ever the quiet observer, studied me with that same unreadable
expression. He always listened first—spoke only when he felt
the question mattered.

"How are we even supposed to find her power?" Luke asked, his voice low, directed at Ragnai, who was absently running his fingers over the tight braids on his scalp. "If I knew," Ragnai said, voice taut with frustration, "I would tell you. Only Hanwi knows the answer. You must follow where they lead."

"They didn't tell me anything I didn't already know, I don't eve know where to begin with that." I huffed, frustrated. "I believe, in time, it will reveal itself." Ragnai said gently. Luke turned to Odina, his voice quieter now, "Why do you think Hanwi chose Pandora as the *last* one?" Odina's face remained composed, but I saw the storm beneath it—uncertainty, curiosity, maybe even fear. She sighed, "I don't know why they chose her, but if what they said is true—if you really are the last chosen one—then the power they've given you must be crucial. Especially for the war they warned us about."

Her gaze found mine, steady and unwavering. "You are a chosen one now. In our culture, that means you are a warrior—someone we hold in deep respect. Though Ragnai is your guide in battle and tradition, he will recognize your place and offer you his respect, sister."

As if summoned by her words, Ragnai lowered himself to one knee before me, his head bowed low in solemn deference. My breath caught as the moment settled into me—heavy and sacred. "I am at your service, sister," he said, voice deep and certain. "As your guide, I vow to fulfill my duty—to see your purpose brought to light." He stayed there, still as stone, the long shaft of his spear resting diagonally across his back, its tip angled toward me. "Thank you," I whispered, the words barely making it past the lump in my throat. Then, with a quiet grace, he rose. Odina turned to address the crowd, raising both her hands. "She is *chosen*!" she boomed.

A roar of applause burst through the air, mingled with

chants and jubilant songs. The Gaythe erupted in wild celebration—whooping, hollering, their voices echoing like thunder. Then, as if driven by a single heartbeat, they surged to their feet and sprinted together through the open arch of the dome, disappearing into the untamed embrace of the Gayle jungle beyond. Amid the chaos, Odina moved to follow the others, her steps quick and instinctive. But after a few paces, she halted, something pulling her back. She turned slowly, her gaze finding us—steady, searching, heavy with unspoken meaning—before she spoke.

"Ragnai and Haggik will wait for you just outside," she said, her gaze drifting to Luke, who nodded before she rejoined her people and headed back to the city. Haggik's eyes lingered on mine as long as Odina allowed, before he too turned and followed her, Ragnai close in step.

I took a deep cleansing breath, "This just gets more and more complicated," I said, my voice trembling as I paced along the grass beneath the enormous black stone overhead. Moonlight cast through the open arcs bathing us in a silvery glow, my shadow following my every step. "Is that all Hanwi said to you?" Luke asked gently, watching me pace with eyes that seemed to search for a way to ease whatever was unraveling inside me. "I told them everything," I said quietly, the words fragile in the space between us. "They said I embody them—and that I have to protect their power from the Dark One." My voice bounced off the onyx walls, returning to me.

"Embody them," he repeated, not quite asking, more like tasting the weight of the words aloud. "Yes," I murmured, coming to a stop and turning to face him. "But I don't know what that *means*."

"I don't either," he admitted quietly. "It doesn't seem like anyone does, but Odina, Ragnai, and Kirro seem to trust Hanwi."

Suddenly, his eyes widened as he looked at me. "What?" I asked, alarmed. "It's nothing," he quickly dismissed. "It's getting late—you should rest." I moved toward the dome's opening, with Luke walking beside me, "I wonder what Ivy would think of this place," Luke chuckled under his breath, "I think she'd have an aneurysm." My eyes lifted toward him as our feet carried us into the jungle. "You cannot tell her about Kehel. Ragnai told us we must never reveal this place," he said firmly, "We gave him our word, Pandora."

"I know," I said softly, "but I don't know what we're going to tell them when we get back to Liarta." I bit down on my lower lip, anxiety swirling just beneath the surface. "That's the least of my worries right now," he muttered. "I'm more concerned about hiding the dark marks on your arms. Your father's going to lose his mind—he'll *kill* me if he thinks I'm the one who did that to you." His voice was low, tense, almost a growl.

We stepped through the arched doorway, the jungle greeting us with its chorus of night sounds—chirps, rustles, distant howls—each echoing off the trees and threading through the moonlit air. "My father isn't going to kill anyone," I snapped, my voice sharp. "I can take care of myself." My jaw tightened, eyes fixed forward, refusing to waver.

Leaned against a tree, Haggik's shoulders were firm and muscular beneath his shimmering scales. Ragnai stood beside him, his spear jutting from his back. Neither of them said a word as we approached. "Once again, I didn't say you couldn't," Luke bickered with me, "But you also have to understand—you are his daughter. His only living relative now. If he's any kind of man worth being, he would find whoever marked you and end them." He grabbed my elbow, stopping us in our tracks and I looked at him as his eyes bore into mine. "I know I would," he said firmly, then dropped my elbow and continued walking.

I stayed frozen for a moment, absorbing his words before jogging to catch up. "Then what should I do?" I asked. "I don't know, Pandora, but you cannot let *anyone* see your arms. Do you know what scientists on Liarta would do if they knew about this power that Hanwi has bestowed upon you—and that you're *half Gaythe, half human*, just as Amy was?" His voice pitched higher.

"Kimi," I corrected, and Ragnai cleared his throat, reminding us that they were there. I chose to ignore him. "Whoever. You know what I mean," he said, his tone clipped with annoyance. "You're no longer safe *anywhere*—neither here nor on Liarta. You no longer have a home. You must stay vigilant because, whether you accept it or not, the Gaythe war has become your war, and the humans on Liarta will stop at nothing to find a weakness to exploit in another species."

Fear crept back up my spine. "They wouldn't," I said briskly. He turned and stopped abruptly in front of me and I nearly bumped into his stationary body. My arms windmilled out as Haggik surged forward to steady me from falling onto my ass. Luke narrowed his eyes at his outstretched arm for a moment, but Haggik remained unfazed, arm still poised to keep me from falling into the jungle floor. "They would," he said his eyes returning to mine. He leaned forward until his face was inches from mine, "Danny Fritz is preparing for war on Liarta. Your father has been doing his dirty work for *years*, Pandora,"

"You're *wrong*," I whispered. "I wish I were," he replied, as he lowered his voice further, leaning even closer, "It's time for your end of the bargain, Pandora. I told you I would help you close your case; now it's time for you to help me close mine. We must return to Liarta and end this war before it starts."

"We still haven't figured out who killed Kimi," I whispered, my voice barely more than a breath. "I know who did," he said, his tone low and certain. My heart skipped. "Who?" I asked, eyes wide, my voice tightening with urgency. "Not here," he warned, casting a wary glance toward Ragnai and Haggik.

Quiet footsteps made the entire group turn to see two nearby Gaythe women had stopped mid-step, their gaze fixed on us. Their slit pupils flickered back and forth between me and Luke. I couldn't tell if they understood English, but I wasn't about to risk it. Not when I'd already learned the hard way that more of them spoke it than I'd first assumed. "Okay," I murmured, reining in the rising tension, "not here."

Without another word, Haggik lifted me effortlessly onto his back, and the four of us vanished into the jungle, swallowed by the night.

Chapter 33

We moved in silence through the dim corridors of the tower, our footsteps the only sound—soft but hollow. No words passed between us. After returning to Kehel almost immediately, Ragnai, Odina, and Haggik had vanished for a private meeting, leaving Luke and me to find our way back to the bunk room alone. We were nearly there when Luke suddenly threw an arm across my chest, stopping me cold.

"What—" I began, but his hand covered my mouth before I could finish, his eyes sharp and urgent. He pressed a finger to his lips, commanding silence. I froze, my breath catching in my throat as he tilted his head toward a door slightly ajar, shadows spilling out into the hallway like ink. Faint voices floated through the crack—too low to distinguish words, but urgent enough to steal the stillness from the air. My eyes followed his as he stared at the doorway, every muscle in his body coiled, listening. Then he glanced at me and beckoned with a jerk of his chin, slipping soundlessly toward the voices.

I hesitated.

"We shouldn't be eavesdropping," I whispered, barely audible. "It's Ragnai and Odina," he murmured without looking back. "We need to know what they're saying—about you." My pulse pounded in my ears as I pressed against the cool stone wall, inching closer until I could feel the heat radiating from the sliver of open space. The voices inside sharpened just enough to recognize their cadence, the way truth always sounds different when people think they're alone. I didn't want to hear it. And yet—I had to.

"Hanwi said she was the last chosen one." Ragnai's voice became audible. "Yes," Odina replied. I looked at Luke, who shook his head at me to stay quiet. I craned my neck, trying to hear better. "What has Kirro interpreted from it?" Odina asked him. There was a loud sigh, seemingly from Ragnai, "He doesn't know what it means, Odina. He said this had never happened before. Hanwi has always told the chosen their purpose. This time, it seems that they are letting her decide."

It felt as if all the oxygen had been sucked from my body. Letting me decide my purpose? That couldn't be right.

"She's different," Odina said slowly, as if weighing each word. "The prophecy mentioned a battle," Ragnai replied, his voice lifting, tight with uncertainty. "Between 'The Dark One' and 'The Moon Child.'" A pause, then, "Do you think it's *her*?"

"If she is, the war is much closer than we anticipated, Ragnai. We must make haste and prepare as best we can. She needs training— a *lot* of it."

There was no response, only the sound of footsteps pacing through the cracked door. "We need to send her back to Liarta. She must find what Kimi discovered that led to her death. It could be critical in this war."

"She is not ready," Ragnai hissed, slamming his fist on the table with a resounding thud. I jumped at the abrupt noise, but Luke placed a hand on my shoulder, keeping me steady. "If anyone knows that, it's me," she growled in response, "we don't have another choice. If Kimi was killed, it was because she knew something someone didn't want her to tell us."

Her voice sounded sad and distant. I glanced at Luke, who shrugged, unsure of what that could mean either. Ragnai bit his tongue as a moment of silence hung tight in the air then, "We will speak with them in the morning. This is now their war, too. You are her *guide*, Ragnai—do not become clouded by emotion. I need you to be the guide I appointed you to be; lead her as such." She said firmly. "As you command, my Queen," he said with resolution.

Before I could fully process it, Luke grabbed my wrist and pulled me into the nearest hallway. He paused there, ears straining for footsteps, eyes scanning the corridor. Then his gaze snapped back to mine. "They're sending us back to Liarta," I whispered, my voice barely carrying as I glanced over my shoulder toward the room we'd just left. "As they should," he said, his tone low but resolute, "They're not wrong—Kimi uncovered something. Something worth silencing. Maybe it was intel on a high-ranking official or details about the war Danny Fritz is orchestrating."

"You still haven't told me about this supposed 'war' he's planning. How do you even know about it?" I asked, raising my fingers in air quotes. "It seems you've forgotten that I was sent by 'The Protectorate' to end the mining of Element X. They plan to use it as a weapon of war." He tilted his head in my direction."And how *exactly* do they plan on using it?" I asked. "I wasn't sure until earlier. Kirro said you cannot touch Element X because it *consumes* anyone it contacts. If they mine enough of it, can you imagine what kind of evil it could do if they *inject* it into someone?" he replied, his brows furrowing in thought.

The blood drained from my face. "What could that even do to a person?" I asked, horrified. "Considering what happened when it merely *touched* you earlier—and you weren't injected—that's not something I'm eager to find out," he said. "Luke, we have to get back to Liarta and stop them." The potential for danger was immense; Element X in the wrong hands was too perilous to ignore. I thought I knew my father and believed he was a good man, but was he? What if it had all been part of the illusion he and my mother had created?

"Come on. We'll worry about it in the morning," he said, and I reluctantly followed him back to his room.

***

I stood at the city's edge, watching the light bounce off the veil. I had been here for hours, mesmerized as the water bent and folded. I wanted nothing more than to reach out and touch it, but I remained frozen, my eyes glued to its shimmering surface. Finally, I took a step—then another—reaching for the light flowing before me. It called to me, promising the vast ocean beyond. My fingers slid across its surface—warm and inviting. Reaching further, I slipped past it into the water. I felt no worry, for I no longer relied on air to fill my lungs; the powers bestowed upon me had made me amphibious, and the water was my home. I kicked my legs, propelling myself forward. The muscles in my legs contracted and transformed slowly into large, magnificent fins of silvery-pink light. They swished against the oceanic current, thrusting me onward. I wasn't sure where I was going, but I knew what called to me, Hanwi.

As I moved deeper, the black skin along my arms bubbled and flowed, replaced by iridescent pink scales that matched the fins emerging from my legs. They were incredible—unlike any Gaythe scales I had ever seen. Further into the water, my legs pushed me faster and faster. The city disappeared into darkness behind me, but I pressed on, trusting I was safe and knowing they wanted to show me something extraordinary. The ocean floor dipped to reveal a cavern deeper than any on the surface of Liarta. Neon fish swam in enormous schools against red coral that led down into the abyss. I floated above the gap.

"Come and see," a voice called from far below. With one flick of my feet, I was pulled down—down, down. All the light seemed to vanish at this depth, and my eyes had to adjust to the darkness. It felt endless until, eventually, I reached the bottom of the cavern. I looked around, my eyes barely able to see through the dimness. What was it they wanted me to see?

A tiny pinhole of light appeared in the darkness—white at first—and then it began to grow until it formed a silver strand winding its way through the shadowy water. I watched as it curled around my waist, then lifted in front of me, coiling and coiling until it formed a face. Hanwi. "Pandora," the face intoned, its voice brushing the water.

"Show me," I pleaded.

"As you wish," it replied, dissipating into particles of light that shot off like fireworks. I covered my eyes against the sudden assault of brilliance, but only for a moment until I realized what had been revealed. Here, in the deepest part of the Gayle ocean, were the largest stone formations ever seen—massive structures of pure, black stone. I dropped my hand, gaping at them. "Protect us," the voice commanded.

***

I awoke with a gasp, lungs heaving like I'd broken the surface of deep water. My skin was drenched in sweat, my heart pounding so hard I could feel it in my throat. For a moment, I didn't know where I was—only the heavy crimson sheets in my fists and the flickering shadows on the walls. Then, slowly, the reality settled around me.

Kehel. Gayle. Just a dream. Or at least, that's what I told myself.

I sat up, my breath still uneven. The bed was too quiet I realized—Luke was gone. The space beside me was cool, untouched. I was alone. I shifted under the sheets and only then realized I was completely bare beneath them. I couldn't remember taking my clothes off. Had I even made the choice to? Exhaustion must've consumed me so thoroughly I'd gone on autopilot. But the dream clung to me like humidity, heavy and impossible to shake.

Images still flickered behind my eyes. The black stone monoliths rising from the seafloor, ancient and unmoving, like sleeping giants. Light had filtered down in beams, illuminating their edges—cold and sacred. I remembered the sensation of being watched, not by something hostile, but by something eternal. Was it really just a dream? Or had Hanwi reached into my sleep and pressed their message into me? They said they were part of me now. That I embodied them. If that was true, then dreams might not be dreams at all. Maybe they were glimpses—memories, warnings, pieces of the truth too vast to comprehend all at once. Still, I didn't understand. Why show me the stones? What did they want from me? My head throbbed. The uncertainty felt like a weight I wasn't strong enough to carry.

I lay back down and pulled the sheets up again, as if they could shield me from the enormity of it all. I sighed and turned onto my back, pressing my palms to my chest as if that might still my racing heart. Right now, I just needed rest. I focused on my breath, counting each inhale, each exhale, until the tightness began to ease and sleep slowly reclaimed me.

Chapter 34

I moaned, rolling over in the sheets. How long had I lain here—minutes, hours? After that strange dream, I'd tossed and turned for what felt like an eternity, but eventually, I must have fallen asleep. The windowless room looked exactly as it had earlier, with the dim light from a floating orb in the corner being the only illumination. Strangely, Luke hadn't returned after asking me to rest. Not knowing the time, I swung my legs over the side of the bed, allowing myself to wake up fully. I blinked in the partial darkness as my eyes adjusted.

I was wearing nothing and all the black whorls of paint were magically gone, no longer brushed along my skin. I blushed at the realization that Luke would most likely return at any moment now.

A lot had happened in just a couple of days here on Gayle, and although I had accepted him as my mate, my feelings for him remained murky at best. Odina had said that once a chosen Gaythe mated, it was for life—but did that rule apply to me, or did she mean the other full-blooded chosen Gaythe?

I rubbed my temples, trying to ease the headache I knew was coming. What would this mean when we returned to Liarta? How would I explain everything that had happened? We were brought here and trusted to keep this city safe—what would happen if we told anyone on Liarta that it even existed? And how would that affect the supposed war Danny Fritz was preparing for? Was it true that my father was working for him, colluding about Element X? He had laid out almost everything in black and white, unknowingly confirming it at the precinct ball.

There it was—the headache I'd been dreading.

My eye twitched, and I groaned while rubbing the back of my neck. We needed to go back to finish the cases we had started. We came with questions, and got their answers. Now it was time to piece together the fragments of answers into the bigger picture, even if I wasn't sure where each piece belonged.

The bed creaked beneath me as I rose, my eyes scanning the dim room for the black jeans and fitted tank top I'd worn when we first arrived on this planet. I found them in a heap near the foot of the bed and slipped into them without hesitation. My long auburn hair hung loose in soft waves, cascading over my shoulders and down my back—I didn't bother tying it up. Lowering myself back onto the mattress, I grabbed my boots and tugged them on, fingers moving quickly as I laced them tight. I tucked the ends in, securing them with practiced ease, every movement sharp with purpose. A knock sounded at the door and I rose crossing the room in a few strides to open it.

Luke stood before me, freshly showered and dressed in black tactical pants and a long-sleeve green shirt. His hair was still damp, and the faint scent of eucalyptus drifted toward me. My eyes swept over him, landing on his striking blue eyes.

"Good morning," he breathed. "Is it?" I asked, glancing around the room. He chuckled, a sly grin curling up his face. He always remained so composed and calm—as if our lives weren't being completely disassembled right before our eyes. "We need to start packing," He said. "Ragnai just told me that Odina's decided we're heading back to Liarta today." he picked at his thumbnail as he leaned against the door frame. His large frame cast a long shadow over mine as light from the hallway seeped into the room.

"*Today?*" I asked in disbelief. "We only just got here. I haven't even started training. She dropped all this world-shifting information on me in a matter of days, and now she expects me to just go back to Liarta like nothing's changed—as if this place wasn't real, as if Hanwi doesn't exist, and as if I wasn't just told I'm the last chosen one, tasked with protecting something I can't even begin to comprehend!" My words tumbled out, heated and emotional, and I felt the familiar panic creeping up my spine.

"She wants us to find out what happened to her daughter, Pandora, and her sister." He said calmly, "She is still the Queen of these people—*your people*—and although we outrank her on Liarta, here, what she says goes. If she says jump, you don't ask how high, you just start hopping."

"Since when were you one to follow rank and rules?" I scowled and narrowed my eyes at him. "Since it affects the bigger picture, not just a measly precinct on a planet whose government is ignorant to its implosion."

"And here?" I asked, tilting my chin up toward him. He sighed and leaned forward, crossing his arms. I felt the warmth of his cheeks radiate to mine, and an inexplicable heat surged through me at his close proximity. "I have no reason to believe that Odina is conspiring against us. We knew when we came here that we would have to go back. We have unfinished business on Liarta that must be attended to, regardless of how you feel about the people here—or the people back home. The fight is just beginning, Pandora. So, grab your things and meet me in the banquet hall in ten minutes. I won't ask again." His minty breath brushed over my lips, and for a moment, it felt as if my lungs had stopped working. How did he have this effect on me?

Irritation flared within me for a moment before I realized he was right. Coming here was only the first part of the enormous can of worms I had opened—*Pandora's box, if you will*—and the only way out was through.

He paused, and silence filled the space between us for a heartbeat, then another. He brushed his thumb over my cheek, and my eyes caught a smudge of black paint on it as he lifted it, "Ah, I missed some." He muttered. I turned the deepest shade of ruddy red that existed and shook my head, clearing my thoughts.

"You are only as strong as you believe you are. If you give up, everything around you will fail." I furrowed my brows and opened my mouth to ask what he meant, but he was already heading down the hall. "Ten minutes!" he repeated over his shoulder, leaving me standing in the doorway, pondering by myself.

I muttered a curse under my breath as he walked away, then turned back into the room and began gathering my things. I stuffed clothes and gear into the backpack—someone, likely Haggik, had already brought it up from the bunk room. With quick, practiced movements, I smoothed out the bedding, a small act of control in the chaos. Then I secured the iridescent blades along my thighs and slid the pistol into the holster at my waist. It was time to go home—whatever *home* meant now.

The pack brushed against my loose auburn hair as I made my way to the banquet hall. The space was eerily silent, and my footsteps echoed in the empty corridors. I padded across a red rug, glancing through open doors and wondering where everyone was. Although this building was often quiet, there was usually a warrior or two coming and going on some duty or training. At the end of the hall, the large wooden doors to the banquet hall loomed before me. I pushed them open and walked into what appeared to be an ongoing briefing.

Luke stood with his back to the door, turning as I entered;

his boots made barely a sound on the shiny white tile. Ragnai was seated at a long table, while Haggik, leaning on the smooth surface beside him, eyed me silently. Their matching spears gleamed, still firmly attached to their backs—it seemed they never went anywhere without them—they probably even slept with them. I chuckled inwardly at that thought.

Odina stood by one of the tall windows along the wall, gazing out. The queen's guards were posted at the four corners of the room, all dressed in tan canvas pants with their spears held at attention. None of them even glanced in my direction. My eyes, however, were drawn to the color Odina was wearing.

Instead of her usual warrior ensemble, she was draped in a deep, nearly black purple—the color of *royalty*. Her dress featured a high collar, with thin chiffon billowing from her shoulders before reattaching at the wrists with thick golden cuffs. A matching golden belt cinched her waist, and slits ran down the length of her skirt, revealing her iridescent, scaled thighs. She looked every bit the Southern Gaythe Queen—beautiful and *deadly*. I glanced down at my own plain black attire and couldn't help but feel that she had, quite effectively, put me to shame.

"Seems like I'm interrupting something," I muttered sarcastically, setting my bag down with a thud. Luke shook his head before turning his gaze back to Odina. "I was just informing Detective Nesnah that we received a distress call from the northern Gaythe tribe's leader," she announced loudly. No one else seemed shocked by the news—perhaps I had indeed interrupted something important.

"The northern tribe?" I asked as I walked further into the room, scooting one of the chairs at the table out and plopping down. I let my hands fall to my lap. "I thought you didn't speak with them," I added, my eyes landing on the two Gaythe men across from me. Ragnai watched me from over the table, and Haggik's scaled hand rested on the tall back of his chair. Neither bothered to respond as I blinked at them. "We don't—unless there are dire circumstances." Ragnai muttered.

"Well, why did they contact you?" I asked. "Dire circumstances," Odina replied dully. I turned, leaning to the side to peer around the back of the chair. "What are the dire circumstances?" I asked, my fingers gripping the wood. I could hear Luke shifting from one leg to the other a few feet away. Odina turned from the window, her long braids twisting in the light. Her hands were clasped behind her back as she took a few measured steps toward the table. She looked every bit the Gaythe Queen—regal, in control. I envied her composure. "The Nephrians have launched another attack," her voice rang through the room.

I paled, "Brykan?"

"No, he sent a group of his frontline fighters to take out their largest city," she said, watching me intently. "What is their largest city?" I asked, turning to glance at Ragnai and Haggik. "It *was* Amarith," Ragnai said, his tone heavy with desolation. "I thought you said it was blasted by their last attack. What do you mean by was?" Dread filled my mind as I took in their wary expressions.

"They came back to finish the job. Their leader wasn't as lucky as I was—it is reported he was assassinated on sight. The northern tribe sent out a distress beacon, asking for aid that I simply don't have the numbers to provide. I don't even want to imagine the aftermath," Odina grumbled. "*Fucking hell*," I whispered, "They're obliterating everything,"

"They have been for some time now, but there are so few of us left after the last wave that I fear it's only a matter of time before they wipe us all out. The only thing I can offer them is a tribe merge—but they've been a separate tribe for more than a millennium. For them to merge with us would be incredibly painful for both sides," her voice filled with regret and sadness. I turned back to face her, anger flaring in my eyes. She knew all of this was happening here on Gayle, and yet she's still sending us back, even in the midst of it all.

"Why are you sending us home when there's a more important war happening right here?" I demanded, slamming my fist onto the table with a clang. She remained unfazed by the noise. "Because I need you to do a job for me."

"Let's hear it then," I muttered.

"We do not have enough people—Pandora, our healers are overwhelmed, and Brykan is taking more of our warriors every day. I need you to finish the job I sent Kimi to do. Convince the Liarta government to send aid against Brykan and the Nephrians," Odina said, watching me.

"Danny Fritz will never go for that, Odina. The only way Danny will aid anyone besides his own planet is the day he's dead," Luke said gruffly. "I don't care what you have to do to convince the Liarta government to lend aid," Odina hissed. "You fucking *do it*."

Luke bristled at her sudden command, "You want me to murder the president of our home planet? I'm sure the citizens would gladly follow the advice of the person who assassinated their leader,"

"Because you're such an honorable soldier, are you?" Odina spat at him. "Or were you sent to Liarta *merely* to shut down the mining operation—like you told Pandora?"

My head whipped in his direction. "What is that supposed to mean?" I whispered. "Pandora," he coaxed gently. "No, don't patronize me. What does she mean by that, Luke?" I demanded, my voice rising. "It's not what you think it means—and it won't sound that way when I explain."

"You better start explaining then," I growled, grinding my teeth. "Right *now*." He released his arms, which had been crossed over his chest, and glanced at Odina again. "Don't look at her—look at me," I hissed. "What are you not telling me?" He pressed his lips into a fine line and said nothing.

"I just learned from Ragnai that Detective Nesnah here is a Protectorate officer," Odina spoke for him. My eyes remained fixed on his face as his expression hardened like stone. "Do you know the authority that Protectorate soldiers have, Pandora?" Odina asked. The air in the room felt heavy as I forced it through my lungs. "Pandora," she repeated. "No, I do not know their full authority," I said quietly, my gaze still locked on Luke. He didn't move, barely breathing as he blinked back at me. "Protectorate soldiers are sworn to kill a single target and until that mission is complete, they cannot return to base."

"What does that have to do with anything?" I asked. She stepped over to stand beside me, leaning forward so that her lips were mere centimeters from my ear. "Have you asked Detective Nesnah who his target is?" she whispered, ensuring only I could hear her. My eyes widened. "Who is your target?" I demanded loudly.

Luke closed his eyes, and I could hear the sharp inhale of breath through his nose. "Pandora, you don't understand I'm not just a Protectorate soldier I'm the—" he started, but I cut him off. "I won't ask again," I spat, venom dripping from my words. He opened his eyes, pleading with me. I shook my head, tears streaming down my face. If it was this difficult for him to tell me, I already knew the answer.

"Harrison Vaughn." His voice rang through my ears.

My father. My father was his intended target. I stood motionless, silent—so silent you could have heard a pen drop. No one dared to breathe. My heart felt as if it had stopped completely. "My father is your target," I managed to say, inhaling shakily. "Yes," he replied, still unmoving. "You're not to return to Cappurn until you kill him," I demanded. "Yes, and to dismantle the Element X mining," he breathed.

"Why does The Protectorate want my father dead?" The question reverberated in my mind as I felt my teeth grind together, a subtle vibration resonating through my skull. "I cannot tell you." His reply was cold and unyielding.

My nostrils flared as I stood there, and before I realized what was happening, I was moving. The room blurred around me as I rushed forward. The blades, neatly tucked into my pockets, hissed as they slid from their slots into my fists. My fingers closed around their hilts—one in each hand—as my feet carried me onward.

I no longer cared who he was. He had deceived me—not by outright lying, but by withholding the most crucial truth. He was a sworn Protectorate assassin, bound to kill my father. I had accepted him as mine and had shared intimate moments with him, all the while knowing his duty was never to me. His duty was to end another's life—a life that had meant everything to me, that had built me, created the world I lived in, and given me life. And now, he was sworn to take it away.

My blade sank into his shoulder up to the hilt, and I screamed—a sound so guttural and animalistic that I had never uttered anything like it before. I screamed and screamed. I raised my left hand to drive the other blade deep into his throat, but he caught my wrist, wrenching it upward barely missing his nose by an inch.

I roared in his face, spitting in defiance, but he squeezed so hard that the blade slipped from my grasp, clattering loudly onto the floor. I wrenched the blade from his shoulder and reared back to strike again, but this time, Ragnai grasped my arm.

"Stop it!" His voice thundered through the banquet hall. He yanked me backward as Haggik rushed to Luke's side, clamping a hand over his bleeding wound. "Let that traitor fucking *die*!" I screeched. Luke fell to one knee, Haggik's hand covering his wound. His head dipped low, obscuring his face as blood dripped onto the white tile. Crimson dots splattered before him, one after another, and I bared my teeth in his direction.

"Pandora, control yourself," Odina's voice pierced the chaos. I refused to look at her, shaking with anger. He hadn't even tried to fight back—he had the audacity to do what he did without resisting. What a fucking *coward*.

Pulling against Ragnai, I bellowed, my voice echoing off the surrounding walls. It was so loud that the enormous emerald curtains hanging from the windows swayed with the noise. Ragnai held me firmly against his chest, his arms wrapped tightly around mine. I fought hard against him, but he did not budge.

Luke finally lifted his head, his eyes scorching flames over my body. Haggik followed his gaze, his eyes widening as they reached me. I stilled. "I'm sorry," he whispered. "I should have told you." His voice was so low, so wretched. "That's just one thing on the very long list of things you should have done," I spat. "I know," he whispered.

"Why is your target, my rejected mate?" Odina asked from beside Ragnai, who still hadn't let me go. "It is Protectorate orders," he replied quietly, unable to meet her gaze. I yelled a string of curses in his direction. His eyes pleaded with mine as he placed a shaky hand on the floor. Although he wasn't going to die from that wound, he continued to pour blood onto the tile. In my peripheral vision, Odina narrowed her eyes at him. My feet dangled a few inches from the ground, my back pressed against Ragnai's chest.

"If I set you down, are you going to launch yourself at him

again?" he breathed into my ear. "Yes," I replied snarkily. "Then I'm going to hold you here until you calm down."

"Calm down?" I hissed. "Yes," he responded. "We need him alive, Pandora," Odina said, turning to me. Her deep violet sleeves ruffled with her movement. "Why?" My eyes flickered to hers as she stepped in front of me, blocking my view of him. "He's Protectorate, and although I'd love nothing more than to sink metal into his chest, they're on our side. If we kill him, they won't be."

"How do you know they're on our side?" I breathed. "They sent doctors to try and reverse the curse Brykan laid on our people," she replied. "If they have a reason to want Harrison dead, then it must be a damn good one."

"They can't have a good enough reason to assassinate him," I said. "They just can't."

She shook her head and turned to look at Luke again. "It seems the only one who knows why The Protectorate wants your father dead is him," she said, pointing at Luke angrily. "And as much as I wish I could slit your throat and let you bleed out right here in my banquet hall, I know my place—and I know The Protectorate. If you kill one of their soldiers, they don't play around. They'd nuke this entire planet just for one of you."

My eyes widened. I had always believed the Liarta government to be the most advanced of all the planets. However, if Odina was worried about The Protectorate having nuclear capabilities, I had been clearly mistaken. How had I been in the dark about what was going on with other planets' governments? The citizens of Liarta barely even knew the Gaythe existed. It had all been kept under wraps. What were they not telling us about the human civilization on Cappurn—the planet Luke came from—and why were they keeping it a secret?

"Take him to the healers. They leave this afternoon," Odina ordered Haggik. He nodded, helping Luke up from the floor and dragging him out of the room through the great doors. Ragnai finally released his grip on me, and my feet sank to the floor as my body sagged as if weighed down by a ton. Hopelessness flared in my chest along with a surge of anger—so much anger. Hot, blistering tears streamed down my face, and I hurried to wipe them away. I vowed that I would no longer be weak. I would no longer depend on anyone else. I would *choose* my destiny—and he would have no part in it. I swore it to myself.

"Listen to me," Odina said gently, placing a hand on my shoulder as she led me back to the long table. She eased me into one of the chairs and then sat in the one beside mine. Ragnai watched warily from a few feet away, silent. "You must return to Liarta. Find who killed Kimi and convince Danny Fritz to lend aid by whatever means necessary. You can sort out whatever you feel about Detective Nesnah after we have won the war," she said softly. Then she turned to Ragnai, lifting her hand in his direction. The gold cuff around her wrist gleamed.

"Hand me your spear," she ordered. He tipped his brow toward her and slid the spear from its sheath along his spine. The ebony rod landed in her open palm as he bowed his head to his Queen. She swiftly wrapped her hand around the wooden grip, rose from her chair, and, with one foot, pushed it back before standing before me.

"Kneel," she commanded, her purple eyes darkening with intent. I slowly rose from my chair—its legs scraping against the floor—and knelt before her. My knee pressed into the cold stone, and my eyes dropped to the floor. "Pandora Vaughn, as your Queen, I hereby sanction you as one of my Gaythe warriors. May your life serve me and my people until your last breath," she said softly, her voice washing over me. I lifted my eyes to meet hers. "My life is yours, my Queen," I declared.

Her lips twitched—I couldn't tell whether it was a smile or a scowl—but she nodded in approval. "Give me your hand," she ordered. I extended my open palm toward her, and her eyes swept over the black skin the stones had permanently marked on my body. I swallowed hard, waiting for her next instruction. She then lowered the sharp end of the spear toward my hand, slicing from my thumb to my pinky.

I winced at the sudden pain, though it soon eased. She handed Ragnai back his spear, which he sheathed while unable to tear his eyes away from us. Pressing her thumb into the cut along my palm, she smeared my blood onto her scaled skin. "With your sacrifice, I wear your blood," she declared. Pressing her thumb to her forehead, her finger left a crimson thumbprint between her eyebrows. "Should you die in battle, your life will be honored as a sacrifice for me."

Flipping my hand over, she placed her palm on the back of my hand. "Go to Liarta. Save my people. Save *your* people." I turned my gaze toward Ragnai, who knelt on one knee and inclined his head toward me. "I will serve you as your warrior guide. May your life be long and your death be swift," he uttered before rising again. A heavy sense of responsibility settled on my shoulders as I stood. Odina smiled at me, her sharp, needle-like teeth peeking from her full lips. I had no words in that moment, but I knew this was only the beginning of a long and very *ugly* war.

***

The walk to the healer's den wounded my soul. I wanted nothing more than to leave him here to rot, but I had two problems with that. First, I didn't know how to fly the ship by myself, and second, although no one knew everything that transpired on Gayle these last few days, someone was bound to notice him missing—and I was not about to get wrapped up in a conspiracy involving the death of one of our detectives. It was no secret that I had hated him, and at this point, I wasn't convinced I no longer did. I still hated him—even those piercing blue eyes, how his body felt against mine, and the brush of his warm fingertips.

My feet stopped abruptly in the hallway. What was wrong with me? Even after learning that he was sworn to assassinate my father, I still couldn't help but think of him with a twisted tenderness. I pinched the bridge of my nose. It was going to be a long, enduring flight home.

Focus, Pandora—you have a mission. A mission that does not remotely involve him, aside from warning my father that an organization called The Protectorate was hot on his tail.

"Fuck," I hissed to myself, forcing my feet to carry me forward. What disaster had he entangled me in? Every layer I peeled back revealed more blood, bodies, and lies. I had wiped the blade that had sunk into Luke's shoulder and returned it to its place along my thigh. It was such a shame I hadn't been quick enough to sink the other deep in his throat.

The pack on my back shifted its contents as I trailed down the twisted staircase to the healer's den. As I approached the slightly cracked wooden door, gentle voices floated through the air. I pushed it open, peeking inside, and saw Luke, shirtless, sitting on a chair facing the door while Manika worked. I inhaled sharply as my eyes drifted over his bare chest. His eyes lifted to meet mine—regret flashing in them—and my heart thundered in response.

Too late, he had his chance, and he had obliterated it.

"You really meant to plunge that blade into him," Manika said, wrapping his wounded shoulder tightly with tan tape. "I *meant* to do far worse than slice his shoulder," I huffed, leaning against the wall near the door. Hanging herbs brushed my scalp as they moved out of my way. Manika abruptly turned to me, her eyes blazing. "He is your *mate*," she growled, pointing a finger in my direction.

"Was," I said, crossing my arms. "I kept it to myself to protect you," he snapped. "I don't need a protector! I don't need you!" I hollered, pushing off the wall and taking two determined steps toward him, anger boiling in my veins. Manika stepped in front of him. "You need him way more than you think you do. If you kill him, it will *kill you*," she warned. I scowled, unyielding. "It's your grave you're digging." She shrugged and then turned back to him. "Keep this wrapped for the next few hours—it should speed up healing. But since you sliced through several muscles in that shoulder, it might still take a few days before it's fully usable." She instructed, and he nodded, "Thank you," A small smile curved up his lips as she patted his uninjured shoulder with a knowing look, "Good luck—you're gonna need it,"

I fought the urge to roll my eyes. He pulled a long-sleeve black shirt over his head, and I smirked; the green one he had been wearing must have had a ginormous hole in it. "You'll probably have a scar there," she continued, her back turned to me. Her long braids cascaded over a knitted cream shawl wrapped around her shoulders, reminding me of a grandmother tending a wound after a fall from a bicycle.

Sadness panged as I realized why I had never met any of my family—never had that kind of grandmother. My family had been here, kept from me, fed the lie that they were banished for being together, forced to start over on their own. When I returned to Liarta, there would be one long, uncomfortable conversation with my father. I needed answers, and he was the only person alive who could give them to me. "May Odina's strength be with you," she said, then turned to me, "To both of you."

I blinked, unsure how to respond, as she took my hand. "You are fierce, but remember, with true strength must come mercy. Find yours." With that, she wrapped her shawl tighter around her arms and brushed past us, heading to the back room. We watched her leave as the door shut gently behind her. My attention snapped back to him.

"Ragnai sent me to fetch you. He should have the rest of our belongings—they're waiting for us," I said as he rose from his seat. I followed his gaze as he stepped toward me. I tensed, my fingers brushing against the pistol grip peeking over my waistband, out of habit. He stopped in his tracks.

"I mean you no harm, Pandora," he said softly. I lowered my hand to my side. "I know you don't understand right now, but you'll see why I kept it from you in time. This is just the beginning—there's a long road ahead, and you can either fight me the whole way or choose to trust me."

"I will *never* trust you," I hissed. I forced my face to remain impassive, though my words wounded me deep within my soul. In the recesses of my mind, I sensed him standing at a door—a door representing our connection. Even though I longed to shut him out, he remained, his palm resting on its wooden surface. I moved toward it in my mind, its dark grain mocking me.

"*Let me in,*" he whispered from the other side. "*No,*" I replied firmly. Turning on my heel, I left him standing in the healer's den, watching me walk away without another glance.

Chapter 35

Ragnai and Haggik stood silently waiting for us at the city's edge as we approached. Haggik's eyes remained fixed on me while Ragnai cleared his throat. "Humans, as much as I have enjoyed your company here, it is time for your departure," he said. I bore no visible injuries, but the weight I carried was etched deep within me. My shoulders sagged—not from the pack slung across them, but from the quiet, relentless heaviness that had taken root inside. The darkness clinging to my clothes was only a reflection of the one shadowing my thoughts.

This past week had reshaped me—tempered me into something tougher, yes, but also more guarded. It had cracked open the foundation of everything I believed, forcing me to question the people I once trusted without hesitation—those I'd laughed with, confided in, called my own.

A part of me longed for Ivy—for the comfort of her presence, the simplicity of our friendship. But would she even recognize me now? Would she trust me, knowing what I've seen, what I've become? And if I tried to explain would the twisted truth of my past make any sense at all?

Pushing down my thoughts, I faced Ragnai. "It's time. Let's go," I said. He nodded dipping his head in my direction, "I must inform you, intel from the surface has been spotty, but there are confirmed groups of Nephrians near the northern tribe. I hope they haven't made their way to us yet, but we must be extra cautious when we breach to avoid attracting their attention."

Today, Ragnai looked nothing of himself. He still wore his usual tan canvas pants, but they were now reinforced with thick leather guards that hinted at the gravity of what lay ahead. His bare chest—typically exposed without care—was now hidden beneath a fitted leather vest, slotted with an arsenal of blades. Four across his chest, two on each flank.

As he turned, I caught sight of a line of seven knives strapped down his back—each so dark they seemed to soak in the light like miniature black holes. His arms were bare, save for thin leather bands wrapped around each bicep, each one centered with a small, dark stone—pure Element X. His ever-present spear was slung across his back, now joined by a sword nearly its equal in size, its shimmering edge eerily similar to the radiant blades Odina had gifted me.

I swallowed hard, suddenly hyper-aware of the twin blades strapped to my thighs. My fingers brushed their hilts, checking that they were secure beneath the sleek lines of my black pants. Ragnai wasn't just ready for war—he was a walking weapon.

Haggik, too, was heavily armed. He wore a matching leather pant and vest set, but instead of rows of blades, he carried his spear and a ginormous mace. Strapped to his back in a similar fashion to the other weapons. The sheer size of the mace was astonishing—bigger than Haggik's head and fashioned with spikes longer than any of my fingers. The dark grey metal seemed to whisper violence and it made my pulse quicken. Luke appeared to share my thoughts as he casually placed his palm on the grip of his pistol at his hip, his fingers twitching.

"Be quiet, be fast, and get the *hell* off the planet as quickly as you can," Ragnai warned, stepping forward for me. His eyes locked onto mine, "Be ready to run,"Haggik then approached and wrapped an arm around my waist, pulling me close as my pack rustled against me. I nodded firmly, "I'm ready." Ragnai turned to Luke, who bobbed his head in agreement. "It's now or never," Ragnai declared before pulling Luke onto his back. Ragnai barely shifted before bending his legs and launching himself into the veil. It stretched for several feet before bursting, letting them pass. It snapped back into place as they disappeared into the black water beyond. Haggik's eyes met mine one last time, and then he leaped after them.

The water was warm, rushing past us as we sped through its depths. With the power flowing through me, I was no longer concerned about holding my breath. Instead, my attention focused on our extraordinary surroundings.

Massive, cavernous coral formations flew by at dizzying speed while brightly glowing fish darted frantically out of our path. Some were colossal, larger than any vehicle I'd ridden in on Liarta, their eyes as big as my entire body. Others were smaller than a fingernail but just as swift, spinning alongside us, their fins glittering like tiny mirrors in the light. I tightened my grip around Haggik, who stared resolutely ahead toward Ragnai and Luke, positioned several meters above us. A trail of bubbles rose steadily in their wake. Below, Kehel shrank into a speck of illumination on the ocean floor. But then my breath caught, my thoughts stuttered, and my blood ran cold.

Barely a mile from Kehel lay a vast, gaping fissure carved into rock and coral. Darkness seemed to seep from it like ink in water, yet its depths shimmered unmistakably with silver brilliance. My heart raced. There at the bottom sat the very stone I'd glimpsed in my dream.

Element X.

Endless miles of it stretched untouched across the ocean floor, glowing silently with unimaginable power. In that instant, I understood—the heart of Gayle itself empowered the Gaythe.

Dread twisted sharply in my gut. This was no dream, it was reality. If Luke was right, and Danny Fritz sought war using pure Element X, discovering such an immense source would fuel his ambitions. He would stop at nothing to possess it.

I could tell no one what I'd seen. No one could be trusted with such devastating potential. Did Odina realize what lay beneath her ocean? She must know. Did Ragnai? Haggik? Was this the real reason the Nephrians chose Gayle as their new home? Odina had said they coveted Gayle's power—was this the power she meant? My uncertainty intensified, flooding me with a deeper, colder fear the longer I pondered these troubling questions.

We erupted through the surface, emerging into the familiar crater.

Silence.

We exchanged wary glances. This was definitely not good. The usual jungle chatter that blanketed the surface of Gayle was gone—as if even the smallest creatures sensed the sinister threat approaching and had retreated deep into their burrows and crevices, desperate to avoid the coming massacre.

Haggik released my waist, and I waded carefully toward shore, climbing slowly out of the water into a low crouch. I pulled my pistol from my waist and waited, my pulse hammering in my ears. No sounds came, only the rhythm of my breathing.

Luke followed quietly, pistol already drawn. Behind him, Haggik and Ragnai emerged silently, the only sound a faint whisper as they unsheathed their spears. Adjusting my pack tightly against my back, I crept toward the tunnel in the soil. Above us, palm trees leaned over the crater, swaying gently in the breeze. My gaze shot upward, body tensing at the soft rustling of leaves. We all froze, eyes fixed upward. The breeze passed, and the trees fell silent again.

Releasing a slow, quiet breath, I continued toward the tunnel. My fingers sank into the soil as we moved, each muted step feeling unbearably loud in the oppressive quiet. I paused at the tunnel's edge, scanning carefully for any signs of movement or danger. The jungle remained eerily still. Not a soul in sight.

I waved the others forward. Luke emerged behind me, weapon raised and ready, eyes sharp as he scanned the surroundings. Ragnai followed next, then Haggik, their spears gripped tightly, eyes alert. They moved silently, watching, waiting—aware that danger might strike at any moment.

It must have just rained. The air felt heavy and thick with moisture that quickly beaded across my skin. I wiped the sweat from my forehead and shaded my eyes, squinting upward as I took a moment to bask in the precious Aurelios light. How could they live at the bottom of the ocean without it? The thought seemed unbearably unnatural.

I turned toward Luke, forcing myself to ignore the resentment burning in my chest. "Do you remember which direction the ship was?" He pointed roughly south. "Should be about two miles that way," he said. "But it'll take time, and we need to be careful and methodical." His eyes never lingered, continuously scanning our surroundings for threats. "We'll escort you as close as we can," Ragnai interjected, his face serious. "But once you power up the ship, we'll have to run like hell. Everyone within miles will hear it and come charging." I bit my lip anxiously. "Then let's hope we're faster than they are," I said, and Luke nodded grimly. "Let's hope." He muttered. With that, we crept into the jungle, each step carrying us closer to danger.

The underbrush bent silently beneath our feet as we moved steadily southward. I carefully avoided the brightly colored flowers gaping at us, grateful we hadn't encountered any Vipyrs yet on our trek back toward the ship. A worrying thought crept into my mind as we pressed onward. "What will we do if they've already ransacked the ship?" I asked Luke who had led the way. He glanced back briefly. "Cross that bridge when we get there," he replied coolly, turning his attention forward again.

I mimed a scowl at the back of his head and huffed quietly to myself. Behind me, Haggik chuckled softly, reminding me to keep my emotions under control. We weren't safe yet—I needed absolute focus. Luke had always been so arrogant, so cocky. I swallowed the urge to voice my frustration aloud, knowing our bickering would only put Haggik and Ragnai in unnecessary danger.

We continued onward in tense silence, Aurelios beating through gaps in the dense canopy overhead. After nearly an hour, Luke abruptly raised a hand, signaling us to halt. Everyone froze instantly, breaths held. Directly ahead, blocking our path, stood figures capable of draining every ounce of warmth from a person's soul.

Nephrians. They were *here*.

This Nephrian differed from Brykan—not nearly as large, yet equally terrifying. He wore a heavy, billowing black robe even in the stifling jungle heat. His pale face was so white it seemed almost translucent, blue veins spiraling visibly across his temples.

A wave of goosebumps prickled down my arms as he turned slightly, revealing those empty, gaping black eyes. If he had hair, I couldn't see it—like Brykan, this Nephrian's head was concealed by a deep hood, from which only his sharply pointed, crooked nose emerged.

My lips curled back involuntarily, nausea rising in my gut. Just seeing him summoned vivid memories of Brykan's iron grip around my neck atop Mount Akasari. My skin burned again where his hand had closed around my throat, the ghost of pain causing me to grit my teeth.

The figure drifted slowly along, his dark robes brushing silently across the jungle floor. The soil itself seemed to recoil from him, plants shriveling and turning black at the slightest contact. My breath caught painfully in my chest—not merely from fear of his ghastly appearance but from the dark power flowing from his fingertips.

Like Brykan, black tendrils of shadow twisted around him like smoke, coiling outward, lifting stones and boulders effortlessly into the air. Each rock exploded into fragments, scattering debris across the jungle floor. He was searching for something—but what?

Haggik's warm breath brushed my neck. Turning ever so slowly, I caught him pressing a scaled finger urgently to his lips. Time froze as we crouched motionlessly, watching. The Nephrian hadn't noticed us yet. If luck favored us, he would continue his path without realizing our small group was huddled in the brush mere feet away. My trembling hands threatened to betray me, and I clenched them tightly, begging my nerves to settle. Any careless movement could give us away. Who knew how sharp these creatures' senses were.

Inches in front of me, Luke was frozen like a statue, his fingers resting lightly on his pistol grip. An eternity seemed to pass as another boulder rose, hovering silently before shattering midair, fragments raining down noisily.

Lift, smash. Lift, smash.

Slowly, he moved farther away, continuing his destructive search. When he finally drifted several yards further, I allowed my fingers to relax slightly, breathing again despite the burning ache in my lungs. Luke turned his head cautiously, checking we were still with him. I gave a slight, tense nod. He raised a finger to his lips, mirroring Haggik's earlier gesture. One by one, we all did the same, acknowledging silently that our survival depended entirely on silence.

Satisfied that we understood the importance of silence, Luke quietly sidestepped off the main path, slipping beneath the dense vegetation. We followed close behind, crouched low enough that my legs burned in protest. We kept the distant figure of the Nephrian to our right, still visible through gaps in the foliage.

From this distance, I hoped any accidental sound we made would be masked by the explosions of shattered rock echoing through the jungle. I brushed branches aside, sweat now streaming freely down my face. This planet was unbearably hot. Luke's shirt had darkened considerably, soaked beneath his pack straps. He raised a hand suddenly, signaling us to halt. We froze, straining to listen.

A low hum was building somewhere far off, rapidly growing louder and louder. My pulse spiked as the humming swelled into an overpowering roar, vibrating painfully in my ears. Our eyes all drifted slowly upward.

A massive ship thundered across the sky, casting the jungle into shadow. My jaw dropped, eyes wide with shock. It was enormous—nothing like the human ships back on Liarta. Shaped like a giant diamond, its metallic grey hull tapered sharply to a point, likely for docking, while countless windows and doors dotted its gleaming surface. It was so large that as it moved overhead, it eclipsed Aurelios completely.

Wind surged violently around us, whipping dirt and debris into my eyes. Shielding my face with my arm, I peered upward just as countless hatches simultaneously opened along the ship's colossal hull. Hundreds—no, thousands—of smaller fighter ships burst forth, streaking out into the atmosphere.

In the distance, even from here, I could see the Nephrian

we'd been avoiding lift his hooded face toward the ship. His sinister grin widened, sharp needle-like teeth glistening black as he raised his arms and unleashed a deafening, otherworldly screech.

It was the worst sound I'd ever heard—a piercing screech, like nails scraping violently across a chalkboard. We snapped our hands over our ears, grimacing against the pain. Ahead of me, Luke squinted upward, his eyes darting frantically from one fighter ship to another.

There were so many, a relentless swarm flooding the sky. One after another, they poured from the massive hull. How many were there? The jungle, previously dead silent, erupted into deafening chaos. Luke turned suddenly, blood draining from his face. His mouth opened, and I heard him clearly through the roaring noise.

"Run!"

I didn't hesitate. My legs launched me upright, and I burst into a frantic sprint. Branches slapped at my face, whipping and scratching my skin as we tore recklessly through the jungle. Haggik's and Ragnai's pounding footsteps propelled me faster, adrenaline fueling every step. I risked a glance toward the Nephrian and instantly regretted it. He had stopped screeching, his arms slowly lowering to his sides as his hooded face snapped directly toward us. A chilling, sinister smile spread from ear to ear.

Before I could gasp a warning, he was moving—closing the distance with terrifying speed. I finally drew enough breath to scream and pointed wildly toward him. Luke, Haggik, and Ragnai turned their heads, eyes widening in horror. But it was too late for stealth. Our only hope now was speed.

We ran harder, faster, sweat stinging my eyes, pouring into my mouth, soaking my back—but I ignored it all, pumping my legs to their absolute limit. Still, the Nephrian gained on us with terrifying efficiency. We'd be dead if we didn't reach the ship in moments. Ahead of me, Luke vaulted effortlessly over a fallen log. I tensed to maneuver around it, but it was too late, I hadn't anticipated it.

My foot caught beneath it, and I slammed into the jungle floor. Air exploded from my lungs with a painful gasp, stars bursting in my vision. Ragnai leapt over my sprawled form, narrowly missing my head. Haggik skidded to a halt, spinning around just behind me.

Groaning, I rolled onto my back, dirt streaking my skin as pain radiated through my chest. I propped myself onto an elbow just in time to see the Nephrian bearing down on us—twenty feet, closing fast. Haggik roared, swinging his massive mace high above his head, the sound so fierce my teeth rattled and skin prickled. Yet the Nephrian was unfazed, still closing the distance. Ten feet, five feet...

WHAM

Haggik's spiked mace slammed into the side of the Nephrian's head, sending him hurtling through the air like a ragdoll. He collided violently with a palm tree before crumpling to the jungle floor. My breath caught sharply in my throat—but he didn't stay down long. He sprang to his feet again with unnatural agility, lunging toward us. Cursing, I drew my pistol and fired.

Bang! Bang! Bang!

My aim was true; all three bullets struck him squarely in the head. Black blood poured down his pale skin, but he kept charging. My hands shook violently. What kind of creature was immune to bullets?

"The only thing that stops them is Gaythe scales!" Ragnai roared behind me. "Well, that would've been good to know earlier!" I screamed back, thrusting my pistol into its holster and sliding the blades from my leather corset. I'd hoped to fight from a distance, but clearly, close combat was my only choice.

The Nephrian collided with Haggik, his gnarled hands gripping tightly as they struggled. "Pandora, we have to *go*!" Luke shouted urgently, but I couldn't tear my gaze away from the fight. Haggik and the Nephrian tumbled furiously in the dirt, leaves, and debris flying in every direction. Fists flew wildly, robes flapping with every brutal move. Haggik's fist smashed into the Nephrian's nose, breaking it with a satisfying crunch, but before he could strike again, the Nephrian's knuckles slammed into Haggik's temple.

Haggik roared, spit flying from his teeth, then wrapped his arms around the Nephrian, lifting him off the ground. He slammed him down hard, but the Nephrian countered immediately, kicking Haggik off and sending him flying. I watched helplessly as Haggik crashed to the jungle floor, sliding twenty feet before grinding to a halt. Blood dripping from his crumpled ghostly face, the Nephrian advanced on him, a sinister smile returning.

Panic surged through me. "Haggik, get up!" I screamed, tears streaming down my cheeks as I sprinted for him. Haggik groaned weakly, his head rolling limply to the side. "Haggik!" His eyes snapped open just as the Nephrian leaped onto him.

The roar around us was deafening, so loud it shook my bones and blurred my vision. Black steam poured off the Nephrian's hands, cascading ominously before he slammed them down onto Haggik's chest. My heart stopped as the life slowly drained from Haggik's face. I didn't think—I just moved. My legs burned, lungs on fire, blade raised high as I sprinted toward them.

A guttural roar tore from my throat, desperate and raw. But before I could reach them, I saw Haggik's hand slip to his thigh, drawing out a long, slender, iridescent blade.

Everything slowed to a crawl.

He gripped the hilt tightly and thrust upward with fierce determination, driving the blade deep into the Nephrian's chest. Straight into the forsaken creature's heart. The blade pierced through, erupting from the creature's back as my sprint slowed to a stunned halt.

The Nephrian gasped, the sickening sound bubbling from his throat as blood poured from the deep wound in his chest, drenching Haggik in thick, black liquid. His body slumped lifelessly onto Haggik, who shoved him away and rose shakily to his feet. My stomach twisted as I watched Haggik grip the blade lodged in the Nephrian's chest and pull it free. It scraped harshly against bone, a horrible grinding sound that sent chills down my spine. Haggik lifted his eyes to meet mine, his expression fierce and determined. "Go. *Now*," he commanded.

I didn't hesitate.

Turning swiftly, I ran, knowing the others would follow as we sprinted desperately toward the ship. He had taken the brunt of the attack for me. I'd been careless, tripping over a fallen log I should have seen. Haggik could have easily left me behind, but he didn't—he'd stopped and fought off the Nephrian, risking everything to save my life. My heart thumped painfully with gratitude, knowing I would forever be in his debt. Even though we'd known each other less than a week, he was family now.

Finally, we burst through the trees into the clearing, and relief nearly brought tears to my eyes. Our sleek, silvery-black ship sat untouched, exactly as we'd left it, nestled in the shallow crater left by our rough landing. Luke sprinted to the ship, yanking open the cargo door. He threw his pack inside and reached urgently for mine. I slid the straps off quickly, tossing it toward him, and watched as he effortlessly hurled it into the hold. Ragnai rushed over, gripping my shoulders firmly. "Go now," he said, his voice tight with urgency. "Fly back to Liarta. Don't return until you bring aid."

I nodded quickly, swallowing the painful lump in my throat. My mind raced with worry—what would happen to them? Would the Nephrians destroy them before we returned?

Ragnai seemed to read my thoughts. "We'll hold them off as long as we can," he said softly but urgently. "The fate of our people lies in your hands." Haggik stood quietly nearby, his expression heavy with worry. When he saw me looking, he stepped closer, his voice calm and steady. "You are a Gaythe. The fire *inside* you will always burn brighter than any flames *around* you. Let it roar—and *burn them all to the ground.*"

Tears blurred my vision as I launched myself at him, wrapping my arms around his thick neck. He staggered slightly under my sudden embrace before gently lifting me from the ground and burying his face against my shoulder. I squeezed tighter, refusing to let go and acknowledge that this might be goodbye. "Thank you," I whispered, meant only for him.

As I began to pull away, he murmured something in my ear so quietly I almost thought I'd imagined it. My eyes widened, stunned, but before I could question him, he gently placed me back on my feet.

"Pandora, let's go. *Now!*" Luke called sharply, standing halfway up the metal ladder into the cargo hold. "Go," Haggik repeated softly, smiling warmly through eyes full of strength and resolve. "We'll wait for you." I forced myself to turn away before my emotions overwhelmed me.

I raced up the rungs two at a time, quickly swinging into the ship. Luke and I stood together at the open hatch, looking out at Haggik and Ragnai, who watched us in return. "We'll be fine," Ragnai assured us, waving confidently. "Go now, before you're trapped here." They both lifted their hands, waving goodbye as

Luke shut the cargo door behind us with a firm, final click.

The door hissed sharply, sealing shut behind us. Luke swiftly tightened the cargo net and dashed toward the cockpit. I followed closely, my muddy boots squeaking across the smooth floor, leaving a messy trail of jungle dirt in my wake. We dropped quickly into our flight seats, securing the harnesses and pulling the straps tight. Luke flipped switches rapidly across the control panel as I slipped on my headset.

Instantly, the ship hummed to life, lights flickering and instruments buzzing to readiness. I watched Ragnai and Haggik vanish into the thick green foliage through the windshield, sprinting back toward Kehel. I shut my eyes briefly, whispering a silent prayer to the powers that be.

Keep them safe. Please let them make it home.

Luke entered flight mode, his fingers darting expertly over the controls. "It's now or never," he said, his voice clear through my headset. Red lights flashed, signaling the engines had warmed fully. Luke engaged the boosters, and with a gentle shudder, we began to hover.

Gayle's surface slowly fell away beneath us. As we rose steadily upward, I looked out at Mount Akasari standing proudly in the distance, its peak seeming to wink defiantly—ready, perhaps, to slice open the Nephrian ship looming ominously above it.

Leaning forward, I stared upward at what seemed like millions of Nephrian fighter ships buzzing furiously through the atmosphere. "It might be a bumpy ride," Luke warned, gripping the steering column and pushing it forward. The ship surged upward, Gayle rapidly shrinking beneath us as we climbed sharply into the sky. Our wings tilted, angling us away from the planet.

"Hold on tight!" Luke shouted, propelling us straight into

the chaotic swarm above. The ship shook violently, jostling me against the harness as fighters narrowly missed our hull, streaking past in blurs of black and silver. Far above, the colossal Nephrian mothership lumbered forward, too massive to maneuver quickly enough to chase us down—but the nimble fighter ships were another story. A cluster of twelve immediately broke formation, streaking directly toward us.

"They're coming!" I shouted, heart pounding, eyes fixed on the swarm racing in from the left. "Hold them off!" Luke yelled back, dodging another fighter with a sharp roll. "How?!" I screamed frantically, searching the dashboard for answers. "The mounted machine gun!" he barked, swerving again to miss an oncoming ship narrowly.

My eyes darted across the controls and landed on a large red button beneath a protective glass cover. Flipping open the lid, I slammed my fist onto the button. Two control levers emerged instantly, swiveling into position on either side of me. A huge, intimidating machine gun deployed from the ship's nose, its long barrel glinting menacingly ahead. I gripped both levers, aiming carefully with the left joystick, swinging the barrel toward the four fighters speeding straight at us.

My breath caught.

I yanked the right lever back, and bullets roared from the gun, rattling the entire ship with each powerful blast. Three fighters exploded immediately in bright fireballs, but the weapon suddenly clicked empty, leaving one last enemy hurtling directly toward us. "He's not stopping!" I gasped. The Nephrian pilot was on a suicide collision course, racing directly at our cockpit. "Reload!" Luke shouted, pointing urgently. "The blue button!"

I slammed my hand down on it. With a reassuring clink, a fresh ammunition belt slid smoothly into place. My heart stopped as I aimed again, locked onto the approaching fighter, and squeezed the lever. The ship rattled fiercely as bullets streamed forward, shredding the enemy craft into a fiery cloud of debris.

Fragments scattered across our windshield.

"Hyperspeed—NOW!" Luke yelled. Without hesitation, I grabbed the lever and pulled hard. Space blurred around us as we rocketed forward, hurtling toward Liarta and away from the chaos behind.

Chapter 36

The ship rattled and shook violently—but then, suddenly, everything fell quiet. We glided smoothly through space, and the chaos behind us became a distant memory. Gayle shrank rapidly into nothingness, disappearing into the darkness as hyperspeed carried us swiftly toward Liarta. A profound sense of loss tugged at my heart. I hoped desperately that they'd be safe, that I'd see them again soon.

Silence stretched between us, punctuated only by the faint hum and flicker of the dashboard lights. The universe stretched infinitely through the windshield, stars shimmering quietly against the dark expanse. The ship's sleek, silvery hull slid gracefully through space, the landing beams folding neatly back into their housing beneath us.

Slowly, I removed my headset and placed it gently on its hook. Beside me, Luke tapped a few controls, activated autopilot, and then took off his headset. "Well," I murmured softly, breaking the silence, "that could've gone better."

"It could've gone worse," Luke countered quietly, leaning back against the headrest, eyes closed. My voice lowered, heavy with worry. "They'll never survive an attack of that scale."

Luke opened his eyes, turning slowly to face me. "They've survived this long. Trust that they know what they're doing." His voice softened, "besides, they have Odina now. She'll lead them through." I nodded slowly, trying to let his confidence ease the ache in my chest. But I couldn't shake the feeling that, no matter how strong a leader she was, they couldn't truly escape what we had just barely survived. "How effective is a captain leading a sinking ship?" I muttered. "More effective than a sinking ship with no captain," I ground my teeth.

Smart-ass.

He stood from his chair, boots scuffing softly against the floor. Just like before—on the journey to Gayle—we faced each other in the narrow hallway, now on our way back to Liarta. I'd hoped that when we returned, I'd have fewer questions and less bitterness toward him. Instead, every passing moment only intensified my confusion, deepening my resentment toward the man standing before me.

Soft lights flickered on at the base of the wall, casting shadows across his features. Luke angled his head slightly downward, eyes darkened, unreadable in the dim glow. "You don't trust me," he said quietly, more of a statement than a question. He hesitated, a flicker of regret briefly crossing his blue eyes. "I get it. I wasn't exactly forthcoming with you."

I crossed my arms tightly over my chest, leaning back against the wall, face deliberately blank. I wouldn't make this easy—let him dig his own grave. Luke sighed softly, almost to himself, "I didn't have a choice, Pandora."

"We always have a choice," I snapped, throwing his words back in his face. Luke stiffened, visibly irritated, before leaning toward me and closing the space between us. His hand flattened against the wall beside my head, his arm rigid as he angled his body closer, eyes darkening dangerously. "The decisions I make aren't always my own," he growled softly, "sometimes, they're made for me. I owe a debt to some powerful people back on Cappurn—the same people who sent me to Liarta with a mission."

"The Protectorate?" I asked, my voice tight. "Yes." His jaw tensed sharply as if admitting that much might physically wound him. "Why are you indebted?" I pressed, flattening my shoulder blades against the wall attempting to put distance between us—but gaining little. Luke exhaled heavily, his voice dropping lower, "It's complicated."

"You want me to trust you, yet you're still not telling me anything. All you offer is cryptic half-truths." I shook my head bitterly.

"Dammit, Pandora," Luke growled, frustration edging every word. "I could tell you everything right now, but you wouldn't believe me— and it wouldn't even make sense. You have to see it yourself. You need to reach your own conclusions—your own path." His eyes narrowed, fierce and searching, but I didn't flinch. I'd been a detective long enough to know precisely how to handle a man like him. The moment you gave ground, even an inch, respect vanished forever.

My lips pulled back in a cold, defiant sneer, "Your intimidation tactics won't work on me. My father is the commissioner. You? You're just some nobody detective who messed with the wrong woman." My voice dripped venom as I stepped forward, closing the space between us, "When we get back to Liarta, I'll see that you pay for what you've done. I won't eat, won't sleep until you're chained to a wall in solitary confinement for the rest of your miserable life. Death would be a mercy you don't deserve." I leaned closer, hissing my final words, "How's that for a fated mate?"

Yet even now, even with this fire blazing between us, Luke stood relentlessly at the edge of my mind, palm pressed firmly against the locked door inside me. Anger flared across his face as he straightened, pulling away. Oddly, his withdrawal stung, leaving an unwanted feeling of rejection in my chest. My face heated, embarrassment briefly threatening my resolve.

His voice sharpened, slicing through the silence, "Danny Fritz will tear everything down. Your precious Liarta is a ticking time bomb. Your father will oversee everything you love being dismantled piece by piece. Do you really think his deceitful ways ended when he abandoned his mate on Gayle for another woman? Do you really believe they loved each other?" He scoffed bitterly. "You're lying to yourself, Pandora. Everyone else sees the truth. Everyone but you. Why? Because you wish things could be different? Because you wish you'd never left Liarta—that you could live safely in your little bubble before your mother was murdered?"

His words slammed into me, knocking the air from my lungs. Tears blurred my vision, but I refused to let them fall. "When we get back to Liarta, nothing will ever be the same again," Luke pressed on mercilessly. "You can't pretend the past week never happened. I certainly can't. I won't return to believing that my only purpose is to serve The Protectorate. And I definitely can't go back to a life without you." He paused, studying my face intently, watching his words take root deep within me. "The choice is yours now. Lie down and accept the lies, or stand up and fight for what's right. I can't make this decision for you. You have to *choose*—your father or your people."

His words weighed heavily on me, suffocating every last bit of resistance. My hands clenched into fists, nails biting into my palms. I couldn't do it—I couldn't choose between them. If Luke was right, Liarta would descend into chaos. If he was wrong, I risked losing the last family I had left. I couldn't gamble on the hope that the Gaythe would stand by me if everything fell apart. No, I needed answers. I needed to know exactly what trouble my father was caught in and how to save him from it.

My father was a good man. Whatever he'd gotten himself into

wasn't by choice. I couldn't condemn him—not without proof.

"I—I can't." My voice cracked painfully, betraying my weakness. Turning away sharply, I stifled a sob, desperate to keep control. Luke reached out instinctively, and I slapped his hand away. "Don't," I snapped, voice trembling. Without another word, I stormed off toward the bunk room, slamming the door shut behind me.

I dropped onto one of the bunks, the mattress sinking beneath my weight. Lying on my back, arms limp at my sides, everything felt unbearably heavy. I had nothing left—no strength to fight Luke, no energy to battle the Nephrians, no resolve to face whatever my father had gotten himself tangled up in. Nothing. Even my eyelids felt heavy as I took slow, measured breaths, willing myself toward sleep. But a quiet, persistent beeping pulled me back just as I started drifting. I opened my eyes, irritated.

What was that noise?

I sat up, legs swinging off the side of the bed, straining to pinpoint the source. Narrowing my eyes, I scanned the room. White cabinets, tightly secured, lined the walls—nothing unusual. Dropping to one knee, I glanced beneath the bunk: only blankets and pillows. No luck there. Standing, I angled my head toward the door. The beeping sounded clearer now, coming from outside the room.

Moving past the bunks, I cracked the door open slightly and peered down the hallway. A thin sliver of light streamed into the room. Up ahead, Luke was absorbed in the cockpit, busy with the controls and headset firmly over his ears. He clearly couldn't hear the alarm. How long had it been sounding?

I padded into the hallway, following the noise toward the cargo hold at the rear of the ship. The beeping grew louder as I knelt beside the cargo net. Shifting through the gear we'd hastily tossed inside during departure, I located my pack and pulled it toward me. The sound was definitely coming from inside. My stomach tightened as I quickly unzipped the largest compartment and reached inside. My fingers closed around my communicator, and dread pooled in my gut.

Ivy.

I'd completely forgotten to send correspondence back to Liarta. This was going to be unpleasant. With a wary glance back toward the cockpit—Luke still oblivious—I gently retrieved the communicator, secured the pack under the net, and hurriedly retreated into the bunk room, sliding the door shut behind me.

The door clicked shut behind me as I sank heavily onto the bunk. The indicator light at the top of the communicator flashed urgently, its rapid blinking mirroring my anxiety. Sliding my finger across the side button, the screen flickered to life, and my heart immediately sank.

Fifteen messages from Ivy.

I quickly scrolled through them. Most were routine updates about the investigation on Liarta, but the final message was a video attachment marked urgent. A knot formed in my stomach as I bit my lip, hesitating briefly before tapping it.

Ivy's familiar features appeared as a shimmering hologram above the communicator, her face cast in a hazy blue glow. Her eyes seemed to stare directly at me, filled with worry and impatience. Taking a shaky breath, I pressed play.

"*Pandora, I don't have much time,*" Ivy began, glancing nervously around her before her holo leaned closer to the camera. Her voice dropped to an urgent whisper. "*Things have gotten completely out of control here on Liarta. Hundreds of people have gone missing just this week in Raos alone. We don't even have enough detectives to handle all the reports. Everyone's working five or six cases at once, and we're barely making a dent."*

My breath caught as I watched, helplessness gripping me. Ivy sounded rattled—scared, even—and she was tougher than granite.

"*Y*ou need to come home, Pandora. Now." Her tone was sharp, her eyes pleading. "*Your father is launching a city-wide manhunt for you. Yesterday, he interrogated me for eight hours, threatening to pull my badge if he discovered I knew your whereabouts. He's also been grilling everyone at Precinct 12 about Detective Nesnah. I don't know what can of worms you've opened, but you'd better close it—and fast."*

Ivy glanced anxiously off-camera again before continuing. "*I think Danny Fritz is planning something. He's acting strange, and yesterday, I saw him arguing fiercely with his son Adam. I couldn't hear everything, but I distinctly heard them mention something about the bigger picture."*

Sorrow filled Ivy's expression as her voice softened. "*I miss you, friend. Wherever you are, I hope this message reaches you. And whatever's happening—I just hope you're alive and come home soon."*

"*Ivy, what are you doing?"* called an unfamiliar voice from somewhere off-camera. Ivy whipped her head around. "*Nothing! I'm coming!"* she called back, panic flickering briefly across her face. She turned urgently toward the camera one last time. "*I've gotta go. Hurry home—I need your help,"* she whispered sharply, and then the hologram vanished.

I sat frozen, blinking at the empty space where Ivy's face had just been. The weight of my decision to leave Liarta came crashing down on me. I'd known it was a gamble, but now it was clear I'd drastically underestimated the consequences. This wasn't just trouble. It was a nightmare—and I was right in the center of it. There was no fixing this now. My only choice was to return home and face whatever awaited me. Switching off the communicator, I slipped it under the bunk. There was nothing more I could do except sleep, rest, and mentally brace myself for the storm ahead. I lay down with a sigh, my back turned to the door, and let exhaustion carry me into a restless sleep.

The rest of the flight went about as expected. Luke didn't push for conversation, and I didn't mention Ivy's recording. He could deal with his mess—I had enough on my plate without sorting out his problems, too. Even if he was still assigned to my mother's case, I'd figure it out alone. I didn't need him—I never had. For now, I had to stay smart, strategic, and trust no one. Nothing was certain anymore.

Before long, Liarta came further into view, its familiar swirls of blue and green looming ahead as I sat stiffly in the co-pilot seat. My fingers tapped anxiously on the armrest. Luke glanced at me sideways. "Everything good?" he asked. "Peachy," I snapped back, keeping my eyes forward.

His eyebrows lifted slightly in response, but he wisely said nothing more. Shaking his head, he returned his focus to the approaching planet. "I don't know what we're returning to," he said evenly, "Be ready for a rough landing."

I nodded tersely.

"Oh—and you should probably put this on." Luke tossed me a black, long-sleeved shirt along with matching flight gloves.

I scowled as the items landed in my lap. "And what exactly are *these* for?" I muttered. "Well," he said dryly, irritation edging his voice, "unless you'd prefer explaining why your skin is pitch-black from fingertips to shoulder blades, you might want to cover up until we come up with a better plan."

Crossing my arms defiantly, I huffed in frustration. "Suit yourself," he muttered, placing the headset over his ears and returning to the controls. "*Hell*," I hissed, relenting as I quickly pulled on the shirt and gloves.

They felt bulky, and I grimaced at the uncomfortable weight. A thin sliver of dark skin remained visible between the sleeve and glove cuff, but thankfully, it was barely noticeable unless someone was looking closely. I tugged at the sleeve anxiously, adjusting it to cover the exposed area.

Sliding my headset into place, I took a deep breath and steadied my nerves. Liarta grew larger and larger through the windshield, anxiety coiling tightly in my gut. I swallowed hard, forcing myself to remain calm despite my pounding heart. What's the worst that could happen, right? Luke flipped on the long-range radio with a slight click. Static buzzed briefly before smoothing into silence.

"This is Detective Nesnah and Detective Vaughn," he announced calmly, emotionless. "Liarta towers, do you read me?" His voice revealed nothing—not at all matching the storm of emotions swirling within me. His gaze remained steady and composed, focused solely on guiding our ship toward whatever awaited us below. A tense silence stretched after Luke's transmission, broken finally by a crackling sound as someone answered from the tower.

"This is Liarta Towers. Detective Nesnah and Detective Vaughn, please land *immediately* at Precinct 12's docks." Luke and I exchanged worried glances. Precinct 12's docks were reserved strictly for police craft or dire emergencies.

A wave of unease slithered up my spine, and I fidgeted anxiously in my seat. Liarta loomed closer now, lights from the cities twinkling across its metallic gold surface. It gleamed brightly in the Aurelios light, almost blinding me, but otherwise looked exactly as we'd left it.

"Confirm docking at Precinct 12," Luke responded calmly. "Two minutes to the atmosphere."

"Affirmative," the tower replied sharply. Luke didn't look at me, merely guiding the ship toward Raos with steady hands. Buildings rose rapidly in the windshield as we approached, and I braced for the usual violent jolt upon entering Liarta's atmosphere—but it came with only mild turbulence, nothing like the rough landing we'd experienced on Gayle.

My relief vanished in a puff as Precinct 12's docks came into view, lit up with countless red, white, and blue flashing lights. My jaw dropped. It looked as though every single squad car in the precinct had assembled, waiting for our arrival. Luke adjusted the radio to a different frequency, leaning forward into the mic, "This is Detective Nesnah, requesting clearance to dock at Precinct 12."

The voice that responded froze my blood in an instant.

"*Detective Nesnah*," my father's familiar voice echoed over the speakers, cold and authoritative, "Land your ship at dock seven. Leave your cargo behind, and exit with your hands above your head."

I knew my father would eventually discover what happened—and that he'd be angry—but my palms grew damp as I wondered exactly how angry he might be. "Yes, Commissioner. Dock seven," Luke replied evenly, guiding us toward the flashing red guide lights lining the tarmac.

The ship settled gently onto the dock, but I remained glued to my seat, frozen in place. My hands gripped the dash so tightly that, if not for the bulky flight gloves, my knuckles would surely be stark white.

"Detective Nesnah, exit the ship immediately with your hands up!" The voice boomed over the loudspeaker, rattling the ship's windows. Luke unclipped his harness and stood up beside my seat. I looked up at him, feeling suddenly small beneath his steady gaze. "Any last words?" I asked softly, my voice barely audible.

Blue eyes met green, locked in a heavy stare. "I don't regret a thing," he said simply before swiftly turning toward the exit.

Scrambling to free myself from the harness, I hurried after him, leaving my headset abandoned on the floor. Luke swung the door release upward. It hissed sharply, sliding open to reveal a wall of flashing lights and the massive crowd awaiting us.

Aurelios was just beginning to set in Raos, painting the sky with vibrant orange and crimson streaks, casting long shadows across the tarmac. Under any other circumstances, I would have paused to admire its beauty—but this was far from a joyous homecoming. My father stood rigidly at the head of what seemed like hundreds of police vehicles, anger radiating from him in palpable waves. Even the muddy-brown suit he wore seemed to vibrate with rage. Several officers took cover behind the cars, weapons aimed directly at us as though we were dangerous felons.

My stomach twisted in knots, but Luke remained unfazed, holding my father's furious gaze without flinching. My eyes quickly scanned the crowd until I found Ivy and Chance at the far back. Ivy was pale as a ghost, her eyes wide with worry, while Chance's hand rested firmly on her shoulder—likely to prevent her from rushing forward into possible gunfire.

Even from here, the badge at Ivy's hip glared accusingly at me. Neither of them moved or revealed any emotion, their gazes shifting silently from me to Luke and back again. I could almost hear Ivy's unspoken question echoing across the distance.

What happened?

But I was too exhausted, too empty, to offer any reassurance. Could I even pretend to her that I was okay?

Next to my father stood a visibly irritated Lieutenant Smith, his jaw clenched tightly. Luke's brother. Smith's hand slid casually into the pocket of his charcoal-grey slacks, causing his matching suit jacket to shift slightly. He glared sharply at Luke, unblinking. Luke stayed perfectly still at the top of the ladder, his expression unreadable. He was likely weighing his options—but at this point, I wasn't sure we had any left.

"Hands up, *detective*," my father growled, stepping toward the ladder. Luke descended slowly, deliberately, then turned and raised his hands above his head. "What am I being arrested and charged with, Commissioner?" he asked calmly, his voice steady and controlled.

I climbed down behind him, feeling the eyes of every officer watching our every move. Radios chirped quietly in the background, reminders of the sizable crowd witnessing this spectacle. My father's eyes narrowed dangerously at Luke. "Kidnapping, tampering with evidence, and possession of a stolen vehicle," he snarled, jaw clenched tight. My stomach twisted. I wanted to see Luke behind bars—but not for something he didn't do.

I stepped down the last rung, gripping my fists tightly at my sides as my conscience wrestled with itself. "Turn around and lock your hands behind your head," my father ordered, pulling out a pair of handcuffs from his pocket. Luke complied immediately, clasping his hands behind his head as he turned slowly, his shirt lifting just enough that the grip of his pistol became visible above his belt.

"Kidnapping?" I finally blurted out, disbelief coloring my voice despite my anger. "He didn't—"

"*Quiet*, Pandora." my father cut me off sharply. I bit my tongue, fighting the urge to protest further. Shuffling footsteps and quiet radio chatter reminded me of the enormous crowd watching our every move.

"Is that pistol your only weapon, Detective Nesnah?" my

father demanded, still wary. "Yes, sir," Luke replied calmly, unmoving. "Is there anything else that can stab, poke, slice, or otherwise hurt me on your person, detective?" He asked roughly. Luke blinked before responding, "No sir."

Harrison nodded to himself, seemingly satisfied with that answer.

"Walk backwards *slowly* toward my voice," my father ordered, a pair of handcuffs clinking together was the only sound as everyone collectively held their breath. Luke was silent, and my heart raced wildly as I stood frozen, watching the scene unfold.

Then, suddenly, something shifted. A strange stillness enveloped me, and Luke's voice slipped quietly into my mind, clear and intense. *"You will see. Trust no one, tell no one about what happened."* In my mind, Luke stood impossibly close. The heat radiating from him washed over my skin, his gaze piercing my soul. His blue eyes softened, filled with an emotion that made my throat tighten painfully. *"You'll understand soon enough,"* he whispered fiercely. *"I will find you."*

He leaned forward, and though our physical bodies never touched, I felt the heat radiating off him, felt his breath grazing mine. His nose brushed gently down my own, sending shivers racing down my spine. His lips, soft and unbearably warm, hovered a mere breath away from mine. Confusion tore through me—I wanted him *desperately*, and I hated myself for it.

His lips brushed softly against mine, barely touching, igniting every nerve ending in my body. I gasped silently, breathing in his scent, overwhelmed by the longing and frustration building within me. Then, suddenly, he pulled back, retreating into the darkness behind my mind's door. *"I will find you,"* he repeated urgently. Then the door slammed shut, wrenching me back into reality, leaving me breathless and confused as I watched him calmly walk backward, hands locked behind his head, toward my father, ready to face whatever came next.

I gulped down ragged breaths as my father advanced on Luke. Without hesitation, he grabbed Luke's arms and threw him to the ground. The impact sent a dull thud echoing off the pavement, and I winced, a small, involuntary moan escaping my lips.

"You're under arrest, Detective Nesnah," my father declared, snapping handcuffs over Luke's wrists. Luke turned his face just enough to meet my gaze but didn't say a word. I could only watch in horror, my hand clamped over my mouth to stop myself from speaking—saying something I might regret later.

My father crouched down, his slacks brushing against the asphalt, his mouth just inches from Luke's ear. His voice dropped into something dark and dangerous, something I had never heard before. "Now, between you and me, Detective Nesnah," he hissed. "I will uncover every single terrible thing you've done in your miserable life, and I'll bury you so deep behind bars you'll never see Aurelios light again. You took my daughter—my only child—and if I weren't surrounded by this many people right now, I'd put so much lead in your body that you'd sink to the bottom of the deepest ocean on this planet."

A wave of nausea rolled through me. This wasn't the justice I had meant when I told my father Luke would end up behind bars. And the man crouched before me, spitting venom through clenched teeth, wasn't the father I knew.

"*Only* child?" Luke murmured, angling his head toward him.
"Shut your damn mouth," my father snapped, his grip tightening. He yanked Luke off the pavement with a fistful of his shirt and shoved him toward the line of officers standing nearby.
"Take him to the precinct. Do not let him out of your sight!" he ordered. Two officers seized Luke's arms, leading him toward an open squad car. He didn't resist. He didn't speak.

Harrison turned to me, his face flushed with anger. "Your badge, *detective*," he growled. My gaze snapped to him. "My badge?" I squeaked, my hand instinctively resting on the pocket that held it. The long-sleeve shirt and flight gloves felt stifling as his irritation grew. "Your badge," he repeated, holding his palm toward me. "*Now.*"

I swallowed hard, reached into my pocket, and pulled out the shiny bronze badge labeled 'Detective.' It gleamed in the fading light as I handed it over, the words 'Precinct 12' no longer evoking the pride they once had. I gingerly placed it in his hand. His fingers curled around it, his eyes fixed on the badge as if it held the power to condemn me.

"You are hereby relieved of your detective duties at Precinct 12. You will need to collect your belongings tomorrow," he said, sliding the badge into his pants pocket. "Dad, I—" I began, but he cut me off with a look of disappointment that silenced my words. "Go home. I will deal with you later," His glare softened unexpectedly as he added, "Pandora, I'm relieved you're home."

With that, he turned sharply on his heel. His shoes tapped on the asphalt as he strode toward the officers holding Luke. Harrison swung the car door open, roughly shoved Luke into the backseat, and slammed it closed. Luke managed one last glance at me through the rear window before the car slowly pulled away. My heart sank, and with it, I sank to my knees. Everything—everything was being taken from me.

I buried my face in my hands as the officers filed to their cars and departed. The flight gloves bit into my skin, but I didn't care. I remained motionless, tears streaming freely down my cheeks. I hadn't noticed Ivy and Chance approaching until I felt a soft hand on my shoulder.

"Pandora?" Ivy said, her voice gentle. I was still lost in a trance. "What happened?" she asked, and I finally raised my face to hers.

Her eyes were bloodshot and puffy, and her blonde hair was disheveled from a messy bun, a stark contrast to the organized woman I'd known for years.

Standing just a foot behind her, Chance crossed his arms, his stern expression unmistakable—he was displeased, though I wasn't sure why. Ivy lifted my elbow and embraced me tightly, her fuzzy teal sweater tickling my chin as I returned the hug. "I thought you both were dead," she whispered, her grip tightening. "Me? Dead? You underestimate me," I chuckled softly, trying to lighten the mood. "You're an asshole, you know that?" she retorted, though the corners of her mouth twitched into a tentative smile. "We have a lot to catch you up on."

Chance bristled in my peripherals, "Yes, but maybe you should start with what the hell happened to you," Ivy shot him a pointed glare over her shoulder, "Chance, relax. We literally thought she was dead just a few hours ago."

"I haven't forgotten that you knew where she was going even before she left—and you refused to tell me. I'm so mad at both of you that I could spontaneously combust!" He hissed, and Ivy tensed.

"I'm sorry," I said, meaning every word, "To both of you. I shouldn't have asked you to keep that secret, Ivy, and I'm sorry for asking her to keep it from you." My throat felt raw as I spoke. As the last officers left the tarmac, Ivy glanced around, shivering and rubbing her arms. "Should we go elsewhere to discuss all this?" she asked. Chance's jaw tensed as he narrowed his eyes at me, "How can you know we can even trust her?" I narrowed my eyes in return. "What do you mean, trust me?" I asked, cocking my head to the side and furrowing my brows, "Why wouldn't you be able to trust me?"

The words left my mouth before I could stop them, and I immediately regretted it as Chance's only response was a gesture toward the enormous ship still sitting at the dock. He pinched the bridge of his nose. "Just get in the car, Pandora," he ordered, pointing to his white detective sedan parked nearby. Ivy intertwined her fingers with mine. "He will come around," she whispered, nudging my shoulder. Then she glanced at our hands.

"Why are you wearing those ridiculous gloves?" she asked, raising our hands to eye level. I quickly withdrew my hand. "My hands were cold," I blurted, and she stopped dead in her tracks. "Your hands were cold?" she repeated, narrowing her eyes further. "Yes," I admitted with a gulp. She paused, and I opened my mouth to say something—anything—but she simply turned and continued toward the car. My feet felt like lead, refusing to move.

"Well, are you coming?" Chance called, standing by the open driver's door. My mouth had run dry as I searched for words, but none came. Forcing myself to move, I closed the gap between the car and me and slid into the back seat.

Aurelios sank over the horizon as we pulled out of Precinct 12's dock. The sky was a deep navy blue, almost purple as it kissed her goodbye. I propped my elbow on the car door and rested my cheek in my hand, feeling utterly numb from head to toe.

I no longer knew who to trust—what was truth and what was a lie. I had been so sure I wanted Luke behind bars, yet the image of him being shoved into the backseat kept replaying in my mind. I shouldn't feel this conflicted about a man I hated, though I knew I always had. So why did I let him convince me otherwise? Why did I let him persuade me to accept him as my mate when deep down I knew there was no going back? Our destinies were now intertwined, whether I liked it or not.

We wound through the city as cars passed by on the interstate.

After a week on Gayle's jungle terrain, watching civilization whizzing past the window felt surreal. Up front, Ivy and Chance exchanged no words with me—or with each other. I bit my lower lip, mentally kicking myself. I knew asking Ivy to keep my secrets wouldn't sit well with him, but I had done it anyway in my desperate search for answers.

Everything had come wholly unraveled, and I was the only one to blame.

Chapter 37

As I remembered it, the driveway to my cabin was bumpy and familiar. Dust trailed behind the white sedan as Chance drove us along. I was exhausted, yet I knew the night was far from over. I had so much to explain, armed with very little concrete information.

I had trusted Ivy with everything—even my life on multiple occasions—but now I wondered if I could trust her with something this monumental. Something so beyond myself when the threat of war loomed overhead, and the lives of countless Gaythe and humans were at stake. She had always been my person, my rock. Yet, for the first time, I found myself questioning that certainty.

I gazed out the window at the blue planet hanging in the sky, silently praying that everyone on that vast orb was safe. A sudden jolt from a pothole at the back of the driveway snapped me out of my reverie.

My cabin came into view, its exterior shrouded in darkness. Nestled among the trees, it nearly blended into its surroundings—just as I had intended when I chose this secluded, secret, and safe location. But now, a chill crept up my spine as I remembered I wasn't safe here. Someone had broken into my house and left a note on my counter. I hadn't mentioned it to Luke, though perhaps I should have. Maybe he would know who was behind it.

The gravel crunched as we came to a stop, and Chance shifted the car into park. I took a deep breath, then opened the door and climbed out of the backseat, ready to face whatever awaited me at home.

In the dark of night, rain began to fall. The drops plinked softly off the cabin's metal roof, creating a gentle orchestra of sound. I lifted my face to the sky and let the cool droplets trail over my cheeks, a welcome relief after the oppressive heat and humidity of Gayle. Here on Liarta, spring meant rain. A slight breeze brushed against my neck, and I lowered my gaze to see Chance and Ivy standing on the front porch under the awning, watching me intently.

"You hate the rain," Ivy observed. I blinked at her, then remembered that before Gayle, I had despised rainy days. But now, the rain felt therapeutic, washing away the weight of recent events. Clearing my throat, I muttered, "I guess I should unlock the front door now." I trailed up the wooden steps to the door.

Using my fingerprint, as usual, I unlocked it, yet the house felt distant and unfamiliar—so much had changed. The person I was when I left no longer existed. The door whooshed open, and we stepped inside. Ivy and Chance hung their coats on the rack by the door as I slowly wandered toward the kitchen. The note still sat ominously on the counter, but I ignored it, passing it as I moved down the hallway. Neither Ivy nor Chance followed.

Gradually, the lights flicked on automatically, bathing the house in a soft, pale yellow glow. I paused at my bedroom door, my hand resting on the bronze knob, and craned my ear down the hallway, wondering what they might say once they thought I could no longer hear them.

"She seems off." I heard Ivy's soft voice. A second of silence spanned between them. "Of course, she seems off. Something obviously happened." Chance said, and I heard the sound of a bar stool being slid against the floor and the weight of someone sitting down on it. "Did you see how they were looking at each other?" Her voice filtered in pitch, perhaps nervously. "Yes." Was all he replied. "I've never seen Commissioner Vaughn that angry." Her voice got even lower. "Of course, he's angry. His only daughter left Liarta without his permission to go to another planet that is at war with a completely different species, Ivy." He bit at her. I heard her sniffle, and Chance sighed heavily. "We need to figure out what kind of situation she's in because, unfortunately, you decided to keep her whereabouts secret this whole time. We're heavily involved now."

"What about Detective Nesnah?" she asked.

"What about him?"

"Whatever she's involved in, isn't he involved too?" she replied somberly. "Detective Nesnah can rot in the cell they locked him in. He broke so many rules and crossed so many lines. For all we know, he convinced her to go to that wretched planet with false information from the start," he said, irritation seeping into his tone. "She crossed just as many lines and rules, Chance, and you know that. Why are you so dead set on handing Pandora a different fate than his?" she challenged.

My eyebrows furrowed in frustration. Clearly, she wasn't making a strong case for me at this moment. "Why are you so dead set on defending him?" Chance hissed. "Because something feels different, Chance. We have absolutely no idea what went down on Gayle with them. We need to talk to her," she insisted.

I heard a bar stool scrape against the floor and footsteps echo into the living room. After a few seconds came a sigh, followed by the clanging of pots and pans—as if someone was about to cook. Carefully, I rotated the knob beneath my fingertips and eased into my room. It was dark, but through the back wall of windows, the moon filtered in with a silvery glow.

My bed lay unmade, the emerald sheets and comforter carelessly thrown aside. I pulled off the flight gloves and looked at my hands. The dark skin absorbed all light, but when I flipped my hand back and forth, I noticed an almost iridescent sheen beneath the darkness, reminiscent of Gaythe scales. I pursed my lips in worry but shook it off when I saw the communicator on my wrist blinking repeatedly. I activated it, and Mayra's hologram appeared above my wrist, her light a pale blue.

"Detective Vaughn," she stated. "Just Pandora, Mayra. I've been demoted," I corrected.

"I will correct your title, Pandora. Is there anything I can assist you with, Pandora?" she asked, tilting her AI head to the side. "Can you please reboot into my main house system and ensure all the safeguards are still in place?" I requested. "Indeed. Please insert my capacitor chip into the hard drive," she instructed. "Okay, hold tight, Mayra."

I removed the card from the communicator—her hologram flickering out—and plugged it into the access port on the wall. The indicator lights flickered before settling on green. "Rebooting now," Mayra's voice echoed throughout the house.

"Ah, hell! Pandora, you couldn't have left Mayra in the communicator?" Chance hollered from the kitchen. I chuckled. He had never liked AI—especially Mayra. Something about her sassy demeanor always unnerved him. "Not unless you want someone breaking into my cabin!" I hollered back. There was some grumbling and a few indiscernible words, followed by the clatter of pans as Chance resumed his cooking.

Mayra's hologram reappeared to my left, her silver bobbed hair brushing her shoulders as she turned to face me. "Is there any additional way I can assist you?" she asked, her gaze drifting to my marked skin.

After a brief pause, she looked back at my face. I started to peel my gloves off, "I really need to hide these, Mayra," I said as quietly as possible, lowering my voice in case anyone was eavesdropping. Mayra nodded, her purple eyes meeting mine. "I can fabricate a pair of synthetic gloves that match the rest of your skin."

"You can do that?" I asked, my mouth agape. "Yes," she replied matter-of-factly. "It's how AIs repair ourselves after sustaining damage to our components." She tilted her head as if amused by my confusion. "By all means, then, Mayra—if you think that will work," I said.

Raising her silver hand, she held it palm-up. Slowly, particles began to materialize out of thin air—tiny specks of light resembling fireflies—that coalesced first into fingers, then the rest of the hand, and finally the arms. I gawked as two tan silicone sleeves formed and dangled from her hand, her gesture inviting me to take them. "You can sleep and bathe in the sleeves, but be careful around chemicals and solvents, they will degrade the material."

I gingerly picked up one sleeve, weighing it in my hand. It felt weightless, as if made from the air itself. I cocked an eyebrow at Mayra, but she said nothing. I laid the gloves on the bed and peeled off my long-sleeve tee. Picking up one glove, I held it to the light. It was completely opaque and matched my skin color exactly.

Carefully, I slid my hand into the glove so as not to rip the material. It skimmed over my skin like velvet, barely noticeable. Once the sleeve was fully on, I released its hem. Immediately, the material bonded with my skin so seamlessly that I lifted my arm close to my face, marveling at its realism. I was certain no one would notice—except maybe Luke and Mayra. The hem of the silicone sleeve lay flush against my shoulders, melding into my skin until it seemed as though the marred skin had never existed. I carefully donned the second sleeve and walked over to the mirror.

Rubbing my arms, I marveled at how natural they felt. Had I not applied them myself, I wouldn't have suspected I was wearing anything at all. It was as if magic had cloaked my imperfections. "They're incredible," I breathed, and Mayra watched as I examined them. "I'm glad you like them. Is there any other way I can assist you, Pandora?" she asked, her purple eyes glowing. "No, Mayra. Thank you, you are dismissed." I murmured, still studying my reflection.

With that, her hologram faded, leaving me alone with my thoughts. I then began peeling off the rest of my clothes, taking extra care to remove the intricate, iridescent blades strapped to my thighs. He had taken my badge but hadn't bothered to search me for weapons—a rookie mistake.

I rotated one of the blades in my hand. Its hilt fit snugly in my palm, and a thin sliver of moonlight caught its edge. I needed to be careful who saw these, as someone would inevitably try to take them—even my father. Cautiously, I opened my armoire and stowed the blades inside against the back wall. I then draped a hanging white blouse over them. That should suffice for now.

I trailed into the bathroom and turned on the shower. I sat against the counter, waiting for the water to warm up while examining my fingertips. Despite the lifelike quality of the sleeves, they were missing my fingerprints—the ends of my fingers were completely smooth and devoid of prints. I chewed on my cheek, realizing that anything requiring my fingerprint wouldn't work with these on. I'd have to remove them if needed, and for now, I'd keep this secret by avoiding tasks that required my touch.

As steam billowed out of the shower door, I slid in. The

sleeves stayed firmly in place as I bathed, not budging an inch. Mayra had truly outdone herself. When I finally finished showering, I grabbed the fluffy grey towel hanging on a hook and dried myself off. I felt somewhat rejuvenated after washing away the remnants of the flight.

Dressing in grey sweatpants and a white hoodie, I squared my shoulders and left my bedroom to face Chance and Ivy. I hadn't bothered drying my hair—the wet auburn strands clinging damply to the back of my sweatshirt. My white socks muted my footsteps as I walked down the hall into the kitchen, where the aroma of Tyrian food welcomed me.

Chance had prepared pasta, grilled chicken, and broccoli—my mouth watered at the sight and smell of dinner. I was famished.

"Figured you were hungry," Chance said as I plopped down on a bar stool. He slid a plate loaded with dinner over to me. Glancing around, I asked, "Where's Ivy?"

His eyes met mine. "Living room, I think. She said she needed a moment to collect herself," he shrugged as he turned back to the stovetop, stirring something red with a large wooden spoon. I took a giant bite of the cheesy pasta he'd made and moaned—it was so delicious. Glancing over his shoulder, Chance chuckled, "So you were hungry."

I smiled, cheeks puckered from the pasta, and he resumed his work on the stovetop. An awkward silence filled the space between us until Chance broke it with a low, calculated voice, "What happened on Gayle, Pandora?"

I swallowed my bite and gazed up at him, his back turned, wanting to speak but unable to form the words. Instead, I filled the silence by spearing a broccoli head and taking another bite of food. "You know, you'll have to talk to us at some point," Ivy's voice came from behind me.

She stood there with her arms crossed over her sweater. After finishing the last couple of bites, I slid the plate forward on the counter. "I know. I intend to," I replied quietly. "Come sit down," she said, and I followed her into the living room.

Pulling my hood over my head, I sank into the white recliner closest to the hearth. Ivy sat across from me on the green couch, leaning forward with her elbows resting on her knees as she watched me. She had already lit a fire in the fireplace. Its gentle crackling and the dancing flames cast shifting shadows on the walls. I suddenly felt suffocated under her gaze and crossed my arms over my chest. "Whatever you're going to ask, ask it," I said pointedly.

She had spread a stack of papers across the coffee table between us, and one of the folders was labeled "Luke Nesnah." My heart pounded as I realized this conversation was going to be a long one. "This is his file. You should look at it," Ivy said, handing me the thin manila folder. The name burned into my eyes as I read the label on the edge of the file. Taking a deep breath, I lifted the first page, bracing myself for what would come.

Before me lay a surveillance photo of Luke Nesnah. He looked as he usually did—calm, collected—but this wasn't a mug shot. I lifted an eyebrow and glanced at Ivy, who watched me silently. I flipped through several pictures in the file. Most depicted him in everyday settings—the grocery store, the precinct, his car, and even what appeared to be his apartment. Nothing immediately stood out. Was there something here I was missing?

Continuing to flip, I landed on a transcript of a telephone conversation. The words at the top sent chills down my spine. It was a transcript of a private conversation between Lieutenant Smith and Detective Luke Nesnah.

Goosebumps prickled along my neck as I read rapidly. Most of it appeared to be generic small talk—likely intended to mislead anyone eavesdropping or to serve as coded banter I couldn't decipher. But as I neared the bottom of the transcript, my blood ran cold.

Smith: Have you convinced her to travel with you yet?
Nesnah: I met with her after the ball. She is on board.
Smith: Good.
Nesnah: I will report when I have further information and a departure date.
Smith: Luke, remember we need her alive. It is your job to protect her, with your life. All of this means nothing if she's dead.

"All of this means nothing if I'm dead?" I asked hoarsely. "It would seem that was what he said," Ivy replied, plucking a piece of lint from the arm of the couch. "What does that even mean?"

"I was hoping you could tell me." She said sourly. "Who overheard this conversation?" I demanded, flipping the paper back and forth as I searched for any indication of the transcriber. There were no signatures—most likely a measure to protect their identity. I cursed under my breath.

"I'll be honest with you—that's only half of my concern right now," she said, leaning forward with her elbows resting on her knees. "Flip to the last page in that file."

I complied, rifling through various papers about Luke: apartment leasing documents, fingerprints, badge numbers, job lists—until I finally landed on the last page. It was a warrant. A warrant for Luke Nesnah's arrest. I lifted the paper, holding it close to my face.

Wanted: Domestic terrorism and first degree murder

I froze.

"And I was hoping you'd be able to tell me about *that*," Chance's voice made me jump. He stood leaning against the wall behind me, his shoulder pressed against it, arms crossed. "Hoping I'd be able to tell you about *this*?" My voice rose an octave. "Yes," they both answered in unison.

My eyes widened as I stared back at the paper. "I didn't know anything about this," I whispered. "I thought he was just being arrested because he took me to Gayle. There's no way this is right—if it is, he'd be a felon."

All lies.

Ivy narrowed her eyes at me. I knew she was hard to lie to, but I hadn't expected her to be so skeptical of everything I said. She leaned against the back of the couch with her arm draped over the cushions and didn't answer my question. Instead, she stared off into the fire, her thoughts seemingly racing behind her brown eyes.

Breaking the silence, Chance said, "We brought Danny Fritz in for questioning while you were gone. In your absence, it seemed logical for Lieutenant Smith to reassign Ivy as head detective of Amy O'Rayne's case since he didn't know your whereabouts or Detective Nesnah's."

I turned to look at him, still leaning against the wall, as the gravity of the situation settled over us all.

The fire was dwindling into dark, smoldering embers when Ivy got up to add another log. As it hissed and slowly caught flame, she returned to the couch, her expression completely impassive. I reminded myself that these were trained detectives—especially Ivy, renowned for her interrogation skills. This wasn't a friendly reunion. It was an interrogation masked as concern for a supposedly abducted woman. I had to tread carefully. They'd forgotten that I, too, was a detective, well-versed in every interrogation technique taught in the academy.

"You brought Danny Fritz in for questioning?" I asked, forcing a look of surprise. I wasn't shocked they had brought him in, what startled me was that it seemed they'd actually extracted helpful information from him. Unless, of course, they were pretending, trying instead to lure the truth out of me. I would not crack.

"He claims that Detective Nesnah is a Protectorate soldier—a member of a terrorist organization founded on Cappurn. He further alleges that his son paid him to assist in taking over Fritz Corporation," Chance said, settling into one of the spare chairs in the living room.

A genuine look of confusion flickered across my face. "He said what?"

I turned my head around to look at Ivy. My hood slipped off, and my wet hair clung to my face as I pushed it away. "Furthermore," Chance continued, "he also told us that Adam hired Detective Nesnah to kill Amy O'Rayne. Apparently, she possessed some incriminating files—the same files that were in your mother's basement the night she died."

My eyes widened with shock and fear. Everything he had told me—everything he had promised—turned out to be a lie. He had begged for my trust time and again, but he was nothing more than a manipulative murderer. I sucked in a sharp breath through clenched teeth. "That *bastard*," I hissed.

"You need to tell us everything that happened on Gayle," Ivy said again, her wariness finally visible in her eyes. "He told me there was going to be a war," I replied, pinching the bridge of my nose as I finally caved. "That Danny Fritz and my father were planning to use this newly found Element X for nefarious purposes—he said it would be used to create dangerous weapons no one has ever seen before."

Ivy and Chance exchanged glances.

"The purpose of mining Element X is for clean energy," she countered. "It doesn't produce waste like oil-powered machinery. We have no reason to think they'd use it for anything other than that."

As she cocked her head at me, stray blonde strands from her messy bun framed her gentle face. Her knees were crossed, and though stressed, she didn't seem on edge talking to me. I wondered what was wrong with me—I had never doubted the one person in this world I truly trusted. My best friend.

Ivy cleared her throat, "The military boot print found at Amy's crime scene..." Her voice was soft, "It was his,"

"It can't have been," I protested, shaking my head. She sighed and leaned forward, flipping through Luke's file until she pointed at a pair of boots. "These were found in his apartment. They still had mud caked on them that matched the mud outside Fritz Corporation." She indicated the chunks of brown clinging to the boot tread. "It couldn't be..." I began.

"Adam gave him the vecuronium to kill Amy," she continued. "He was about to be caught when your father showed up, and then he disappeared. We believe that the pendant he always wears around his neck allows him to flash." She pointed to a picture of the relic, identical to the one he wore constantly. I cursed and threw the folder onto the coffee table.

"That fucking asshole! He told me Adam gave it to him." I spat, pacing the room. "I told you she didn't know." Ivy hissed at Chance.

"That's why he was trying to find those files. They incriminate him and Adam—not my father and Danny like he claimed." I hissed. All the puzzle pieces finally began to click together, and then a worse thought struck me. The world started spinning, and nausea overwhelmed me.

"If he killed Amy, wouldn't that mean he killed my mother?" I whispered.

Ivy's face went pale.

"We don't have evidence for that yet," she murmured. "But you think he did, too?" I choked out, tears welling in my eyes. "We plan to charge him with it if we can find the right evidence," she breathed.

My anger exploded. I grabbed a vase with a plant from beside the fireplace and hurled it across the room. It slammed into the glass wall behind the couch, shattering into a million pieces. Ivy instinctively raised an arm to shield herself from the dirt and glass debris that sprayed over her. Chance leaped from his seat, rushing to check if she was alright, but I was beyond caring—I roared, throwing book after book at the wall.

The glass groaned as a spider crack formed along it, arcing like a bolt of lightning. The rage inside me was untamable, unquenchable. Chance stormed over, looming over me as the fury took over. "Pandora! You're going to hurt someone!" he hollered, shaking my shoulders as I raised another book, poised to hurl it.

"Pandora!" he shouted again, yanking the book from my hand and pushing me back. My socks slid across the hardwood floor as I stared at him—or perhaps through him. "You need space," Chance said, rising, though I barely heard him through the ringing in my ears. Ivy cautiously stood from the couch, and my arms sagged at my sides as I tried to catch my breath.

She cautiously approached me and then gingerly wrapped her arms around my neck. I didn't move. "We will leave these here. These copies are for you. We're both here for you, Pandora, and when you are ready, we can talk more about what happened while you were on Gayle." She said.

She leaned back and caressed my face with her palm. Pain and despair shone in her eyes as she looked at me, at her best friend whose life had completely fallen apart over and over again. "We can put him behind bars for the rest of his life, Pandora. I will see to it that it happens. For Esme."

I shut my eyes, the tears rolling freely down my red cheeks. She swiped her thumb over one of them, smearing it slightly. "You've asked for justice for her. Let me give it to you." Her voice was gentle and soothing.

I pulled her in, roughly burying my face in her neck, and sobbed. I don't know how long we stood there, but it was a very long time.

Chapter 38

I sat curled up on the couch, eating the last tub of ice cream from my freezer. Chance and Ivy had left hours ago, but I couldn't sleep. The anguish I felt was indescribable. Impossible to contain. I lifted another spoonful of mint chocolate chip to my mouth—my favorite flavor—but it tasted bland and disappointing tonight. Glancing at the clock on the fireplace mantle, I noted it was midnight.

The moon blazed through the glass wall, its light refracting through the spider crack that now stretched from the floor to the ceiling. I took another spoonful of ice cream, glaring at its audacity to be beautiful, patterned like a delicate snowflake against the shattered glass.

The fire had long since died, leaving only grey ash and smoldering embers in the pit, but I remained, knees pulled to my chest, hood pulled over my head, drowning my sorrow in sugar because I couldn't sleep. Who could, after learning who killed their mom?

The thought nauseated me, and I set the spoon down in the now-empty bowl. The clatter of metal on porcelain echoed through the quiet room as rain streamed down the window, collecting in the crack I had made. I sighed, knowing I'd eventually have to fix it or end up with a swimming pool in my living room every time it rained.

Taking a deep breath, I prepared to head back to my bedroom

and try to sleep again, but my thoughts were interrupted by a gentle knock at the front door. Detective instincts kicking in, I grabbed the hidden pistol stashed under the coffee table and crept toward the door. A figure appeared just behind the fogged glass.

"Pandora. It's just me. Open the door," came my exasperated father's voice, as though he knew I was right on the other side. I opened the door with one hand on my hip, casually holding my pistol away from him. He leaned against the door frame, one arm crossed over his chest, his other hand tucked in his slacks pocket.

"It's late, and you almost became very unalive," I muttered. "I know, but we need to talk," he said, trying to push past me. I placed a hand on his chest, stopping him in his tracks, "You've been lying to me. Do you think you can just show up at my house and demand entry?"

He paused. "I'm sorry. I want to explain everything," he said, placing a hand on my shoulder. I sighed and shook my head. "Go ahead then," I let him pass as he removed his suit jacket and hung it by the door. It closed with a thunk, the sound echoing through the quiet house.

My hair had dried entirely by now—auburn waves hanging loosely over my shoulders. I toyed with it in my fingers as I followed him into the living room, stashing the gun back in its secret compartment. "It's cold in here," he murmured, tossing another log onto the fire and watching it catch slowly. He lowered himself onto the couch, and I remained standing, watching him.

"Where would you like me to start?" he asked, his eyes searching mine. "Literally anywhere," I muttered and he sighed with resignation. "Okay, let's start with Detective Nesnah." He patted the couch beside him, inviting me to sit, but I eased myself into one of the fluffy white chairs across the room, choosing to remain silent. He hung his head for a moment, then began.

"We've had surveillance on Detective Nesnah for months now. We believe he's part of a terrorist organization on Cappurn called 'The Protectorate.' From what we understand, their mission is to dismantle the Liarta government and seize control—they want to impose a dictatorship here. We believe they're using Element X to create mutant soldiers to take up arms for them. There have been countless reports of missing people here in Raos, and we suspect The Protectorate is behind these disappearances for their human experiments."

I curled my lips in disgust, "What kind of human experiments?"

"We don't know yet," he admitted, "but we do know they're very interested in our Element X mining on Feros. We believe Detective Nesnah was sent here to undermine the operation and eventually seize control for himself."

I ground my teeth together in irritation. The more I learned, the more I realized I did hate him. He had manipulated every bit of information to his benefit. I swallowed my anger attempting to regain my level headed detective composure before speaking again, "Tell me the truth about the files."

He paled slightly. "The files are evidence of the experiments that The Protectorate is conducting. I couldn't let Detective Nesnah get his hands on them. They're our only evidence against them and he would have destroyed them, so I hid them. I didn't have another choice." I ground my teeth, "So everyone keeps saying. Where did you hide them?" His fingers rested in his lap and I watched him with a guarded expression, "With Danny at Fritz Co."

"And you trust him?" I pressed. "Yes. He helped me obtain

them,"

I narrowed my eyes. There Danny was again, heavily involved in this mess. Regardless of how involved he was, I had to tread lightly. Because going to bat with someone with his reputation and resources as his disposal was risky, if not downright foolish, and one mistake could cost me everything. Including my badge. Permanently.

"How did he help you obtain them?" My voice wavered slightly but I stifled any note of apprehension. "He had connections that implicated Detective Nesnah and The Protectorate. I needed a solid reason beforc the Raos Government would allow me to start an investigation." I shifted forward in my chair, my tone laced with suspicion. "Well, that's both convenient and *suspicious*,"

He sighed, pinching the bridge of his nose. "It's his son," he muttered, "Adam is conspiring with The Protectorate. They offered him control of Fritz Corporation—framing Danny Fritz for the Element X experiments in the process." I bit my lower lip, confused. It was what Ivy had claimed earlier, but none of it made sense. I'd known Adam for a long time, and while he was conniving, I wouldn't have assumed he was clever enough to orchestrate such an elaborate scheme. "Why would Adam undermine Danny when he is set to inherit Fritz Co. anyway?" I questioned, nonchalantly picking lint off my sock.

"I'm sure he wanted it sooner," he replied slowly. "Besides, it would be in his best interest to be on The Protectorate's good side if they try to infiltrate the local government. Better to be a friend than an enemy." He glanced at the empty ice cream bowl on the table—the spoon still sticking out—but offered no comment. "Unfortunately," he continued, "when I went to Fritz Co. to hand over the files to Matilda, Danny's secretary, I was shocked to find my daughter sitting behind the desk."

My eyes snapped up to his.

"I have made many mistakes in my life, Pandora," he said, his tone heavy with regret. "Not telling you that you had a half-sister is one of my biggest failures." I set my jaw firmly as tears began welling up in my eyes but I quickly rubbed the cuff of my sweatshirt over them, anger and hurt mingling in my thoughts. "You knew about her this entire time and didn't say anything? Did mom know about her?" I asked.

"Yes."

I buried my face in my hands. "If you knew about her, why didn't you go back for Odina?" I whispered through them. His expression grew sad and his voice was soft when he spoke again, "I loved your mom. I don't regret that decision because if I hadn't left with her, I wouldn't have you."

A forced, somber smile appeared on his face as I peered at him. I couldn't decide whether I was angry or heartbroken. I looked out the glass wall behind him into the dark forest beyond and longed to disappear into its depths—free from the wretched humans and their catastrophic decisions. I blinked realizing I had been staring out the window for some time now. "Say something," he urged, placing his arm over the back of the couch and tilting his head toward me. "If you were Odina's mate, who was Mom's?"

The question seemed to catch him off guard. His forehead creased with concern as he replied, "She never told me, and I never asked. It wasn't important at the time, and we certainly didn't want to dwell on the past. All I know is that he died sometime before I met her." I nodded slowly. He was finally talking, not hiding any information. Layer by layer, it felt like I could start breathing again.

"Did Amy know it was you?"

Although I wasn't officially assigned to the case, finding out what happened to my sister was something I couldn't let go. Who would've wanted her dead? And was it be connected to these files somehow?

"She did," he said. "In the shock of seeing her there, I forgot about the files on her desk. I fear she may have gave them to Adam, and he killed her to tie up loose ends. I've already told Ivy to bring Adam in for questioning again and to dig up whatever dirt she can on him. Danny and I want to see him and Nesnah permanently behind bars, Pandora." He ran his finger through his salt-and-pepper hair. "Detective Luke Nesnah will be a bigger problem, though. He's sly and has covered his tracks better. We'll need to do some digging to get more on him."

I swallowed, my thoughts churning in my mind. Why would Adam hire Luke to kill Kimi, only to then practically beg me to go to Gayle and investigate her case—knowing full well it would eventually lead me to uncover the truth that he'd been the one to hire him in the first place?

If he had hired him.

A seed of doubt planted itself in my chest, one I couldn't will away, and in that moment I silently cursed myself for becoming a detective. Thankfully, my father didn't seem to catch the flicker of doubt that passed through me. "Which brings me to some questions I need to ask you," he said calmly. I nodded—I should trust him because he's my father—but Luke's voice echoed in my mind fanning the fiery flames of doubt.

Trust no one, tell no one.

Something was going on—something my father didn't want me to uncover—and I'd bet hard money that Luke was the only one holding the truth. Who was the real killer? Who was my father protecting? Luke might be the only person who knew, but locked in a jail cell, he couldn't do a damn thing about it.

I thought back to when we landed back on Liarta, how calm

Luke had been. He had known he was going to be arrested. He had known my father would come for him, but if he had why would he let him take him. My eyes widened as the realization struck. It was a ploy to make my father reveal his hand.

He was going to make a run for it.

The thought tore through me, leaving me pale. If he escaped, he'd only be digging his own grave. Danny and Harrison would stop at nothing until they caught him again. Before thinking my words tumbled out of my mouth, "Where is he right now?" I mentally kicked myself, shoving a proverbial foot in my mouth. Confusion flickered across his face. "He's in booking at Precinct 12 right now. Why?"

"Who is watching him?" I continued, my stress rising though I tried to conceal it. "I have everything under control, Pandora. He's been denied bail—he won't be released anytime soon, and he certainly won't be able to get out." His eyebrow lifted as he looked at me, "Why do you ask?"

"Nothing. I'm just—I'm just making sure," I replied quickly, then snapped my mouth shut. He sat completely still, his jaw twitching slightly. I bit my lip and shifted my eyes to the forest outside, hoping he wouldn't press further. "Well then," he began, shifting slightly on the couch. "As I was about to ask, what did Detective Nesnah say to convince you to go to Gayle with him?"

My heart felt as heavy as lead. He hadn't convinced me—in fact, I had convinced him. This felt all wrong. "He told me we needed to go to Gayle to solve my case—which, at the time, I didn't know was about my half-sister," I said cautiously. "And whose ship do we have docked at Precinct 12?"

"Adam's," I said curtly. "Adam Fritz?" His eyes widened.

"The one and only,"

He shook his head and let out a low chuckle. "I thought you were smarter than that, Pandora."

"He made quite the argument," I said.

He rose from the couch and placed another log on the dying fire. It quickly hit the burning ash and burst into flames. He sighed as he began pacing the room, eventually stopping by the glass window. Placing a finger on the spider crack I had caused earlier that evening, he asked, "What happened to your window?" I met his gaze evenly, "I happened."

He pursed his lips, staring out into the forest like I had moments ago. His hands were clasped behind his back as he pondered his next question. It was still raining, and the trees drooped in misery, mirroring the weight on my sagging shoulders. "Is Odina alive?" he asked. "Yes, why do you care?" I replied quietly.

He didn't turn to look at me—he simply hung his head slightly, resting a hand on the glass window before him, "I never meant her any harm," Lowering his arms to his sides, he turned to face me. I pulled my knees to my chest and wrapped my arms around them, my chin resting firmly on top. "Did Detective Nesnah mention The Protectorate when you were on Gayle?" he asked. "Yes, he said he was with The Protectorate and that he'd been sent to interfere with the mining on Feros." I deliberately left out that I knew he was sworn to kill him. He scoffed and shook his head.

"Idiot," he breathed, "He tried to convince my own daughter to take his side. What a damn idiot. I should have never let Smith assign you to Amy's case," he muttered. "It was too late to change it by then. I just hoped it wouldn't come to this."

"Hoped that I wouldn't find out she was my sister—and your daughter?" I asked, narrowing my eyes at him.

It's not what you think it is, Pandora. I just figured it would be easier if that burden was mine to carry, not yours." He took a deep breath, leaning forward and placing his hands on the back of the couch.

"The truth always comes out in the end, no matter how hard you try to bury it, Dad." The words spilled from my mouth like hot fire and they tasted bitter in my mouth. There were secrets I was keeping from him too, things I was purposefully leaving unsaid. Maybe I was more like him than I ever realized. I had always been told I was the spitting image of my mom, but as I grew older, I saw just how much he had shaped me—how he had molded the way I think, speak, and act.

A somber smile tugged at his lips. "You're right, Pandora. I'm sorry," he said.

"Sorry doesn't even begin to fix the disaster I'm caught up in—something you could have warned me about—but it's a start," I glanced at the clock on the wall. It was already two in the morning. His eyes followed mine, and he cleared his throat. "I guess I should let you get some sleep. I'm sure you're tired. We can continue this conversation tomorrow when you retrieve your things at the precinct."

"Are you really decommissioning me?" I asked the fight completely resolving from my shoulders. "Until this whole thing blows over, yes. I can't risk you being in the middle anymore—it's time you sat this one out." I rose from the chair and followed him to the front door. He slid his suit jacket on and reached for the door but paused. I stood there with my arms crossed over my chest.

Suddenly, he turned and pulled me into a swift hug. I stiffened in surprise before wrapping my arms around him. "I truly am sorry, Pandora. From now on, no more secrets. It's just me and you," he murmured quietly in my ear. "No more secrets," I whispered back. Before we could speak further, he released me, briskly opened the front door, and strode out to his car without looking back.

Chapter 39

I tossed and turned all night, irritated and restless. Finally, I had enough at five in the morning and dragged myself out of bed. Rubbing my eyes and fighting the dark purple bags forming beneath them, I realized it was time to head to the station and retrieve my belongings.

Did everyone already know I'd been removed from my position? They must have—people talk. With the sheer number of officers present at Dock 12 when we landed, word would have circulated the precinct at least a couple of times before I had a chance to say anything.

Sitting on the edge of my bed, I took a deep breath. "Mayra," I called out. "Yes, Pandora, how may I assist you?" came her monotone response as her hologram appeared before me, yet her ever-present smile shone brightly.

"What is the weather like today?" I asked, looking up at her. Her violet eyes dimmed for a moment as she searched her sources. "It's somewhat chilly this morning—about 60 degrees—but this afternoon it will be closer to 68," she chimed. We'd only been away a week, but it felt strange to experience such brisk weather compared to the sauna that was Gayle. "Thank you, Mayra," I said dismissively, and she vanished.

Opening the armoire, I selected a black turtleneck sweater, jeans, and chunky boots—no need for office attire since I was merely retrieving my things. I sighed deeply. I had been with this precinct for ten years, and being demoted by my father felt like a punch to the gut.

I was a good cop. I cared about my job and my coworkers, but in the end, none of it mattered. It didn't matter if my intentions were good or just. It mattered which lines I had crossed, and that was that. Although most police work was legally very black and white, I couldn't help but wonder if life was almost always in the grey. Continuing to adhere to a black-and-white governmental system quite possibly could be our downfall.

I shook my head, clearing my thoughts—I was beginning to sound like my mother. She always said that the color we all wore was grey, even if we claimed black or white. Perhaps we were just varying shades of grey, and maybe she was right—because, as much as I had resisted the idea, I had yet to meet someone who was utterly one-sided.

I pulled the sweater over my head, pinning my auburn waves in place with a hair clip. Some stray strands stubbornly framed my face, so I let them hang loosely. My boots echoed through the empty house. It felt unbearably lonely—the silence clinging to the walls was almost deafening. I remained motionless in the kitchen for what felt like hours, wondering if this was what my life had come to. The handwritten note sat eerily on the counter still.

I am not who you think I am.

Before I could drown in my thoughts, I briskly walked through the kitchen, grabbed my bag from the counter, and strode out the front door without looking back.

***

As I entered through its front doors, the precinct felt less welcoming than usual.

I rounded the giant indoor fountain as Margaret eyed me from behind the front desk. "So, it's true—you're back," she said, her cherry-red glasses sliding down the bridge of her nose. Her grey hair was pulled back into a neatly coiled bun that aged her. She clucked her tongue at me, "You've been the talk of the precinct this week." I grew even more irritable the further into the day I went. Chewing the inside of my cheek, I closed my eyes. "I don't have my badge, Margaret. Can you let Ivy know I'm here to get my belongings?"

I refused to take the bait.

She raised an eyebrow at my attitude but gestured toward the white chairs in the lobby. "Take a seat, I guess. I'll let her know. I didn't think your father had it in him to strip you of your badge," she said, then picked up her telephone to call for Ivy. "Honestly, me either," I muttered.

Plopping down on one of the white chairs, my boots scuffed against the dark tile. The shiny black surface echoed the dark marks on my skin. I glanced at my fingers peeking out from the cuffs of my sweater. No one could tell I was wearing silicone sleeves, but worry gnawed at me—they wouldn't last forever, and without fingerprints, I'd have to come up with an explanation if I was ever to regain my father's trust.

A migraine began to form, and I rubbed my temples. What a nightmare everything had become—it all felt like a terrible fever dream. If I weren't currently benched in my precinct lobby, I might have dismissed it as nothing more than that.

"Pandora," Ivy's voice rang out over the tile. Her blonde hair was in its usual slicked-back, tight bun, and the collar of her high-neck mauve blouse brushed against the base of her hairline. Her black slacks skimmed the tops of her matching pumps as she stood waiting. The Precinct 12 detective badge on her hip glared at me from across the room. I didn't want to, but I looked into her eyes. Desolation reflected back at me.

She had been here nearly as long as I had, and we'd shared desk space ever since she was hired. Today wasn't just about being released from duty—it felt like the end of the partnership I'd forged when she started the class after mine.

"Let's go, I suppose," I sighed, standing up from the chair. Margaret said nothing further, just watched us with her knowing gaze as we brushed past the desk. I figured if she tried, she could probably gossip about an inanimate stone wall. Gritting my teeth, I folded my arms over my chest. Let them talk, let them think they knew me. So be it.

"Did you get any sleep last night?" Ivy asked as we rounded a corner. Her blouse ruffled slightly as we walked, and the steady clack of her heels kept me anchored in the moment. "No," I muttered. "I heard your father paid you a visit." Her brown eyes met mine over her shoulder as she continued. "How did that go?"

"About as well as expected, I guess. I need to tell you more about what happened on Gayle—what my father involved himself in," I said in a lower voice as two uniformed officers gawked at me while we passed. "I'm free tonight. We should meet at Lady Emerald," she said, her shoulders rising with a sigh.

"A bar is the last place I want to be right now," I muttered. "I get that, but it's the only place I can guarantee that whatever we talk about gets drowned out. I don't trust your cabin anymore," She raised a hand, silently signaling me to wait.

I stopped in front of the atom scanner's light but didn't

step into it. Ivy stepped forward, and the scanner's AI dinged giving her the green light. "Ivy Zephyr. Detective. Business," She announced in her formal voice. "Detective Ivy Zephyr. Identified," the AI confirmed, its voice even toned. She waved for me to step forward.

"Visitor. Pandora Vaughn," I identified myself and tried not to cringe as my voice emerged hoarse. The light began scanning my feet, and I kept my hands down at my sides, staying as still as possible. Then, the light faltered as it reached my hands.

Oh shit—the gloves.

Ivy narrowed her eyes at me from beyond the scanner and tapped her toe against the tile. Her mouth pressed into a thin, tight line. The scan finally finished, the blue light fading away. "Pandora Vaughn. Identified," the device announced before shutting off.

Sweat formed at my temples as I casually pushed the sleeve of my sweater down, trying to act nonchalant though Ivy's gaze was fixed on me.

"What was that about? I've never seen that light falter on anything before," she asked, her head cocked to the side as she stared at me. I just shrugged and briskly brushed past her. "You know, one of these days, you're going to have to tell me the truth, Pandora," she called after me, her voice trailing off as I moved ahead. I heard her heels clicking as she caught up. "Yeah, that's what everyone keeps saying," I muttered as we reached the back office.

The usual hustle and bustle of the precinct fell silent as everyone turned to watch us standing at the door. Even Casey Lament—the neighborhood junkie—paused his taunting of the officers in his holding cell. My lips thinned.

"Well, well. If it isn't the detective turned traitor," he drawled from the back of the cell. He leaned against the metal bars, one foot crossed over the other, one arm folded over his chest, and the other resting on the bar. He looked as though he was out smoking a cigarette—except he wasn't holding a lit roll of carcinogens between his fingers. A small part of me felt strange seeing him like that. Detective Nesnah had once looked at me in exactly the same way. I shook off the memory and tried to ignore him.

"Oh, I see—ignore Casey because he's just a crazy druggie," he continued as I walked along the cell toward my desk. He pushed off the wall and followed me as far as he could. "Can't give me the time of day, Pandora? Whatever happened to that tall, handsome detective I heard you ran away with? I'd love to strangle the life out of him for what he did to me last time we were here—he walloped me good, even split my lip open."

This was the thing with druggies, they always talked themselves into trouble. They just couldn't keep their mouths closed.

"I heard they were going to execute him for *treason*," Casey added, his malicious grin stretching from ear to ear, exposing all four of his teeth. Having had enough, I slammed my palms against the metal bars of the holding cell. "Say one more word, and I'll make sure it's *you* in that execution chair instead of him," I hissed.

Somewhat surprised at my outburst, Casey blanched and backed away. "Just trying to make small talk, geez. Women are so sensitive," he snorted, then shrugged as he sank back onto the metal bench bolted to the ground inside the cell. I ground my teeth together audibly.

"Shut your mouth, Casey, before I shut it for you," I heard Chance call from his desk. Casey scoffed but clammed up, saying nothing more. I turned to find the entire precinct, watching our interaction. "Don't listen to him," Ivy whispered, gently ushering me along. "Carry on," she half-shouted across the desks, and soon everyone found something else to do.

"Are they really going to execute him, Ivy?" I whispered, panic starting to flood my system. "That's what the prosecutors are going for, yes," she replied, glancing at me. "You seem torn by that information. I figured you'd be relieved to see him gone—after all, you hate him."

I rubbed my temples and groaned. "It's *complicated*," I murmured. "How *complicated*?" she asked, raising one eyebrow. *"Complicated,"* I repeated.

She shook her head. "I don't know how long you have to collect your things, so be fast. I don't want to deal with Lieutenant Smith's wrath today." Lieutenant Smith—Luke's brother—must be working to change the charges from execution. He must have some sway. "This is all moving very fast. He was only arrested last night," I said quickly as I pulled the chair back from the desk that used to be mine. "I've been told he doesn't have an attorney—he's self-representing."

My eyes flicked to hers, "Why would he do that? He's not a lawyer. He's a detective." Ivy's shoulders rose in a shrug, "I don't know. I asked the same question."

"Who is the prosecutor?" I asked. After a pause, she raised her eyes to meet mine. "Your father."

I pinched the bridge of my nose, already knowing the answer—I just didn't want to hear it. Part of me wondered if it was indeed an act of vengeance for "kidnapping" his daughter or if he was using Luke as a warning, an example of why no one should ever mess with him as commissioner. "I'm not surprised," I said. "I'm not either," she replied softly. I bit my lip, then stopped myself remembering what Luke had said about that bad habit.

A rush of heat filled my face as I shook my head to forget the memory of how his fingers had brushed my lips. Ivy plopped down in her seat, shuffling some papers on her desk, and glanced at me as I ran the back of my fingers over my tomato-red face.

"Everything good?" she asked, raising an eyebrow. "Yep," I replied absentmindedly, waving a hand in her direction as I opened the desk's top drawer. She scooted a cardboard box toward me with the toe of her shoe. "I brought this to put your stuff in," she said, still watching me with those brown eyes. In her other hand, she held a manila file with several papers peeking out.

"So..." she drawled as I pulled items from the drawer—my nice pens, notebooks, a precinct protocol handbook, handcuffs, and a stapler. "*So?*" I echoed as I moved on to the second drawer.

My hands felt numb as I continued emptying the desk, my body moving as if someone else were controlling it. "The bar tonight?" she asked, tucking the folder under her chin and tilting her head to the side. Her nails, freshly painted bright pink, stood in stark contrast to the drab folder. "Do I have a choice? Or are you just telling me to go there?" I asked. "When have I ever been able to simply tell you what to do?" she replied with a slight, teasing grin. "Never. But I do like to give the illusion that I do what people ask me to,"

She chuckled, her laughter easing my nerves just a bit. After watching me for a moment longer, she added in a nearly apologetic tone, "We'll figure it out, Pandora. It will be fine,"

I gritted my teeth. "*We* aren't doing anything. *You* have a case to solve, and *I* have a father to deal with."

"You know what I mean, Pandora. Don't be cross with me. I didn't choose to be assigned to this case. In fact, I'd avoided it ever since you left because I didn't want that kind of heat—but as luck would have it, here we are," she said, slightly irritated.

She tapped her brightly colored nails on her desk, and I scowled at the noise. I opened the last drawer, pulling out all the remaining files—mostly solved cases I had worked on that still needed to be filed with Cathy, the forensic record keeper. I thumbed through them carefully, making sure I didn't miss anything. They were mostly homicides, but I stopped abruptly on one name in particular.

Aiya Malone.

I sucked in a breath through clenched teeth. The woman who had been brutally murdered by her husband, Raj Malone—the same man who had attempted to assassinate me in the bar parking lot. I glanced around the room; no one was watching us. I quickly slid the file into the box of belongings and covered it with other office supplies.

"What are you doing?" Ivy whispered, her eyes widening as she darted a look at the file in the box. "You can't take files when you're not assigned to a case," she added nervously, glancing around to see if anyone had noticed. "The man who tried to kill me in Lady Emerald's parking lot is the same man who killed his wife—Aiya Malone," I said quietly. "He said someone had paid him to kill me."

"Yes, but you shot him. He's dead," she said, shaking her head. Thin blonde strands escaped from her tight bun, framing her face. I scowled in annoyance. "Ivy, you're a detective. Use your detective brain," I said. "I am," she countered. "How do you plan on finding the person who hired him to kill you if you don't have access to the precinct files?"

A feral grin spread across my face, and she blanched. "Oh no. Absolutely not," she huffed, crossing her arms. "You are not using my badge to get files," she hissed low enough not to draw attention. "Come on, Ivy. Are you really just going to let someone off the hook who tried to kill your best friend—purely for the precinct's sake?" I rolled my eyes.

She narrowed her eyes, tapping her nails against the desk again. "Fine," she muttered. "Thank you!" I grinned, stacking the rest of the files on the desk. "The rest of these need to be filed, but when you're there, can you ask for Raj Malone's criminal file?" I added, batting my eyes. She bared her teeth at me. "It's a good thing you're my best friend. I should gut you for this after what you put me through this week," she snapped, standing up to retrieve the files, "Did you grab everything?"

"I think so—oh, wait!" I reached for the last item on my desk. A framed photograph of me, my father, and my mother. It had been taken at my father's commissioner swearing-in. He looked striking in his navy blue uniform and cap, the white of his shirt matching the brightness of his smile, every pin on his shirt standing out against the dark fabric. My mother wore a deep teal dress with a square neckline and long sleeves. The dress hugged her waist and flowed gracefully over her hips.

She gazed up at my father, her smile nearly contagious even in the photograph. Her red hair billowed in an imaginary wind, revealing the delicate pearl jewelry she had chosen. I, too, looked at my father with pride in that moment—the mocha brown A-line dress I wore hugged my waist and flared at the hips, giving me more movement than my mother's dress. My hair was neatly tucked into a low bun, and thin gold hoops dangled from my ears. The three of us looked so happy. Even as I stared at the picture, rage blossomed in my chest. It had all been a lie. A single tear slipped down my cheek as I stood there, lost in the memories and the betrayal.

The door to the back holding cells suddenly burst open and slammed into the wall behind it. The abrupt noise startled me, and my head whipped toward it and in the same breath a part of me wished I could disappear from existence altogether.

There stood Detective Luke Nesnah, roughly escorted by two uniformed officers. I swallowed hard as I watched them push him forward and groaned when I realized who was trailing behind him—my father.

"Don't try anything stupid," my father hissed as he watched Luke struggle against the officers holding his arms. Luke's hands were cuffed behind his back, but I knew him and those frail pieces of metal wouldn't keep him contained for long. I stood motionless, eyes wide. Ivy's gaze flickered from me to Luke and back again, silently asking what was happening. I shook my head, indicating my own uncertainty. She then returned her focus to the pair.

"Oh, Commissioner Vaughn, do you not just love flaunting your authority over everyone here?" Luke taunted, clearly trying to provoke him in front of the entire precinct. "Continue talking, Nesnah, and you'll just keep digging your grave for me," my father growled, a clear warning as he slammed the door shut again. Luke continued to struggle, making a show of defiance.

"Digging my grave for you?" he hissed. "You'd like that wouldn't you. Less dirt on your own hands, hmm? Tell me Commissioner Vaughn, how many graves have *you* dug? Mine hardly is the first one, is it?" his teeth glinted under the fluorescent light.

My stomach began to roil, and my mouth went parched. "Careful what you say, Nesnah. You don't know who you're talking to," Harrison warned him a second time. "I know *exactly* who I'm talking to," Luke retorted under his breath, his voice barely audible despite the tense silence of the room.

My father swept around the officers, pointing a finger directly in Luke's face. "You will cooperate, Nesnah, or you will get the execution chair," he thundered, his nostrils flaring angrily. I held my breath, waiting for Luke's response, but he remained silent.

Instead, a sinister smile spread across his face as he glared back at my father. Harrison clenched his fists at his sides.

"Take him to maximum holding until the trial, and do not take your eyes off him for one second!" he roared. The officers obeyed and continued pushing him forward. I clutched the picture frame against my chest as I watched them drag him away.

My head felt fuzzy, and the world seemed to fade as I stood in the recess of my mind near the wooden door. There he stood, the door wide open, blinking at me. "*Don't believe a word he told you. I will find you,*" he said as the door slowly closed on its hinges, I was left alone.

For the first time, I placed my hand back on the door. "*Please, don't leave me,*" I whispered.

Before I could hear an answer, I was jolted back to reality. My eyes pleaded with his back as if I were trying to warn him that they were going to execute him. His spine straightened. He paused in his struggle for a moment, then slowly turned his head until his blue eyes met mine—blue on green. The officers continued to drag him out, but he never broke our gaze. I took a sharp breath and reached for him through the door in my mind, stretching as far as I could.

"*Run,*" I whispered. He nodded once and then disappeared through the doors.

Chapter 40

The weather had finally warmed up enough that a simple dark green t-shirt, skinny jeans, and boots were all I needed as I trudged through the bustling city sidewalks. My hair was pulled back in a single long braid that swayed with each step as I glanced for traffic before crossing the street. I shoved my hands into my pockets as my crossbody bag thumped lightly against my hip.

Bar-hopping wasn't really my scene, but this place had become our usual hangout outside the precinct. I passed a group of street dancers, the pulse of rap music pounding from a box speaker behind them and vibrating through my chest. There was no line outside the bar tonight—not surprising for a Wednesday. Fridays and Saturdays were always their busiest.

I pushed open the glass door and stepped inside. The place was quieter than our last visit, with patrons spread thinly between the bar, high-top tables, and booths. My eyes scanned the room until I caught sight of Ivy's blonde hair poking above the back booth.

She sat with her chin resting in one hand, flipping through the menu. Ditching her office attire, she had opted for a chunky mauve sweater and black skinny jeans, and my eyes were drawn to her thigh-high black suede boots. She always looked so put together.

"Hey," I greeted as I slid into the opposite side of the booth.

"Hey," she replied, setting the menu flat on the table. "Did Cathy give you any trouble when you asked for the file?" I asked in a hushed tone. Even though we were at the bar, I was cautious—no telling whose ears might be listening. After my stint on Gayle, I trusted everyone here about as far as I could throw them.

"No, she did ask why it was his file, though," she said as she cautiously slid the enormous manila folder across the table. My eyes met hers as I flipped the folder open. "What did you tell her?" I asked. "I said I was looking into who put out a hit on you and to keep it on the down low," she murmured, taking a sip of the lemon water that had been sitting on the table.

I scanned the top paper—a mug shot featuring Raj Malone—and my eyes narrowed at him. Who had paid him to off me?

"I ordered you a bourbon, neat," she said, breaking through my thoughts. "Thanks," I replied, my gaze drifting back to her. Before we could get too deep into conversation, a perky, young, carrot-top waitress appeared seemingly out of nowhere. I snapped the folder closed.

"What can I get for you?" She chirped. "Uh, I'll do the angus burger and fries," I said with a smile. "Of course!" the waitress beamed. "And for you?" she asked, turning to Ivy. "The street tacos sound amazing," Ivy replied sweetly, handing the waitress both our menus. "I'll have that right out!" the waitress smiled and rushed away. I took a deep breath. "As you were saying," I said, reopening the folder.

I began thumbing through the endless stack of papers—this was one of the thickest folders I had ever seen. When I had been assigned to the Aiya Malone homicide case, I'd known that her husband was one of Raos' biggest crime lords and if he'd been involved, it would be hard to press charges. He had connections and he always managed to get himself cleaned up before anything could stick.

Yet, despite being richer than any politician's dreams, Raj lost all his money due to the downfall of his organization. He'd poked the wrong bear, and someone had assassinated his entire crew in the middle of the night. Because they were all big crime offenders, no one cared enough to find the person responsible, and his entire legacy crumbled in one night.

In the wake of the disaster, his wife was found beaten to death in their upstairs bedroom. Raj swore that he hadn't been home at the time and claimed it was the same people who had murdered his crew, but further investigation revealed that his wife had threatened to leave him—and in a panic, he had lashed out at her. The horror in that woman's eyes still haunted me. He'd been so reckless, so destructive, that the mere thought of losing his wife drove him to end her life himself.

I shuddered as his image stared back at me from the file. He was brutal, yet until then, he'd always managed to evade the law by having prosecutors drop charges. But this time was different. This was a crime of passion, and when detectives ran the blood found on the hem of his shirt that night, it turned out to be hers.

The evidence was damning—her blood on his clothes and the bruising on his knuckles left no doubt that he had killed her. He had unintentionally backed himself into a corner, and everything had collapsed around him. Ironically, that's exactly how I felt about my own life now—my own hands were the ones that had torn it all down.

"You'll find what Cathy said interesting when I told her that," Ivy said quietly. "Oh?" I lifted my eyes from the papers. "She said Harrison was the last to request his file," I paused, letting her words sink in as the past and present collided in a mess of anger and regret.

My eyebrows furrowed. "What do you mean he was the last to pull his file?" I asked, leaning forward over the table. Ivy snapped the folder shut in front of me, her eyes blazing. "Cathy said she asked him why he was taking a closed file for a felon—a man already given multiple life sentences in federal prison—and he just replied, *my job.*"

She then pulled a small piece of paper from her pocket and slid it across the table with her pointer finger. "I told her to write down the date and time he requested the file."

I took the paper, studying Cathy's feminine, coiled handwriting. "This was two days before he tried to kill me," I said quietly, crumpling the paper and shoving it into my pocket. "I know," Ivy murmured. Then she leaned forward even more, lowering her voice. "Even stranger—she told me that Luke Nesnah had come up to the desk just fifteen minutes after your father left with his file and asked which files he'd requested from her." My eyes widened, "And?"

She shook her head slowly, her gaze dropping before lifting back to mine, "Cathy said he only asked for Raj's file and one other."

"Whose?" I hissed under my breath. "Danny Fritz," she replied quietly.

I leaned all the way back in the booth, my shoulders touching the dark blue padding. "Danny's?" I whispered. She nodded, leaning back in her seat as well. We stared at each other for a moment, mulling over the information. The spunky waitress returned, her orange hair swishing in two short pigtails. "A bourbon, neat for you," she said, setting an amber-colored glass in front of me.

Her eyes briefly scanned the file folder, but I discreetly slid it into my bag. No one needed to know I was in possession of precinct files—let alone Raj Malone's.

"And a Manhattan for you," she added, placing Ivy's drink in front of her. "Anything else I can get you ladies before I return with your food?" The freckles on her nose seemed to dance as she moved. "No, thank you," I said politely, and she whisked herself away. My smile faded as I turned back to Ivy. "Why does he need Danny's file?" I asked, taking a sip of my whiskey. The liquid warmed my throat as I relished its sweet flavor. "That's what I was going to ask you," she replied. I pursed my lips. "I can't think of a good reason for him to need it—unless there's something incriminating in it he's trying to get rid of."

"He signed the bill to allocate funds to the Feros mining three days after you left for Gayle. Do you think it has something to do with that?" I nodded in response, "I definitely don't think it's a coincidence,"

I took a sip of my drink as my eyes scanned the folder in front of me. "There's absolutely nothing noteworthy in here—just a long list of charges he'd managed to wiggle out of conviction over the years," My eyebrows scrunched with thought. Ivy took a swig of her drink, her blonde hair brushing her cheeks.

"I don't think it's about what he wanted to hide," I continued. "I've never trusted Danny. If he wanted his file, it was for a reason. I have a sneaking suspicion it wasn't to cover something up—I think he wanted the file to track down Raj." Ivy paled as she set her drink down. "You don't mean..."

"I think Danny Fritz told my father he needed the file to locate Raj and pay him to assassinate me," I said. Ivy gaped at me, unmoving. "That's a bold move if you're right," she hissed under her breath. "Well, let's hope I'm wrong. But we can't just bring him in for questioning—we'll have to do some sleuthing to figure out what he's been up to." I downed the rest of my whiskey, setting the glass on the table with a thunk.

The waitress returned, setting our food down. "Would you

like another?" She pointed to my empty glass. "No, thank you," I replied. She smiled brightly at both of us. "Well then, enjoy!" she sang before disappearing. "She's so..." Ivy began. "Joyful?" I finished. She grunted in agreement before taking a large bite out of her taco. "I wonder what that's like," she muttered with her mouth full. I bobbed my head in response as I took a bite of my burger. I chewed but didn't really taste it as my eyes drifted to the TV screens behind the bar.

Several random sitcoms played on a few, but every hair on my arms stood erect as I focused on the largest screen. There, on the screen, was a picture of Detective Luke Nesnah.

I set my burger down and pointed at the screen, struggling to find words. Ivy turned in her seat, her shoulders slumping as she realized what I was watching. I listened intently as the bartender turned up the volume.

"This just in, Detective Luke Nesnah escaped police custody today during what was supposed to be a routine transport from Precinct 12's holding cells to solitary confinement. Sources reveal the detective is being charged with murder, kidnapping, tampering, possession of a stolen vehicle, and recently added to the charges was treason."

Suddenly, the burger that I had been eating felt like poison in my stomach, threatening to return back up.

"Commissioner Harrison Vaughn is asking for information regarding his whereabouts with a handsome reward and a warning. Anyone harboring the fugitive will be charged with treason and placed in federal prison. If you know anyone with information or have seen Detective Nesnah, please call precinct 12's hotline at 567-874-3235. Back you to John." The reporter's voice rang in my ears as I tried to process everything that had been said.

He had escaped. He had *actually* escaped.

Ivy's eyes grew wider than her dinner plate. "Pandora," she warned softly. My gaze flickered over the crowd in the bar as panic began to rise. "Pandora," Ivy repeated, placing a reassuring hand on my shoulder across the table. My eyes were wild as they locked onto hers, and concern spread across her face.

"Hey, everything's fine. They'll find him," she said, trying to reassure me. I was frozen in shock. "We should go," she said quietly, pulling out her wallet and leaving money on the table for our waitress. "Grab your things. We're gonna have a good old-fashioned sleepover tonight." I slid from the booth as she wound her arm through mine and led me out of the bar.

***

I stood in front of the glass window in my bedroom, the knitted white pajamas offering little warmth to my frozen body as I ruminated. All the lights in the house were off, and it was quiet. After we got home from the bar, Ivy had taken couch duty. She'd claimed that if Luke Nesnah ever stepped foot in my house, she would "flatten him herself." But I knew that nothing would stop him, given the right motivation.

He was Protectorate—trained to lethal ends.

My eyes grew heavy as I stared out into the forest. The trees were dead still tonight, with not even a whisper of breeze, and I felt as though something was staring back. I stared anyway, letting whatever was watching me do its work. My entire life felt like a ticking bomb, and no matter how many times I tried to defuse it, the countdown continued. The horror of watching that clock count down seared into my brain.

I raised an open bottle of whiskey to my lips and took a long swig.

I was drunk, and despite Ivy's pleas for me to sleep, I couldn't. I was drowning my sorrows in alcohol, just like every other normal person would in my situation. My mother was dead, my newly discovered family was under attack on a different planet, I had inexplicable powers I couldn't control, my father was deeply rooted in a political nightmare, and a dangerous man I barely knew was my fated mate.

I lifted the amber bottle again, and it sloshed, spilling a little on the wooden floor. "Here's to you, Mom," I slurred before downing another hearty swig.

I paced back and forth, the hem of my pants swished along the floor with every step. I was sure Ivy was probably asleep by now and I didn't want to plague her with my problems. These burdens were mine to bear, yet I felt so achingly lonely—wrapped in depression and grief, trapped within the walls of my own mind. I moaned, pressing my palm against the armoire to steady myself as the world began to spin. I crumpled to the floor, setting the bottle down.

What had my life come to?

Pulling my knees to my chest, I leaned back against them in deep self-loathing when I almost didn't hear the soft *click* of the bathroom window opening. But I did.

I burst to my feet, spinning around to face the sound. I didn't have to guess who it was—I already knew. I had known he would come. I had known that I loved him just as much as I feared him. Deep down, there was a part of me fated to be with him—a part that would always be tied to him—that would always *yearn* for him. I knew what he was sworn to do and hated him for it, yet that fire could not be extinguished or removed. My heart raced as he paused in the doorway, leaning slightly to one side. His eyes caught mine.

Blue on green.

"There are better things to do than to drink yourself to death, you know," he quipped, a smirk tugging at the corner of his mouth. I blinked at him, unable to form any words. I was far from my right mind, but I tried anyway. "Who said I was trying to do the best thing with my time?" I slurred, swaying slightly. The abrupt motion made my head pulse, and I pressed a hand to my temple, groaning. "Yeah, you're not going to feel great tomorrow," he murmured quietly.

"*So*, Detective Nesnah—you escaped just to come hassle me about my nightly activities?" I inquired, raising a brow and immediately regretting it as my headache throbbed in response. He inclined his chin, crossing his arms and one ankle over the other, clearly relishing my moment of weakness. "Sure, if you believe that," he smirked, his tone dripping with derision. I growled in response.

"Wipe that smile off your face. Don't you know you're a wanted *felon*? If Ivy hears our little conversation, she'd probably just kill you herself instead of calling someone to arrest you." He chuckled and I narrowed my eyes at him, "Well then, you might want to keep your voice down," I studied him leaning against my bathroom door frame—this was the so called dangerous fugitive on the run chuckling at my drunken state.

He had ditched his old clothes for a black hoodie, joggers, and red high-top Converse. I squinted further, wondering where he had gotten all those clothes. "What's on your arms?" he asked curiously. "A makeshift solution," I retorted as I stepped closer, "Why are you here?"

"Hi, honey, it's so good to see you too," he drawled. "Oh, stop it," I hissed, pointing a finger at him. "You just broke into my house. Why. Are. You. Here?" I slammed my hand down into my palm to emphasize every word. From his hoodie pocket, he produced several files, holding them up in the air.

"I found the files," he said softly, his eyes never leaving mine. "What?" I asked, my gaze darting to the folders as I licked my lips. "The files your father hid, I'm holding them in my hand." he said. I inhaled sharply as my chest grew suddenly heavy. "Where did you—oh, it doesn't matter. Give them to me."

I rushed forward, but he lifted the files further out of my reach. "Ah, ah," he cautioned, bending his face forward mere inches from mine. I lowered the arm that had reached for them.

"First, you need to listen to what I'm about to tell you," he said. I rolled my eyes but kept silent. "These files confirm everything I suspected about your father and Danny Fritz."

"I'll finally get some answers, especially since everyone seems so intent on feeding me conflicting versions twisted from the truth." I said irritably, gesturing for the files. He raised them even further out of reach.

"Pandora, these are not *good* answers," he said softly, angling his head toward me. "All I ask is that when you look through these, you remember that none of this is your fault and you couldn't have done anything to change it." His voice was gentle as he leaned in, and his closed lips nearly brushed against mine.

The alcohol I'd been drinking before he arrived took hold, and I swayed, reaching for something to steady myself. Luke caught me, wrapping his arms around my waist and pulling me closer. "I can't stay, but I will be back. I promise," he breathed into my ear as the room seemed to sway like a stormy sea. I felt incredibly dizzy and disoriented—his face becoming a blur of color.

Suddenly, I felt as if I was being moved, gently placed into bed, and a comforter was laid over me. Spinning, spinning—everything was spinning. "Drink some water when you wake up. You'll be alright," he murmured then everything went dark.

Chapter 41

I woke with a jerk, snapping upright in bed. Realization hit as I frantically scanned my room—but there was absolutely no trace of him having been here. A pounding headache slammed into me, and I moaned, covering my eyes from the bright morning Aurelios light—or rather, the bright afternoon light.

How long had I been asleep?

My mouth felt like it was filled with cotton as I smacked my tongue against the roof of my mouth. I needed water.

I turned to get out of bed, and my eyes landed on a stack of files left on my bedside table. A small sticky note taped to the top was the only label it bore. I peered at the unfamiliar handwriting in front of me.

Do with this what you will. It changes nothing for me.

My eyebrows clenched as I heard stirring in the hallway. I quickly shoved the files under the bed when I heard a gentle knock at the door. She couldn't know she'd missed him in my house last night—I had to keep that trinket of information to myself. I cleared my throat, smoothing my wild, unkempt hair before answering, "Come in." I called and Ivy stepped into the room.

She'd changed into the spare clothes she kept at my house—her beige tank top and blue jeans hinted at a casual morning change. Her blonde hair, now free, brushed the tops of her shoulders, though it was neatly tucked behind her ears.

"How are you feeling?" she asked, eyeing the bottle of whisky still on the floor where I'd left it. "Truthfully, I've been better," I complained leaning back against the pillows behind me.

"I brought you some water," she said, holding up a glass in her hand. "Thanks," I murmured as she set it on the table. "Will you be alright alone for the rest of the afternoon? I need to run to the station for a meeting," she asked, her brown eyes settling on my face. "I'll be fine. Thanks for taking couch watch last night," I replied, picking up the glass of water and gulping it down. "Of course. I'll be back later with dinner. Call me if you need anything—maybe take today to rest. It's been a long week, yeah?" she added. I nodded in response, though I couldn't focus—the files under the bed felt like a molten flame threatening to devour the entire room. "Okay, see you later," she said, closing the bedroom door behind her. I waited until her footsteps faded and the front door closed before reaching under the bed.

The files felt like ice in my hands, trembling slightly as I stared at them. These were the files Luke had been searching for, and he'd left them here with me. Why hadn't he stayed? Taking a deep breath, I set the stack beside me and picked up the top file. It was labeled with a "12."

Cautiously, I opened it, but I couldn't have been prepared for what I found underneath. It looked nearly identical to a criminal file—name, date of birth, home address, ethnicity, family names, felonies, misdemeanors, all the standard information. But as I kept reading, I became increasingly confused.

Species- Human
Experiment 12- Failed

"Why would species be included, and what experiment

failed?" I wondered aloud as I thumbed through the file, confused. I eventually landed on a page featuring a picture of a woman. Her eyes looked sorrowful as they stared directly at the camera. Her body was thin, worn, and tired—nothing more than skin and bones. Her brown hair was matted and tangled, and her eyes, which might once have been a vibrant blue, now appeared a dull grey.

Injection 1.2ml given IM @ 08:00 January 29th 3040.

Injection of *what?* I flipped through more pages, mostly what seemed to be documentation of the events that preceded after the injection.

Vomiting noted by patient @ 20:00.
Seizures noted by patient @ 21:30.
Time of death 02:00 January 30th 3040.

I drew back from the paper. Time of *death?* What files did he bring me? Nausea coiled deep in my stomach. What had my mother gotten hold of that she wasn't supposed to see? I hurriedly rushed to the very last picture. It was a morgue photo of the woman the file was on—her eyes fixed in a permanent, haunting gaze.

Experiment 12- Failed.

I sucked in a breath. She had been an experiment. The woman had been a medical experiment. The files my mother had been hiding were proof that these experiments were taking place. I looked at the stack of papers—there had to be at least ten files here—but this one was labeled number twelve.

I skimmed through the files: twenty-five, eighty-two, eighty-seven, ninety-five, ninety-six, one hundred and one. They weren't in numerical order—no, these were not *all* the files, just a few. I frantically opened each and every one.

Experiment 25- Failed
Experiment 82- Failed
Experiment 87- Failed

I cursed, throwing the files back into the stack as I grabbed the last one and whipped it open. This one was different—much larger than the others. I opened its front cautiously. A young man with jet-black hair stared back at me. He looked nothing like the woman in the previous file. His skin appeared fuller but pale white, and his eyes were a stone gray—still muted but not as lifeless. As I took him in, a gasp escaped my lips.

Black streaks streamed from his neck, emanating from a single black dot. They curved and coiled, spidering off in wild, frantic patterns, inching up and warping over his chin. This man had a wild look in his eye—so different from the desperate, pleading expression of the woman. A deep, instinctive fear coiled in the base of my stomach as I flipped to the very last page.

Experiment 516- Success.

I cursed and flung the file across the room. It hit the glass wall, sending papers scattering like rain. Fuck. Fuck. *Fuck*. Whoever had killed her had been involved in these experiments—and wanted to keep her quiet. If something like this got out, it would trigger mass hysteria. Then Ivy's message from the ship hit me hard.

"Things have gotten wildly crazy here on Liarta. People in the

hundreds have gone missing in the last week here in Raos. We don't have enough detectives to fill all the missing people reports. They're having us work on five or six cases at the same time, and we aren't making even a dent on the list."

Someone was kidnapping people—by the hundreds—and I'd wager my bet that it wasn't The Protectorate behind these experiments.

I rushed out of bed, hurriedly gathering scattered papers from the floor. What were the results of these experiments? What precisely defined a "successful" experiment? Finally, I picked up a piece of paper that clearly outlined the criteria.

Strength test- Success.
Hearing test- Success
Weapon welding- Success
Speed test- Success
Agility test- Success

The air in my lungs whooshed out in one fell swoop. These weren't just any medical experiments—these were military experiments. Someone was creating mutant soldiers, and by the looks of it, they had been successful. I trembled as I held up the final piece of paper with the man's picture plastered on the front.

Feros Officer 001

Luke had been right. War was coming, and they were preparing for it now. Not only were they gearing up for conflict here, but they were also abducting humans on Liarta—subjecting them to experiments to create soldiers for a war nobody truly understood. My thumb brushed over the word

Feros, and it hit me like a freight train.

The mining funding was never intended to secure long-term energy solutions for Raos. No—the money was earmarked to fund the mining of Element X and its experiments when injected into humans. The pieces of the ugly puzzle fit together in the most horrifying way. I clenched my teeth and forced calm into my breathing.

He had been right all along—about Danny Fritz, about my father's involvement. There was no way he didn't know about the experiments. He signed off on the funding allocation for the "mining" on Feros. I gagged. My father had sanctioned the mistreatment of all these people—every single one of them, all five hundred and sixteen. I ran full speed into the bathroom and heaved into the toilet.

I had unknowingly opened Pandora's box, and I knew I would never be able to shut it again.

Chapter 42

Aurelios was just starting to set as I flung open my armoire. Luke had promised he'd be back, but he never said *when*—and this kind of information wasn't something I could simply wait around for, hoping something bad wouldn't happen. No, I'd figure this out once and for all. I knew where Danny lived and how to bypass all his security. I'd confront him myself.

It was Thursday—typically, he'd be home drinking whiskey in his study like clockwork. Someone as powerful as he was should try to be a little less predictable, but in this case I'd use it to my advantage. I grabbed everything black I could find and threw it on including a shirt, pants, boots, and gloves. I frantically began pulling my limbs into the fabric. Ivy would be back any minute, and I knew, without a doubt, she'd try to stop me—but how could I explain the past week to her? How could I tell her that my father was a traitor, that he was conspiring and creating mutant soldiers?

The thought made me shudder.

Tucking my pistol into the waistband of my pants, I secured it in place. I hoped I wouldn't need it, but given who I was visiting tonight, I'd rather have it and not need it than vice versa. The last thing I did was tie my long auburn hair into a braid that cascaded down my back. There was not a chance in hell I'd let my hair get me caught doing nefarious and illegal things.

I took one long look at the full-length mirror hanging on my wall. I hardly recognized the face in the reflection—hardened, determined, and burning with anger. I almost stepped out the door but then stopped. I reached deep into the armoire, my fingers brushing against the smooth wood until I found them. I moved the blouse covering them aside and pulled them out into the dimming evening light.

They were just as beautiful as they'd always been—their edges shimmered with iridescent scales, sharp enough to cut through bone. I carefully sheathed them at my sides and stuffed the files into a small black backpack I'd kept under my bed. Slinging the straps over my shoulders I set my jaw firmly. It was time to pay Danny Fritz a *visit*.

I closed my front door and slipped into the forest.

It was dark now, and I was grateful that the night would help cover my tracks. The trees seemed to hum harmoniously, their leaves whispering in the slight breeze. It was a warm night—late May always felt more pleasant than the warmer and more humid June. I'd always felt safe in the forest, cloaked in the shadows of the trees. I remembered running barefoot through the brush as a child, carefree and wild. Now, though, my chest tightened at the realization that I would never remember that childhood the same way.

Car lights appeared down the driveway, and I rushed behind a tree, just wide enough to conceal my entire body. I eased my body against the bark, leaning out just enough to see who had arrived. Ivy's car pulled up to the house. The headlights swung through the trees, and I quickly pulled my head back, determined to remain unseen.

The vehicle came to a stop, and she stepped out, her shoes crunching on the gravel. I had mere minutes before she would realize I was gone, but I couldn't run off into the forest just yet—if I did, she would see or hear me. Ivy retrieved some takeout from her backseat, and I leaned forward further to ensure no one else accompanied her.

Suddenly, a small branch snapped under my boot, and I hissed, tucking myself deeper behind the tree. Bathed in the shadows, I was reasonably confident she couldn't see me—but then her eyes snapped in my direction. I froze, my pulse pounding in my ears. She narrowed her eyes and raised a hand to shield her gaze from the cabin's lights.

Do not move, I thought desperately to myself.

After a moment, she shook her head, seemingly deciding it was nothing, and continued toward the house. I waited until I heard her fingerprint the door shut before I turned and sprinted into the forest. I'd chosen these boots for a reason—they were light and nimble as I raced forward. I knew this path; I'd run it every day for police academy conditioning. Though I could barely see in front of me, I never faltered, never fell.

This was *my* forest.

I forced my legs forward despite the burning discomfort, and in the distance, I could barely make out Ivy screaming my name.

Chapter 43

I sat at the edge of the forest, huddled behind a tree watching who came and went from the house. Danny Fritz's place was enormous—so much so that the title of mansion might have been more appropriate. It had three stories and resembled a Roman colosseum more than a typical house.

Constructed entirely of beige stone, large pillars accented the wrap-around porch, and meticulously groomed shrubbery dotted the grounds. The pathways leading to and from the house were hand-laid cobblestones that likely cost a small fortune; that kind of brickwork was rare these days, and anyone still skilled in it would charge an arm and a leg. The area was well-lit, and I searched in frustration for a way in without being seen.

Danny had several security guards on rotation. Two at the front gate, two patrolling the cobblestone paths, and one posted at the front door. The guard shack sat near the corner of the property, just outside the fence. From there, I could see inside through its window, and no guards were posted within. I chewed on the inside of my cheek. If I still had my badge, I would have marched straight up to the front gate and demanded to speak with him. What would they have done? Deny a Raos detective access?

I shook my head. They probably *would* have. Danny Fritz was so well connected that he could do whatever he wanted without ever bending the law—apparently, even my father, the commissioner, wasn't immune.

I grumbled to myself. He would be next, and I'd have to have a very lengthy conversation with him—a conversation that would likely resemble an interrogation rather than a casual catch-up between a father and daughter. One of the radios buzzed to life.

The officer closest to me slipped an earbud in and spoke lowly, "Go ahead." I heard him murmur, "Mmhm. Mmhm. Yes, sir," as he nodded. His partner remained vigilant. I backed further into the shadows. The last thing I needed was for them to alert Danny that I was here before I could get the upper hand.

The man on the radio looked almost familiar. He wore a grey uniform like our precinct officers, his cap covering most of his hair, but the sharp edge of his clean-cut peeked out at the bottom. His hair was jet black, and as his eyes swept over the tree line where I hid, I noticed they were a pale grey. I tilted to the side as he turned his head, catching a glimpse of black streaks trailing from the stiff collar of his uniform.

Shit.

The mutant officer was here on Liarta. This was going to make things significantly more complicated.

I gave my head a quick shake, refocusing on the guards stationed at the front. They shared a few brief words before the Feros guard pivoted on his polished heel and started toward the house entrance. A smirk tugged at the corner of my mouth as I watched him go, his partner blissfully oblivious to my gaze. With him alone now, it was my chance to slip over the fence. I tugged my gloves higher up my arms, making sure they were secure, and decided—this was the moment.

I crept toward the corner of the property, my feet whispering against the grass. I was still under the cover of the trees, but there were several feet of open ground I'd have to cross before I could slip behind the guard shack. I crouched at the very edge of the tree line behind a bush. The guard made large, sweeping motions with his head as he scanned for intruders. I needed to divert his attention for a moment while I slipped past.

Scanning the ground, I found a rock about the size of my palm. I picked it up and tested its weight. Heavy, but not too much so—just the right size for a diversion. I swung my arm back and chucked it deep into the forest. It arced through the air just a faint whizz in the dead of night, then abruptly found it's intended target crashing loudly into a tree.

The guard's gaze snapped toward the noise and I hunkered in place just a whisper of my breath as the only sound escaping me. I had mere seconds. He walked toward the disturbance cautiously, his flashlight aimed at the trees. "Who's there?" he demanded, shining his light further into the forest.

I didn't wait to see what else he would do. My legs heaved my body upwards and I sprinted as quietly as possible for the fence.

Bunching my legs like a coiled spring ready to be released I leapt for the fence, my hands grasping for purchase as the cold iron bit into my palms. I pressed the tread of my boot against the metal, propelling myself over the top onto the cobblestone path. I cringed at the small thud my feet made as I hit the ground on the other side.

Pausing, I listened for any commotion, peering slightly over the hedge in front of me. The officer was halfway toward where I'd thrown the rock, his light still poised on the trees. With one hand resting on his pistol as he swung the light back and forth, I didn't wait to see what he would do next—I was already on the move.

I dropped to a crouch and crept along the shrubbery, straining to catch every sound, every breath. My heart hammered in my chest, and my palms sweat inside my gloves, but I pressed on. Here I was, a detective whose career was built on putting people behind bars, and I was now committing some of the very crimes I once charged others with.

Before I became a homicide detective, I'd worked in multiple departments; as a new officer, I was often assigned to the dispatch response team. On my very first shift, I arrested someone for trespassing. If I hadn't been so focused on staying completely silent, I might have chuckled to myself. But this wasn't a laughing matter—potentially, the entire human race was at risk right this very moment. I needed to find out what Danny was plotting and stop it.

I soon came to a fork in the path. One trail led straight to the mansion's front door, another veered to the left around the back of the building, and the third, to the right, led beneath an open window. I did a double take.

An open window?

I blinked slowly, rubbing my eyes in disbelief. Why would he leave a window open? Choosing the path to the right, I crept forward slowly. My boots barely scuffed the stones as my eyes scanned the area. I hadn't heard any alarms or shouts—perhaps the guard at the front really had dismissed the disturbance as nothing. Fortunately for me, the spotlights didn't quite reach underneath the window, and as I approached the sill, I blended thoroughly into the shadows below. Just a whisper in the night.

I froze, straining to catch any sounds from inside the building. The sudden rhythm of approaching footsteps made me curse under my breath as I dropped flat to the ground. Heart pounding, I scrambled beneath a low hedge beneath the window just in time, as two patrolling officers appeared around the back of the house.

"What do you think of the new guy?" one officer's deep, gravelly voice asked. "Who? Markian?" a higher-pitched male voice echoed back. "Yeah, him," the first replied. Their footsteps grew louder, and I peered through the underbrush of the hedge, watching their boots emerge just feet away from me before they stopped in front of the window.

I held my breath, hand clamped over my mouth, paralyzed in place. My throat felt like it was closing in, each breath a shallow, panicked effort. "I think he's a prick," the second officer sniffed as his gaze turned toward the first. "I've been on Fritz security for five years," the first continued, clearly irritated, "and this son of a bitch decides he wants to skip the entire ladder and go straight for personal security for the man himself within the week. If you ask me, he's cocky and under-qualified."

"Yeah, he seems off, but I can't put my finger on it just yet," the second man said quietly. My brows furrowed. Did they not know *what* he was? Danny kept it a secret even from his personal security—and I could use that to my advantage.

"We should keep moving," the first man said, and they continued their path toward the front of the building. I released the tension in my shoulders and exhaled as I scrambled back into a crouch. Time was no longer on my side. The longer I stayed, the higher the risk of being discovered. I reached up with my hands and they barely touched the bottom of the windowsill. I cursed again to myself. How was I supposed to get inside?

Glancing around, I spotted a small, off-kilter ledge adjacent to the window. I pressed the toe of my boot onto it and looked up. The sill was still incredibly high, but with this little lip, I might be able to jump. I took a steadying breath, bunched my legs, and released swiftly.

My chest hit the sill with a thud that knocked the wind from my lungs as my feet scrambled for purchase. Although I was adept at sparring, I was no assassin, and sneaking around was far from my forte.

Finally, I grappled up the wall, hoisted my legs over the sill, and lowered myself through the window. Not my most graceful moment, but it would have to do. I looked around the room—a library of sorts with floor-to-ceiling books.

The lighting was dim, with only a few candles artfully placed among the deep red mahogany furnishings. Every book spine in the library was adorned with gold cursive lettering that glimmered in the candlelight. Most volumes were neatly numbered and arranged, except for a few resting on a small reading desk beside a textured olive sofa. The floors, a deep red with a striking sheen, rivaled the richness of the mahogany furnishings—I could almost see my reflection in the polish.

A lit cigar smoldered gently on the desk, releasing delicate curls of smoke into the air. Someone had been here, and recently.

I narrowed my eyes at it, wondering if the owner was coming back. I inched forward, the floorboards creaking ever so slightly under my weight, and glanced at a book at the top of the stack closest to the couch.

The History of Gayle, Volume Seven.

I blanched—who needed to know anything about Gayle right now?

Suddenly, the doorknob rattled slightly, and my eyes darted around the room, searching for somewhere to hide. I slipped behind the bookshelf nearest the chair as silently as possible. From this concealed spot, the door was out of sight, but I still had a clear view of the chair. The door opened, and footsteps entered.

I angled my ear toward the sound, straining to pick up any details. The steps had measured pauses between them, suggesting someone tall—most likely a male. They weren't heavy, but they weren't light either. A slight click indicated a thick heel, perhaps a loafer, and the soft rustle of what sounded like linen fabric indicated slacks.

A man.

The footsteps approached in my direction, and a large hand—adorned with a ginormous gold ring set with a deep black stone—reached for the cigar. Indeed, it was a man, but my eyes were drawn to that stone. I had seen it before, somewhere.

He leaned forward and I waited with my breath caught in my throat trying to see who it was, but before his face came into view, he pulled back and crossed to the other side of the room. He firmly shut the window and puffed on his cigar. The thick, molasses-like aroma wafted, mingling with the room's candlelit shadows.

"You know, Detective, if you wanted to talk to me, you could have just asked instead of hiding in my study," the voice said, and my throat ran completely dry. I didn't dare move, didn't dare breathe. He couldn't possibly be talking to me.

"Ah, we're beginning with the silent treatment, are we?" he chuckled, a low rumble echoing off the spines of the books surrounding me. "You see, Detective, you thought you would come and question me—but you have fallen into my cunningly woven web." His voice sent chills down my spine.

I reached for the grip of my pistol. "Ah, Detective, I wouldn't if I were you. I wouldn't want to ruin my library. Why don't you come into the light so I can see you better?" His tone was slimy, making my fingers go cold. I cautiously stepped out from behind the bookcase as he came into view.

He wore grey slacks, a short-sleeved white button-up popped open at the collar and brown loafers that matched his belt. I had never seen Danny Fritz so *informal.* His dark hair was tousled as if he'd run his hands through it, and his dark brown eyes met mine. He stood by the now-closed window, turning slightly to face me with a cigar in hand. He held it at his face, smirking before taking a long, deliberate draw, letting the smoke drift toward me.

"You have always been so beautiful, just as your mother was," he said with a smile that was anything but friendly—more like a predator toying with its prey. My mouth pressed into a tight line.

Say nothing, my brain screamed, and for once, I listened.

"Tell me, Detective, why did you plan this lovely visit to Fritz de Casa?" His head tilted as he scrutinized me. I had never realized his features were so distinctly of Tyrian descent, but in this light, there was an undeniable resemblance—dark, sharp, and accented by centuries of human ancestry.

I did my best not to react under his piercing stare. My hands were clenched at my sides as I contemplated my response. I was effectively trapped here, with him blocking my quickest exit—the window of which I entered.

My eyes flicked to the door as I weighed every possible escape. I might reach it before he caught me, but that would mean dashing through Fritz Manor—a maze to me, though he likely knew it by heart.

He clucked his tongue. "I wouldn't," he said with a sinister grin. "I have my guard posted outside the door right now, and if you try to run, he's been ordered to kill you on sight."

I gulped, frozen in place.

"Now then," He purred, "I asked you a question, and it's impolite to ignore your host's inquiries." He took another drag of his cigar, tucking his other hand into his pocket. I turned my head back to face him, the weight of my auburn braid brushing against my back. Finally, I managed to force out, "He's not human, is he?"

It was all I could manage. "Who isn't human?" he waved the cigar in the air as if he couldn't possibly know whom I was referring to.

The candlelight suited him well, casting shadows that made him look much younger than he was, yet they couldn't hide the sinister nature behind his smile. When I had met Danny Fritz, I knew he was someone to fear—someone whose path you never wanted to cross. It didn't matter who you were. If you stood in his way, you were nothing more than collateral damage. That was how he built his entire empire and wealth—the more resistance, the more he enjoyed flattening you in his wake.

"The guard," I said, watching him closely. "Whatever do you mean, Detective? If he wasn't human, what would he be?" The corner of his lips twitched. "Whatever you made him into, I guess," I muttered, my voice barely audible. He fought the smile, nodding his head slowly. "He's human, *of sorts.*" He remarked, setting the cigar down in another ashtray and placing the hand in his other pocket. I remained where I stood, glued to the very spot. "You're kidnapping people. People with lives, with families—"

"I'm not kidnapping anyone," he interrupted, and I snapped my mouth shut. "I offered them a place working for me— all they had to do was subject themselves to a little experiment. You see, Detective, it's all about give and take. I offer them something, but first I must take. First, they must prove themselves worthy of the prize," he gestured silently toward the closed door and the mutant guard standing post. "He just happens to be the first to actually do so."

"You're taking their lives," I whispered, unable to mask the horror and disgust I felt for him and his experiments. "That's entirely up to *them*. I can't force anyone to have a will to live, Detective. I merely subject them to an experiment that gives them the choice to fight and be stronger—or give in and be overtaken." He fixed his eyes on me as the gears spun in my head.

"You mean subject them to pure Element X?" I hissed, "Yes." He nodded, his feet unmoving, "If you had the choice to become the greatest version of yourself, wouldn't you?"

I shook my head roughly and jabbed a finger in his direction. "You're *poisoning* people!" I yelled, my eyes flaring. One of his eyebrows lifted.

"Poisoning people? I'm merely speeding up their evolution," he remarked, taking a step toward me. "Besides, Pandora, why should I stand around and let the Gaythe have all the superpowers while we humans have none?" He hissed, baring his teeth. I lowered my hand and backed away a step.

"I know what you are," He glanced at his thumbnail as if utterly uninterested in our conversation.

"What *I* am?" I spat, gesturing to myself wildly.

"You come in here and accuse me of poisoning people, but in reality, I'm giving them the same choice that you were given—the same power that thrums through your veins. Your mother had it, you have it, and your father and I are going to reclaim it for the humans who never got that same option," he said with blistering conviction. "You think you're *entitled* to superpowers beyond human capability because of your ancestral lineage? *Please*, Detective, do continue arguing that I'm the bad guy when you, standing before me, are much more of a hypocrite."

My mouth opened and snapped shut once, then twice, as I forced my brain to formulate words. "Is that not what you want, Detective? *Justice?* You took an oath—is that not part of it?" his voice lowered to a simmer as he ran his tongue along his exposed teeth. "This isn't justice," I whispered, "this is the start of a *war.*"

"So be it then. Humans have been the lesser species for far too long. We may not have innate abilities like the Gaythe, but we're

human. What we lack in aptitude, we make up for in creation," he sneered, and my breath caught in my throat.

"You're willing to create monsters under the guise of forcing human evolution?" I whispered, my voice trembling. I was so tense that my toes had gone completely numb, and a tingling sensation crept up my legs. He took another step toward me, creating just enough space for me to escape through the window if I caught him off guard. "Yes, and your father agrees."

I forced my legs to move, backing away, but I didn't get far before hitting the olive sofa's edge. I mentally cursed myself for getting trapped in this library with him. The long sleeves I wore began to feel suffocating as he inched closer. I held out my hands. "Do not come any closer," I warned. "Or what?" he barked. "You gonna use those powers on me, just as Esme tried to do?"

A sneer curled his lips and I blanched, raising a pointed finger at him. My teeth clenched in fury. "Repeat her name, and I will cut you down where you stand," I hissed, my voice low and dangerous but the threats were empty and hollow. And he knew it. It only seemed to stoke his insanity further, like he was itching to tear open the gaping wound in my heart. "Such ferocity, such anger. You *are* your mother's daughter," he murmured, his tone shifting into a low, sultry caress. I peeled my lips back over my teeth, my hand falling to my waist again.

I was paralyzed, unable to move any other part of my body as he shifted even closer. "Tell me, Pandora, where do you put it all?" he asked, now so close I could see his pupils flare and contract in the candlelight. "Put what?" I gritted through my teeth. "Your *anger*." He lifted a hand to brush an auburn fly away from my cheek in the most intimate way possible.

My lips trembled with terror at the touch—his hand was warm but far from inviting. As he trailed the back of his fingers down my cheek, my skin prickled, charged with an unsettling current. The question he asked sank into my mind.

Where *did* my anger go?

He watched me closely, eyes wide with curiosity, then nonchalantly slipped his hands back into his pockets. "You are so much like her, yet also like your father—a blaze of fire ready to engulf everything in its path, *wild* and *unpredictable*. That uncontrolled power is the last strand of rope that will be used to noose your neck. Cut it down, or it will hang you," he said.

Silence fell between us as we stood just a foot apart. I could hear my pulse pounding in my ears, growing faster with every beat. "Are *you* going to cut me down, then?" I dared to whisper, a shred of defiant bravery breaking through the oppressive silence. He chuckled, his head dipping before he raised his eyes to meet mine again. "Did Mr. Malone not pay you a visit, Detective?"

I blinked, my brain struggling to form a coherent thought. "Mr. Malone? As in— you did send him to kill me." My voice cracked despite my efforts to remain steady. His eyes shone with something that might have been interpreted as sadness, but I wasn't naive enough to believe it. I ground my teeth together. The vibration was a welcome sensation compared to the lingering touch of his skin against mine.

"The only way to ensure that a wildfire doesn't engulf everything it touches is to put it *out*," he murmured, tilting his head slightly. I shifted my jaw to the side, pressure building in my temples. "Just wait until my father hears that you tried to kill me," I warned.

With that, he leaned his head all the way back and guffawed. "Going to sick your father on me? I have him so tightly leashed he has to beg when he needs to take a piss." He spat in my direction, and I winced. "No, no. Your father does exactly what

I say when I say it."

A smile crept across his face, "That's why I told him it was time to end your mother's life. She was no longer useful and was beginning to become... *unpredictable*."

I stiffened at his words. "Say that again." I hissed. "That's right." He grinned, "Your *father* killed your mother."

Suddenly, the world began spinning again, and I felt violently ill. I bent forward, clutching my stomach. "All he had to do was put a sedative in her tea, then give her one final paralyzing injection of vecuronium. It was the *perfect* murder." He was inches from me, his smoky breath roiling in my nose. "No," I hissed, glaring up at him, "No, my father wouldn't do such a thing."

"Oh? Would you like to ask him yourself? I think he just actually just arrived." I heard a door slam closed almost in punctuation to the statement deep within the house and muffled conversation filtered through the library walls from the floor below. Danny's back straightened watching me as all the remaining blood drained from my face. "Should I call him in here to set the story straight?" A feral grin curled up his lips.

I forced myself to breathe, to remember my training. He was bluffing—trying to get under my skin. He couldn't possibly be serious. My heart pounded uncontrollably, and for a moment, it felt as if the very skin beneath my silicone gloves was burning. The door within my mind burst open, slamming against the wall.

"PANDORA, WHAT ARE YOU DOING?" Luke roared in my head and I flinched at the sudden intrusion.

Danny's brows furrowed quickly in confusion as I just about jumped out of my skin. I fixed my gaze on Danny as my mind and reality melded together, making me dizzy.

"I was trying to question him," I replied, exasperated but my mouth never moved. *"You're going to ruin the entire plan!"* Luke

shouted, his blue eyes blazing with fury in my mind. *"I don't know what I'm doing—I'm in way over my head!"*

Panic set in as my eyes darted around, searching for an escape in the real world. *"You have to get out of that house right—fucking—now!"* he shouted, but I wasn't listening. I was already making a run for the window.

Danny lunged, but I slipped past him, his hands grasping at air. In a panic, I threw the window open and, using every ounce of strength, launched myself toward it—my chest just barely clearing the sill. A burst of hope ignited inside me, hot and fierce—only to die instantly as Danny caught hold of my boots and yanked me back inside.

He grabbed me by my arms, slamming me against the wall and pinning me there. "I wouldn't want you to get away before I can make this a memorable family reunion," he growled, his breath hot and invasive. Desperate, I thrust my head forward, striking his throat.

He coughed, releasing his grip just enough for me to break free. I spun around and lunged for the window again, but he was quickly on me—this time, his whole body pressed me into the wall. "Where is your lovely Commander Nesnah right now, anyway? He seems to have gotten away," he purred in my ear.

"Commander?" I choked out, my throat pressed firmly against the sill. "Do you mean Detective?" I countered and he sniggered in my ear. "*Oh?* He didn't tell you?" He purred. "Tell me what!" I screamed, pressing my hands against the wall as I fought for my life. "That he's the *Commander* of The Protectorate."

Before the words fully registered in my brain, I lifted my heel and drove it straight into his crotch. He crumpled to the floor with a groan. I hurled myself through the window falling with the grace of a baby giraffe and landing squarely on my back. I moaned and rolled to the side—nearly a two-story fall wasn't part of the plan. Thankfully, the files firmly secured in my backpack took the brunt of the impact sparing my spine. Stars dotted my vision as I braced my palm against the dirt and pushed myself up.

"You don't have much time! Get up!" Luke's voice echoed somewhere in the corner of my mind. I turned to see the window, where Danny was leaning over the sill, his face as red as a tomato as he glared at me. His mouth opened in a shout, "She's here, boys! Get her!"

I cursed as I forced myself off the ground, my spine radiating pain. I burst out from the hedges, my feet stomping on the ground. There was no time for stealth—I needed to get out of here before I got caught. Frantically, I whipped my head back and forth, searching for the best escape route. *"By the front gate! Hurry!"* His voice folded into my mind, and I sprinted to my right, back toward the front.

My boots pounded against the cobblestones as I ran as fast as I could. But before I could cover another ten feet, the mansion's front door flew open.

"Stop right there!" a booming voice commanded from the doors. I turned in horror as the mutant officer, still in his grey uniform, stood with both arms outstretched. Black tendrils of smoke whipped from his hands, hurtling straight for me. I gasped and backed away while keeping my eyes fixed on him. A sinister grin curled on his face as Danny Fritz came running up behind him. "I told you, Pandora. I told you not to run. You're mine now."

The black tendrils lashed out, wrapping around my wrists and burning on contact as I glanced desperately toward the front gate—the only glimpse I could catch was the spiked top of the iron, peeking through the greenery. He began pulling me toward the door by my wrists, my heels desperately seeking for purchase on the cobblestones.

"Don't fight it. Come to the dark side, Pandora," Danny coaxed, his eyes gleaming wild and unhinged. "Never! I will never join you!" I screamed, kicking as hard as I could. My arms tingled and vibrated as I reared my head back and roared as loudly as I could. Then, in one swift, unexpected motion, the tan silicone sleeves ripped from my skin and flew across the path.

The mutant officer was thrown backward as he lost his grip on my hands, and something within me *awakened*. I lifted my hands toward the looming doors of Fritz Manor as a deep rumble built in my chest.

"I was right! You are a Gaythe!" Danny hollered, directing the officer toward me. "Catch her right now, you worthless piece of shit—we can't let her get away!" he hissed at the officer, who began sprinting toward me. And then, in an instant, everything went completely silent.

Absolutely no noise filled the air except for the steady thump of my heart—thump, thump, thump. Pain seared along my arms as their color shifted from midnight black to blazing silver. Light burst from my palms in streams of moonlight so bright it shook my vision. The officer skidded to a stop, but it was too late.

The light slammed into his chest, launching him straight into Danny. I couldn't contain the surge as it flowed and grew, setting everything around me on fire. The hedges erupted in silver flames on contact. I whipped my hands down and turned to run, the heat of the raging inferno searing my back as I sprinted for the gate.

"What did you do!?" Luke's voice screamed in my head. *"I don't know!"* I shouted back, my voice raw as I ran even faster. The silvery flames spread quickly as I rushed through the hedges toward the front gate. A large potted plant came crashing down in front of me, and I yelped as it nearly singed the back of my

braid. The iron fence loomed ahead, and beyond it, a black motorcycle was parked.

"You set the whole damn place on *fire*!" He hollered through the iron gates, arms outstretched in exasperation. "I didn't mean to!" I panted as I rushed to the gate and whipped it open. I rushed to him and his eyes darted over me frantically. "Are you hurt? What happened?" Luke's hands flew to my face, turning it from side to side.

His eyes, a fierce blue against my green, bore into me. "I'm fine," I managed to say, though I trembled in his grasp. He was in that familiar black hoodie, cargos, and converse—his tousled hair and wild eyes conveying his frenzy. "What in the world were you thinking!?" he whispered, his eyes darting around at the growing inferno behind us. "I wasn't," I murmured, my voice barely audible as I clung to him.

He dropped his hands, his gaze roaming over me, assessing for damage. "What happened to your arms?" he asked, suddenly noticing I was glowing with a silvery hue. "Something came out of me," I replied, turning my arms over to examine them.

A large crash erupted behind us, accompanied by screaming voices as people searched for us. Luke turned to the motorcycle and produced a white helmet. "Put this on," he ordered, shoving it into my hands. I slipped it over my head, my auburn braid falling loose down my back. He tugged on his black helmet, then swung a leg over the bike. "Get on. *Now*," he growled.

I clambered onto the back and placed my feet on the pegs. Luke leaned forward and revved the engine snarling it to life. "Now, hold on," he called, his voice rising over the roar of flames and the engine. I clenched my eyes shut and wrapped my arms tightly around his torso, clinging to him like my life depended on it.

Gravel sprayed behind us as we sped down Fritz Manor Drive,

trees flashing by in a dizzying blur whenever I dared a peek through my lashes. I had no idea how fast we were going—and I didn't care to find out.

I turned my head just enough to catch sight of the towering silver flames licking the gate—and just beyond them, the man with jet-black hair. A wild, feral grin spread across his face as he slowly raised one hand in an eerie, mocking wave goodbye.

Chapter 44

We raced down the roads, darting through traffic with ease. A persistent tingling ran through my arms as I held tightly to Luke's chest. He twisted the throttle, sending us surging forward as the night became a blur around us. My braid snapped wildly in the wind, and I tucked my head close to his back, careful not to knock our helmets together. I had grown up on motorcycles, but never like this—never this fast.

I couldn't see the speedometer from where I sat, and I didn't dare look. Just the thought of it was enough to unsettle me. Though I was as tense as a rock, Luke was as fluid as liquid, weaving back and forth as if we were flying. His hips shifted the bike beneath us while streetlights flashed across my visor.

"Where are you taking me?" I hollered above the roar of the wind. He didn't answer, only pushed us faster. Sirens whined in the distance, and I dared to look behind us. Flashing red and blue lights appeared on the road, closing in fast.

"Luke...," I warned through our mental link. "On it," he replied, deftly swinging us between a black SUV and a white sedan. He used the SUV to block their view as we slowed to traffic speed. "What happens when they catch up?" I asked nervously, glancing over my shoulder.

The speedway lights whipped past, flashing in my vision as headlights flickered and danced around us. "They won't," he said calmly, keeping his speed steady. The lights grew closer, and a bead of sweat formed at the base of my neck. They were close enough now—I could count eight cop cars. It seemed Danny had in fact called in the cavalry. I ground my teeth together.

"LUKE," I said, panic lacing my tone, "You might want to hold on." He murmured through my skull, and I didn't dare ask any more questions. I just gripped him tighter as we raced on. He pulled the clutch in, losing some speed, my helmet clinking slightly into his as I heard the familiar clunk of the gearshift dropping.

I blanched, "You better not,"

I could see his smirk as the door was wide open in my mind. He rushed forward, one arm winding tightly around my waist. He brought his other arm up, furling it in the base of my loose coppery hair. He lifted my head toward him, our lips brushing slightly. They parted in a gentle gasp.

"Do you trust me?" he murmured into my lips. "Yes," I whispered. "Then hold on tight," he commanded.

He revved the throttle and dumped the clutch as we blasted forward. The sudden movement jolted me, and the wind tore against my clothing as we hurtled off the speedway, curving through the off-ramp. I shifted with his weight, guiding the bike closer to the pavement. The foot pegs grazed against my legs, and I squeezed my eyes shut until we evened out again.

Out of the corner of my eye, I spotted the end of the off-ramp and glanced back—the flashing lights were closer now, but they hadn't made it onto the ramp yet. Then, suddenly, he killed the headlights, plunging us into darkness. I blinked quickly, struggling to adjust to the sudden loss of light.

"WHAT are you doing!?" I roared into the darkness, but he only chuckled—a sound that wrapped around me like a warm blanket. If I had thought he was a good motorcyclist on the freeway, what he was doing now in the dark was on another level entirely. He swung us from side to side, careening through the city streets with only sporadic street lamps to guide us as we flew by—just shadows in the night.

His confidence and decisiveness was unsettling. It was clear he had done this countless times before, maneuvering through the maze of streets purely by muscle memory. The thought of him regularly tearing through traffic like this made me shudder—the cop in me recoiling at the sheer recklessness.

I pushed the thought aside as we finally careened into an alleyway and Luke brought the bike to a complete stop. The engine cut off with a final hum as I started to swing my leg over to dismount, but his hand shot out, gripping my knee firmly and stopping me.

We were tucked into the shadow of a building, its dark silhouette melting into the night around us. Sirens grew louder, my heart thrumming in response. We stayed completely motionless, frozen in place as he steadied the bike on the balls of his feet.

The sirens came closer and I tucked my glowing arms in to conceal the light. I lifted my head over his shoulder as the cop cars went roaring past on the street—eight of them, their lights a blur of red and blue. His hand still rested on my knee as I clutched mine to my chest, silently begging my heart to slow. We couldn't have gotten away just like that—again. This was becoming a regular occurrence with him—racing from the cops. Hell, we *were* cops.

He finally gestured for me to dismount and I lifted my leg, sweeping it over the bike's rear fender as he held it steady. Glancing around, I suddenly became aware of where we were—the forgotten city of Oracle. The air felt heavy with silence and the hairs on the back of my neck rose as I absorbed the eerie stillness. Not a soul was in sight. A few flickering street lamps cast an uneasy glow, barely piercing the darkness.

I lifted my gaze to the looming structure in front of us—ten stories tall, completely dark. Several windows were shattered, the glass littered across the pavement. The dark gray bricks blended into the shadows, almost invisible in the low light.

I took off my helmet, blinking as my vision adjusted. The surrounding buildings were abandoned too—a restaurant with broken tables and chairs scattered across the front terrace, what appeared to be an old convenience store with gas pumps out front, and several other shops along both sides of the alleyway. Nothing was left but the skeletons of what had once been a bustling town.

Luke directed his bike forward, concealing it behind a blue dumpster on the left side of the alley. He swung his leg over the bike and strode toward me, tearing off his helmet. I stood still, helmet in hand, unsure of what to say.

A soft, pale silver glow still lingered around my hands, casting faint light across our faces in the darkness. Though unsettling, the glow felt oddly soothing, and his blue eyes reflected it with a quiet intensity. He extended his hand, and I reluctantly passed him the helmet. He tilted his head slightly, eyes scanning me as I hurriedly smoothed down my frizzy flyaways.

"This way," he murmured, already crossing the pavement toward the looming, dark building. I followed close behind, my eyes darting nervously around. As if sensing my unease, he glanced back at me. "No one's around on this side of town. Three blocks over, there's a drug gang, but I haven't had any trouble with them lately." I stiffened as we stopped in front of a door secured with a numbered padlock. "A drug gang?" I repeated, my voice an octave higher in disbelief. "Yeah," he replied casually, punching in the code.

The silver lock snapped open, and the door creaked loudly

on its hinges. The sound echoed through the alley, grating on my nerves. "Old door," he muttered, motioning toward the dark hallway beyond. "If you think I'm going first into an unlit hallway after the night I've had, you're out of your mind," I said, shooting him a pointed look, arms crossed. "Fair enough," he sighed, rolling his eyes as he stepped through the doorway. He paused just inside, waiting, "It's either come in or stay out here with the drug gang,"

Without another word, I slipped inside after him.

The door clanked shut behind us, and he flicked a switch on the wall. The overhead lights flickered stubbornly before flooding the long hallway with a dim, wavering glow. He hung his helmet on a hook beside the switch and ran a hand through his tousled, curly brown hair. I stood awkwardly nearby, fiddling with the straps of my backpack. I opened my mouth to say something, but he lifted a finger, silencing me. "Not yet. Someone might be listening. We need to get to the briefing room," he said quietly. "Excuse me?" I asked, my brows pulling together in confusion. But he didn't answer—just turned and walked down the hall.

His red Converse squeaked against the cracked tiles, and I weaved around bits of rubble to keep up. His black hood bounced slightly with each step, and even through the sweatshirt, I could see the tension in his back and shoulders. He reached a door leading to a concrete stairwell and held it open for me. "Where are we going?" I asked, my voice echoing against the cold walls. "Up," he replied simply, already climbing.

The building was eerily silent—no hum of power, just the occasional flicker and sputter of the dying incandescent lights. He reached the second floor and immediately continued upward. I followed close behind, our steps syncing on the cement stairs. "How high up are we going?" I asked again, pressing for any hint of information. "Ragnai was right—you really do ask a lot of questions," he said with a smirk, not slowing down as we neared the fourth floor. "I'm a detective. It's what I do," I muttered under my breath and he chuckled. His shoulders lifted in a shrug and his eyes glanced over me briefly as we rounded yet another landing.

We climbed past the fifth floor, then the sixth, and finally stopped in front of a red door on the seventh. Another silver numbered padlock secured it. He punched in a code, and the lock clicked open. The door swung wide. But before we could step inside, a male voice erupted, shouting from within.

"Had you lost your damn mind!?" the man roared. From behind him, I saw Luke's head tilt slightly to the side, unbothered. The door slammed shut behind us, the sound hitting like an exclamation point. "Did you have any idea how many people were looking for you right now, and you decided to go for a little joyride!?"

Wait—that voice. I recognized it.

"I was... upheld," Luke said, fumbling for words. I narrowed my eyes at the back of his head, willing him to sense my glare. *"Upheld?"* I asked through our mind link. *"Yes—upheld. Or would you prefer 'distracted' instead?"* he replied, punctuating the sentence with a quiet snicker.

"What was so fucking funny?" the man snapped, his voice rising. "Harrison had nearly the entire precinct out searching for your dumb ass. My phone hadn't stopped ringing for the past hour. Where the hell were you!?"

As Luke stepped aside, the speaker finally came into full view. The commanding presence, the voice—everything clicked into place.

Lieutenant Charles Smith.

He looked completely different than I was used to—dark

brown jeans, a white t-shirt, a denim jacket, and clunky motorcycle boots. My brows lifted. I hadn't realized Smith rode a bike, too. His gray eyebrows and mustache twitched as his sharp blue eyes landed on me, and he stiffened instantly at the sight. I'd never noticed how much they resembled each other—I should've connected the dots a long time ago. Though Smith was older and grayer, they shared the same solid build, confident stance, and those soft, startling blue eyes.

I offered a sheepish smile.

"Dear God, you brought the commissioner's daughter," he growled, spinning on Luke, who was now casually leaning against a table beneath a cluster of large, glowing monitors. I took a step farther into the room, but Luke raised a hand to stop me. I shot a quick glare at him but didn't advance. "Why did you bring the commissioner's daughter?" Smith hissed, his glare so intense it could've set Luke on fire.

"Our little friend here decided she wanted to pay Danny Fritz a visit tonight," Luke said with a shrug, crossing his arms over his chest. "I intervened." He cocked his head, muscles in his shoulders tensing slightly beneath the fabric of his sweatshirt. "You did WHAT?" Smith roared, snapping his attention back to me. I bit my lip, ready to explain, but Luke lifted a finger without looking at me.

"Don't answer that," he clipped. Smith pinched the bridge of his nose, exasperated. "Why the hell is she glowing, Luke?" Before anyone could respond, Charlie's phone buzzed loudly. He glanced at the screen, snarled, then turned back to Luke, unwilling to divulge what the message on his phone said.

"Ah, that," Luke said casually, ignoring the brief intrusion. "She's Gaythe, like I told you. Honestly, Charlie, I figured you'd be able to keep up better than this." Charlie narrowed his eyes at the jab.

"Charlie?" I echoed, just between us. *"Brother, remember?"* Luke replied with a subtle sideways glance in my direction. *"Right,"* I muttered, more to myself than anyone else. "Last time I checked, Luke, Gaythe don't fucking glow. So I'll ask again—why is she glowing?" Charlie said, his voice sharper now, laced with frustration. Luke shrugged and gestured toward me, "You'll have to ask her."

My eyes widened as Charlie's gaze turned to me with blazing conviction. He raised both eyebrows, clearly waiting for an explanation.

I cleared my throat. "I... I don't really know what happened," I admitted. "One second I was normal, and then my arms just—felt strange. Like something surged through me. A burst of power or energy or something."

Charlie's face went pale. He took a step back, staring up at the ceiling as he dragged in a deep, heavy breath. "Why is Fritz Manor currently burning to the fucking ground?" he muttered the question to no one in particular.

"I think I set it on fire," I said, my voice coming out thin and squeaky as I wrung my hands, desperately trying to shake the lingering tingling sensation. "I'm sorry—did I hear that right? You set Fritz Manor on fire?" Charlie's eyes lowered again as he stared at me, incredulous.

The glow around me had faded slightly since the initial outburst, but a faint silver shimmer still clung to my skin. Everything felt prickly, like my body had been asleep and was only now waking up. The silicone sleeves were gone—completely disintegrated. There was no getting those back. And after that night, I had an unsettling feeling that Danny Fritz would find me, with or without them.

Charlie's phone rang again, and the red climbing up his face deepened to an angry, mottled shade. "He's going to kill me," I

whispered under my breath. "He's not going to kill you," Luke
said calmly, though his posture tightened. Charlie planted both
hands firmly on a desk at the far end of the room. "He may not,"
he growled, "but I sure will."

"Touch her, and I'll chop off your hands," Luke replied,
deadpan.

Charlie merely sighed heavily, and my face burned bright
red at that, the heat radiating all the way to my ears. Trying to
ignore the tension, I glanced around the room. Dozens—maybe
hundreds—of monitors lined the walls, casting cool light across
the space. Only two chairs occupied the room, and in the far
corner, a small cot lay unmade, a mess of tangled blankets tossed
carelessly over it.

"What was this place?" I asked, scanning the glowing screens
around the room. Some displayed live footage from various
spots around Raos, but most were trained on the precinct
and Fritz Corporation. That immediately set off alarms in my
head—there weren't supposed to be cameras outside of Fritz
Co., and I knew for a fact the precinct didn't have internal
surveillance. So where were these feeds coming from?

"Somewhere you shouldn't be," Charlie snapped. Luke rolled
his eyes. "It is a Protectorate forward operating base... sort of,"
he answered, but Charlie didn't let up. "Do you have any idea
how many people are going to be looking for her? You are
already labeled an escaped felon, and now you've gone and
kidnapped the commissioner's daughter—again."

Luke's mouth pressed into a tight line as he said, "I didn't
kidnap her—you're being dramatic. She got on my bike
willingly."

I snorted, and both of them turned toward me. "I mean, it was
either die or get on the bike—real tough decision," I said, my
voice thick with sarcasm.

"Not now," Luke snapped at me, his tone clipped. Charlie gritted his teeth. "I knew involving her was a mistake," he said, jabbing a finger into his own chest. Luke's expression went flat as he growled, "Watch who you're talking to, *brother*."

I half expected Charlie to snap back with something cutting, but instead, he lowered his hand and returned to his desk without another word. "We need her," Luke said, crossing one ankle over the other like this was all just a casual conversation. Charlie eyed him, "Do we need her—or do you need her?"

Luke leaned forward, locking eyes with him, and I felt my breath catch. "I need her," he said lowly, the words laced with intensity. My fingers began to tingle again, a soft buzz of energy building in my skin. I clenched my hands into fists, trying to quiet the strange sensation.

"You're making reckless decisions, Luke. Think of The Protectorate," Charlie warned, holding his ground. "I am thinking of The Protectorate," Luke replied, his voice dark as he continued, "And The Protectorate needs her."

The tension in the room simmered down slightly, though the energy clinging to me didn't fade. My skin felt raw, exposed under their scrutiny. "And why exactly does The Protectorate need the commissioner's daughter?" Charlie pressed.

I slowly put a hand on my hip and tilted my head. "You two realize I'm still in the room, right?"

Both of them turned to look at me, as if suddenly remembering I was indeed present. "I need a Gaythe in my ranks," Luke said, ignoring my comment, his tone casual but deliberate. My eyes widened, "You need what in your—who?"

"I need you to serve The Protectorate," he answered, brushing an imaginary piece of lint from his sleeve. I threw my hands up, palms out. "Wait, wait, wait. You want me to serve The Protectorate—the organization I didn't even know existed until, like, last week?"

Luke shrugged, "Do you want allied military support for the Gaythe?" he asked, and my arms dropped to my sides. My stare was hollow as I contemplated.

"At any cost... that's what she told me," I finally whispered. "This is your cost," he said simply, letting the weight of it settle in the silence. Charlie stepped forward again, "Why do we even need an alliance with the Gaythe, Luke? Our problems are here—on Raos."

I cut in softly, "They won't be here soon," and Luke's eyes drifted to mine as if in answer. "The experiments," I whispered. He nodded, allowing me to continue. "Feros isn't rich in any kind of stone that would hold Element X. They mainly have basalt—grey, not black, and rich in iron. In fact, there's so much iron on Feros that it has changed the rock's natural color from grey to a rich red." I was partially ranting, trying to fill in every gap left by the questions I'd been asking myself this whole time. "Actually, it doesn't make sense to mine there. Why would they be mining on Feros if Element X is what they seek?" I asked.

Luke stood straight and walked across the room, our eyes following his every step. He pointed to a screen overlooking a loading bay for transport ships. "Because they're not mining on Feros—they're setting up a forward operating base and planning on nuking Gayle to reap its resources, Element X, in the aftermath."

I watched in horror as truck after truck loaded massive pallets onto the cargo ship on the screen. "Is that the— headed for—" I began, my voice trailing off in disbelief. "The nuke headed for Feros? Yeah," Luke replied flatly, pressing his palms to the desk and lowering his head, "I've been trying for months to prove they were conducting illegal experiments on Raos civilians. I've been searching for those files forever."

My face drained of color—the files. The ones in my backpack. The same ones I'd nearly lost when I torched Fritz Manor. Without thinking, I yanked the bag off my back and hurled it at him. He caught it midair in one smooth motion, clutching it tightly to his chest.

"You found the files?" Charlie demanded, eyes blazing. "I did—while you were off kissing ass or whatever it is you do," Luke snapped, scowling at him. "Fuck you! I was trying to clean up the disaster you caused when you dragged the commissioner's daughter by her heart strings all the way to Gayle!" Charlie roared.

"Once again, I have a name," I cut in, shaking my head. Luke bit his lip, trying to hide a grin, but Charlie's fury didn't fade.

"The files won't matter if the charges hold. If they catch you they'll execute you before you even start to untangle the mess they've made." He growled, and Luke bared his teeth in silent challenge, but I ignored both of them, my pulse pounding.

"No one was getting executed," I said firmly. "Not you, and not Harrison." I slammed my fist into my palm for emphasis. Both of them stared at me. "What does she mean?" Charlie asked, glancing at Luke. "Aren't you still expected to execute my father, Commander?" I asked, my tone sharp. Charlie smirked now, the smugness returning to his face.

"Oh, she's a smart one, Luke. You've got your hands full," he drawled. "Shut it, Charlie. Who told you I was commander?" Luke demanded, his eyes narrowing as they locked onto mine. "Danny Fritz," I said, my jaw tightening as Luke's eyes sharpened, locking onto mine. "What else did he tell you?" he asked, his tone low and controlled.

I froze as the memories surged back—the weight of Fritz's stare, the grip of his hands on my arms, his breath hot against my neck. A wave of nausea rolled through me, and his words echoed in my mind like a nightmare I couldn't wake from. "Pandora?" Luke said, his voice gentler now. "He said... he said my father killed my mother," I whispered as a rush of emotions slammed into my chest all at once.

It felt like my heart might combust on the spot—because deep down, I had known. I had known all along that he had killed her—I knew I shouldn't trust him. Odina knew it, Luke knew it, Ivy knew it. I just hadn't wanted to admit that my father could do something so twisted, so vile. He had slipped a sedative into her tea, and when she fell asleep while reading, he had given her a paralytic injection at the back of her spine, causing her to stop breathing and her heart to cease.

Tears streamed down my face in giant, wet rivulets. Neither of them said a word as anger built in my chest. "Say something! Say it's not true!" I screamed, but my words were swallowed by the heavy silence. Charlie lowered his head, and Luke pressed his bottom lip between his teeth.

"She was everything to me. My light, my joy—my life-giver. She was the moon and the stars that lit up my night sky. Her laugh sounded like Christmas bells and music, and her eyes... they held the weight of her world." I took a shaky breath, my voice cracking as the truth settled. "And now she's gone." Another breath. "And he killed her."

"I know," Luke said quietly. "You knew?" I asked, my voice rising in disbelief. "Not for sure. Not until right now," he replied softly. Charlie closed his eyes, refusing to meet either of our gazes. He leaned back against a bare grey wall again, his hands shoved in his pockets, his expression distant and clouded with thought. Luke ran his tongue over his lips and looked at me.

"I told you I'd get justice for Esme—and I still will," he said gently, holding me steady through our mind link. *"I just don't want him dead,"* I whispered, resting my head against his chest

in that shared mental space.

In the real world, we were still just staring at each other, motionless. The silence stretched long enough that Charlie's features twisted in visible confusion.

"I want him behind bars for the rest of his life," I muttered. Luke exhaled slowly. *"I swore to a lot of people back on Cappurn that I'd kill the leaders of Revolution X,"* he said softly, running his fingers through my hair—at least in our mind. *"If you kill him, I will leave."* I told him through the link, meaning every word. The bond we shared—one I hadn't dared to sever—hung in the balance. Severing it would shatter me. But I would do it. Time stretched. His heartbeat echoed through the bond—steady and stubborn.

Finally, Luke blinked slowly, eyes locked on mine. "I won't kill him," he said, his audible voice breaking the silence. Charlie's eyes snapped open, his head whipping toward Luke like he'd been slapped. "What do you mean you won't kill him?" he demanded, voice razor-sharp. I held my breath as Charlie stepped forward, fury flaring in his eyes, "Luke, you knew this was the endgame. You have to kill Danny and Harrison when this mission is over. That's what The Protectorate exists for. You don't get to just—not do it."

"I didn't say I wouldn't kill Danny, but if she doesn't want me to kill Harrison, I won't kill him."

My heart threatened to beat right out of my chest. "Luke." Charlie leveled with him, getting between us. "You are the commander of The Protectorate, and as much as I respect that, what you're deciding is a mistake. They need to be held responsible for their actions." He hissed.

"And they will," I said, lifting my chin. "Help me put them behind bars, and I'll help you get to them," I said, my voice feeling like gravel. Charlie's head whipped back and forth between us. "The *point* of The Protectorate, Charlie, isn't to assassinate Danny and Harrison," Luke said, his voice steady. "It's to end the years-long experiments on the people of Liarta and prepare for the interspecies war that's coming."

He pointed to the screen, drawing Charlie's eyes toward it, "And we still can—as long as we intercept that ship before it leaves Liarta. We need damning proof to put them on trial publicly, here in Raos. The only way this ends with both of them still breathing is if we lock them away for life." He stepped around Charlie and looked me dead in the eyes, "I told you I needed your help, Pandora—but the choice is yours. He's your father."

I froze as the weight of his words settled over me.

"We're on a clock now that Danny knows you're involved," Luke warned, "He's going to push to expedite the shipment—and have you arrested for trespassing. Maybe even arson, considering you left his house in a pile of ashes." My stomach dropped. "Based on your intel, when does the ship leave dock?" I asked, eyes flicking to the monitor. "Tomorrow night—but they're still waiting on a shipment of plutonium," he answered. I nodded slowly, narrowing my focus on the screen. "Are we at risk of that nuke going off here on Liarta?" I asked. He shook his head. "I was worried about that too, but from what we've gathered, they're assembling it on Feros to minimize the risk of accidental detonation."

"Will an explosion like that reach Kehel?" I asked, my nerves tightening with every breath. "It shouldn't but it's possible," he replied, "I'm more concerned about the radiation fallout afterward. It will be so intense, they won't be able to surface without a radon purger." He finished, and I closed my eyes, a small bit of relief mingling with worry.

At least Kehel was most likely safe—but how long could they

survive stranded down there without returning to the surface? My eyes snapped open.

"No," I whispered. "No, no, no, give me those files." I rushed forward, shoving Charlie aside. He scowled, but Luke shot him a try it and see what happens look. I was so caught up in the horror that I almost forgot what I had skimmed earlier about Feros Officer One.

Confusion crossed Luke's face as he handed me my backpack. I unzipped it and dumped the contents onto the counter, rifling through the files as fast as I could. Papers scattered everywhere—falling to the floor, the desk, even floating in the air. Charlie lunged in, grabbing them like they'd combust midair.

"Fuck. I'm sorry," I muttered, bending down to sift through the chaos. Luke crouched too, gently sorting the mess of documents scattered around. Our hands reached for the same file at once; our fingers brushed, and a spark of electricity shot up my arm, making it pulse with silver light. He pulled back, leaving the file in my hand. "Thanks," I murmured, forcing my eyes away.

I flipped through the pages rapidly, stopping at the last one and started reading aloud: "Strength test—success. Hearing test—success. Weapon welding—success." I paused, feeling their eyes on me, frozen and waiting. "Speed test—success. Agility test—success. Radioactive endurance—success."

They both inhaled sharply. Luke's eyes darted to the screen showing the ship. "They're not just mutant soldiers. They're intended to be Element X miners," he said, slamming his fist on the table. It rattled with the sudden assault. "They're going to bleed Gayle of every atom of Element X that exists and create soldiers who can outlast and out endure any weapon." His words echoed my thoughts, making me feel sick.

"They are the new weapon," I whispered, horrified, "This

will end humanity as we know it. They'll mass-produce the injection, and we'll become slaves to our own government."

"We have to stop that shipment before it leaves for Liarta." His eyes locked onto mine. I nodded firmly, "Tell me what I need to do."

"As much as I'm enjoying this little chit-chat, I have to leave you two here. Harrison's asking for backup at Fritz Manor." Charlie brushed past me, his shoulder grazing mine. "Do me a favor," He muttered under his breath. "Don't set anything else on fire tonight, okay?"

I swallowed hard and offered an apologetic smile. "Heard," I mumbled. Then he strode out the door, slamming it behind him with a groan of protesting hinges, leaving me and Luke alone.

Chapter 45

I gaped at the long list of contents for the shipment heading to Feros. "Do you know how much money is being dumped into this?" I asked, skimming over the fourth page. "Billions," Luke replied flatly, leaning against the wall with his arms crossed over his chest.

Charlie had left to handle the chaos at Fritz Manor, leaving Luke and me to devise a plan to stop the shipment from leaving Liarta—and we had just over twenty-four hours to do it. "How has no one seen this happening?" I asked, eyes widening as I flipped to the fifth page.

"They hide the money allocations behind publicly accepted fronts—new atom scanners at Precinct 12, new ships, infrastructure updates across Raos—you get the idea. They've done an excellent job concealing where the actual money's going,"

He ran a hand through his hair until a brown curl fell over his forehead.

"You told me before the funding only went to Precinct 12. Are none of the other precincts getting updates?" I asked. "The only precinct being audited by the city is Precinct 12. So unless they wanted to be flagged, they had to sink some money into it as a scapegoat. None of the others got anything," His eyes trailed over my body, and I tensed.

"So, Precinct 12 is the scapegoat," I mumbled, locking eyes

with him. His gaze slid back up to my face, "Exactly, if it doesn't look like the rich investors of Raos are putting their money into something worthwhile, they'll lose all their funding and—"

"And lose the ability to mine for Element X," I finished.

He nodded and pushed off the wall, stepping beside me and gesturing toward the screen showing the loading dock. "What the rich investors of Raos don't realize is that most of their money is being funneled into this," he said. I bit my lip, and his jaw tensed as he leaned on the desk, lowering his head toward mine, "We could do a lot, but we weren't stopping this on our own. This was a layered operation—we needed backup."

His scent overwhelmed me. Eucalyptus and sandalwood. I inhaled sharply as he leaned even closer, our noses brushing, "As much as I'd love to see you light that entire ship up, that would also take the whole dock down with it. We need a plan—one that includes your friends."

I bristled, "Ivy and Chance?"

He straightened and glanced at the monitor, "Can you convince them?" His voice was measured in the question. I chewed on the inside of my cheek, considering. It sounded insane—an A-tier conspiracy. Ivy might buy in. But Chance? Only if Ivy was completely on board.

"I can try," I said, my gaze following his to the monitors, "Is this what you've been doing when you're not at the precinct—reconnaissance?"

"Mostly, yeah," he replied. I tilted my head, pulling back slightly, "Recon on who?"

"Mostly Danny Fritz and your father. And some of you," he said without a hint of apology. I stiffened, heat rushing to my cheeks. "You've been following me?" I asked, incredulous. His expression didn't shift, "Yes,"

I blinked slowly, "Can I ask why?"

He exhaled, straightening and leaning one arm against the desk beside us, "When I came here from Cappurn to stop Revolution X, I didn't know where to begin. I started with Danny Fritz. That trail eventually led me to your father. Around that time, I found out your mother had recently died." His voice tightened as he went on, "Charlie moved here long before the revolution began—he was the first in our family to leave Cappurn. He returned briefly to deliver intel then brought me back with him. When he warned of a revolution starting on Liarta that could spark an interplanetary, interspecies war, I knew I had to intervene."

He paused, emotion flickering across his face. "I started building a team to support the Gaythe and stop their extinction. Charlie believed that if the revolution spread, it would seal their fate. And I believed him. The Protectorate exists to keep all species and all planets from tearing each other apart. I didn't fully understand what I was getting into at first, but I knew someone had to step in—before we destroyed everything."

"You started an entire assembly to police the planets and species that resided on them?" I asked, then added, "By yourself?"

"Of course not." He let out a low chuckle in response, "I'm just one man leading the machine. Every nut, every bolt, every spark plays a role—and a vital one. Right now, we're closer to universal extinction than ever before, and The Protectorate is the only group actively working to stop it." His gaze sharpened, "what started as a revolution to protect the Gaythe from the Nephrians has evolved into something far bigger than me—bigger than us, bigger than our existence. It's become essential if this universe has any hope of surviving past our lifespan." He slipped a hand into the pocket of his cargos and said quietly, "You have to decide if that's worth the sacrifices you're going to make."

"What are the sacrifices I'm going to have to make?" I asked quietly, fingers fumbling with the end of my long auburn braid.

"I can't tell you exactly what sacrifices you'll face," he said, offering a faint, tired smile, "everything comes at a cost though including universal peace—I just don't know to what extent that will be."

For a moment, I saw the weight he carried, the responsibility carved deep into his shoulders. The burden still bewildered me. "Why do you care if the universe exists beyond our lifetime?" The question slipped out before I could stop it and a wave of sadness washed over his face. "Because I hope that someone from our ancestry would have done the same. I hope that one day my kids get a world worth exploring."

The vulnerability in his voice didn't come easily. His posture stiffened, discomfort flickering in his eyes. "I hope for that too," I murmured.

A long silence stretched between us while I sifted through the mountain of information I had just uncovered. "If we're going to do this," I said at last, lifting my face to meet his, "we need to do it right. It has to be by the book."

"What do you propose?" he asked, tilting his head. "My badge was rescinded," I said bitterly. "I can't make arrests—but Ivy and Chance can." The gears in my mind began to turn, pieces of a plan falling into place. "Go on," he prompted. "Are Danny and my father planning to oversee the final confirmation of goods on the ship before it departs?"

"Yes. According to my intel, they'll be there about an hour before the ship launches for Feros tomorrow night. Why?"

"If we catch them there—with the supplies for a nuclear bomb on board—Ivy can arrest them for terrorism. That would be it. Game over." As I spoke, Luke's eyes blazed a brilliant blue. "So what exactly are you proposing?" he asked again.

I started pacing, my boots echoing softly across the worn grey tile. "You and I break onto the ship, confirm what's inside. Once we have proof, we hide out until Danny and my father show up. Then we call Ivy and Chance for the arrest." He watched me, eyes sharp as I moved. "How do you plan to get onto the ship unnoticed?" he asked. "How many guards usually patrol the dock?" I countered. "Four," he replied, a grin curling at the corner of his mouth.

Silence settled between us once more as the plan solidified—one that might save us all... or plunge everything into chaos. "Fine, we snag one—you steal his badge keys, get inside, and gather the information we need to formally charge them while I keep watch of the other three," I said. His brow lifted as his voice dropped low and serious, "It's not a terrible plan, but we only get one shot. This is it."

"I know," I replied, meeting his gaze as his eyes narrowed, studying me in silence. "There's only one thing left before we execute the plan," he said, the grin spreading further across his face and I stopped pacing and turned toward him. "What's that?" I blinked slowly, waiting."You get to convince your friends to help arrest the Liarta President and Raos Commissioner."

Right—and there's that. *Piece of cake.*

Chapter 46

My house rested in stillness, cloaked in shadow, every light extinguished—yet I knew my friends better than they knew themselves. I knew their patterns, knew their tells. They were waiting for me, hidden in the dark.

A breeze sighed through the trees, and I blinked against the velvet dark, my gaze fixed on the windows in silent prayer. The forest hummed a slow lullaby, its branches groaning like old cellos, each note a secret carried on the wind. Even the grass seemed to listen, swaying gently, each blade bending and rising in time with the breath of the night. Behind me, Luke crouched close, his presence quiet and solid. His breath coiled in the crisp night air, a warm tether on my shoulder—anchoring me.

"You're sure they're here?" he asked through the mind link. I nodded subtly. *"I know them,"* I replied. I heard his chest lift, then lower in thought. *"We've been here for an hour, and there's been no sign of anyone in the cabin."* His voice was calm and soothing, wrapping around my mind, and I caught a glimpse of him in the corner of my vision as he scanned the area for the fifteenth time in the last five minutes. I narrowed my eyes at the window that overlooked my bedroom. Surely, any moment now.

Suddenly, a dark shape appeared—a person. I nudged him gently with my elbow. *"I told you,"* I said, snarkily. He scooted closer, his chin grazing my shoulder. *"Who is that?"* he asked, his pupils flaring in my peripherals as they focused on the figure in the dark. *"Ivy,"* I answered.

I didn't need to see the full shadow to know it was her—she was the one who would be waiting at my house for my return. And I knew we couldn't just traipse through the front door; she most likely had my father on speed dial, oblivious to the implications. No, we needed to catch her by surprise. An idea flickered quickly in my mind, and a grin bent the corner of my lips.

"How did you manage to get into my bathroom the other night?" I asked, curiosity puckering at the edges of my question. His head tilted gently toward me, his chin brushing my shoulder again. "Want me to show you?" he audibly whispered, his voice carried on the breeze through the trees. A flash of white teeth appeared in the darkness as he smiled at me. I narrowed my eyes in irritation. "If I didn't, I wouldn't have asked,"

I rolled my eyes once then we returned our gaze to the large bedroom window, waiting for the figure to disappear. It stayed completely still, as if watching the tree line for any movement. I knew these trees, this forest—this spot was a blind area from that window. Thankfully the breeze rustled the leaves just enough to create a hum of natural white noise and I knew the sound of our footsteps would be lost in the wind—just as they had been an hour ago when we crept through the trees to survey the cabin.

The memory of every time I cursed this very spot when I looked out from it myself came flooding back. I never expected to be sitting outside my house in the shadows, but then again, I never anticipated the chain of events that led us here to begin with. A part of me ached for the person I no longer was, but there was no returning to how things were before. The only way out was through—and I had to see it through.

The wind picked up in speed and my auburn flyaways whipped across my face. She would leave any moment, and we would have to move quickly—just like the wind. My legs started to go numb as I crouched further behind the tree, but I hadn't heard a single complaint from Luke. I imagined the recon he had done must have been far more uncomfortable and prolonged than this. There was still so much I didn't know about him, and although I was permanently bonded to him in a way I wasn't entirely sure how to feel about, I was confident of one thing—he had been telling the truth. We needed to stop the call for interspecies war, the experiments on innocent humans, and the looming threat of a Nephrian takeover. And with every passing second, this mission felt more urgent than ever. I was pulled from my thoughts as the figure moved deeper into the house, disappearing from view.

I opened my mouth to give directions, but before anything could come out, Luke was darting towards the cabin, slipping from the cover of the trees. I cursed under my breath and scrambled after him, darting beneath branches that reached out to lick at my face. Though we left the darkness of the woods behind, thick clouds shrouded the moon, casting the cabin in midnight-muted gray light—just enough to see a few feet ahead, but not enough to reveal our creeping silhouettes. Even the grass seemed to hush beneath our steps as we glided across it.

Luke pressed himself against the side of the house, and I mirrored him, my shoulders meeting the chill of the dark brick. We wound our way along the wall until we reached the bathroom window. Luke drew a blade from his thigh and wedged it into the seal along the glass pane. I watched as he eased the window open with practiced care, lifting the pane just enough for my body to fit if angled right. He flipped the blade over with his free hand, its razor edge slicing through the air, then slipped it into the sheath in one sharp movement.

"Ladies first," he cooed, motioning me forward. The voice reminded me of Adam for a moment, and a blush heated my cheeks, but I ignored it. He kept his hand on the window, holding it open as I stepped up, planting the heel of my boot on his knee to boost myself. With both hands gripping the sill, I hauled myself up and swung one leg through until I was straddling the frame. I glanced down at him as he waited, steady.

"Stay here until I say otherwise," I whispered, then slipped inside. The window snapped shut behind me, but I didn't wait to confirm if I was the only one who heard it as I moved through the unlit bathroom, my footsteps dead silent. My reflection caught in the mirror startling me—a pale face, shadowed and sharp with focus, my auburn hair sticking up in wild, rebellious tufts. I smoothed it down with one hand and continued forward, avoiding the creaky floorboards I had memorized long ago. Ivy might have been a detective, but she didn't know this house like I did—like it was part of me.

I slipped through the bathroom doorway into my bedroom. Everything was untouched—even the bed was still unmade from that morning. As I crept forward, my eyes caught on a piece of paper peeking from beneath the armoire. Most likely one of the papers that fell from the experiment folders. I crouched, reaching for it, and stared at the image printed on the page.

A woman—gaunt, skeletal, barely human—gazed out at me, her hollow eyes pleading. The knot in my stomach tightened. I would never be able to save her. Her fate had been sealed long before I understood the stakes, long before I could fight back. Still, the sorrow hit me like a wave—sharp, cold, and merciless. The paper flittered from my hand, coming to rest quietly on the floor once again.

I straightened, leaving the paper where it was, and moved

toward the partially cracked door. Pressing my ear to the gap, I listened—nothing. My brows knitted together. Where did she go?

Sliding my fingers into the crack, I eased the door open, slow and silent. It swung without a sound, and my heart pounded harder in my chest. The silence was absolute. Eerie. Picture frames on the wall caught fleeting glimpses of my reflection like fragmented mirrors as I crept down the hall toward the kitchen. I peeked around the corner—empty. No one.

The hairs on the back of my neck bristled. What if she was on the phone with my father right now? Did she see us out in the forest? The dark wood floor swallowed my shadow as I slipped through the kitchen and into the living room—and that's when I saw her.

I froze.

She was sitting in the center of the couch, hands folded neatly in her lap, staring straight at me. A single lamp on the side table cast a soft light over her face. She was wearing the same beige tank top and blue jeans from that morning. Her blonde hair fell loosely around her shoulders, unmoving, as she sat still as stone—only her eyes blinking. Her chest rose with quiet, measured breaths, but her lips were pressed into a firm line, her gaze locked on mine.

"Hi," I managed, voice rough as I rose from my crouch. "What did you do?" she asked, her tone flat, her jaw tightening as her eyes narrowed. "I need you to listen to me," I said quickly, "I can explain."

"You better start talking right now, or I'm calling and telling him you're here," she snapped, her voice sharp with bitterness and rage. She lifted her phone, and I caught the name—Commissioner Vaughn—glowing on the screen. Just one press away. "Please," I whispered, raising my hands in surrender.

She paled the moment she saw them—my arms no longer shimmering silver, but had reverted to their deep, unnatural black. She gulped, the only motion she made as she stared, eyes wider than dinner plates.

"I just need you to listen," I said, steadying my voice. "Then you can decide whether or not to call him. But I know you—and I know that if you believe what I'm about to tell you, you won't."

Her eyes narrowed, but she lowered the phone to the table, crossed one leg over the other, and stayed seated, her posture rigid. She refused to move, as if any shift might betray something. "Start talking," she muttered.

"We found her mother," I began, choosing the simplest piece first. "Amy's?" she asked, arms folding tightly across her chest. I licked my lips, nerves rising. "Yes—and we found Odina."

"And?" she prompted, her tone clipped and cold. The soft lamp cast long shadows across her face, sharpening her features in a way I had never noticed before. Her brown eyes seemed darker, more intense, framed by the green fabric of the couch. "Amy's real name was Kimi," I said quietly, "She was Odina's daughter. That's why she was half-Gaythe."

I wrung my hands, fingers trembling, unable to stop. Ivy's gaze dropped to them, and she watched like they might erupt into flames. Her voice was hushed as her eyes lifted to mine, "Who is her father?"

My heart slammed against my ribs. The words stuck in my throat, thick and dry. I couldn't say it—I didn't want to be the one to shatter that part of her. She had always admired my father. Looked up to him. She wanted to be Raos' commissioner—just like him. She chased the dream he had for me, the one I never wanted. In so many ways, she was the daughter he wished I'd been. I had pursued police work because I was supposed to. She did it because she believed in it. And she had always been better at it than me. My throat burned as I finally forced the truth out, "My father."

Her eyes flared open. "What do you mean, your father?" she whispered. "Amy was my father's daughter—my half-sister," I replied. She didn't move. Didn't even blink. And in that moment, I wished I could disappear—sink into the floor, vanish beneath a rock, anything to escape the weight of her stare. "How did you find that out?" she finally asked, her voice barely audible. "I DNA-matched to Odina on Gayle," I said softly. Her eyes widened even more, "Does that mean you're—"

"Half-Gaythe, yes. My mother was her sister."

We sat in silence, staring at each other while the clock on the wall ticked away every agonizing second. Each click seemed louder than the last, marking the space between us. "Is that what's wrong with your arms?" she finally asked, her gaze drifting down to them again. I held my arms out in front of me. They trembled as I searched for the right words.

"There's a power on Gayle they call Hanwi. They manifest as black stone—and, in its rarest, purest form, as a liquid so dark that light doesn't reflect off it. That stone form is what they call Element X here. It's extremely dangerous." My eyes locked onto hers, unflinching. She bit her lip, then glanced away, her eyes settling on the family photo hanging on the wall—the one of me, my father, and my mother. The same photo that used to sit on my desk back at Precinct 12.

"I didn't know at the time," I continued slowly, "but they called to me, asked me to touch them—and when I did, they marked me, transferring their power into me. I think the leader of the Nephrians is trying to steal the power from the Gaythe." My words felt foreign and raw in my throat.

"The leader of the Nephrians?" Her head snapped toward me. "Brykan," I replied, shuddering at the name. "How do you know who he is?" she demanded.

"He appeared to me—threatened my friends, my family. He said if I didn't go with him when he came, he'd kill everyone," I said, my throat raw, thick with emotion. The truth finally spilled out, but I was only halfway there. The worst was still coming.

Suddenly, she launched off the couch, pale as a ghost, stumbling backwards over the furniture in a panic. A vase crashed to the floor, shattering with a deafening crack. I whipped my head toward where she was gaping—and saw Luke leaning casually against the wall, arms crossed, watching us.

"I told you to stay put!" I snapped. He shrugged like I was overreacting. "Seemed like you had things under control. Thought I'd join the fun," he hummed. Ivy jabbed a finger in his direction. "I don't trust this traitor for a second. Have you heard what your father has said about him?"

"Yes. Ignore him for now," I said quickly, waving him off and turning back to her. But she had already raised her phone, finger hovering over the dial button.

"Ivy, don't. I meant what I said—if you want to call him when I'm done explaining, you still can, and I won't run. But you have to hear everything first. Then you can judge," I said, the words rushing out in a heated torrent. She glared at Luke for a long beat, then swung her eyes back to me. "Keep talking—I'm staying right here." She bit her lip and glanced again at Luke, who tilted his head and smirked, arms still folded like we were in the middle of some casual debate.

I shook my head—what an *ass*.

"Listen," I pressed on, locking eyes with her, "the people going missing in Raos are being subjected to illegal experiments with Element X." That grabbed her. Her eyes flicked up to meet mine, sharp and alert. "How do you know that?" she asked.

"The files that went missing from Commissioner Vaughn's

basement are documents detailing the experiments they're conducting," Luke said, his voice calm and even—too calm—while my heart hammered in my chest like a hummingbird's wings. If we didn't handle this perfectly, everything would fall apart. "And why should I trust you?" Ivy hissed at him. "I saw the files myself, Ivy," I snapped.

"You can look for yourself." Luke shrugged again, unfazed, and pulled the files from his hoodie pocket, tossing them onto the table. Ivy didn't move—just stared at the stack, her body rigid, her blonde hair wild and tousled. Her eyes locked onto the documents like they might combust at any second.

"Please, Ivy," I said, softer this time. She glanced at me, then slowly lowered her arms. She stepped toward the table, her gaze never leaving us, and picked up the top file. As she opened the first page, the color drained from her face. "Believe us now?" I asked. Her lips parted slightly, curling over her teeth as she breathed out, "Who is conducting these experiments?"

"Danny Fritz," I said quietly, "and my father."

"Why?" she asked, her voice barely a whisper as her eyes lifted to meet mine. "Danny wants humans to be the dominant species in this universe," I said bitterly. "What does Element X do to them?" Her voice was hollow as she sifted through the pages.

"It turns them into super mutant humans," I said as I watched her face carefully. "There were so many people... Are they all mutants?" she asked, her voice unsteady. She wobbled slightly, and I crossed the room quickly, reaching out to steady her. I guided her to the couch, and she didn't resist as we both sat down. "No," I said, gently closing the file in front of her. "There's only one we know of who survived." Her beautiful brown eyes met mine, filled with the same sorrow I had been carrying for so long. "Where are they?" she whispered.

"He's at Fritz Manor, working as one of the guards. They label him Feros Officer One," I said slowly. "Feros Officer One," she repeated, her gaze swinging to Luke. She was incredibly pale and her skin prickled with goosebumps. I swallowed mirroring her gaze on Luke.

"The experiments are being conducted on Feros and they're not mining there like they claim to be," he added. "What are they doing, then?" she asked. "Creating a mutant army to take over Gayle and extract the raw Element X buried deep in its largest ocean," he replied.

I watched as he crossed the living room to stand in front of us, "There's a shipment of supplies for a nuclear bomb leaving Liarta for Feros tomorrow night. They plan to nuke Gayle and then reap its resources after everyone there is left for dead."

Well he sure didn't sugarcoat anything. I shot him a glare, "My people—*my people*—are going to die. And if they don't nuke them, the Nephrians will slaughter them all,"

I no longer knew what time it was, but my body ached with exhaustion, and I could see hers did too—her shoulders slumped under the weight of everything we had just laid bare. "The files were hers," I murmured, my voice barely audible. "My mother's. Danny had Harrison kill her because of them."

Tears brimmed in her eyes, "Your father killed your mother?" Her voice trembled.

Before I could respond, she leaned into me, her arms wrapping protectively around my torso, and all the composure I had clung to shattered. I broke down in her arms, the grief and betrayal pouring out in sobs I couldn't contain. I didn't have to explain the agony I felt. She knew. She knew my mother had died fighting for what was right, protecting people who had labeled her a traitor.

My mother had been a powerhouse of a soul, a light in the bleak corners of this world—and he had extinguished it without hesitation. She pulled back, her eyes searching mine.

"Who killed Amy?" she asked. I turned to Luke. He knew I had enough information—he knew who did it and why—but was waiting. Waiting for me to confirm what I already suspected. "Someone I'll bring to their knees in retribution for ending her life," I said, still holding onto Ivy's shoulders.

I had known from the moment I had been told that my father killed my mother. I knew why Amy had died, and by whose hands, but that wasn't important right now. That would have to be put on the back burner. "We need to stop that shipment, Ivy. We need you," I told her. She looked from me to Luke, and his blue eyes blazed as he nodded.

"What do you need me to do?" she asked, her brown eyes blazing.

***

Luke and I stood in the doorway, watching as Ivy drove off, her car kicking up clouds of dust along the gravel drive. We'd spent the last few hours sketching out a rough plan, with the intention of locking down the details tomorrow, and she'd promised to get Chance on board first thing in the morning. She gave me a quick parting squeeze before hurrying to her car, and disappeared down the road.

I closed the front door with a soft hiss and finally exhaled the breath I had been holding all night. It was the earliest hours of the morning and my body was began to protest as I stretched my spine, still haunted by the memory of that brutal landing outside Fritz Manor. Luke rubbed the back of his neck while lingering in the entryway.

"We should get some rest," I murmured, though I didn't move.

His mouth was set in a firm line as he stared out the window, eyes distant, like he was still tracking her taillights down the drive. "Tonight might be our last night alive if the plan fails," he said quietly, and fear slithered up my spine.

"I know. If we fail, they'll kill us," I replied, my voice barely louder than a breath. The silence hung thick between us. His eyes caught the faint light—icy blue, glowing almost unnaturally—and his jaw flexed. He rolled his neck, then lifted his head to meet my gaze—blue locking with green. My breath caught. "What?" I asked, my eyes tracing the strength in his shoulders. I bit my bottom lip, and he drew in a sharp, sudden breath.

"Fuck it," he muttered before launching forward. I gasped as he lifted me straight off the floor, his hands firm at my hips as he carried me through the house toward the bedroom. He kicked off his sneakers and pulled my boots off along the way, leaving them behind somewhere in the kitchen. "What are you—" I began, but didn't finish.

His mouth crashed into mine, silencing everything. His lips were warm, urgent, and searing against my skin, and the world blurred around us. The bedroom door slammed into the wall as he pushed through, lowering me onto the bed with a gentleness that contradicted his hunger. Our lips broke apart in a breathless gasp. His eyes darkened, jaw tense as he watched me. I licked my lips and retreated up the mattress, pulse racing. "If tonight is my last night alive, I want to be with you," he murmured. "I want to be *inside* you."

My body melted at his words. I pressed my thighs together as a tight coil of heat and desire wound in my stomach. Outside, the clouds finally parted, and moonlight spilled into the room through the towering window, bathing everything in silver. "You're *mine*," he growled, and every nerve in my skin hummed in answer. Mate or no mate, this man made me feel things I didn't have words for.

The black markings along my arms began to tingle as he pulled his shirt over his head and tossed it aside, fingers running through his hair. His chest rippled in the soft light, drawing my gaze to the dark pink stab wound still healing on his shoulder.

My heart stuttered.

His eyes followed mine. "Ignore it—it was justified," he said, lowering his head to graze his nose along my collarbone. "I sank a blade into you, convinced you were wrong... and you were right." I murmured into his hair, and he lifted his head slightly. "Well then, maybe you can make it up to me." A smirk played on his lips, eyes sparking with a flicker of humor.

I reached up, fingers grazing over the lines of his chest, resisting the urge to pull him closer. He drew in a sharp breath, then leaned over me, placing his palms on either side of my head, eyes burning into mine. "You're so beautiful," he whispered.

Blue on green. Breath on breath.

My heart slammed in my chest, the air between us electric, every part of me echoing with the intensity of this moment.

"Oh, the wonderful things I want to do to you, Pandora," he murmured, his voice wrapping around my thoughts like silk. I shuddered as it sank in. He leaned in, our noses brushing, and my eyes widened—not in fear, but in defiance, daring him to rise to the challenge. He hummed low in his throat before kissing me softly.

"I want to relish you," he breathed, then lifted his face and slowly pulled his hands away from either side of my head. His knees settled on either side of my hips as he tucked his fingers into the waistband of my pants and eased them down, taking his time. A shiver raced through me as the cool air hit my skin, leaving me in nothing but my panties. Goosebumps rose along my legs as he dragged his thumb along the inside of my thigh, stopping just centimeters from my most sensitive spot.

I swallowed, watching him, unable to find the words. His eyes—so blue in the soft light—focused intently on my reaction.

"Take your shirt off for me," he commanded, his voice husky. I obeyed, lifting my black shirt over my head and tossing it onto the floor along with my pants. His gaze raked over my nearly bare body, and he reached up to pull the hair tie from my braid. I shook my head, letting my auburn waves fall around me on the bed like a halo. He hissed under his breath, "Fuck, the things you do to me."

He reached up, one hand gently cupping my breast over my bra. With the pressure, my nipple stood at attention as he guided his thumb further up and over my panties. He traced slow, deliberate circles over me, and my hands clutched the sheets tightly at his touch. Desire built in my core, my insides throbbing in anticipation. He chuckled as he reached behind my back to unclasp my bra. My breasts fell free as he tossed it onto the floor.

Lowering his mouth to my right nipple, I sighed as his tongue circled it in slow, deliberate strokes. Then, slipping a finger beneath my underwear, he softly strummed his thumb along my most sensitive spot, intensifying my aching need. He moved slowly, savoring each movement and I brought my hand to my mouth to stifle a moan.

"Moan for me," he coaxed, his voice sending shivers down my spine and his eyes sparkling at my response. A finger slid into me, then another, drawing me tighter under his careful guidance. "Fuck, you're wet," he groaned, and I hummed in response, my back arching off the mattress as I clutched the sheets until my knuckles turned white. The pressure built and built as he pumped his fingers slowly. I yearned for release, my mouth hanging agape with pleasure.

"Not yet, *love*," he finally murmured, pulling his fingers away. I groaned with irritation—but it was short-lived as he lowered his hands to his pants and slid them off. His cock sprang free, and I gasped.

"*See*, this is what you do to me." His voice slithered into my ear as he leaned forward, his mouth colliding with mine. My fingers fumbled into his hair, and his tongue caressed my bottom lip. The pressure—the sweet pressure he had built—returned with a vengeance.

I tore off my panties, discarding them, then wrapped my thighs around his waist, pulling him close feeling his arousal press insistently against me. He shifted slightly, rubbing the head against my clit, and I moaned breathily into his mouth.

Before I can change my mind, I thrusted my hips forward, sending him over onto his back. He didn't resist as I climbed up his body. He pushed his head back near the headboard as his hands rose to hold my waist steady. I reached down and took his full, erect length in my palm—he was so hard. He hissed through his teeth as I moved along his shaft, coaxing him further.

"If you don't stop that, I will take you right now," he growled, and a grin curled up my face. I leaned forward, our faces nearly touching as I eased the head of his arousal toward my entrance. He slid into me, and we both moaned as I lowered myself completely onto him. He stretched me entirely, and I leaned back, placing my hands on his chest. His eyes were wild, searching mine as he wriggled his hips beneath me.

"*Ah*," I coaxed softly, and the corner of his mouth twitched with amusement. I began moving slowly, savoring the sensation of his rigidity inside me. I tightened with every twitch of his length as my hips rose and fell, his hands guiding me as he watched intently. I leaned my head back, my fingers splayed on his chest, and the pressure built again.

My vision grew hazy as I lost myself to the rhythm of riding him, his hands caressing my ass, encouraging me. Faster and faster, I rose him, our breathing quickening into short, forced gasps. I felt it coming—a wave of pleasure—and I pushed even harder. Finally, that wave of release washed over me, and I screamed with delight as I climaxed and before I could say anything else we were moving.

He sat up, holding me to his chest and rotating my back against the sheets with a thud. "My turn," he murmured with a smile spreading across his face as he leaned forward, tucking his nose beneath the soft part of my ear. Lights flashed in my vision as the wave of my orgasm persisted, continuing as he started thrusting in and out of me. I whimpered, my legs shaking as I surrendered completely to him. He lifted his hand to grasp the headboard, thrusting harder and faster until I was wound up once again.

At that moment, I couldn't tell where my body ended, and his began—we were like two puzzle pieces fitting together in the most glorious harmony I had ever experienced. He nuzzled his lips against the soft part of my neck, and I wrapped my arms around his chest, gently digging my nails into his skin. The pressure built as he rocked his hips, sliding in and out in the most delectable, friction-filled rhythm. "Cum for me again—and this time, I want you to say my name," he whispered.

I exploded around him, coming wholly unraveled, and shouted his name into the night. He rumbled in response, finally finding his release.

He rolled to my side, and we both heaved for air. I laid a hand over my chest, waiting for my heart to slow its frantic pace as a heavy silence settled between us, our eyes still wild and searching in the afterglow.

He was the first to break the silence. "Whatever happens, I need you," he said quietly. I blinked slowly as the post-sex bliss began to ebb away. "I need you, Pandora," he repeated, his breath warm against my skin. I raised a hand to his face, my thumb gliding along his chin as the rough stubble prickled my fingertip. "I'm right here," I whispered, my brows furrowing.

"I've been working to take down Revolution X for years, and if this plan doesn't go through tomorrow, it could be the end of everything." His voice dropped low, sending shivers down my spine.

I propped myself up on one elbow to look at him. "Then we take them down by their kneecaps and shove them behind bars for the rest of their miserable lives."

He took a heavy breath before his eyes drifted upward to stare at the ceiling, but he didn't interject. "And pray to the powers that be that they stay there," I murmured as I plopped back down, pulling the covers over us.

Chapter 47

I woke tangled in arms and legs as Aurelios rose over the horizon, its light streaming through the canopy of trees. I blinked against the brightness, raising a hand to shield my eyes. There wasn't a cloud in sight to dull the blinding Aurelios pouring through the window. The horizon was painted in a burnt orange that gradually lifted into a pale blue as it climbed through the atmosphere.

After a few more blinks, my eyes finally adjusted. The room remained dim—it was still early—and as I looked around, I noticed discarded pieces of clothing scattered across the floor. I blushed as I turned to my side.

Luke lay prone on my emerald sheets, the comforter barely covering him above the hips, revealing his large, muscled back in the soft morning light. His face was turned toward the bedroom door, and I resisted the urge to run my fingers through the crown of his thick, curly brown hair. His strong arms were wrapped around the pillow beneath his head, and I could faintly hear his gentle snoring.

Cautious not to wake him, I peeled the covers off myself and slid out from under the arm he had draped around my waist. He stirred slightly, and I paused halfway off the bed, but his soft snoring resumed a moment later. I crept into the bathroom and softly closed the door behind me.

Rubbing the sleep from my eyes, I started the shower and

brushed my teeth. It had been incredibly late when we finally fell asleep, but there was no time for sleeping in on a day like today. I showered quickly, letting the warm water cascade over my shoulders. Closing my eyes, I relished the moment, unaware of the ramifications of everything about to transpire today.

"You're up early," Luke said, his voice echoing softly off the white tile. I startled, bumping my elbow against the shower's glass door with a muted thud. I grumbled, clutching my now-throbbing arm, and he chuckled, his eyes warm and captivating. "Is there room for me in there?" he asked, padding barefoot into the bathroom. Even with sleep still clinging to his eyes and his hair plastered sideways from the pillow, he looked strikingly handsome.

I stepped back and held the door open for him. He pulled off his boxers and eased into the water beside me. My eyes lifted to meet his; they were like twin oceans, swirling with blue light and quiet depth, and I felt completely adrift in them. He tilted my chin up with his thumb, leaning in until our lips grazed. A smile tugged at the corner of his mouth as I reached around him, my fingers digging gently into his shoulders.

His lips met mine with velvet softness that quickly sparked a slow-burning heat between us. The water rippled around us as he pulled me into his chest. My body melted into his, our bare skin pressed together in an intimacy that made me wish I could stay in that moment forever. He pressed his tongue against mine, coaxing me to reciprocate. I surrendered to the sensation, our tongues dancing in a slow, passionate rhythm.

A low moan escaped me from deep within as he lowered his other hand to my crotch. His fingers traced lazy circles along the apex of my thighs, sparking a small fire in my core. Yes, I could definitely have stayed here forever. He pulled back, his eyes heated and wild as he examined me. "As much as I'd love to stay in this shower until our skin turns pruny and red, we have work to do," he murmured, tilting his head at me. I grumbled in reluctant agreement, leaning my head back against the tiled wall. With a playful, childish look, he quickly washed himself and stepped out of the shower.

"Don't be too long," he snickered, grabbing a towel from the hook. I sighed with resignation, finishing my shower and stepping out, knowing that despite the lingering warmth and the tenderness between us, reality was waiting just outside.

***

"That's too far from where you'll be posted—it'll take us over fifteen minutes to get there." Ivy grumbled as glared at me crossing her arms. "Where do you propose you wait, then? If we're doing this right, you need to be far enough away so a cop car nearby won't raise suspicion." I waved my arms in exasperation. Luke and Chance just stared at each other, leaning against opposite walls of my living room, arms crossed.

We had been at this for an hour, trying to formulate a plan that wouldn't get us all killed or tip our hand too soon, and the afternoon was slipping away. Time was not on our side. Aurelios now bathed the cabin in warm, golden light that fragmented through the spider crack I had made in the glass.

Ivy's hair shimmered, and her brown eyes narrowed as she continued, "It won't matter if it takes too long. If we can't get there fast enough, Harrison and Danny will have time to dip out before we can catch them."

I plopped down on the green couch, letting my head fall against its back. My hair spilled over the cushions like a wave of crimson. "Please, boys," Ivy drawled. "Don't both talk at the same time." She rolled her eyes, darting them between Luke and Chance, who had been mostly silent until now.

Chance shifted from one foot to the other in his tan tactical pants, which made his sandy blonde hair look even lighter. His plain white shirt caught at his hips, revealing the Precinct 12 badge clipped to his belt loop, and just above his opposite hip, the grip of his police pistol peeked out. Ivy glanced at him, silently pleading for him to speak. His pale, hazy green eyes drifted from her to Luke, who stood across from him. I chewed on the inside of my cheek, waiting for someone to break the stalemate.

Finally, Chance sighed, his eyes landing on me. "Are you sure everything he told you is correct?" he asked. I nodded, "I saw it all with my own eyes. He's telling the truth—even if I don't want it to be."

Chance returned his gaze to Luke, who merely tilted his head toward him adjusting his jaw as if deep in thought. He shook his head as if not fully convinced, but willing to stand down. Finally, he took a few steps forward to the map on the coffee table in front of us. "If we wait on Caplan Street, adjacent to Moore Lane—which is basically a straight shot to the dock—it takes us less than five minutes to get there," he said, dragging his finger along the map to indicate the route, stopping at the shipping dock's location. All our eyes fixed on the map as we scrutinized the surrounding streets.

"That might work," I said, lifting my head from the couch. My auburn hair framed my face as I pressed a finger to my lips in contemplation, "They should take Crescent Street from the precinct to the dock, completely bypassing Caplan Street. From that angle, they wouldn't see you parked at all."

"What if they're coming from Fritz Manor?" Ivy asked, her eyebrows rising as she gestured toward where the partially burned mansion would be on the map. "If they take Green Road from there, it leads to Moore Lane and still bypasses Caplan Street. But if they take Blackbird Road, that leads right through Caplan Street—and they'd pass us,"

She pointed at the third road that completed the rectangle connecting Fritz Manor to the dock. I sucked in a sharp breath, "We'll just have to hope they take Green Road and bypass Caplan Street. If you wait elsewhere, it takes too long for you to respond."

Luke's eyes locked on mine as I turned to him—*blue on green*.

"What do you think?" I asked, chewing on my cheek again. He finally pushed himself off the wall, running a hand through his hair, "I think it's the best shot we have, but I'll be honest—something about this still doesn't sit right with me." His gaze drifted along the route from the precinct and back again. I nodded, glancing back at the map. "We only get one shot, so if anyone has a better plan, speak now."

All three of them looked at me, but only silence followed. I took a deep breath, exhaling slowly through my nose and closing my eyes, "We've got a few hours to prep. Ivy and Chance, head back to the station and act like everything's normal—no one can suspect anything's going on. Luke, you and I need to gather supplies here and be at the dock when they arrive."

They all nodded, exchanging tense looks. "If it all goes south—"

"It's going to be fine," Ivy assured me, placing a warm hand on my shoulder. A small, forced smile tugged at her lips. "The best outcome is that we arrest our president and my father. The worst? They get away and obliterate an entire planet and species for its resources. Nothing is fine," I muttered, and she slowly retracted her hand.

"That's not what I meant," she said quietly. "I know. But we have to be realistic. This isn't some heroic plan to save the entire universe—it's a salvage mission to prevent things from getting worse. This is just the beginning of what will most likely be a long legal battle to put them behind bars. Cross your T's and dot your I's, because the people we're up against have every wildcard in their back pocket, and believe me, they're more than ready to use them,"

Luke tilted his head in agreement, his eyes flashing with appreciation. "One last thing," he said as I rose from the couch. He glanced at each of us, but his eyes stayed locked on mine.

"If this goes south, get her out." His voice was firm, and Ivy and Chance exchanged worried looks. "If it does, we get you both out," Ivy interjected, her brows furrowing. Luke shook his head and raised a hand. "I'm trained for this kind of combat—she's not. If we get caught, you do everything possible to get her out. Understood?"

The breath in my lungs turned to ice as I watched my friends stare back at him.

"Understood," Chance finally said. I blinked, feeling the full weight of the mission settle in. I had put myself—and all of us—in grave danger with this plan, but I had no other option. The only way to stop them was to implicate them publicly. It was time for us to do what we did best, play detectives.

Chapter 48

Perched atop a neighboring building in our all-black gear, we had conducted surveillance for several hours. From our vantage point, we watched cargo workers enter and exit the ship, oblivious to our presence. Dressed in identical orange safety vests, they methodically loaded pallet after pallet of unmarked cardboard boxes. With every jolt of the forklift over the uneven dock boards, I tensed—there was no way to tell which pallets held fragile or hazardous materials, and it seemed the workers either didn't know or didn't care.

This dock was the only place in Raos where spaceships parked beside the roiling water. While Precinct Twelve's dock sat in an open field, this one nestled against the tawny boulders of the Pearl Sea cliffs. The lingering warmth of the day quickly vanished, replaced by an evening chill that swept over the murky blue water. The gentle lapping of ocean waves against the wooden posts of the dock served as a soft reminder of the treacherous depths below.

Before us stood one of the largest spaceships I had ever seen—a deep charcoal-gray vessel accented with gleaming silver. Its hull was a mosaic of countless panels in various shapes and sizes, punctuated by over a dozen windows nearly half my height and four boarding ramps.

As Aurelios set, the ship's running lights flickered on, casting a glow over the massive vessel and the dock below. The sky, typically overcast on this side of the city by the sea, cleared to reveal a vast expanse slowly dimming into a warm orange light. I shifted from one foot to the other, careful not to lose feeling in my limbs as we lay in wait.

Though my career as a detective had often thrust me into the spotlight, I relished slipping through the shadows—unseen and unstoppable. The evening breeze caressed my exposed arms, the short sleeves of my black shirt offering scant protection as the setting Aurelios sent a shiver down my skin. I wore form-fitting black pants lined with pockets, my pistol nestled against my abdomen and the iridescent Gaythe blades fastened to the outside of my right thigh. But it was my boots that truly defined my style.

Jet black, mid-calf high, and laced up the front.

They embodied agility, silence, and durability. I prided myself on being an honest detective turned phantom of the night, perfectly blending into the darkness. My gaze shifted to Luke, who merged effortlessly with the dark brick wall behind us. Clad head-to-toe in black—a mirror image of my own attire—his cargo pants, shirt, and combat boots let him vanish into the shadows like a silent knight on watch. With his back turned, he peered through binoculars, scrutinizing every package being loaded, his striking blue eyes fixed on the ship as his brow furrowed in concentration.

We hadn't spoken a word during our stakeout, each of us locked in our own focus. With roughly fifteen minutes left before Aurelios fully set and the workers clocked out, every second stretched longer. My eyes adjusted to the quickly fading light, and I rolled my neck, savoring the slightest movement after hours of stillness.

"Still no sign of the plutonium package?" I whispered into Luke's ear. He lowered his binoculars, turned slightly toward me, and shook his head. "Not yet. They have been receiving more delicate shipments after their shift ends with a much smaller crew," he replied. I pressed my lips into a thin line and tucked my arms close to my chest. I should have worn more layers, but the weather that time of year was unpredictable.

Suddenly, a loud siren blared across the dock, signaling the end of the shift. Luke and I slid further behind the brick wall as we watched the workers file out one by one to the time clock mounted beside a utility shed. They hung their safety vests on hooks along the wall before making their way to the parking lot several yards away. The sounds of car engines turning over and tearing out filtered into my ears, but we remained posted in our concealed spot. I glanced at my watch—just after six o'clock.

Narrowing my eyes, I spotted a group of three dock workers moving sluggishly as they clocked out and gathered their belongings. I tapped Luke on the shoulder and nodded toward them. His eyes caught who I pointed to. "That's them," he murmured, creeping along the wall for a better vantage point. I followed, my boots barely whispering against the pale grey cement. "It's always the same three for every special shipment," he noted, raising his binoculars again.

The workers scanned their surroundings for any unwanted attention until the tallest—his short, dark brown hair barely catching the dim light—stepped toward a shed. A heavy padlock secured the door, but he produced a key and unlocked it with ease. I slipped a pair of earbuds from my pocket and held my watch to my face. "Mayra," I whispered. Her face instantly appeared on the screen. "Yes, Pandora?" Her voice echoed in my headset. "Amplify the voices across the dock," I ordered, keeping my tone low. "Magnifying now," she confirmed, then disappeared from view. A moment later, their distant murmurs sharpened in my ear. I handed the other earpiece to Luke, who fit it in place.

"They should be here any minute. Stop wasting time, Chad," the shortest man—his bald, shiny head catching the minimal light—barked as he whacked the tallest on the shoulder. I raised an eyebrow but remained silent. "Here, you be in charge then Gary," Chad snapped, shoving a black radio into the bald man's hand. "Besides, if something goes wrong with this shipment, I'd rather it be on your hands than mine," he argued, and Gary retorted with a roll of his eyes.

The third man grabbed the remaining radio, and a whining noise filled my earbud as he cranked it on, making me wince. "You can argue all night, but when they get here, you better keep your mouths shut and do as they say," the third man—sporting shoulder-length, shaggy brown hair—hissed at them. "Alright, James. Calm down," Gary said, clipping his radio to his hip.

"Radio the guards and confirm everyone's in place—I don't need Markian handing me my ass again tonight," Chad barked at Gary, jabbing a finger into his chest. Gary puffed out his chest in silent defiance. My brows furrowed. Markian? That name rang a bell. I drummed my finger against my thigh, trying to place where I'd heard it before. "I can't stand that guy," Gary muttered. "Figures Danny hired him as his personal bodyguard—his ego's even bigger than the boss's."

I blanched.

"They're talking about the Feros officer," I whispered to Luke, my breath fogging in the dark. "The one who almost offed you last night?" His eyes darted to mine. "I believe so. If he's coming tonight, that slightly complicates things," he murmured. "You'll need to move quickly to get the evidence—or risk getting caught when they arrive," I warned, my eyes never leaving the group as Luke handed me the binoculars. Their weight made my hands dip slightly.

Chad locked the shed again, and the trio moved to the opposite side of the dock. Luke shifted his gaze to the ship, and I followed, noting only a single security guard stationed at the nearest ramp. If we had any chance of obtaining the evidence we needed, it would be when the fewest people were on rotation—but with Markian now in the lineup, our odds of getting out unscathed had just shrunk.

"Go now," I ordered, pointing to the guard. He nodded and slinked off the roof behind me. The ladder creaked as Luke's head disappeared below the brick wall, and I returned my gaze to the ship. One by one, the dock lights closest to the vessel flickered on like fire watchtowers igniting across distant peaks. It was now a race against time to secure proof of their nuclear plans without getting caught.

I pressed a button on my earpiece to switch channels. "Ivy, are you and Chance in place?" I raised my voice just enough for them to hear but not so much that it alerted the guard lingering at the edge of my vision. After a slight crackle of feedback, Ivy's voice boomed through. "We're in place."

"Hold your position," I said, clicking off the return button. "Confirm, holding position," she replied. My heart pounded as I switched channels back, taking a steadying breath. This was it—if this plan failed, we all failed. I leaned forward over the brick wall, scanning for Luke among the shadows. A glimmer of his earpiece caught the moonlight, and I watched as he crept, nearly invisible, through the dock toward the ramp. The guard, rocking on his heels, kept his eyes fixed ahead—ignoring his surroundings.

Their first foolish mistake—hiring imbeciles.

My fingers tingled as Luke edged closer, finally ducking behind a forklift with several unlabeled boxes waiting to be loaded onto the ship. I held my breath, pulse thrumming in my neck. Then he surged forward. In one swift motion, he seized the guard from behind, clamped a hand over the man's mouth, and pulled him down. Only a faint, muffled gasp broke the silence before the guard crumpled like a sack of potatoes. The guard thrashed briefly, but the struggle faded as Luke pressed a cloth over his mouth. Within moments, the guard went limp—unconscious.

I exhaled in relief—one down. Their second foolish mistake—docking their ship here at the Pearl Sea, where the crashing waves masked any suspicious sounds. Luke didn't linger. He hauled the unconscious body behind a stack of boxes, snatched the badge from the guard's chest, and slipped away. One moment he was there, the next he was creeping up the ramp toward the door, badge in hand. My eyes followed him, heart racing, fingertips gripping the brick before me. Just ten feet more, and he was through.

A radio crackled to life as the three dock workers rounded the corner into view. I cursed silently and sank back behind the wall so only my forehead and eyes peeked over while Luke sprinted the last few feet and slipped his body behind an open panel on the ship's hull. The workers moved at a casual pace unknowingly toward their unconscious coworker, their footsteps making the old wooden boards creak in protest.

My breath hitched in my throat—if they noticed he was gone or found the body, we were done for. Every muscle tensed as I held my breath, but they walked right past him—just a few feet away—continuing along the dock and disappearing into the office below me.

Luke's eyes met mine from several yards away as we both stayed perfectly still. The door finally clicked shut, and their voices faded into inaudibility. I exhaled slowly and glanced around. No other officers were nearby.

"Clear," I whispered into the earpiece. "Confirm, moving to the door," Luke replied as he slid out from behind the panel and stepped toward the door. He waved his laminated badge over the reader, which flashed green twice before the panel slid open into a recessed area, revealing a doorway wide enough to pass through. After one last glance in my direction, he disappeared into the ship as the gray panel slid back into place.

Basking in the darkness, I turned and crept to the other side of the building, giving me the best view of Moore Lane. I carefully inched forward, my boots hissing softly against the loose gravel on the cement roof. As lookout, it was my job to warn him if they arrived ahead of schedule. Moore Lane emerged over the brick wall as I raised the binoculars to my eyes. Not a soul was in sight along the road.

This affluent Raos neighborhood was home to uptight politicians and their families. Large houses of white marble and gold lined the street like soldiers in formation. I scanned each one, keeping a close watch for anything suspicious.

Most residents had just begun turning on their exterior lights, illuminating manicured lawns and expensive vehicles in driveways. Despite being so close to the sea, nearly every home boasted vibrant green shrubbery and towering cypress trees that arched over cobblestone pathways—meticulously maintained to withstand the corrosive salty air, a costly indulgence the Raos politicians gladly financed.

I continued along the freshly paved road, counting driveways and mentally logging vehicles that appeared, none of which were running or had anyone inside. Then, Luke's voice crackled clearly in my ear, "First floor clear." I jumped slightly at the sound and, keeping the binoculars in position, asked quietly, "Did you find anything?" I pressed the return button. "No, badging into the second floor," he replied.

"Confirm," I responded, clicking the line closed. Each house along the road seemed larger than the next, and at the very end sat a nondescript dark blue sedan with tinted windows. I narrowed my eyes and sidled up to the wall. It hadn't been there when we arrived earlier. It was just far enough away that even the binoculars could barely make out its windshield. Beneath the cover of night, it was nearly impossible to tell if someone was inside. I locked in, as still as a statue, holding my breath while I waited for any movement that might reveal information about the occupants. A lump of unease grew in my throat, but I pushed it aside.

"Pandora," Luke said through comms. "Here." I barely moved my hand to press the button, keeping the binoculars glued to my face and my eyes fixed on the sedan. "This ship is empty of everything except the few boxes we saw loaded over the last couple of hours." His voice was low and cautious as he relayed the information. My brows furrowed in concern.

"Empty?" I asked, inclining my chin as if it might help me peer through the car's tinted window I staked out. "There are some boxes filled with mining equipment and medical supplies, but that's it. There's no sign of nuclear materials anywhere."

A wave of worry crept up my spine as the earpiece clicked off. I paused, gears turning at record speed in my mind. If the materials weren't here, where were they?

Movement caught my attention in the sedan's windshield. The mirrored surface reflected the silver moonlight back at me, and my blood ran cold as I took a step back, my boot crunching the gravel beneath me. That wasn't just any reflection—it was the lens of a pair of binoculars, and suddenly, the world started to spin in slow motion as if gravity were shifting beneath me. I sprinted for the ladder as the car's headlights blazed on in the distance, lighting Moore Lane up like an inferno.

"Get out. We've been compromised." I hissed into the receiver as my boots gripped for purchase. No response, but I didn't have time to confirm that he heard me. It would inevitably slow me down. I had to get inside the ship. I didn't know who was in that car, but what I did know was the coincidence of missing shipment supplies and someone camping near the dock definitely didn't sit well with me. I finally reached the ladder, stowing the binoculars in my pack as swiftly as possible.

Setting one hand on the wall, I heaved my legs over in an arc and slid down the ladder rails without using the rungs, just like my father had taught me. A small shard of grief stabbed me in the heart at the thought, but I shoved it down and took off in a sprint toward the ship. My feet pounded against the wooden slats, and I prayed to the powers that be that there wasn't anyone out here to hear them.

Careening past the unconscious guard, I hurried up the ramp, my eyes glancing down at the water below, and instantly, I regretted it. The water churned several hundred feet below against the serrated rocks in enormous waves big enough to engulf an entire person. A shiver zinged up my spine, and I charged to the end of the ramp, not risking another peek down. I didn't need the mental image of my body smashed against those rocks.

I darted to the door Luke had slipped through, yanking the handle with force, praying it was still unlocked. The badge reader blinked red, rejecting my attempt, and I cursed, spinning around. In the distance, the sedan's headlights grew closer, and fear tightened its grip around my throat. Think, Pandora, you have to think. There had to be a back door somewhere around here.

"Luke?" I whispered sharply through comms, only getting static in reply. Alright, I'd have to do it myself then. I slid my pistol from its holster at my waist and bent into a crouch. I held it steady as I jumped from shadow to shadow, doing my best to be swift. I didn't turn to see if the sedan had finally reached the lot. I would be gone long before anyone reached the ship.

Pressing my shoulder into the wall, I peered around the corner, cleared it, and surged forward, finding a door without a badge reader on the backside of the ship. Their third foolish mistake—this door didn't have a badge reader but instead, a code reader. One that Mayra had hacked plenty of times before. Excellent.

I lifted my watch to my face. "Mayra," I spoke, and her figure illuminated in front of me in pale blue. "Pandora." She chimed, tilting her head sideways in inquiry. "Decrypt this door, please." My words spilled out hurried and garbled. "Decrypting now." She dinged in response before disappearing. The code box blinked once, then almost reluctantly, the door clicked open, and air whooshed out of my lungs in relief as I slipped inside, shutting it firmly behind me.

The ship's inside was nearly bare, with only metal sheathing covering the walls and plain grey tile lining the floors. The lighting was unhelpful as half the fluorescent bulbs were burnt out. Why would they use this ship if it was this broken down and needing to be decommissioned? I edged further down the hallway, quiet as a mouse as it arced into a U-shape that I couldn't see past.

"Luke." I hissed under my breath, my voice echoing off the walls and back into my ears. Pausing, I listened for any noise. Nothing. A sense of nagging dread ebbed with my pulse, and I forced my tensed shoulders to relax. All the training from the police academy came rushing back to me, and I locked in, going into detective mode.

Angling my shoulders, I moved down the hall, rolling through the balls of my feet to mask my footsteps. The only sound was my breath as I focused on inhaling steadily through my nose and clearing my mind of any thoughts. There was no room for thinking in the field—only action. The thinking was what got people killed, and in moments where every second counted, thinking might easily be a death sentence.

"Luke," I said with more indignation than the last time. Again, no response, and I ground my teeth, a door coming into view around the corner. I sidled up to it, pressing my ear to the metal. Not a sound came from inside.

My left hand lowered from my pistol grip to the door handle, but I left it aimed down the hall with my right. I turned the knob, and the door creaked open. I cringed at the sound and peered into the room. Empty other than a desk and a few beat-up foldable metal chairs. Something was definitely not right. I left the room, hurrying faster down the hallway to another door. I listened for a moment, then gingerly cracked it open, too.

Fear sank to the base of my stomach as I saw only a few cardboard boxes tucked away in the corner. I searched door after door, eight in total, only to find the entire hallway vacant and desolate. My pulse quickened as I reached the stairs to the second floor, and the realization hit me like a ton of bricks.

This was no longer a recon mission—this was a retrieval mission, and I was racing the clock to find Luke and get out before it was too late. This was never the ship they intended to use. No, this was a carefully fabricated facade luring us into a trap. I didn't want to think of the numerous amounts of outcomes that were possible if caught.

I slowed my breathing and flipped the channel over in my ear. "Ivy," I kept my eyes up as I talked into the earpiece. "What is going on, Pandora? We haven't heard from you in over ten minutes." Her voice raised in inflection with apparent worry.

"Change of plans," I turned to glance back down the hallway, ensuring I wasn't being followed. "What do you mean change of plans?" She clipped her voice rising in the back of her throat in the familiar way it always did when she was stressed. "I need evacuation. Get to the rendezvous point."

"Pandora, tell me right now what—" But I flipped channels back, cutting her transmission off. She knew her job, and in that moment, I just had to trust that she would do what she promised. The stairs reached a landing and proceeded towards the right as I followed them up, pushing on. There was only one outcome I was willing to allow, finding Luke and getting the hell off this ship.

A high-pitched screech of metal against metal coursed down the second-floor hallway, causing every hair on my scalp to stand on end. I froze in place, my pistol at the ready, as my thumbs began to shake.

"Pandora." An eerie voice filtered down the hall, and my pupils dilated at the noise. I was no longer on offense. It was time to play defense. Slinking up to the wall, I flattened myself into a shadow, willing myself to become a part of it. "Come out, come out wherever you are," it said, and I tensed. The voice was male and taunting, like he was playing with me. "Come out, or your little friend Detective Nesnah meets his demise."

And as if summoned to me himself purely by my fear, what felt like a hand caressed my mind, and I was transported into the room within it. He stood before me, his eyes tearing into mine, blue on green. He reached a hand up to cup my cheek, and I instinctively reached to place mine over his. *"You need to go,"* he said, and I blinked. *"And leave you?"*

"That was the plan."

"That was your plan."

"Don't play games with me right now, Pandora." Luke's jaw

tensed, and he pinched my chin under his thumb. "*Get out.*" And before I could argue, the connection went dark.

I shook my head as I reeled back into the real world. To hell with his plan.

"Come and get him!" he shouted, and the noise of frantic struggling and something heavy being dragged echoed down the hall. I burst off the wall, running for the only door the sound came from. I grabbed the doorknob and turned, but it didn't budge. I slammed my shoulder into it once, twice, and it held.

Fuck.

I stepped back and took a deep steadying breath. I shifted my weight onto one leg, lifted the other above my hips, and drove the heel of my boot into the handle. Hard.

WHAM.

The door burst open, crashing against the wall with force as I rushed in, pistol raised. Immediately, I was met with a cold wind rushing through a portal opened at the top of a red ladder, dead center in the room. I raised my arm, shielding my face as my auburn braid whipped around my shoulders. The cold wind stung my eyes and cheeks as I glanced around the room in realization. This was the ship's control room. They had been watching us the entire time.

Surveillance monitors covered the whole back wall, displaying live feeds of nearly every angle aboard the ship and on the dock—including the roof where we had sat for several hours before boarding. The last strand of hope sank in my chest. I shoved chairs out of my way with a loud screech and bolted for the ladder, praying it wasn't too late. Every rung dug into my palms as I climbed inch by inch until my head rose above the top—and an evil face glared down at me.

"Well, hello, lovely," he drawled. "So wonderful of you to join us." His voice felt like hot coals dragged across an open wound as I inched my way onto the roof, standing before him. The wind picked up, carrying the freezing, salty air of the Pearl Sea over the top of the ship, and I blinked against the assault, steadying myself to avoid falling hundreds of feet to my death.

He was just as terrifying up close as he had been at Fritz Manor, and I tensed at the sight. He looked like a walking corpse—pale, ashen skin, gray distended veins, and greasy black hair slicked back from his skull—but his eyes were the most horrifying of all.

Just like in the experiment file photo, his pale gray irises lifted to meet mine, pupils so dilated the color nearly disappeared into the void. Black streaks stretched from the injection mark on his neck all the way to his chin, and I couldn't help but wonder how excruciating his transition must've been. He was the only one who had survived it.

My gaze drifted to Luke, heartbreakingly still behind him. His eyes blazed with frustration, and his arms hung at his sides—until I looked closer. No. They weren't relaxed. He was using them to balance—teetering on the very edge of the ship's roof. My breath caught, mouth parting in a silent gasp, but Luke gently shook his head, pleading with me not to speak.

Markian's teeth gleamed under the moonlight as he casually gestured his pistol at me. "I would put that down if I were you," he said, rolling his eyes. My gaze snapped back to him, and he inclined his head with a lazy warning—as if he wouldn't say it again. "Now, detective," he said, blinking those soulless eyes. I slowly crouched and set my pistol on the roof, then rose again, hands trembling. "The blades, too." I flashed him a snarl but obeyed, placing them beside my pistol, their iridescent edges catching the light. My heart hammered in my throat, every beat sharp and unnatural.

"Now," he grinned, teeth sharp as tacks, "we can play."

Chapter 49

He teetered, and with every gust of wind, I held my breath. He wouldn't—he couldn't—go overboard. I willed gravity itself to stop existing if it meant keeping him from falling hundreds of feet into the dark, turbulent water below. In a way, he was a force of nature, but the Pearl Sea didn't care. It would swallow him whole and spit his body back out against the tan, serrated cliffs without hesitation. With every painful breath, I forced myself to calm down.

"You look as if you've seen a ghost," Markian's voice cut through the wind, snapping my eyes back to him. "Well, excuse me if you look like a walking corpse. I couldn't quite tell the difference," I snapped sarcastically. His brows pulled together, and he sighed. "I quite like my new look. But what I like even more..." He grinned, and even his teeth looked gray and lifeless. "...is my new power."

"And what power is that, exactly?" I lifted my chin toward him, though my hands stayed up, palms out, keeping him in my line of sight. "The power of a thousand stars. A power people kill for." I fought to keep my voice steady, "It is a power people have killed for, Markian." I said his name, and his eyes narrowed.

"It's not yours to take. It's not yours to wield." My voice lowered, gentle, almost pleading—like I could reason with a madman.

"Remain calm," Luke's voice drifted through my mind, but his

body stayed rigid, unmoving.

Markian ran a pale hand along the slide of his pistol. "It is mine. I took it. And in my death, I was reborn—with power no human has had before. I am the first." His grin twisted. "A pioneer, Danny called me. He told me I would be his most trusted. He promised a life I could never have imagined." A flicker of something—regret?—flared behind his eyes, but it vanished just as quickly, replaced by cold fury.

"I am a nobody. I come from no one and nothing," he said, his voice low and unflinching. "I was homeless, chained to my debts, starving, when he came to me. At that kind of low, even death feels like mercy. But instead, Danny offered me a deal. In exchange for participating in a grueling experiment—if I survive—I'll never have to wonder where I'll sleep again. I get a job, a purpose. For once in my life, I'm finally someone. Someone with power. Physical power." His tone shifted as he stepped forward and stooped, snatching my blades and pistol off the roof.

Luke's eyes tracked every movement, his jaw twitching with tension.

"Humans no longer have to bow to other species with more power. With our technology, we're already the most advanced. And now, with magic? We'll be unstoppable." His grin was feral and my heart felt heavy—like it was filling with lead.

"The participants were all going to die soon anyway," Markian continued. "Most were homeless like I was, living off scraps and pitiful donations from prudes who just want to pat themselves on the back once a year. Why not give them one last shot?" He lifted an eyebrow at me, angling the iridescent blades near my face.

"Why not?" I repeated, incredulous. My arms dropped to my sides. "Because humans aren't meant to hold that kind of power. I'm not meant to hold that kind of power. Humans are already dangerous enough without magic. With it, we're not even comparable to the other species—we'd wipe them out without lifting a finger." I shook my head sharply and my auburn braid whipped across my back throwing me slightly off balance. I swung my arms to recover, planting my feet again glancing at Luke. His eyes widened for a beat before he exhaled, relaxing when I found my footing.

"When I was a young boy," Markian began, his voice almost wistful, "I dreamed of a universe where only humans existed. Where we controlled the narrative. The power. No more worrying about the Gaythe or the Nephrians or their endless wars." He blinked, his gray eyes sharpening with intent. "And to think—I might be the one to lead that revolution." He grinned, sick with triumph and I scowled.

"What a cowardly revolution," I spat. He clucked his tongue, shaking his head slowly, "You still don't see it, do you?"

"See what?" I growled, my fingernails biting into my palms. The most sinister of grins furled along his face, "Danny claims that with your power, they can take over the entire universe. Humans to rule over them all."

I was nearly vibrating with anger as I took a step toward Markian, "Over my dead body will he use me as a catalyst for death and destruction." He didn't even flinch at my movement as he chuckled deep in his throat, "Oh, but it's already too late."

"Pandora!"

I whipped my head around at the sound of my name in a voice I knew all too well—my father. He stood just over the hatch in the roof, his eyes flicking between Luke and me. He was wearing a gray suit and white shirt, his navy tie snapping in the wind. Every fiber in my body screamed at me to run—to get as far away from this man, this traitor, as I could. My very soul burned at the sight of him.

"You," I hissed, baring my teeth. "Pandora, please," he said, taking a step forward, "Just come with me, and I can explain everything."

"Come with you?!" I screamed into the wind as it whipped my hair across my face. "Yes, please, Pandora," he pleaded quietly. "Why should I trust anything that comes out of your mouth right now? You've lied to me my entire life—about everything. I looked up to you, practically worshipped the ground you walked on, only to find out you're a cold-blooded killer and conspirator."

Something flickered in his eyes at my words—hatred? Surprise? Guilt? I didn't know, and I didn't care. "I will never come with you, and I will never trust you again," I hissed. Gone was the emotion and softness I once associated with him. "You misunderstand, Pandora," he said, his expression smoothing into a placated calm, "You either come willingly, or you'll be forced. The choice is yours."

"I'd rather die where I stand," I hissed, and he shook his head slowly. "Wrong choice." Markian laughed, and before I could react, he slammed the butt of his pistol into the back of my head.

Pain exploded in my skull, and I dropped like a sack of stones, my shoulder thudding hard against the roof. I scrambled to get up, but my father moved faster, yanking me up by my bicep and pinning my arms behind my back. I thrashed, kicking at his shins with the heel of my boot.

"I wouldn't if I were you," he growled into my ear. "You are no longer my daughter, it seems—and Danny would love nothing more than for me to end your life right here."

A cold shiver raced down my spine.

"You're nothing more than a coward," I spat back at him, tears brimming my eyes, but I stopped struggling. Markian watched us like a child in a candy store, delighted by the unfolding chaos. "Lovely," he said, clapping his hands once. "Now that we've taken care of that—what should I do with him?" He jerked a thumb toward Luke, still teetering at the roof's edge. "I don't care, Markian," my father sighed. "Get rid of him."

Markian's teeth gleamed as he smiled, brazen and cruel, before turning and stomping toward Luke.

"No!" I shrieked and started fighting my father's hold again. "If you don't cut it out, I'll have no other choice than to bind your hands," he seethed as his fingers wrapped tighter around my wrists. "Don't do it!" I screamed. "Let him go, and I'll go with you! I'll do whatever you want." My breath came ragged and sharp, my lungs burning with every intake.

"My, my, that's one hell of a deal. Anything?" Markian purred as he casually drifted closer to Luke. "Anything!" I shouted in a panic, my heart racing. Markian tilted his head to the side like he was contemplating letting him go, "As interesting as that could go, I believe that deal is offered far too late." Then he turned, lifted one of his boots, and kicked him squarely in the chest.

His body arched backward, feet soaring into the air as he plunged off the ship's roof, and I roared into the night sky before everything abruptly faded to dark.

Chapter 50

I didn't know how much time had passed—only that my head throbbed. I sat up, and the pulsing in my temple turned into a full-blown pounding. I winced, raising my fingers to my head as if that might somehow ease the pain. My eyes blinked against the darkness as my memory returned in crashing waves. Markian. My father. The shipment. It had all been a trap.

Luke.

I reached for the bond within my mind, only to find an empty recess where his door should sit. My heart plummeted to the pit of my stomach. Luke was dead. They killed him. Panic rushed through me as I scanned my surroundings.

I was in what looked like a cell—but definitely not one from Precinct 12. I'd never been in this building before. Nothing about it was familiar. It was bathed in darkness, the only light trickling in from a small portal window in the cell door. The walls, floor, and ceiling were made of sleek, polished metal. Aside from a toilet in the corner and a thin, worn mattress across from it, the room was completely bare.

I was still in my long-sleeved shirt and pants, but my boots, belt, and weapons were gone. My bare feet stung against the cold metal floor as I attempted to stand. My body shook with the forced movement, but I grit my teeth and steadied myself to search for a way out. Four small panels, each only a couple of inches wide, sat flush in the middle of the room, forming the corners of a square.

I dropped to my hands and knees and crawled over to them. In the darkness, my marred arms seemed to vanish beneath the shadows, and I fumbled at the seams, struggling to see anything in front of me clearly.

Finally, I pressed my fingers into one, and it popped up with a faint click, revealing a metal loop roughly an inch wide. I furrowed my brows and pressed the others. The same result—each panel revealed a single loop. I dug my fingers into one of the holes, searching for a mechanism or latch—but found nothing. Frustrated, I snapped the panels closed and rose slowly to my feet.

I swayed slightly, shaking my head to clear the haze. There was no mirror in the room, but judging by the swelling on both my temple and the back of my head, I figured I'd been knocked out—likely leaving a nice bruise in both spots. I took two large steps forward and reached the back of the cell.

I brushed my palm against the wall—it was cool to the touch, just like the floor. Probably metal. Aluminum, most likely, since that was what was used in our standard jail cells. But none of the rooms I knew were completely enclosed like this one. I dragged my hand along the wall until I reached the corner.

Crossing the seam, I continued along the second wall—this one to the right of the door—then over the next junction and stopped at the door itself. There were no hinges on this side. Just a rectangle cut directly into the wall. The door must have swung outward, the hinges hidden on the other side, sealing in whoever they wanted locked away.

The portal glass was two panes thick. I was tall, but even so, I had to lift onto my toes to peer through it. The hallway beyond reminded me of a hospital—plain white walls and glossy white tile. Absolutely no one was in sight. In fact, aside from the sterile walls and the endless tile, there was nothing visible from this angle. I rapped my fingers against the glass, trying to get someone's attention. Silence.

I pressed my ear to the door, hoping to hear anything—footsteps, voices, even a hum of machinery—but again, silence. I loosened the tie securing my braid and ran my fingers through my scalp, trying to relieve the pressure it left behind. The memory of standing on the ship, watching Luke's body pitch off the roof, crashed back into me, dragging a wave of emotion in its wake.

Fear welled up in my chest, tightening like a vice—but I closed my eyes and took slow, steady breaths. Panicking wouldn't help me. And it certainly wouldn't change the outcome of his death. My heart stuttered. No. What I needed now was a way out of this cell.

I lifted my face to the ceiling—most of it bathed in shadow since very little light made it into the room, save for the portal window in the door. Like the rest of the room, the ceiling was metal, but about twenty feet above my head, a black dome camera sat in the center. A small green light blinked at its edge—the only sign it was recording. I narrowed my eyes at it. Of course I was being watched. I returned my gaze to the door. Raising my hand, I knocked on the metal surface, the sound echoing off the walls.

"Hello?" I called, then waited a few seconds, straining for any reply. I looked back up at the dome camera on the ceiling. "The least you could do is tell me why I'm here," I quipped in its direction. It didn't respond—obviously, it was an inanimate object—and I huffed at myself for expecting anything else. I banged a little louder on the door with my fist. "Hey!" I shouted, knocking again.

Suddenly, a face appeared in the window, and I jumped

back, startled. His eyes were dark, pupils nearly swallowing them whole, and his shaggy blonde hair puffed around his ears beneath a gray service cap with a black brim. He was pale—extremely pale—and he didn't blink as he stared at me through the glass. "Why am I here?" I asked, my voice sharper and more defiant than it probably should be, considering I was locked inside a metal, impenetrable box. He still didn't blink, but the lock mechanism on the door clicked, and I watched as it pulled outward, swinging into the hallway like a ship's flight door.

He stepped into the doorway, his body blocking the hallway light and casting me in shadow. His uniform matched the cap, and even in the dim lighting, I could tell it was the same one Markian wore at Fritz Manor—steel gray with buttons down the front, matching slacks, and shiny black boots. The pleat on the trouser legs was crisp, even as they draped over his knees, the hem brushing his shoes. The cuffs of his long-sleeved shirt were tight around his clenched fists, and the sharp collar jutted toward his hard-set chin.

Taking a step back, I raised one of my hands in his direction. "Don't touch me," I hissed, and he took a large sigh. "I won't touch you unless you do something stupid," he hissed back at me, venom dripping from his tone. I blanched, stepping another foot behind me, but watched as he sidestepped and another figure moved into the door. The salt and pepper hair was the dead giveaway, but my heart lurched in my chest as soon as I realized who it was.

"Pandora," Harrison said softly, his eyes lifting to meet mine. I stood frozen in place as I watched him take another step into the cell. "You," I whispered, mainly to myself, as I gathered the shreds of dignity I had left and lifted my chin indignantly. The blonde officer took several strides to the corner of the room, turning his face towards us and clasping his hands behind his back. He stood silent, in wait. "Now," Harrison said, placing his hands in his pockets, "You have two options and *only* two options."

My eyes flickered from him to the officer and back, but I didn't respond. *Stay calm.*

He tilted his head some and inhaled a sharp breath through his nose. "You are going to tell me *exactly* where Odina and the rest of the Gaythe are on Gayle, how you obtained your power, and where the rest of the Element X is located," he said calmly. I counted to ten in my head, the numbers blurring together as I stared back at him.

He didn't move, didn't flinch as he stared at his daughter, his only living daughter, but I knew that was no longer who I was. I may have been his daughter in blood, but I was no longer his daughter in soul. No, I was merely a pawn in a power war. Just a single, small pawn with no power, no sway in the outcome of thousands of lives, both human and Gaythe. No, if he wanted that information, he would have to take it, and even then, I would let that information *die* with me rather than let him have it.

"And if I refuse?" My throat felt tight and dry as I asked the question because I already knew the answer. My father was one of the most decorated interrogators on our planet. He could make even the most tight-lipped criminals spill their guts at his feet, and at that thought, I swallowed the rock in my throat. He *wouldn't* break me.

He thought momentarily, the muscle in his temple feathering with impatience. It had always done that, even when I was a little girl creating a mess in the house. It was his tell, of sorts, that he was furious but reigning it in. "If you don't comply, we will work the information out of you. Don't make me do that to you, Pandora." Fine, if he planned on interrogating me, then I would make him suffer, push his buttons, and make him lose every sense of self-control he had.

Game on.

"You can try." My voice had no warmth, and as soon as the words left my mouth, his eyes darkened, and he moved sideways, letting another person into the room. This time, it was Markian. His black eyes landed on me. He wasn't wearing the grey cap that his partner in the corner wore, but merely the steel gray uniform that it seemed he never took off. His black hair was slicked back out of his face, but my eyes drifted to the large metal chair with hooks on the ends of all four legs that he carried in with him.

I crouched, backing up towards the furthest wall. My very skin prickled at the sight of him, and I could *feel* his power rolling off of him like billows of steam in the stuffy cell air. He strode to the middle of the room as the door slammed shut in place behind him. Locked in, I was locked in with these *animals.*

My heart started to quicken, its steady beat growing more erratic as I watched him set the chair down, stoop to the floor, and open the four panels I had examined earlier. He pulled the chair forward, the metal *screeching* along the floor. I clamped my hands over my ears at the sudden noise, watching wide-eyed as the hooks on the bottom of the legs snapped into the loops built into the holes in the floor. This was not a regular cell. This was a custom-made *interrogation* room. He used the seat of the chair to hoist himself to a stand, then backed up, facing me at all times. Well, at least he took me as a serious threat, I supposed.

"Sit," Harrison said gruffly. "No," I responded defiantly. He turned his face to Markian, who never took his eyes off me. "Place her in the chair." He gave the command, and I pressed myself further into the wall as he moved quickly with inhuman speed. I barely had time to blink before his hands grasped my shoulders, and I was heaved up in the air, my bare feet dangling below me.

I kicked towards him, landing a blow to his chest but hardly doing any damage without my boots on. I twisted my shoulders, fighting his grip, but my body barely moved as he calmly carried me over to the chair. He plopped me down on the chair, the cold metal surface stinging against any exposed skin. Markian produced a pair of silver shackles from his pocket, locking first my wrists to the arms and then my ankles to the legs. I bared my teeth at him, growling in my throat. He didn't flinch as he looked up at me, his elbow resting on the knee that wasn't braced against the floor.

"Now, now. Haven't you heard not to bite the hand that feeds you?" He quipped in my direction, and I snapped my teeth in his direction. He just chuckled, straightening quickly and returning to stand by the door.

Harrison, *my father*, took a few leisurely strides to the side of the chair. He gazed down at me sidelong as his chest faced the back wall. "You have one last chance to tell me everything, or so help me, Pandora; I will be forced to cleave you in two." He said it gently, too gently. Like coaxing a wild animal into a trap with bait, but I knew that trick. I had watched him interrogate criminals my entire life. I knew his plays and his games, and in this scenario, it was best to keep my mouth shut. I kept my eyes forward, not risking a glance at him, the *man* who raised me. The silence that followed itched my brain, and I fidgeted my fingers against the chair's metal arms.

"I cannot kill you," he began sliding his arms out of his gray suit jacket and slinging it over his arm. He turned on his heel and marched toward the door. I watched wide-eyed as he handed Markian his jacket and returned to look at me. He started rolling his white button-up sleeves all the way to the elbow, folding them in neat sections. "You are far too powerful and useful to kill outright." He continued, and my nose scrunched at being described as a weapon of war. He paused as he finished rolling up his second sleeve. "Where is Odina?" he asked.

"Fuck you." I hissed, jolting my body forward, the shackles clinking loudly. No reaction. "Where are the Gaythe?" His voice was even toned, serene almost. I snapped my mouth shut, leaning back against the chair. If he wanted the information, I certainly wasn't just going to give it to him. No, no. He would have to work very hard to break me, and even then, I would never turn on my people, on Odina. They had trusted me and had shown me their city. No, it was my burden to bear, even in *death*.

Harrison let out a calculated sigh as if to express his dissatisfaction with the inconvenience of this interrogation. "What? You just thought you'd come in here and scare me with shackles and mutant guards, and I'd spew information on a species that you're trying to *murder*?" His eyes darkened, and his jaw tensed in the dim light.

"Oh, there's no *scaring* you. I had meant what I said when I said I would cleave you in two. You will remain here, chained to this chair, until you decide to tell me the information I ask of you. You will not be given food, only water, although we will see how much water you want after today." He said roughly and waved his hand at Markian, who turned as the door clicked and swung open again.

He disappeared somewhere beyond it, returning with a black rag and a bucket of water. My chest tightened at the sight, constricting my racing heart. There wasn't a chance in hell that either of those items were for any kind of legal interrogation. No, this was a full-on prisoner-of-war treatment orchestrated by none other than my father himself. "Where is Odina?" he asked again as the door slammed shut. "I don't know where she is." I lied, and his chin tilted in my direction, a sinister smile forming on his face. "Pandora, I raised you. You can't lie to me."

"Watch me." I ground through my teeth, and he shook his head. "Play this game how you want, Pandora. The outcome won't change." He said, taking the rag from Markian as they both advanced towards me. I stiffened against the chair, shaking the shackles against my wrists, but they hardly moved. "If you fight it, it will get worse." He said before throwing the rag over my face and pushing my forehead back with his palm. His hand gripped my temples, and I fought to push my head back up.

"Where is Odina?" he asked again, and I pressed my mouth into a line underneath the rag. I couldn't see anything beyond the dark fabric, only feeling his hand over my face and the cold chair against my skin. I kicked my feet, trying to find an ankle to jam my toe into, but the only thing I could touch was the metal floor. His hand shifted some, and I heard his breathing against my left ear. "Tell me where Odina and the Gaythe are, and I will release you." His breath brushed over my shoulder, an ominous vow.

A lie, a blatant lie. There was absolutely no way they would release me.

"Go to hell." I hissed, and I sensed his face leave my side. "Wrong answer." He said, and before I could smart back, water was dumped over my face. The fabric sealed itself to my face, covering my nose, mouth, and eyes, and I fought for air, kicking my legs frantically while lashing out with my arms. He waited several seconds before he finally removed the rag from my face.

I snapped my head forward, choking aggressively on water. My auburn hair, now soaked, stuck to my skin across my face and neck, but I willed myself to be silent and endure it. He merely blinked at me, watching my response. I lifted my chin in anger toward my father. Something flickered in his eyes, pride? Respect? I didn't care. It was misplaced anyway.

"Where is Odina?" His voice was like a broken record, repeating the same question over and over again. I didn't move, but my pulse hammered in my throat as I knew what was coming next. He waited hardly even ten seconds before whipping the wet rag over my face and lurching my neck back against the chair. "Where is Odina?"

I thrashed my hands and felt pain against my wrists, but I ignored it and waited for the next wave. Water rushed over my face, sealing my airways again. This time, I *inhaled* the water, and something shifted. Oxygen returned to my brain, and I stopped fighting as hard. I had forgotten that I could breathe underwater, and in that moment there was nothing more I wanted to do than kiss the ground the Gaythe walked on for their inherent gifts they had given me. I stopped fighting, letting the water cascade into me. Then, as quickly as it had been applied, the rag was removed from my face, but I didn't lift my head. I left the water in my nose and throat and moved my gaze to my father, who was now a beautiful shade of white.

"Impossible." He hissed, throwing the rag to the floor. I turned and spit the water right in his face, releasing a soul-wrenching cackle as the water poured over my bared teeth. "It should be, but it isn't." I laughed, turning to Markian, who narrowed his eyes at me. "Shall I go get the other supplies?" He asked my father, who took the back of his hand and wiped the water from his face. "Yes." He growled, then stomped forward, stopping right in front of the chair. He placed a hand on the metal behind my neck, leaning down just a few inches from my face.

Markian disappeared behind my father, and I heard the door open and shut again before he reappeared at his side. Harrison's eye twitched with irritation as he leveled his face with mine. "You are going to tell me everything you know." He whispered, jabbing a finger into my chest. I smiled maniacally, then reared my head back as far as it would go and whipped it forward right into his nose.

Stars burst in the corners of my vision as I was dazed by the strike, but it hit true to my aim as he careened back, roaring as blood poured from his broken nose. Bright red stained the front of his white shirt and I couldn't help myself, a smile curling up my face. "You think this is funny? You think this is a game?" He shouted at me and I shook my head, the motion making me dizzy. "Of course not. War is never a game." I retorted and he cracked his knuckles. "You would rather protect the people that wanted you dead, wanted your mother dead than your own father?" His brows knit together as he took the new equipment from Markian's hands. "I'd rather protect the innocent people, yes." I said, raising the tone in my voice.

He didn't entertain my statement, only advanced back to the chair, wrapping what seemed to be thin metal wire around my wrists and ankles. The wires were decently long, and attached to a big black box with buttons on the front and a screen with numbers that lit up in the shadows of the room. It basked Markian's pale face in eerie green light as he set the box roughly ten feet away from me.

The sound of steady drips of water trailing off the ends of my drenched hair grounded me and I took a deep breath, waiting. "I will ask again," Harrison started, but I interrupted him, "You can ask as many times as you like, I will never give you the information you're asking for." I whispered, my voice low and deadly. "So be it then." He backed up a few steps out of the growing puddle beneath me, then crossed his arms over his chest.

"Charge." He said and Markian pressed a large red button on the control face of the black box. A loud whirring sounded and the hairs on my scalp and arms stood on end. I was as tense as a spring board, waiting. "Where is Odina?" He asked. "She is nowhere, she is dead." I smiled sarcastically and he tilted his head at me, "No she isn't. I would know." He didn't move his eyes from mine as he opened his mouth to give the order, "Shock."

Pain erupted in my hands and legs, traveling up my skin. My head whipped back, and a scream erupted from me, loud and guttural. This was far, far worse than being waterboarded. The pain increased as heat built along my skin, my fingers digging into the metal arms of the chair as my voice cascaded off every wall, slamming back into my body with such force that I felt I was inside an erupting volcano. Spit flew out of my mouth, and my body vibrated with pain. Then, as quickly as it had started, it ended. My head hung down, and I panted large agonizing breaths into my lungs. "Now we're getting somewhere," Harrison said, and I heard his shoes scuff against the floor. I didn't dare look up. I didn't wish to give him the satisfaction of seeing me in pain.

"Where is Odina?" He was starting to sound like a broken record infinitely on repeat. I lifted my eyes just enough for him to see them. "Go to hell." I whispered before lowering my eyes to the floor again. "Again." He said, and pain erupted just as the first time.

I shook violently against the chains, the metal rattling loudly in my ears. The singeing pain blasted up my hands and ankles towards my scalp as the ringing began in my ears. It started low but increased in pitch and intensity over time. How long had they been electrocuting me? Seconds? Minutes? Hours? My body no longer felt my own, and I could no longer hear my screaming through the cacophony of bells reeling through my skull. Then again, it stopped.

Unable to stifle it, a moan released from me as my head whipped forward again. I fought for breath, the feeling like swallowing fire as Harrison's shoes paced in front of me. The ringing subsided as the tapping of his footsteps echoed through the room, and I blinked rapidly, attempting to clear my head. "You're a monster." I moaned, barely loud enough to be audible, but he heard it and stopped dead in his tracks. "Well, that we can agree on," he said low before continuing to pace. "Why did you do it?" I lifted my chin again to gauge his reaction to the question. Unsurprisingly, he was unfazed.

"You're going to have to be more specific than that." He muttered, facing me, his arms crossed. "Why did you kill her?" I asked, licking my lips, the dry skin sticking to my tongue, "Why did you kill mom?" My voice was gritty and raw against my throat. He tilted his head at me, cool, calm, and calculating, nothing like the man I called my father. He tapped his toe on the floor and turned to glance at Markian and the second officer, neither of whom were paying me much mind apart from waiting for orders.

"Your mother," he began, and I swallowed, watching, waiting for answers. "Was one of the most cunning people I had ever met." His voice shifted some as if digging deep within his tainted soul for a long-lost memory. "When I was dispatched to Gayle by the Liarta government to gain intel on Element X before you were even born, I was told to find the leader of the Gaythe and dispose of her. I met Odina and Esme and immediately knew they were both incredibly dangerous. It was a matter of the safety of all the planets, not just Liarta, to eliminate that threat. Under the guise of intel of other interplanetary species, I stayed for months studying them, determining who was the leader and who was the Queen. But your mother and her sister were very intelligent. Neither rightfully claimed the title and they were always within earshot of each other. They were careful and calculated. I kept my distance, only observing, and then one day, I was approached by Odina." He paused. The only sound was my heavy breathing as I watched him still. "She claimed that I was her fated mate,"

My breath caught in my throat, but I remained silent, the chains digging mercilessly into my wrists and ankles. The metal burned against my skin, but I bit my tongue. This was not the worst I would endure. No, these were merely physical wounds. The wounds that lurked deeper *beneath* the skin were far more painful, far more raw, and exposed. "But when your mother claimed the title of Queen of the Gaythe, I denied Odina and took your mother with me instead."

I bristled, my eyes widening as I looked at him. "What do you mean she claimed the title?" I hissed, the detective gears whirring at light speed in my mind. He leaned forward so close our foreheads nearly touched as his eyes darkened. "She claimed she was the Queen and sacrificed herself. Somehow, she knew it would be a one-way mission coming to Liarta and that I would stop at nothing to gain every ounce of information on Element X that I could, including enslaving the *supposed* Queen of the Gaythe herself."

I suddenly felt so sick to my stomach, nausea roiling in its base. "She didn't love you," I said out loud, the final pieces of the puzzle clicking into place. "She didn't love you. Instead, she sacrificed herself and her life to save her sister, the *real* Queen of the Gaythe."

"Yes." His jaw twitched at the admission. "So why did you wait to kill her? Why didn't you kill her when you found out?" I asked, anger building in my chest as I leaned off the chair, the chains against my wrists digging deeper into the marred skin. "I didn't *know* she wasn't the Queen until after you were born. After I had fallen in love with her and built a life with her."

"You expect me to believe you were in love with her, then killed her?" I ground out through my teeth. "I don't expect you to believe anything, but it's the truth. She gave me no other choice," he hissed. "We always have a choice," I hissed, and he just stared at me blank-faced. "I discovered she was stealing confidential files from my office on our Elemental X experiments, intending to frame me."

"Saying she was framing you insinuates that you weren't committing treason in the first place." I retorted. "What you call treason, I call loyalty to my species, Pandora. The Gaythe do not deserve the power they wield, no more than anyone else does. It is so much more complicated than you could ever imagine. We are at a critical point in our evolution, and if we don't advance our civilization, it will cease to exist." He shook his head roughly, his salt and pepper hair flicking over his forehead. "The Nephrians are on a salvation mission, attempting to take over Gayle and every other planet in this system. They hadn't accounted for the core of their planet to freeze, essentially killing everything on the surface. Now, their species will die if they don't scramble to find a habitable planet."

I shifted under the chains as I started to shiver, my body losing heat after being drenched with water. "Why are you telling me this?" I asked as I leaned my head against the chair, my wet hair cascading over the back in large clumps. I could still hear the steady drips of water on the floor. "Because if they succeed in taking Gayle, we will be next." He said roughly and leaned forward, placing his hand on the arm of the chair. He eyed me as I pressed my mouth into a thin line. "It is for the greater good of our species that we find a way to end them." He murmured. "At the expense of my species?" I whispered, and he blinked.

"You are just as much human as you are, Gaythe." He clipped and spit hit me on the cheek. I peeled my lips back over my teeth, "So was Amy." I hissed and my eyes flicked water on my cheeks as I blinked taking him in, *all* of him in. The tense look in his eyes, his hard-set jaw, he was so delicately balanced on the end of his leash that any tug would cause him to explode. Danny had been right. He owned my dad. It was far too late, and he was far too deep into the orchestra of destruction. He couldn't dig his way out, only dig his way down, which meant anyone who had anything remotely dirty on Danny or Fritz Co. was a loose end, even his family.

"*You killed Amy.*" I whispered, the clattering of my teeth vibrating through my voice. He bristled, his eyes widening some. "How did you—?"

"That was one hell of a bluff—you had me believing this whole time that Mom committed suicide, and if Luke hadn't approached me with her autopsy, you probably would have gone to your grave with the knowledge you had been the one to end her life," I paused, and he swallowed. "But to kill your daughter," my face pinched as emotion got the better of me.

"*Diabolical,*" I whispered.

He stilled in front of me, and no one made a sound. Markian and the other officer stayed locked in place. Every breath felt like inhaling smoke, burning itchy air coiling in my lungs, then was released over and over again. I stopped counting the seconds of us staring at each other and waited for what I knew was coming. I wasn't any more special than Amy had been.

In fact, I was far more dangerous, and I had discovered far more than she had. The briefcase that had been manhandled at her murder scene had held those experimental files—I was sure of it. "She took those files, the ones that you left on her desk when you took them back to Fritz Co., and you offered her hush money, didn't you?"

No response.

"Then, when she refused to take it, Danny force-wired it to her account, and you killed her to make it look like she was committing a slight against Fritz Company." The muscle in his jaw twitched and I vibrated slightly as I tilted my head to the side, unable to control the shivering.

"*You* left the note in her briefcase, and *you* left the note in my house to scare me into stopping investigating her case." He straightened away from me, and his eyes became someone I had never seen before, but I kept going. "You have to *stop*. You have to convince Danny to stop. If we continue down this path, it will be interplanetary and interspecies war."

"It was too late," he whispered, looking away from me, and I knew he was gone. There was no stopping what was in motion, at least not from this chair. This wasn't just an interrogation. My heart dropped as I realized if they couldn't get the information they needed from me, this was also going to be an execution. Once again, he had lied.

"You will always take everyone down around you. Regardless of who they are to you. Regardless if they beg you to stop." I was so cold that my lips were beginning to go numb, and I could no longer feel my hands and feet. Thankfully, the shivering had stopped, but I knew that was because my core was too low of a temperature for my body to attempt to warm it back up. I was going to die here.

"Everything has aligned for this very moment. It is too late to stop what is in motion. There is always war, Pandora. We will never be enough to stop it. You have to choose what side you want to die on. What story you'll narrate. There will always be a higher power that levels the others. I will always choose the greater good for humanity. Even if that means losing you," he said. "Even if that means *killing* me," I said in correction. "Yes." Was all he replied.

Silence echoed through the walls, and I closed my eyes. "You have one last chance, Pandora, or we will leave you here to die," he said quietly. "Where are Odina and the Gaythe?" I kept my eyes closed and didn't respond, but I heard the shuffling of shoes and equipment being moved. The wires dangled against my wrists, and I knew Markian was poised to give the final shock. If this was how I went, so be it then. Let my last moment be protecting the lives of the innocent Gaythe they meant to slaughter.

"*Burn in hell*," I muttered under my breath. "I anticipate you'll welcome me at the gate when I arrive." My father's voice bit back before the current struck through my body, and I ceased to exist.

Chapter 51

The world was dark and cold as I forced open my eyes against the flashing white light. If this was hell, it was definitely not as warm as I had anticipated. The smell of singed skin drifted up to me as I attempted to move my body.

Pain erupted everywhere, and my head throbbed as I fought to lift it off the chair. The interrogation room. I was still in the interrogation room; I wasn't dead yet, but I soon would be if I didn't find a way out. The room was even darker than before, the only light coming through the portal flashing in my vision. I squinted against it. They must have been security lights of some kind, but that was the least of my problems right now. I looked at the camera on the ceiling above me. The green indicator light was off.

Scrunching my eyebrows together, I looked back out the portal, my hearing slowly coming back to me. Indeed, an alarm was going off in the hallway, but no other sound came. No rushing footsteps, no shadows crossing over the portal. Just the shrill noise of an alarm on repeat. My head felt heavy and foggy, like I was swimming in a sedative as I leaned forward to assess the situation. The pain sharpened, and I hissed, taking in my wounds.

The wires were no longer attached to me, but huge strips of burned skin remained where they had been on my wrists and ankles. The shackles remained, and as I fought to lift my arms, the metal bit into the burn wounds. I gasped at the sensation but ground my teeth together and put it away. Put the pain away, or I would never get out.

The world started to appear more clearly as my head finally began to unclog. I looked around the room, but there was absolutely nothing left. Just me chained to the chair in the center of the cell. I shook the shackles again, and they clang. My breath started to come in panicked heaves. I was stuck here. I roared, the sound coming from the back of my throat, hot and angry. They had left me here to die slowly.

Power welled in my chest as I screamed, the pain disappearing as magic coursed its way down my arms. I could feel it building, feel it *burning*, and yet I continued to scream, continued to let it funnel, let it build. Heat radiated from my arms as steam curled off my body, the water sizzling away from my skin. The temperature in the room climbed higher and higher until, all at once, silver light burst from my hands.

My vision was obscured by a wall of silver fire that rose like a miniature Aurelios before me, and the very shackles that held me in place melted underneath the flame. I burst from the chair, my body screaming in pain as the flame reached the ceiling and then extinguished completely, plunging the room back into darkness. I stumbled towards the door, grasping my knees with my palms, panting for breath, then gasped as I looked at my hands.

Beautiful, intricate iridescent scales covered the entirety of what had once been black-marred skin. They shimmered even in the dim light, and my breath caught in my lungs. Gaythe—I was the *chosen* Gaythe. I ran my fingers over each scale. Smooth to the touch, like snakeskin, and I blinked and blinked as if they would suddenly disappear altogether.

Beautiful, they were so incredibly beautiful. Loud banging

sounds echoed on the door, and a figure appeared in the portal window. I jumped back into a crouched stance, my muscles complaining at any movement, but I recognized the face. His curly brown hair, tense jaw, and striking blue eyes were wide with panic as they landed on mine, and the bond slammed back into my mind.

Blue on green.

"Pandora! There you are!" His voice rushed as he pulled the door open. The wailing alarm grew louder with the swing of the door, and he rushed into the room. He looked every bit as glorious as he had right before he had plummeted off the ship into the Pearl Sea—dressed in a dark T-shirt, black pants, and boots. He grabbed my shoulders and pulled me into his chest. "I thought you were dead," he said so quietly I almost didn't hear him. "I thought you were, too," I murmured into his chest.

He was warm and smelled of eucalyptus and sandalwood. He leaned back slightly, one hand resting at the nape of my neck as he looked me over, his eyes landing on my arms. My breath caught in my lungs as I waited for him to say something. "They look like they're scales," he said softly, and I nodded. His gaze continued down my arms until it landed on the burn wounds around my wrists. His eyes darkened as he stared at them. "Who did this to you?"

"My father," I croaked, and he returned his gaze to my face as a shadow descended over his features. "He will die for this," he snarled but gently wiped wet strands of auburn hair from my face. "Please don't scare me like that again," he whispered before planting a fervent but gentle kiss on my lips. I lifted onto my toes, winding my fingers through his hair. I didn't care that my body hurt as I kissed him back, but he broke away all too soon, looking behind him into the hallway.

"Can you walk?" he asked, looking down at my legs. "Gods

above," he muttered, and I shook my head. "It's fine. I can walk. I'm fine," I said with as much enthusiasm as I could muster in this scenario. He licked his lips. "We've got to go," he said quickly, then cautiously grabbed my hand and pulled me out of the room.

The tile was slick under my wet bare feet, and I struggled to keep up without falling on my ass. All the lights that had once illuminated the hallway were now off. The only thing lighting our path was the emergency alarm lights, flickering on and off in erratic pulses. We rushed past door after door, each identical to the one I'd just been trapped behind. Every door had a circular portal window, but each room beyond lay in total darkness. I slowed behind him, my heart hammering in my chest. Cautiously, I drifted toward one of the windows and peered inside.

My eyes adjusted to the shift in light as I narrowed them further, stepping closer to the glass. Inside sat a figure at the center of the room. She was petite, long blonde hair cascading over her back. Wearing a plain gray shirt and matching trousers, her skin nearly blended into the colorless fabric—pale and gray.

She turned toward the shadow I cast through the glass, and her pale blue eyes met mine—sad, empty. But worse than that—my breath caught in my throat, and I slapped a hand over my mouth. Jet-black streaks crawled from the base of her neck, winding over her collarbone like ink poured into water. She blinked at me but didn't move as I stepped back slowly from the door.

"Not now. We have to run," Luke snapped, grabbing my arm. We took off again, feet pounding against tile, my pulse racing just as fast. Every door we passed made my stomach twist tighter. We rounded a corner and barreled down another hallway. "Where are we?" I shouted, my voice raw, the soles of my feet slapping the floor with every stride. "Feros!" he yelled over his shoulder.

"Excuse me!?" I shouted again, disbelieving.

How long had I been unconscious that they managed to transport me to a completely different planet?

"How the fuck are we on Feros!" I screamed over the wail of sirens as we burst through a set of double doors. I skidded to a halt, colliding with Luke's back when he stopped abruptly. He didn't answer immediately, just moved toward a cabinet on our left. "They brought you here," he finally said.

The room was circular, cabinets lining every inch of the walls, and a decontamination shower standing in the center. "No shit, but how are you here?" I asked, walking over to him. The tile in this room wasn't the stark white of the hallway but a dusty beige. A fine layer of red dust coated the surface, sticking to my wet heels in clumps and darkening into something that looked disturbingly like blood. An enormous black door loomed to our right, a huge lever bolted into its center. I opened my mouth to ask where it led, but Luke held out a navy-blue jumpsuit.

"Adam. Put this on," he said. I took it from him, stripping off my soaked clothes and yanking the suit on. "Of course he got you here. Are you going to explain what's happening? Where is everyone?" I asked, sliding my arms into the long sleeves. "Evacuated," he replied, then slammed shut the door we had entered through and started rummaging through another cabinet. I zipped the jumpsuit from the waist to the collar, which pressed tightly against my neck. It was plain—no logos or marks—just a single silver zipper. Two chest pockets, four more on the pants, and the fabric was coarse and thick. Probably to protect against the infamous Feros winds from blasting red sand into your skin. The thought made my stomach turn.

Feros. We were really on Feros.

I quickly braided my hair down my back and tied it off with a rubber band from the cabinet where Luke had pulled the suit. He tossed a pair of black boots across the room, and they landed near my feet. "Put those on," he said gruffly, still moving from cabinet to cabinet, opening and shutting each one with methodical precision. I slid my feet into the boots and laced them up tight. Somehow, they fit.

"Why is everyone evacuated?" I asked. He finally stopped, turned to look at me, and said flatly, "Because they're about to launch a nuke." The blood drained from my face, "The nuke?" I choked, and he moved to the giant black door, placing a hand on the lever. "Yes, I had been wrong about the shipment. It was a diversion to kidnap you."

"No shit," I rolled my eyes, and he glared at me. "We have five minutes before it goes off." My pulse quickened. His eyes locked with mine—blue on green. "We have to stop it," I whispered. "I know," he said. His shoulders were tense, one arm braced against the lever, unmoving. "There's a good chance if we try to stop it, we won't make it," he added quietly. I felt my heartbeat pulsing in my fingertips. "The Gaythe don't deserve to die," I whispered. "I know," he repeated. "I can do it myself. You don't have to come with me." I said quietly, and he pushed off the door and closed the distance between us, cradling my head in his hands. I lifted my iridescent, scaled fingers and wrapped them around his wrists.

"Where you go, I go," he whispered, and his lips crashed into mine. They were warm against my chilled skin as he pressed into me. One hand slid down to wrap around my waist, pulling me closer. He deepened the kiss, his tongue brushing my lower lip, exploring. I parted my lips, letting him in. Our tongues moved wildly, desperately, and my heart pounded in my chest. If those were our last moments—just us—they were worth it. My fingers gripped his biceps, hungry for more, but he pulled away too quickly. My skin cooled in the absence of his touch.

"Let's move," he said, rushing to the door. He slammed the lever down, and with a hiss, the door groaned open. A blast of hot, dry air smacked me in the face, and I lifted my arm to shield myself from the wind. It died down a little but still whipped red dust into the room. We ran through the doorway, and my boots immediately sank into the muted red sand. I blinked hard against the sudden brightness, shoulders slacking at the world before me.

Ginormous red rock faces climbed around us, forming a bowl with the building we had just come from sitting in the very center. Luke didn't stop to take it all in—he sprinted toward a metal tower several hundred yards away. The tower held the biggest rocket I had ever seen, and the small, flickering hope I had for stopping the war died the moment I laid eyes on it. That was an enormous nuke. If it launched, it would destroy half of Gayle.

I rushed after him, red sand kicking up behind me. Dust caked my face, and I coughed against it, trying—and failing—to expel it from my lungs. The Aurelios light bounced off the rock faces, casting everything in an eerie red-toned glow. There was nothing around us but massive rocks, the building we had left behind, and the looming tower ahead. Just rocks and sand. This planet sucked.

"Stop!" a voice called from behind us, and we both froze in our tracks. I whipped around to find my father, pistol aimed straight at me. "Detective Nesnah, so kind of you to release Pandora from her cell," he said maliciously.

Red sand blasted into his white shirt, tinting it a dusty pink. A firm hand gripped my arm, and Luke tugged me partially behind him. I peered over his shoulder at my father, who now leveled the pistol squarely at Luke's chest. "You left her to die," Luke growled. "You left your daughter to die—chained in a cell—after you burned her."

A twisted smile curled across my father's face. "We didn't burn her. We electrocuted her," he corrected.

Luke went deathly still in front of me, barely breathing. "The both of you are coming with me. Now," my father commanded, jerking the pistol toward the open door behind him. "I'm never coming with you again!" I shouted, jabbing a finger toward him. His eyes went wide. He lowered the pistol slightly. "What happened to your arms?" he whispered, catching me off guard. I looked down at them, but before I could think—before I could answer, Luke lunged forward. His body moved fast—but not fast enough.

Chapter 52

*C*RACK!

The gun fired, and I screamed as every cell in my body wailed in protest. Luke pitched forward, his face slamming into the sand.

"No!" I screeched, sprinting to him, my knees plopping down in the sand beside his very still body. I rolled him over to find a gaping gunshot wound in the very center of his chest. "No, no, this can't be happening. You were dead, then you weren't. You can't die like this. Not here, not like this." I rambled as I frantically pressed my hands into his chest.

"He's just another detective, Pandora. He is *nothing* and belongs to no one."

"You're wrong!" I screamed, tears pouring down my face, "He's mine! He's mine!" I wailed, and he narrowed his eyes. "Fine, you can die out here with him then." He turned, stomped through the sand into the building, and slammed the door closed.

Sirens started blaring around us, but I tuned them out, pressing my hands harder into his chest. His blood poured over them, hot and sticky, and Luke's face went deathly pale. He slowly blinked at me, lifting a hand to my face to wipe the tears streaking across my cheek.

"You are so beautiful, scars and all." He whispered, and I choked on a sob. "Please, Luke. Please don't leave me." I whimpered, and he forced a small smile on his face. "And to think you hated my guts when you first met me." His voice was garbled, and streaks of blood leaked from the corners of his lips. "Damnit, this isn't a goodbye. Please don't die on me." I sobbed, and in the distance, the rocket flared to life.

Small flames started at the base, and the metal tower folded in on itself, ready for launch. I jumped up, brushing wisps of auburn hair from my face smearing sticky red blood across my forehead. I tucked my arms under his shoulders and lifted him, pulling his back to my chest. He went wholly slack, and I cursed at his weight, dragging him as quickly as I could to the closest boulder I could find. His legs dragged long trails in the sand, leaving wells for his blood to sink into.

There was so much blood.

It covered his entire chest, my hands and arms, and the entire front of me. I set him down behind the rock and grabbed his face. His eyes were set, and his body was limp. I set his face back down and pressed my forehead into his shoulder, sobbing. This couldn't be how it ended. It couldn't be. He had given me so much and asked for so little. He wanted to save my people. He tried to prevent the war. He was supposed to be a hero. I felt the bond between us falter—then *fail.*

He disappeared entirely from my mind, and frantically, I pressed my fingers into his neck and choked—no pulse. It couldn't be over. I wouldn't let it be over. I moved to straddle him, placing my hands over his chest, and pushed hard and fast over and over again. "Breathe, damnit. Breathe." I growled. Again and again, I pressed my hands into his chest for what felt like hours, but it did nothing. There were no signs of life beneath me.

I lifted my arms above my head and screamed at the top of my lungs, only for it to die in the wind. "Help me, Hanwi!" I roared, and I felt my magic stir within me. Before I realized what I was doing, I placed my hands on his chest and closed my eyes. I ran on instinct as I reached for the power within. It was there. I just had to believe that it could save him.

I was the *last* chosen one, which meant I was the source of Hanwi. I didn't need a conduit. I *was* the conduit. It was *me*. I was the power. I was life and death itself. The magic spiraled within, coiling along itself and roaring through my veins. My scales glimmered with power, and my arms tingled with the force but not with fire. No, this power was the raw force of Hanwi. This was the power to *return* life, not take it.

I released the torrent of magic through my arms, and a blinding silver light erupted from my hands straight into his chest. The pendant lying over his chest cracked loudly, and I blasted from the top of him, slamming into the sand several feet away, my shoulder taking the brunt of the pain. I shot up my eyes, landing on his chest, and held my breath and counted.

Ten seconds, fifteen seconds, thirty seconds.

He took a gasping breath, lifting his head off the sand, and I hurriedly crawled through the sand, grasping his face. The bond snapped back with such force I grit my teeth at the sensation. "You're fine, I'm right here. You're fine." My hands shook as I held his face in my hands. His eyes blinked at me, and he gasped more air into his lungs. "How did you—?" but his voice died in his throat as the entire planet's surface vibrated with an explosion.

The *nuke.*

I lay my body over him, burying my face in his shoulder and covering his eyes as the sand roared around us. Luke wrapped his arms around me, holding me to his chest to keep me from flying away. Fire blasted the rock face as an eruption sent the rocket blasting into space. We stayed that way, gripping each other as the rocket slowly disappeared into the atmosphere. I lifted my face as the fire trail behind the rocket disappeared altogether, and the last strand of hope in my heart went with it. War was coming, and we were not ready for it.

Aknowledgements

The most heartfelt gratitude and thanks,

To my amazing husband who was absolutely nothing but supportive the entire crazy couple of years I spent working on this project. To my father who not only supported me and my dreams, but also heavily supported our family throughout this adventure. To my son, who I saw grow so much during the last two years, you are incredible and I hope that one day you are proud of the things your mommy accomplished. To Jennifer Bruce for the incredible artwork and creativity in creating the cover art of my dreams. To my sisters who gave me inspiration for multiple characters and insight into different personalities and the beauty in being different humans all on the same planet. To my friends who lent an ear or a heart to my constant rambling and nerding out to the lore of this story. To my favorite fictional and nonfictional stories to date that helped inspire the world that I created. To Carly Juneau for giving me inspiration for a fiery redheaded detective. To Bronwen Pope who was a friend in a time when I didn't realize I needed one most. To Hannah Brueher who shared my love of fiction and fantasy. To Shelbie Allen for being my hype woman, I hope you like my second book just as much as the first. To Nichole Young for introducing me to my favorite fantasy series to date, it shaped my fire to write my own story. To Brian Peters for the hours of self defense that gave me insight into sparring and self confidence that I needed to create my badass main female character. To Ashley Carrion for being so incredibly supportive of my dream. To my mother in law, Debbie Hansen, for never being blood, but always being a mom. To Nathan Carrion who begrudgingly lended his police expertise when I asked way too many questions. To my beta readers that gave me incredible feedback. To the writing groups and online communities that gave my inspiration. To my public publishing platforms,

To the people who burned me,

And to you, the reader, the dreamer, the one who picked up this book and went through this journey with me. I will forever be grateful for you.

www.ingramcontent.com/pod-product-compliance
Lightning Source LLC
Chambersburg PA
CBHW070259310726
48976CB00005B/1487